FIRST MAGYC

Guardians of the Path
Book One

NICOLE DRAGONBECK

Witching Hour Publishing Inc.

Witching Hour Publishing, Inc.

ISBN-13: 978-1-943121-47-2

Editor: www.CourtenayDodds.com

DEDICATION

Dedicated first to those who believe in
dragons and magic;

second to those who use words to make magic.

CONTENTS

ACKNOWLEDGEMENTS

My list of acknowledgements is much longer than I had originally thought it would be, but that's a good thing. It means my life is full of people I am thankful to have around. On that note, a very big thank you goes...

To Lisa Barry and Courtenay Dodds of Witching Hour Publishing - without their help it would have been much less fun to publish this book, because frankly, I didn't have the first clue. But here it is, and I'm thrilled and grateful for everything they did.

To my mom and dad, for teaching me to read and write, for encouraging me to read and write, and for buying me my first book (The Enchanted Wood by Enid Blyton, still one of my favorites).

To Matthew, for the text which told me to email this lady he worked with who was starting this writers' group. I always suspected he really did love me, but after that I knew. He's still not getting any money.

To Andrew, for using his magic hands to hook up my keyboard to my computer and all of his good advice on who I should kill off. He's also not getting any money.

To Danielle, for bugging me to finish the stories I'd started. One day I might actually finish all of them.

To The Ink Slingers' Guild, for being awesome and fun and so supportive; Lisa for tea and being the greatest den mother ever; Erika for shameless self-promotion and wanting to read after me; Courtenay for funny stories, cat pictures and chocolate cherry martinis; Rhiannon for her enthusiasm and thoroughly inspiring adventurism; Jen for encouraging me to keep the faith. (Of course mermaids exist. Unicorns, too.)

To my friends; to those who read my stuff and gave feedback, especially Felix and Leo; to those who encouraged me and those who put up with me. Special thanks to Felix for the lovely words you'll find on the back cover.

To Sirio, for verse and technical support.

To Brooks, Tolkien, Gaiman, Salvatore, King, Jaques, Paolini, Rothfuss, Rowling, Lewis, Pullmen, Goodkind, Pratchett, Butcher, Lawhead, Martin, and all other amazing authors who took me to other worlds with their words and inspired me to let others into my worlds.

And finally to muses and music; a good song is a kind of magic in itself and I will forever be convinced that in the end, it will be music that vanquishes evil. Rock on!

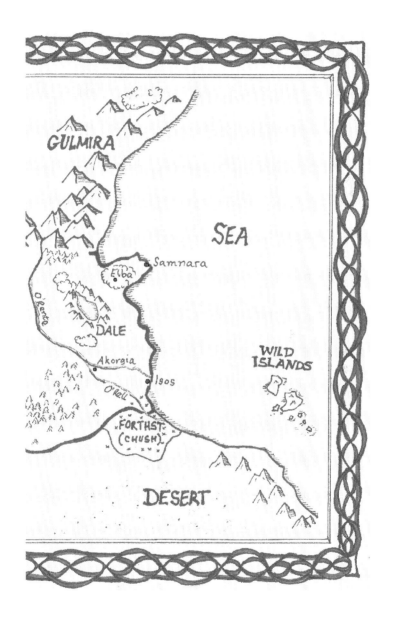

GULMIRA

SEA

Samnara

Elba

Olenta

DALE

Akorgia

O'keli

Isos

WILD
ISLANDS

FORTHST
(CHUSH)

DESERT

The Prophecy of *Aethsiths*

as depicted on the walls of the
Guardians' Hall in the Crescent Temple

The Path Everlasting

Shall ne'er Perish

Yet Waxes and Wanes

As Day's Light gives way to Night's Dark

One Day Will Vanish

Forsaken by People

Faded then put out the Final Spark

Without the Power of Life

All Shall Turn to Death

The Guardians as Named

Though Strong and True

Cannot Rekindle a Dead Fire

In a Place Devoid of the Path

Their most Dire Need

Will bring Forth One

Known as *Aethsiths*

Chosen by the Path

Begotten by the same

Marked by the First

When Future and past Clash

She is the Songstress

Singer of the Song

To revive the Dying Light

From embers or Ashes

Her Voice is the Spark

To Ignite the Golden Flame

With Purpose Now fulfilled

Her magyc will fade

Aethsiths expires

With the First Age

Her life given

To light

The Second Age

Of the Guardians of the Path

DOORS

The fights always started the same way; a sudden chill, a soft rumbling and then an explosion like a late-summer thunderstorm. They were at it again.

Twelve-year-old Ria tried to ignore them, concentrating instead on the book in front of her and the music coming through her headphones.

Deep, deep down in the place Ria only visited in dreams, she knew something was wrong, and if she could only find some way to pull everything together and put it back where it belonged, things would be right again. Maybe they would stop fighting about what they always ended up fighting about, even if it wasn't what they'd started fighting about. Namely, Ria.

Through the chorus of *Picking Up the Pieces* by City of Light, Ria could hear them.

"…that's twice she's refused to go to the session this week, Richard. It isn't *healthy* to be so alone all the time…"

That wasn't true. She had friends at school, Billy Friedman and Miranda Orlo. She ate lunch with them every day, did science projects and art assignments with them. There was the elderly Italian gentleman in 182 she visited every Saturday - he would make foods he called *spaghettini alla puttanesca* and *fettuccine verde con mascarpone* and she would read the newspaper to him. And there was always her dad. Ria knew he tried so hard.

It wasn't that she was being difficult on purpose, it was just that sometimes it was hard to manage her two skins. One was the person they wanted her to be and the other was who she really was. The first was just too tight to fit into comfortably, and made Ria feel as though she were suffocating. Ria hoped that one day they would all believe her when she told them that she wasn't lonely, it was just better for her to be alone. Yes, she missed her mother; no, she didn't dwell on death. Her father believed her, Ria knew, but there was always someone else, the stepmother, the school counselor, even the well-meaning lady with the shrill voice in number 196.

One day they'll believe me.

Ria sat on her bed with her headphones on, a book filled with the tales of wizards and valiant warriors lying on her lap, and she squinted at the paragraph blurring in front of her. She swiped the back of her hand across her eyes and focused on the page. The Queen's handmaiden was about to reveal the truth and the secret of her powers to the young prince.

Something thudded against the wall behind Ria and despite her resolve she jumped. She closed the book with a snap and tossed it on her pillow. The fate of the prince was going to have to wait. Turning up the volume of the music had proved to be just as futile as trying to read. Ria sighed. The air in the apartment was stale and charged with negative energy. It was time for her to leave. Some fresh air would do her good.

She pulled on the pair of shoes that sat under her bed for easy grabbing and stuffed her iPod into the pocket of her jeans. Walking to the bedroom door, Ria held her breath as she grabbed the handle as though it might bite her and turned it. She pulled the door open a crack and peered through with one eye.

Through the dying notes of the song she could hear shouting. She wished the band would hurry up with the outro and get on with the next song. She crept down the short hallway, pointedly turning her head from the light pouring out of the kitchen. Still, Ria couldn't help but see her father and step-mother out of the corner of her eye, anger twisting their faces into people she did not recognize, their words punctuated with sweeping gestures and curses.

Ria grabbed her purple jacket from the hook behind the door and let herself out of the apartment. She dismissed the idea of leaving a note before it had fully formed. It wasn't as if they would even notice. The thought was bitter, and it left a similar taste in the back of her throat as she closed the door behind her. The tarnished 192 on the door glared down at her, seeming to admonish her for the uncharitable thought.

Smelling of litter box and cigarette smoke, with water spots adorning the ceiling like old bruises and the too-narrow carpet worn through, the hallway was in no better shape than the apartment. Ria tapped her fingers along the pitted wall in time to the music as she walked. At the top of the dark stairway in the middle of the hall Ria paused and decided she didn't really feel like going outside after all.

She continued down the hallway to the very end, which was dim and stuffy. Passing the last door, she took several more steps and settled down in the corner under a window which had not been cleaned in some time. The layer of grime blocked most of the light and gave the little that managed to slip through a thick, sticky quality that blunted the corners of everything it touched, making the world soft and distant.

Ria liked that. It was quiet and no one would come here to disturb her. Drawing her knees up to her chest, she closed her eyes and let her head fall back. The wall was hard and unyielding, comfortably solid behind her back. As she sang along under her breath, her troubles melted away into the music. It made her feel better when she sang and her head moved a little in time to the song, one of the Silver Knockers originals called *Trapped Between Worlds*. In the safe space marked by the boundaries of sound, Ria let her thoughts wander.

They wandered down a familiar path, well worn by their little thought-feet. What would life be like if her mother hadn't died? Would it be different now, more like it was then, not lacking some basic necessity which had no name yet was as vital as oxygen to a beating heart? It was always at this point that Ria reached the constant impasse, her thoughts faltering and freezing up as she tried to puzzle out what it was that was missing, her mental feet stuck in a sucking morass which she couldn't move beyond. Tears welled up behind her eyelids as she fought to get free of the consuming thought.

Little by little, Ria became aware of something else, something which pulled her thoughts out and into the real world again. *Holy Fire* by Demons in Disguise syncopated through her headphones, but it was only in the silence after the song ended that she heard the foreign melody that vibrated through her.

Ria listened hard, cocking her head to better pinpoint

where the sound was coming from. When the next song on her iPod started with a crash of drums and power-chords Ria almost fainted with fright. She ripped the headphones from her ears and sat in the dimness, her heart pounding, the song a faint buzz coming from her lap. She slowly turned the volume down and listened again. In the emptiness, Ria realized she had *heard* nothing. Instead, the melody was there, flowing around and through her soundlessly.

Ria stood and clutched her headphones tightly as she looked around. The thin walls of the apartment building made it painfully easy to hear anything and everything, and to know exactly where it was coming from. The sounds of yelling and fists being slammed on tables coming from the direction of number 192 intruded in a rude manner and Ria felt her concentration slip.

The music seemed to come from directly around or maybe a little above Ria's own head, which did not help her pinpoint the source of the ethereal strains of the song. She was distracted again, this time by what appeared to be a door which floated in front of her eyes, but disappeared the instant she focused on it.

Only after squinting for several moments at the spot where it had been did Ria see the shape of a door in front of her where there certainly was not *supposed* to be a door. The door moved back and forth, moving closer and then farther away. It looked old. No, it *felt* old, as though countless thousands had come through to what awaited on the other side. Ria's skin tingled.

The door was as difficult to place as the music. It looked to be *in* the wall, but not part of it, or it could have been behind the wall and visible *through* it. When Ria reached out to touch it, all she came into contact with was the rough, pitted and slightly greasy wall of the apartment building, but at the exact moment that her fingers brushed the wall, the door gave an excited little jump towards her.

For the briefest second, the door came into focus; a pattern of gilded leaves ran down the left side, shining against the warm wood, the grain making mysterious shapes and faces, the ornate golden handle pleading to be turned.

The instant Ria withdrew her hand, however, the door fell back to its semi-there state, floating somewhere it could be seen but not touched. Ria bit her lip. *This is precisely the type of thing which gets people into trouble and mixed up with things that they should never be involved with,* she thought. *At least in books.*

But, Ria reasoned, e*verything turns out alright for them.*

Things like that don't happen here anymore, a prudent voice said meanly. *Nothing turns out alright here.*

Ria ignored the advice and put her hand against the wall. The door leapt forward again. She willed it closer and, like a shape rising from the depths of the ocean, it began to solidify out of the wall.

Most of those shapes have teeth, prudence warned and the door sank back a little into the shadows.

Shut up, Ria thought. "You don't have to be so negative all the time," she added aloud.

The door responded immediately to the sound of her voice and surged forward. Whatever had been holding it back fell away like a blanket being flung off but the door refused to come all the way. Ria had the distinct impression that it could sense her fear.

"Come on come on come on come-on-come-on, a little bit more," Ria coaxed the door. She used the same voice that she used on the shy rabbits which hid in the bushes along the path outside, and just like one of the creatures, the door crept forward.

Pulling it out felt like dragging a wagon with no wheels uphill and Ria stood tense, every muscle in her body trembling, sweat beading on her temple, oblivious to all else but the door. A last heave sent Ria falling back to crash against the wall behind her. In the opposite wall the door now stood, firmly there and beckoning her to open it. At last, Ria could pinpoint the source of the music. Haunting notes slipped from behind the door, flowing like fresh water, painting the world in silver and diamond.

Her chest heaving, Ria gazed at the door wide-eyed and slowly righted herself. The door looked as though it had come out of a fairytale. The wood of the door was polished to a golden gleam, and it did not belong with the other chipped, pale green doors in the apartment hall. She touched it lightly, delighting in the soft warmth under her hand. She thought that her hand should leave an imprint, but when she pulled away, there was nothing.

Ria hesitated for a long moment, debating with herself as the music tugged at her. One part of her said that she should walk away and leave it, another part knew that it was *right* to surrender to that beautiful melody. Ria swayed to the music, her fingers tapping the rhythm on her thigh. She looked down the corridor once, her eyes flicking past the door of the apartment she had fled, and the song made up her mind.

Biting her lip, the melody resonating pleasantly in her chest, Ria knocked, a sharp rap with her knuckles that sounded too loud in the empty corridor. Immediately the melody ceased, the silence shattering the fragile veneer the melody had given the world into a thousand crystal shards. It made Ria feel strangely lost. From behind the door came sounds of scurrying, a series of bumps, and then silence.

Ria waited and as the silence grew, she became impatient. She knocked again, then reached out and turned the handle. The door swung outward. Ria took an automatic step back, and looked up to find a man staring down at her with a quizzical expression in his startling eyes.

A slim man of slightly greater than average height, he leaned with one hand against the frame as he looked down at her without moving. A strange blue light from the room behind him bent around his frame in soft rays. Midnight hair stood haphazardly in oiled spikes atop his head and gold eyes gazed at her with unveiled curiosity. He wore a black shirt, unbuttoned at the throat, along with dark grey slacks and a black leather belt with a gold buckle. Shiny Italian-looking shoes adorned his feet. His full lips twitched in a half-smile as he regarded her for a long moment before speaking.

"May I help you?" he asked with a courtesy practiced only by storybook knights and well-bred young men in English romances.

Ria didn't have any sort of plan in mind after knocking; she had not really been expecting anyone to answer.

"I…I…" she stammered as she groped for a place to begin an explanation.

Her eyes darted to the room behind him, through the odd blue light and to something in the corner. An ornate acoustic guitar leaned against the arm of a reddish sofa that sat against the wall.

"You were the one playing!" Ria exclaimed, her eyes lighting up as they devoured the curves of the instrument.

The man's extraordinary eyes flicked over his shoulder to the guitar, and his smile widened.

"So you did feel me playing?" he asked, straightening with a jerk. "I wondered. Did you bring the Door?"

"I'm not sure," she answered.

Something was strange about what he'd said, but Ria

couldn't put her finger on it. The guitar was beautiful, gleaming chocolate, bronze and silver. Ria fancied she could still hear crystal notes dancing through the air, but that was impossible because no one was playing the guitar.

"So you didn't call the Door?"

"No," Ria said. "No, I don't think so."

"I see." The look he gave her pierced deep into layers Ria kept hidden from sight. "Won't you come in then?"

"No, I don't think so," she said again, all training about strangers making her cautious.

"Of course," he said, looking disappointed. He put his hand in his pocket and nodded at the wires in her hand. Very faint strains of a rock song came from the headphones. "What are you listening to?"

She looked down. The white wire was almost invisible against her clenched hand, and though the song was faint, it was so familiar she knew it instantly. "Um…this is *Supernatural Eyes* by Castaway."

He looked nonplussed.

"They're an Indie band," she said and shrugged a little self-consciously.

Something about him made Ria need to perform her best and be of use. Why she wanted his approval, Ria couldn't say. He nodded, but Ria had the feeling it was only because he had no idea what else to do and not because she had provided information he needed. Her shoulders sagged, his disappointment infecting her.

"You like music?" he asked.

She nodded, perking up. Music helped her to forget her troubles and sometimes, at least in her mind, it seemed as though it could do more, if only she knew how to use it. Ria had never voiced this thought to anyone and she certainly was not going to tell a stranger she'd just met, but something in the man's eyes made her think perhaps he knew nonetheless. Ria couldn't help smiling at him and he smiled back, his eyes thoughtful and far away. Then he looked straight at her, his gaze as piercing as a sunbeam.

He must have seen something in her eyes, because he gave a sharp nod of his head and asked, "Would you tell me please, if there is anyone else about?"

Ria looked up the hallway. It was deserted. Looking back at him, she shook her head.

"I really think you'd better come in. It's quite important." He smiled as he spoke.

She looked down the hallway again and her eyes gravitated to the door of her apartment. Shadows moved in the square of light under the door and she could still hear them faintly. A sort of helpless sadness infused her. In its wake rose a reckless desire to leave her horribly topsy-turvy life all behind.

"Alright," she said, steeling her twelve-year-old nerves and gathering all the courage she could muster.

He stood aside as she walked in. He smelled good, clean and fresh like soap and a spring morning.

"Won't you close the Door behind you?" he asked.

She did. The door closed with a soft click, and the blue light in the room flickered and disappeared.

Gesturing for her to take a seat with a wave of his hand, the man disappeared through a cased opening in the back wall.. Looking around, Ria saw only the sofa and a small coffee table in the room. The walls were devoid of picture or decoration, giving the room a lonely, uninhabited feel.

She sat down, knees pressed tightly together, as far from the guitar as she could, though she was acutely aware of it sitting at the other end of the sofa. She played with her headphones as she waited and tried to rationalize what she was doing there.

Ria didn't consider herself stupid or impulsive, and even her curiosity didn't usually cause her to do something this obviously senseless.

Even as she thought about it, Ria realized she might be dreaming. The room itself, and everything in it, felt unreal. The couch seemed to give way under her as if it were not really there and looking down she could almost see the floor through it. The strange idea that it was made of musical notes occurred to Ria. She shook the thought away and the sofa became more solid.

Just as Ria noticed she was jiggling her feet with apprehension and stilled them by force of will, the man strolled back in and handed her a little box of chocolate milk with a candy-cane-striped straw.

"I found this in what I assume is the kitchen," he said. "I've tasted it and it doesn't appear to be poisoned. I apologize for the lack of hospitality. It's the only thing there is. I haven't felt the need to eat since I arrived here so it didn't occur to me to look."

The statement was made even stranger by the way he said it - he put the emphasis on odd parts of words and his inflection wasn't a hundred percent correct. Ria made no effort to make sense of it and simply nodded and took a sip of the chocolate milk. He was a little unusual in an unsettling sort of way, but a warm aura around him and something in his eyes and his smile made him quite likable.

Still, Ria started and drew away when he pulled the coffee table over so he could sit down on it. Face-to-face and eye-to-eye, she found his gold eyes were captivating and soothing, wrapping her in a pleasant blanket of security. The colored light had returned and was lurking in the corners of the room and she tried not to pay attention to it as he looked at her intently.

"Do you have a name?" he asked.

"Ria," she said.

"Ria," he repeated, tasting the word as he drew it out, rolling the 'r' slightly.

"Short for Maria," she told him. "What's your name?"

"I am called Cedar Jal." He held out his hand and she shook it. His grip was firm and he held her gaze. "Would you please tell me what you felt beyond that Door?"

She sat bolt upright and pulled her hand from his, an electric tingle running from her head to her feet. *That's it!* "You keep saying 'felt'," she stated.

"And?"

"And that's exactly what it was! I thought I was hearing something, but that didn't really seem right, and I couldn't think of what it was, but it was *feeling!*"

Cedar sat back, and smiled. "That is exactly what I wanted to hear. Can you see any other Doors here in this place, other than that one?" He pointed to the door she had just walked through.

Ria looked about the room and wondered if that was a trick question, but there was only the one door. She shook her head, not knowing what reaction to expect. He sighed and rubbed his chin.

"That presents a bit of a problem I'd hoped to circumvent, but no matter," he smiled again. "I'm very glad you appeared."

Ria gave him a tentative smile in return, unsure if that required a response. Standing abruptly, Cedar retrieved the guitar from the other side of the sofa, then sat back down and set it on his knee. He fiddled with the pegs for a moment, his fingers settling over the strings as lightly as a breeze. His right hand caressed the neck as his fingers danced over the frets, and he started to play.

The song was beautiful, but it was the melody which

lay under the sound that held Ria enthralled. It resonated in her very soul and she was carried away as the intangible fibers of her being were strummed in time to the notes. A distant crash and a faint yell made Cedar pause and turn his head. Ria came back to the room around her with a jolt when the music stopped and she closed her eyes.

"They're at it again," she said, her face growing warm as the sounds continued. "Sorry." The need to explain overcame her reticence to speak. "I know they argue about me, but I don't mean for them to. I just don't know how to explain to them that I'm fine. Even if I did, they probably wouldn't listen. I just wish they weren't so loud."

As she finished, there was a screech and a door slammed. Ria winced.

"It's not your fault. The Walls are so thin here," Cedar said, patting her knee. He smiled crookedly. "You'd think that would make it easier."

"Easier?"

"Well, that's the thing, isn't it?"

She stared at him, knowing very well he meant something more than what he was saying, but it escaped her. "What do you mean?"

"Easier to get out."

"Get out?" Ria asked. "You mean you *can't* get out?"

"I'm afraid not," Cedar said. "If I could, I would have, believe me."

"Why can't you get out?" she asked, already assuming the worst. *He'd probably been locked up here for something terrible.*

Her thoughts must have been apparent in her expression, because Cedar gave her another one of his disarming smiles. "It's not that bad. I actually don't fully understand why I can't get out, and that's most of the problem." His teeth gleamed and his eyes looked at her hungrily. "I need your help, Ria."

She eyed him, a trace of suspicion flaring in her chest, but with it came the other feeling, the one she couldn't name but could only describe as *familiarity*. It was the same feeling Ria had when she pressed against her mother's chest, the warm smell of wood and spices and other things filling her nose and the warm beat of another heart lulling her into a blissful comfort without thought or care in the world. "Help with what?"

Cedar stood and tossed the guitar carelessly onto the sofa beside her. It bounced and started to slide. Ria gave a squeal and quickly grabbed it, expecting her fingers to burn. They didn't and the silver strings glittered in the oddly shifting light as she placed it reverently on the coffee table. Her eyes slid to the man in front of her, who was moving through the purple and blue light-shapes as if he didn't see them.

"I have been trapped here for far too long. It was a mistake that I even arrived here. But I did, and unfortunately, I am stuck here. *Was* stuck here," Cedar said as he paced restlessly, one hand in his pocket, the other punctuating his speech.

She watched him with her eyes wide, her mouth hanging open slightly. Ria sensed a story behind the words, a long and complex adventure that she longed to ask about, but she wasn't sure she should know the answer. It smelled of the things she read in her books and it pulled her, enticing her forward where otherwise she might not go.

Cedar turned to her with a sharp click of a black boot. "I want to go home. I *need* to get home. It is quite imperative." He gazed at her, his expression frank and earnest, and more than slightly compelling.

"Where do you live?" she asked, to keep from saying, "Of course I'll help you!" which was what she wanted to do.

"I live in a place called Demona."

"Sounds like a fancy name for hell," Ria said before her mind could sensor her tongue.

Cedar threw his head back and laughed out loud, his eyes crinkling at the corners and his lips pulling back to show all of his very neat, white teeth. "You know, that is not completely inaccurate."

Ria's eyes flickered around the tiny room and counted the shapes in the light then returned to his face. "Then why do you want to go back?"

He took her hand and gave it a gentle squeeze. "Because Demona needs me." He pulled his hands away and looked down at his lap. "And possibly every other world as well. Like the one out there." Cedar jerked his head at the door.

"Sounds serious," Ria said. A tense current ran under the man's cordial demeanor, something which would eventually snap, and Ria saw in the shadowy depths of his gold eyes that this was not a man that it would be smart to make angry.

"It is," Cedar nodded. "Though it helps if you don't think about it too hard."

She studied him, trying to judge how much she could press him. "Demona is not very close, is it?" she asked at last.

"Well, not really. It depends on how you look at it," he said, choosing his words carefully. "But it won't take long to get there, I'm fairly sure."

"And you need me because…?"

"Because I can't get out of here by myself. I've tried. If my intuition is correct, you can help me."

"Okay. Let's go then."

Ria stood up and marched across the room. She

stopped at the front door and looked back at him expectantly. Cedar had not moved.

"Unfortunately, it's not that simple. I wish it were - I would have been gone long before now, and without troubling you. I can't just walk out. You see, that Door was not made for me," he said. "Watch."

He went over and reached out to open the door, turning the handle and pulling. His fingers slipped over the handle and the door didn't move, even when he tried it a second and a third time.

"You may need to help me," he said, his smile forced over a clenched jaw.

Ria looked at him, her eyes narrow. He didn't look like he was faking it. She reached out and opened the door with no difficulty. Cedar took a deep breath and extended his arm through the doorway. It disappeared up to the elbow. Ria screamed in shock and threw her hands in front of her face.

"Hey, hey, hey," Cedar said. He pulled her hands down and knelt down so he was looking up at her. He showed her his own hand and flexed his fingers. "Look. It's fine."

"What is going on? Why did that happen? How…?" she demanded, her voice breathy. Her eyes darted wildly between his arm and the corridor beyond the door. The conviction that she was now trapped there with him made her throat constrict. Suddenly the dilapidated corridor was beautiful in the same way as something desirable utterly beyond reach.

His eyes followed her gaze. "Don't worry. You can leave anytime you want."

Ria looked at him and tried to determine the intent behind his words. She didn't think he was lying, but he also said he needed her in order to get out. Why would he just let her go like that?

Cedar stood up and gestured at the door with a wan expression. Ria took three quick steps and was in the safety of the corridor. She touched the wall and found it solid and reassuring. She looked back inside the little apartment at Cedar, who stood just beyond the threshold with his hand in his pocket, edged in blue light again. He gave her a small, sad smile.

"Simple, isn't it?" he said. "No harm done at all."

The way he said it made small tugs at her heart. Cedar shrugged at her and it was this helpless gesture which convinced Ria that he did not intend to hurt her. "If I don't come back, what will you do?" she asked him, stalling.

He tilted his head to the side and smiled. His smile was very charming. "I'll keep playing. I've been waiting for someone like you for as long as I've been here."

"Like me?" Ria found that hard to believe.

Cedar nodded. Ria stood in the middle of the corridor. She could hear water running in one apartment, a T.V. and radio in another, and somewhere else two girls were giggling. She listened hard, but she couldn't hear any yelling or objects being thrown and shattered. Stepping closer to the doorway, she pointed at him.

"Do the thing with your arm again," she ordered.

Cedar obliged. Ria stepped even closer and examined the air where his arm should have been from half a dozen different angles while he stood patiently. She couldn't see his arm in the corridor at all. When she waved her hand, she didn't feel anything either. She frowned. "Is this what you meant when you said the walls are so thin?"

"Yes, a little," he said, pulling his arm back inside the room. He rubbed it gingerly, grimacing slightly. "The physical walls," he rapped the wall inside the flat with his knuckles, "and the *meta*physical Walls." He wagged his fingers out the door and they promptly disappeared.

"I don't know that word," Ria said, frowning. "I'm only twelve."

"It means the Walls you can't see or feel with your body."

"So then why can't you get out?"

"I'm trapped here," he gestured to the room, "halfway between, I think. I am here, but not quite. I didn't exactly have all my attention on what I was doing at the time, and things didn't turn out how I had intended, to say the least."

"What happened?"

"That is a long story Ria, longer than I really have time for," Cedar said and looked at her impatiently. Ria caught a glimpse of the ice just below the surface and it made the room suddenly cold. "It would really help me if you would come back inside now."

Despite the chill, Ria nodded. As she stepped inside, the light changed from blue to purple. Cedar took her arm and led her across the room.

"Come. We have a few preparations to make."

"What do you need me to do?" Ria stood with her hands clasped, too curious to be afraid, but imaginative enough to be a little nervous.

"Actually, I just need some of your blood Ria." Cedar took her to the sofa and sat her down, then knelt in front of her.

She considered this for a moment. Blood was important, but she'd had cuts and scrapes before. None had been that bad. "What are you going to do with it?"

"Well, I'm going to use it to get out. Magyc doesn't work in all worlds, you see, except First Magyc, and that requires a little of the right kind of blood." He took a knife from his boot. "This may hurt just a little. Close your eyes for me, won't you Ria?"

She did as he asked, electrified by the mention of magyc. He bared her arm, firmly but very gently, and made a small cut halfway between her wrist and elbow. With a shriek of surprise, Ria's eyes flew open. She watched in fascination as bright red blood welled up and spilled over.

Cedar caught it in a glass vial the size of his thumb. When it was full, he sealed the vial and put it in the pocket of a white jacket lying over the back corner of the sofa. Pulling a narrow strip of cloth out of another pocket, he wrapped her arm and showed her how to put pressure on the wound.

"It doesn't hurt," she told him, hoping to ease the worried frown from his face.

He smiled, but his eyes were still haunted by a faint shadow of something, doubt, hesitation, maybe regret, Ria couldn't tell.

"That's good," he said. "Now, I want you to come with me."

"To Demona?" she asked.

"Exactly."

She frowned and glanced over her shoulder, toward her apartment. That had not been expressly mentioned, but Ria liked the idea. Something about it made sense, on a level below thinking or computing.

"Just for a little while. What do you think?" Cedar prompted, his voice soft.

Ria felt a curious sensation of warmth envelope her. It made her feel safe. She glanced up at him and saw him looking at her, his eyes now a darker, molten gold, and she knew that he was somehow influencing her feelings. Ria didn't really mind. She was certain that if she really didn't want to go with him, he would not be able to force her and would have to let her go. Ria suspected if he wanted to hurt her, he would have done so already.

"Okay," she agreed, and smiled at him.

No one would miss her if she was gone for just a little while, and if she went with him she would be able to find out about the feeling of familiarity she had whenever she looked into his eyes or heard his guitar.

Cedar smiled back, but it didn't quite reach his eyes. He leaned over and took the white jacket and slid his arms into it, then grabbed his guitar with one hand and reached under the sofa with the other. He pulled out a red case, into which he placed the guitar. Slinging the case across his back, Cedar scooted closer to her.

"Now this *is* going to hurt, but I promise that everything will be alright." His gold eyes were cool and his hands were warm, matching the words.

He was right. It hurt a lot when he slid the knife across her throat.

All thought fled from Ria's mind and her breath hissed out. She couldn't remember how to take another one as she fell into his arms. The front of her white shirt and his white jacket were suddenly red. He said something, but she didn't understand him. Her arms and legs were cold and she tried to press closer to his warmth.

The world became a kaleidoscope not so much of color but of shades, blending and blurring in geometric patterns of fantastic design. With a kind of fascinated detachment, Ria noticed there was now a second man standing there, a tall thin figure that had not been in the room before. *All sorts of things were just appearing out of thin air today* was the only cohesive thought she could manage as her attention drifted without direction or cause.

Cedar spoke with the second man. Ria could feel the vibrations of Cedar's deep voice with her head pressed against his chest, but she couldn't hear the words. Cedar was adamant, the other man calm and sure.

An argument ensued, which Ria was sure she was the subject of and she felt a distant twinge of annoyance. The man made a gesture with His hand and Cedar fell silent. The man remained calm while taking smooth strides forward. Cedar shoved the man in the shoulder with one hand and sent Him backwards. Even the man's stumble had grace in it.

Cedar was breathing heavily, his heart thudding on the other side of his ribs. As the man righted Himself, Cedar said something that made the man pause. Cedar spoke faster and somewhere in his words, something came out that made the man fall still.

After a brief pause, the man gave a slow nod and stood back. Cedar edged around Him, clutching Ria tight. Ria's eyes looked straight into the man's for the briefest instant. She almost saw Him, but He faded into the swirls of shadow and light. He lifted His hand in a grave salute and then disappeared. Ria knew something important happened.

"Okay, we're good," Cedar whispered into her ear, his voice surprisingly clear as he shifted her gently and turned to the door. "We're going to be alright."

The corridor was grey and drab and as they moved closer to the door the colors flowed together and the corridor disappeared, draining into the emerald green of a forest clothed in springtime.

Ria became hyper-aware of everything around her. The color of the leaves, vibrant against a sapphire sky; the gold of his eyes; the twittering of startled birds as they took flight; the smell of dirt and wild roses; the softness of the ground when he lay her down; and the discordant 'clang' when he chucked the empty guitar case to the side.

"Okay, okay, okay," Cedar whispered as he brushed her hair back. His fingers came away red.

He pulled her head into his lap, against the hard soundboard of his guitar. His words had no meaning for her as his voice breathed into her ear, but his breath smelled sweet and the notes from the guitar enveloped her, consuming her body in a fire that burned for a split second before freezing.

When Cedar gently touched three fingers to her throat the fire leapt to the point where his fingers touched and escaped her mouth in a tortured scream. Her voice cut off as though someone clicked a mute switch, her scream echoing away into the trees. Ria sat up, gasping. She pushed his hands away and clutched her neck.

It was as soft as a baby's cheek, with neither scratch nor scar. Her shirt was perfectly clean as was his immaculate jacket. She looked at Cedar, her eyes accusing. He smiled at her, his skin pallid and the sunlight seemed to go straight through him, illuminating his bones. Dark shadows had swallowed his lovely golden eyes, turning them a dull umber. He fell weakly beside her, eyes closing. His fingers fluttered and then he was still.

The whole world went still with him. All Ria heard was her own breathing and her steadily beating heart. She looked at him, lying with his legs bent under him and his arms by his side. She scooted slowly closer and got to her knees next to him. When she pressed her head to his chest, she could hear faint pattering. She shook him gently, but he didn't move. Suddenly the silence was sinister and she was very aware of how alone she was.

"Cedar. Cedar!!"

He mumbled, rolled over and curled into a ball. His

breathing evened out, but he did not rouse. Ria sat next to him, pulled her knees to her chest and hugged herself tightly. She would watch over him, she decided. That was the only sensible thing to do.

The sun moved across the sky and disappeared behind the trees. The sky filled with fire, and soon after with diamonds. Presently Ria's eyelids began to droop and she fought sleep.

As the night deepened it grew cold and Ria huddled closer to Cedar, her teeth chattering softly. The trees became lost in shadows, and the shadows were not empty. Music would help keep those unseen things at bay. She felt for her iPod, but it was no longer in her pocket. She must have lost it in the transition, and the loss of her constant companion deepened her solitude.

Squeezing her eyes shut, determined not to see anything that might be lurking in the trees, Ria curled up next to Cedar, and despite the sounds in the night, fell asleep with the reassuring thought that perhaps this was just a dream.

Ria woke the next morning when a spear of sunlight darted down and pried her eyes open. She saw green leaves waving gently above her, edged in shining light that illuminated motes in the air. Cedar's jacket lay over both of them. She stirred and wriggled from his embrace.

At some point during the night he must have gotten up and made a fire, for coals were still smoking in a small pit nearby. The chill of night had not worn off, but the sun played pleasantly over her skin, and she shrugged out of her purple jacket to enjoy the sun to the fullest. Ria looked closer at the place she found herself in.

Something in the air or the sky, something which was too small to be seen, too subtle to be touched or heard told

Ria in no uncertain terms that this was not the same world she had lived in all her life. The air was unfamiliar to her lungs, thick and viscous, the sunlight brighter and even the ground felt as though if she put her ear to it and concentrated, she would hear somewhere deep within it a beating heart of stone.

The small clearing was something out of a fairy story, small, bright and perfect. Straight, slim saplings grew just in front of giant, gnarled trees which ate the sunlight. Ria bit her lip, looked around to make sure no one was watching and then pinched herself on the arm. It hurt more than she intended and she whimpered. *So I'm not dreaming. I could be dead, but I don't think that dead people get hungry.*

Breathing in a deep breath of fresh, tart air, Ria was a little surprised to find she would be perfectly content to stay in this place forever. The lack of any worry or desire to return home put a buoyancy in her chest that bubbled up into a delighted giggle. She clapped her hand over her mouth and looked back at Cedar, hoping she hadn't woken him. He hadn't moved, hadn't even stirred and if she hadn't been able to see his ribs moving up and down, he could have been dead for all she would be able to tell.

Retrieving the guitar from where it had fallen when he'd collapsed, Ria lay it at his head and sat down cross-leg next to him. He looked peaceful when he slept, and the light shadow of stubble on his smooth face made him look strangely youthful. His eyelashes were thick and dark and gave his angular face a masculine beauty which was easy to miss when he was awake. Ria tried to guess how old he was, but her gut and her eyes kept giving her different answers.

She was lost in watching him when, without warning, he sat bolt upright, eyes open, hands out. Ria screamed and threw herself backwards. Cedar looked at her with a bemused expression, and stretched. His hair was mussed and a leaf stuck out from behind his ear. His eyes gleamed warmly, nearly returned to their former bright hue.

"Good morning," he greeted her cheerfully. "By the Path, I'm starving!"

Her stomach grumbled an agreement, but she said nothing. Instead, she watched him warily as he got to his feet and cracked his spine with a satisfied grunt. She wondered how they would get food in the middle of a forest. Cedar walked over to the fire and within moments, he had woken it and the orange flames were dancing merrily. Then he went over and slung the guitar over his back.

"I'm going to get something for breakfast. I'll be back momentarily. Stay here."

"Are you going to leave me here?" Ria blurted out as he began to turn away, the fear jumping to her mind and coming out her mouth when he took his first step away.

Realizing that he could do just that made the security she had felt minutes before disappear. The thought of being left alone in this world that she found both new and familiar terrified her beyond imagination. He paused and turned his head back to look at her, his eyes veiled by an impenetrable shadow.

Cedar opened his mouth to speak when a crude spear buried itself in the ground just in front of him, spraying his trousers with dirt. Before Ria could react, he leaped over to her in one fluid motion, the guitar sliding off his shoulder and down his arm, and pulled her to him as another spear struck the ground where she'd been sitting. She looked around, her mouth frozen in an 'o' of surprise. Out of the trees stepped a handful of people, all of them carrying rough spears and leering.

Ria counted six and some of them looked very strange. Two were clearly not human, one very skinny with dark skin and white hair, the other slouched, chubby and bald, but their features were gross and uneven. The shortest was hairy, with little eyes that glinted from underneath an overhanging brow. The tallest one had pointed ears and his unpleasant smile revealed his teeth were pointed as well. Two ordinary men stood with the first four.

Cedar had his guitar in hand as he surveyed the newcomers. "I really wasn't expecting company."

The small dark-skinned one with a large nose and even larger ears grinned. He was missing several teeth, the rest were slightly pointed. "May the Path keep you," he said, straight-faced, though his eyes were mocking. "Will you invite us to share your fire?"

"No, I think not," Cedar replied, his voice quiet.

He had gone cold and rigid, and his eyes burned with an icy fire. For the first time, Ria saw fully the forbidding exterior she had glimpsed in the room between this world and the other world. She fought the urge to shrink away from him when her eyes fell upon the guitar. It was humming slightly, an eager sound that ignited the air around them. Cedar's fingers were white as they gripped the neck tight enough to warp the strings and Ria's eyes widened as she watched the guitar shimmer away into a longbow of mahogany and gold.

In a second Cedar had it up and drawn, his left hand next to his ear, the knuckles of his right pointed at the closest of the intruders though no arrow was nocked, nor was a quiver in evidence. The intruders shuffled and hefted their spears. Some of them chuckled softly, their dark little eyes glittering with something less than warmth, but two of them, the tall one and the dark one, took a step back and glanced at each other with uneasy expressions.

Cedar nodded at the line of scraggly figures. "I wasn't able to get much of a look at your world. Some things here may be not be familiar to you. Do you know what each of those is?" he asked Ria.

She knew what he meant, but she looked at each again to make sure then shook her head.

"Pay attention." Cedar's fingers did a little dance on the taught bowstring and Ria shivered. An arrow appeared in his hand, fletched with golden light.

"Elf." The tall one went down with an arrow in his neck, his pointed teeth bared in a grimace of pain.

"Goblin." The stunted one with large ears and dark skin looked down in surprise as an arrow sprouted from his chest. Dark purple blood stained his ragged shirt.

"Troll." The chubby one's whole body jiggled when the arrow struck him, his tiny eyes rolling up in his bald head as he dropped to the ground.

"Dwarf." The stout, ruddy man with mounds of tangled hair on his head and face glared and snapped the shaft of the arrow that went into his shoulder. The arrow was quickly joined by two more, and the dwarf managed to stagger forward one step before he fell face-first to the ground.

"And of course, your average man." Cedar gestured at the two remaining aggressors, brothers by the look of them, blond and bearded, gaunt of face and too thin. Neither of them had a chance to lift a spear before Cedar's arrows took them down.

The bow slid down through Cedar's grip. It shimmered as his fingers ran over its length and it was the guitar that landed on the ground. He gazed at the fallen bodies with a haunted shadow in his eyes. The bodies did not move when Cedar walked up and nudged them with the toe of his shoe. He looked so sad that Ria stepped closer and took his hand. He squeezed hers, but his dark expression did not disappear, and an odd protective instinct surged in Ria.

"What did they want?" she asked.

"Food, most likely," Cedar said. "Money. Our clothes." He looked tired again. "I wasn't going to wait around to find out, not since…" he stopped suddenly and shook his head.

"Why…why…"

"Why did I shoot them?" Cedar looked down at her. "Because they would have killed us."

"What are we going to do with them?"

"What do you mean?"

"Shouldn't we bury them or something?" Ria looked down at the crumpled bodies.

"Bury them?" Cedar looked amused. "It would be more respectful to burn them. The dwarfs believe that fire consumes the spirit and sends the body back to Mother Eyrth where it belongs. The elves believe that the sparks carry their souls to an afterlife among the stars where they are watched over by the Moon." He began dragging the bodies together, piling them on top of one another, his words punctuated with grunts of exertion. "The goblins are rumored to eat their dead after roasting them over a fire for three days and nights, in order to benefit from the wisdom and experience of the deceased. And I don't really know what the trolls think."

Ria stared at him, fascinated horror written over her face. "How do you know all that?"

"Part of the job description," Cedar said with a shrug. He gave her a lopsided smile. "I've been around a while. We should finish our business here quickly and leave. There may be more of them around."

"More of them?" Ria looked at the pile of bodies. "Who...what are they?"

"Vagabonds, thieves, cutthroats," Cedar said as he heaved the last one onto the pile.

"Are there lots of bad people here?"

"Not bad," he contradicted gently. "Just misguided. Everyone follows the Path in his or her own way, but some ways lead to more unhappiness than others do. Tell me Ria, do these look like happy men?"

"They're dead."

His laughter startled several birds from their roosts. "I suppose that puts it more clearly than anything else."

The bodies were piled like logs. Ria helped Cedar clear an area of ground and build a ring of stones to provide a firebreak, then watched Cedar set them alight with no more than a wave of his hand. Flames licked hungrily at their clothes and then their flesh. The smell reminded her she was hungry and her stomach rolled in protest at the thought of eating something that could talk. Cedar would not leave until the bodies were ashes, which did not take long for the less-than-natural fire to accomplish. He extinguished the last embers with another wave of his hand and then nudged her away.

"Let's go," Cedar said, rubbing a hand across his eyes.

She followed behind him as he made his way through the forest. She had so many questions she felt like they were leaking out of her nose and ears. *Who is he? What was that guitar? What is this place? How did he do that with the fire?* Lost in her thoughts she didn't see him stop and ran into his back. She peeked around him.

Through the trees, a few meters away, she saw a road.

With slow deliberate steps, Cedar walked on with Ria

trailing behind him then stopped in the middle of the road. He stood, his hand in his pocket, and surveyed the road with a thoughtful expression. It was only visible for a short distance in both directions before the trees swallowed it. He looked at the sky, counted something silently on his fingers and was lost in thought for a time before glancing up the road a final time. He nodded sharply to himself and then knelt down in front of her.

"Now, I would like to send you home without delay, but I'm afraid I might need a little more rest, not to mention some food. So, you will have to stick with me for just a little bit longer."

His gold eyes looked at her earnestly. Ria didn't mind staying with him, but didn't say anything. Cedar put his hands on her shoulders, mistaking her silence for something else.

"I'm going to send you back," he tried to reassure her. "And I'm not going to leave you."

He took Ria back into the trees, in sight of the road but hidden from the view of anyone who might pass. "Now, I'm going to get something for us to eat. Stay here. There's no one about."

Ria nodded and settled herself under a tree, keeping half an eye on the road; she thought he would want to know if someone went by. As she waited, thoughts of the burning bodies they had left in the forest, Cedar's guitar-bow, and First Magyc ran through her head. She looked upwards at the sliver of pale moon, bleached by the past-noon sun hanging overhead, and wondered if it was watching over the elf.

Cedar returned soon, stepping out of the trees on silent feet, a brace of pigeon in one hand. His other arm cradled half a dozen small apples against his side, and his guitar hung on his back.

NICOLE DRAGONBECK

Ria watched him make a fire, this one with wood and tinder and flint, clean and skewer the birds, then set them over the flames. Not too long after, the tantalizing scent of roast pigeon drifted through the air. Cedar handed her one of the crisp, browned birds and sat down next to her. Sitting beside him, in complete silence, Ria found her hunger had been replaced by a knot in her stomach made of questions and mysteries. She picked at the tender meat and avoided his eyes, unsure how to resolve her quandary.

The farther Ria went the less she understood and the more obvious it was to her how dependent on him she was. It irked her how helpless she was. Back home, she could at least go to her corner or disappear into her music. Here, she had nothing.

Cedar sighed and she looked up at him. "We can't go on with you being afraid to speak to me. That's not going to work," he said, a little crease between his eyes.

"I'm not afraid," she said.

It was mostly true, yet her hand automatically went to her throat. The same expression which had been lurking in Cedar's eyes before flashed across his face, and this time Ria recognized it as consternation.

"Right. That. Perhaps I should try to explain," he said.

"Demona is a world of the Path and that means magyc will work here, but in other worlds not touched by the Path, a person can only make First Magyc, or Blood Magyc as some call it, work. I needed your blood to get out of that place I was trapped in. There was nothing else I could think of."

"Why didn't you use your own blood?" Ria asked accusingly.

He was silent for a long time before he looked unflinchingly at her. "At times I thought about it. I even

34

tried it once and it took only the one time for me to realize the amount of blood required would kill me."

"How did you know it wouldn't kill me?" Ria asked.

"I didn't."

The flashback was so vivid it held Ria motionless, the cold knife drawing a line of fire across her throat. *His eyes were cold and his hands were warm.* He had known exactly what he was about to do and Ria had mixed feelings about that. The sense of betrayal and a profound knowledge that he had done only what he thought was right twisted in her stomach as her hands twisted in her lap, neither gaining supremacy over the other.

"Then why did you do it?" she asked at last.

"Ria, I know I took a chance with your life, and some would say I had no right to do that, but," he sighed. "I had a feeling. It's difficult to explain."

"Try," Ria demanded, growing more desperate to reconcile the tumult of emotions his actions evoked. *If I've actually trapped myself with a psychopath…*she wouldn't let that thought run its course. It had nowhere to go but darkness and terror, and that wouldn't help her.

"I…" he stopped, and reevaluated his choice of words. "Why did you agree to help me and come to Demona?"

Ria had to think that one over for a little while. His comparison didn't make sense, and yet at the same time, she knew that logic could be overruled by something more instinctual, more powerful and compelling than reason. A warm glow settled in her stomach and she gave him a little smile. "I guess I had a feeling."

He returned her smile. "You see? Besides, I did protect you from Death, and bring you back."

She could not argue with that. "Did you use your blood to do that?"

Cedar shook his head. "No. Magyc is complicated, and has rules just like physics or mathematics, and one such rule is that only specific blood will work. The right type of blood is quite valuable here. Or it was when I left. Who knows what it's like now." A pensive frown flitted across his face.

Ria stared at him in confusion. He caught her look, and shook his head. "Don't worry," he said. "Nobody will be wanting your blood."

"What do you mean?" she demanded.

"I used it all."

She frowned. The memory of her shirt, wet and sticking to her skin flashed past her eyes, and she suddenly felt pale and sick. She looked down at her hand. It was trembling, even though it looked perfectly normal.

"What are you saying?" she said slowly, pressure stinging behind her eyes. "Am I empty?"

His eyes widened. "No! No, no. It…I…"

He pulled the knife out, the same knife that he'd used before, reached over and grabbed her right hand. She tried to pull it away, but he held it firmly as he nicked the tip of her finger. A drop of red welled up.

"See?" He smiled.

Two tears slid down the sides of her face and she gave a trembling sigh of relief.

"I thought you were going to tell me I actually was dead," she confessed, holding her wrist with one hand, carefully balancing the blood on the tip of her finger, watching the drop grow bigger.

"You're not dead," Cedar said firmly. "I promise. Death is a very blunt character. You would know with complete certainty if you were dead."

He sighed again, a weary sound that made Ria feel old just listening to it, and he sat back, pulling his guitar to his lap and starting to play. Reverberating through her, the notes carried the strange melody which was felt and not heard. The melody illuminated the whole world, but in a different manner than it had illuminated the other world that was Ria's.

That had been silver and glass, this was all gold and fire. Ria gazed all around, drinking in the vivid sights, until she caught sight of the blood on her finger. She raised her injured finger and blinked, staring at the drop of blood.

"There's something wrong with it," she whispered.

That brought him up short and the music died away. Cedar cocked his head to one side.

"What do you mean?" he asked staring at her hard.

"It's glowing. It *was* glowing. I think."

He sat back, shock plain on his face. "How do you mean *glowing*?" he asked carefully.

"It looks," she looked up at him, "Gold."

"Impossible," Cedar breathed.

"What?" she asked, admiring the vibrant light within her blood which turned the drop into a glittering ruby.

"Nothing," he muttered and looked down at his guitar with a little frown. He strummed gently as he stared into space. Ria sat quietly so as not to disturb his mulling, sensing he was thinking important thoughts. She gently rubbed the drop of blood away and watched Cedar's long fingers flow over the strings.

"Would you like to play?" he asked suddenly.

"I don't know how," Ria said and looked at the guitar wistfully.

"I'll show you. Here, put this finger here, this one here and that one there," he instructed. "Now, strum like so."

She brought her hand down. The chord rang out, clear as crystal, yet empty. Ria frowned. "It doesn't sound like when you play."

"First you learn to play, then maybe I'll teach you to play like I do."

"Do you really think I can?" Ria's asked, enchanted with the idea of being able to make the music that protected and bolstered her.

"Yes, I believe you may be able to," he said carefully. "If you can see the Path that way."

She smiled and strummed again. Cedar's gold eyes were molten as he watched her, his expression a mix of confused hope and doubt, but Ria was too enthralled with the guitar to care.

He showed her a few more chords and then looked up at the sun. "We should go."

She put the guitar over her arm as he wrapped the rest of their meal in large leaves he found on a vine and put them in his jacket. He covered the fire with dirt and dusted off his hands. Ria took the hand he offered and they made their way to the road.

Walking at a leisurely pace down the middle of the road, Ria tried to take in everything all at once, the small yellow and white flowers which grew between the huge trees that stretched up above them, the blue sky patchy between many shades of green. Everything was so *real* that it made the other world, her world, feel like a grainy, two-dimensional picture. Ria didn't want to think about that world when the one here was so fascinating. Deciding it was a good time to probe just a little, she looked up at Cedar.

"So, what did you need to get back here for?" she asked.

"How is your history?" he replied.

Ria gave him a look. "I know *my* history. But I don't think your history and mine are the same."

"Good point. I'll have to keep that in mind. Well then, things were in a bit of a mess when I inadvertently left. I have to fix that by collecting the pieces of a magycal artifact called the Amber Torch and return it to its place at the Crescent Temple."

"Why?"

"That's quite a tale."

"I'd like to hear it," she said, shifting the strap on her shoulder and looking up at him. "And we're not doing anything else."

He smiled widely. "No we're not, are we? Very well. Several years ago," he paused to collect his thoughts, "the Amber Torch was broken and the other Guardians and I were forced to go into hiding. Events transpired and I was cast away to a Void between Demona and your world, where I was delayed for a time. I'm not sure for how long." He looked around. "It was the end of winter when I was last here, and now it is the middle of spring, which means it could have been several weeks or it could have been almost a whole year. Time is strange sometimes. Now that I'm back I must find the other Guardians in order to figure out what happened and set everything straight, put everything back the way it's supposed to be."

Ria felt his last words physically hit her, they matched so closely to her sentiments, and she decided she might believe in fate after all. "So we're going to find the Torch?"

"Not exactly. I have a hunch that my friends have gone to a place called D'Ohera."

At the exact instant they both stopped. Ria choked on the bitter air and Cedar pulled a face like he had just bitten into a lemon. The air was cold though the midday sun was shining above them, and Ria felt malignant forces at work on her body, pushing and pulling at it, trying to crush it into a dense lump.

"What happened?" she said in a small voice as she stepped closer to him.

"This is Demons' work," Cedar said slowly. "Why don't you give me my guitar?"

She handed it over to him immediately, clutching the red case to her chest as if it could protect her. He took the guitar and held it at his side by the neck.

The longbow shimmered into being.

Cedar looked around carefully, his eyes taking on the cold burn they had when he had faced the motley attackers that morning. He pushed up the sleeves of his black shirt.

"Come."

The word was terse and made all of Ria's senses heighten. He took her hand and led her off the road, through the trees. He made no sound as he moved and she attempted to be just as silent, but each time she put her foot down something crackled or snapped. The forest had gone silent as death and her breathing echoed loudly in the emptiness. Cedar stopped.

"Wait here."

Ria didn't want to let him go, but she made herself pull her hand from his and watch him slip into the trees with his golden bow drawn taut. The silence pressed on her from all sides. The world was cloaked in shadow though the sun still shone brightly. Ria peered into the trees trying to see where Cedar was. She felt vulnerable and exposed, and wanted the comfort of his presence, but he was gone.

Unable to stand being alone in the deathly silence anymore, Ria crept after him. The trees pressed close, their branches catching her clothes and the air stole the warmth from her body. Evil lurked there, pressing the air from Ria's lungs until she was gasping for breath when she emerged onto the road. Cedar was nowhere to be seen, but sounds came from just beyond where the road started to curve so Ria trotted cautiously in that direction.

"Ria!" came Cedar's exasperated groan. "I told you to wait!"

He was crouched in the middle of the road, one leg stretched out, leaving all his weight on the other leg on which he balanced with an effortless grace. He drew the bowstring and sent a golden arrow streaking into the trees and out of sight. A screech echoed back and Ria jumped.

"What's that?"

"Later. Right now I need you to go back and wait for me."

Then she saw the blood.

Ria ran to him. Cedar looked unhappy with her but she ignored him.

"You're hurt!" Ria said with an quick glance at his leg.

"Not badly," he told her firmly. "Listen, right now is *not* such a good time. Damn and Demonfire!"

Ria looked up when the Demon rounded the corner. Half-moon talons made furrows in the ground as it stalked towards them. Hunched over, it stood as tall as a man. Its head was small, the rest of it thin and sinewy, extra joints giving it an angular and ungainly appearance. Uneven spines criss-crossed down the creature's back and crimson eyes shone over a frighteningly human mouth full of inhuman teeth.

"*Guardian!*" it hissed, sending shivers down Ria's spine.

With one arm and without losing his balance, Cedar pulled Ria behind him and shot at it. His arrow melted into gold sparks when it hit the Demon's abdomen and the Demon howled in pain, blinking its eyes rapidly.

"Ria, can you please do what I said?" Cedar asked, his

teeth clenched. "I need to concentrate."

Ria crouched down beside him. Her stomach turned at the sight of blood pouring out with each beat of his heart and drenching the dark grey cotton of his pants. Cedar moaned and his next arrow went wild, over the Demon's shoulder, to melt into the air. His smile was grey on his pale face. "Perhaps a different tactic."

His hand caressed the bow and he pulled the guitar into his lap. The notes sounded as tired as he looked, like autumn leaves stirred by an apathetic wind. He didn't stop playing as he shrugged out of his jacket, finger-picking as he pulled off the right sleeve, hammering on and off against the frets as he slid his arm out of the left. Jacket hanging over his knee, he threw his hand along the strings and sent a wave of sound thundering through the air. Then he turned to her, grabbed her by the shoulders, and began to speak.

"Ria, I need you to listen to me very carefully. Take my jacket and go back to the trees. There's a little money in the pocket, for what help it will be. Follow the road out of the forest and over the hills; find someone, anyone, and ask them to take you to a town called D'Ohera. Find a woman by the name of Victoria Meech at the Tales Mane. Tell her what happened here, she will help you."

A cold hand gripped Ria's stomach as she grabbed the jacket without thinking. She glanced over her shoulder at the Demon still held at bay by the last chord Cedar had flung at it.

"What are you going to do?"

He paused before answering, taking his hands from her shoulders and placing them upon the guitar once more. The music was louder than his voice, making Ria lean closer to hear. "After I finish my business here I'll be right behind you. I'll meet you on the way or find you there."

A dissonance in the melody, as though sharp nails were shredding her bones, made bile rise in Ria's throat. She didn't know how or what, but something was telling her that Cedar didn't mean what he was saying. "You're lying, aren't you?"

Cedar looked at her quizzically. "How did you know that?"

"You can't play properly. It didn't feel right."

Something akin to hope flickered in his eyes and he brightened for a moment. It was quickly extinguished by a blunt and stubborn rejection. When the Demon hissed, one forelimb breaking through the bars of sound, he looked tired again.

"D'Ohera. Tales Mane. Victoria Meech. Now *go*."

His fingers began to play a different tune, this one compelling, the notes building on each other like waves until what felt like a tsunami crashed over her.

Ria stood slowly. Her heart was being torn in two; she wanted desperately to stay at the same time she was being pushed away. The Demon, temporarily forgotten, screamed and snarled at them but was unable to come closer. The same music that ordered Ria to leave slipped around the Demon in intricate chains to bind it in place.

Ria took a step away-

-and another and another. In the middle of the fifth step Ria stopped, her foot hovering just above the ground as she fought the compelling strains. She could feel the music pushing her like a strong wind. She could almost see it, the shades of color glowing gold and blending into one another like an iridescent watercolor. Using every ounce of her will, Ria turned against it.

Cedar still knelt in the middle of the road, his hair

black against too-pale skin. His shirt sleeves were rolled up, revealing slim wrists and sharp fingers. The Demon stood barely five paces from him, its teeth bared and muscles taught as it fought to be free of the music. Ria could see the spirit of the bow in the substance of the guitar, shining brilliantly as the notes flew straight and deadly as any arrow.

Ria watched and the jacket in her hand dropped from her lax fingers, as she became entranced by the fiery gold sparks and swirls all around her. Then she heard it, the voice of the music. It spoke to her too softly for her to understand the words, but it was imperative that she get the message. She leaned into it.

The further Ria opened her mind to let the music in, the more it imbued everything around with a burning pulse. It was too much and distracted her with its intensity and magnitude. Ria closed her eyes and tried to concentrate. She reached out to catch the music, but it slipped away as a shadow beset by a lantern.

The harder she tried to hear it the faster it ran away. Tears rolled down her cheeks as she realized the music was fading the closer the Demon came. She wasn't going to be able to help Cedar and he was going to die. Her shoulders slumped in defeat, she fell into the music and let it carry her away. In its golden arms, she was finally able to hear the voice clearly.

Opening her eyes, Ria repeated the words in a whisper. They slipped from her lips like molten starlight and a lion's roar. She didn't recognize them or understand what they meant but the Demon screamed, its multi-jointed arms flailing as if it was trying to brush off an incorporeal attacker. Ria felt her heart rise, filled with elation. She grasped again for the words and again they flitted away like fireflies. The Demon stepped closer, its talons reaching out. Ria forced herself to relax, forced herself not to watch, and let the words come to her.

She spoke in time to the music, deliberate as a tightrope-walker's steps. Cedar heard her and his head turned as she approached and stood beside him. She stared at his fingers as they flew over the strings of his guitar. He closed his eyes and his head fell back, but he did not fall and his fingers did not falter.

The Demon lay on the road writhing. Within the Demon, amber light tinged with bloody shadows flickered wildly with a dark beauty. The Demon glared at them with red eyes and hissed something unintelligible. The sound slid like thorns through its clenched teeth and ripped through the music, sundering it into a million pieces. Cedar cried out in pain as his arm spasmed and the music died.

Startled, Ria's voice caught in her throat. The gold light dimmed and began to bleed away. Freed, the Demon pulled itself up to its full height, towering eight feet over them. Its triumphant screech was painful in the overwhelming silence.

Cedar collapsed, the guitar falling from his hands with a discordant bang.

The golden glow disappeared altogether and with it the voice, leaving Ria alone once more. She screamed and shook Cedar, begging him to get up. He opened his eyes and tried to focus on her. His fingers twitched and his mouth moved. She bent close to hear what he was trying to say.

"Listen," he whispered, his voice paper-thin.

"I'm trying!" she sobbed, not listening to anything but the frantic pounding of her own heart.

"Just listen." He grabbed her arm. His grip was strong, but only for an instant and then his hand fell away.

"I don't know how to!" she said.

"Of course you do," he said with the hint of a smile. "What do you think you were doing before?"

Ria shook her head in disbelief. The Demon stalked towards them, ignoring her. It was not her it was concerned with as it began to crush the guitar under its feet, grinding the splinters into the road.

"But you're not playing!" Ria wiped her face with the back of her hand. "You're not playing! I can't hear the words!"

"Ria, just listen! You don't *need* the music."

Only the strength in his eyes kept her from breaking down and curling up in a ball to shut the world out. It was all wrong, but Cedar believed. That had to be worth something. Ria took a deep breath and listened.

Call them.

She listened for the music, but it was gone, silenced. Something else, something she could only comprehend as a vast, powerful silence which was not so much the absence of the song but a precursor to it, filled the air instead and suddenly, somehow, she knew that *this* was what Cedar called the Path.

Call them.

Ria started to speak again with the foreign words. She still didn't know what meaning they held, but she could feel the compelling intention under the sound and syllables, pushing, pulling, commanding, *creating.*

Call them.

Ria did. With every utterance her voice grew stronger, wiping out everything else but her mission.

A strapping blond young man with strong, square features and a pair of fur-lined drums strapped to his back appeared next to her. Dressed entirely in furs from boots to knee-length pants and vest, he gazed at her with clear sky-blue eyes. He stood casually on one leg, the other tucked behind the first, his arms crossed and a surprised expression on his guileless face.

"Hello," he said with a courteous nod.

Ria stared at him and faltered slightly in her shock. The man looked around and seemed to take in the situation with aplomb, though his eyes lingered on Cedar and the Demon.

"I would continue singing if I were you," he said, nodding at her encouragingly, his voice warm and gentle.

Ria continued. The second to appear was a small man with a polished violin against his neck and the bow in his hands. His dark hair was long and swept to one side with streaks of silver, green and violet. His black leather garb was threaded with the same colors. Thin lips curved up in a wicked smile, and his black eyes sparkled in a sharp face shadowed by stubble.

"What's all this?" he said, sweeping his bow in a savage arc to encompass the scene.

Ria didn't waste breath answering, instead closing her eyes and continuing to speak the magyc words, knowing one more remained to be summoned. When the words ran out and she opened her eyes, a slim woman with long auburn hair braided with gold string and feathers had arrived.

The woman's breaches were white suede and her white silk shirt, edged with lace, flared at the sleeves. Teal eyes danced with latent laughter and her unlined face had a kind patience that belied how ancient she was. Her ears curved up to pointed tips and she clenched a slim silver flute in one hand.

"Hello boys," the she-elf drawled. Her eyes fell on Ria. "And girl? What is going on?" She reached down and held out a hand to Ria. "Did you bring us here, young lady?"

Ria nodded, too drained to say anything, her mind empty now that she had unleashed the words given to her. She reached out to take the she-elf's hand. Their hands touched and then passed right through each other.

The she-elf looked dismayed. "By the Path, we do not have much time."

"Listen to me very carefully." Teal eyes bored into Ria's grey ones, the steel in the elf's gaze much louder than that of Cedar's. "We have been brought here by the Path, but our bodies are elsewhere. As such, we will be of little help to you."

Ria glanced behind her at Cedar's inert form which lay defenseless in the shadow of the Demon as it howled and tried to shred the strings of the guitar between its teeth.

"What do I have to do?" she whispered.

"She can't kill it," the violinist spoke up. "She's not strong enough, apparently. Why else would she waste the effort to call us here?"

Ria rankled at his words and decided she didn't like him, even though she hadn't technically met him yet.

"Banish it," the drummer said. "She can banish it."

"If she hurries," the she-elf added.

"How?" Ria asked.

"Listen, just like you did before. Let the Path use you," the drummer said. "We will help as much as we can."

Doubt filled the emptiness in Ria's mind but now she knew enough not to pay attention to it. She took a deep breath and closed her eyes. The tap of a drum was joined by the haunting notes of a flute and violin, so faint the sound was only the whisper of a memory, but it was enough. The amber light that was the Path grew in her again and Ria let it use her, her lips and tongue moving, no longer trying to hear the words, instead letting them flow through her.

She spoke faster, her voice rising and falling in time to the primordial rhythm given to her by the Path. The Demon dropped the scraps of the guitar, driven into a dance of agony. It writhed spasmodically, its claws scratching deep grooves in the dirt road. After a moment spent trying to fight Ria, it tried to crawl away as it shot glances drenched in hatred back at her. Finally, it collapsed and lay still for a moment, then raised its head with effort.

"I will remember you, *Aethsiths*," it hissed, the guttural voice breaking.

Using its claws, the Demon tore through the very air itself, opening a fissure into a dark Void which reeked of Demons. It climbed into the Void, screeched once more over its shoulder and then followed the echoes into nothingness.

The early-evening sun infused the air with new warmth, and a breeze carried a fresh, sweet smell to wash away the acid air the Demon had brought. A bird began a joyful trill as the forest around them returned to life. Ria sank to her knees, devoid of strength. The strangers she had called began to melt into the fading amber light.

"Tell Cedar when he awakes that we will search for him," the she-elf said and smiled with ghostly lips. "The Guardians will be together again."

Looking around, Ria saw Cedar behind her. She didn't remember moving away, but she must have chased the Demon as it retreated. Feeling as if she had a mountain resting between her shoulder blades, Ria rose to her feet and clumsily walked to where Cedar lay unmoving. The splinters of his guitar looked like matchsticks, cold and lifeless. She touched his arm and his eyes opened, the gold submerged in a dull film.

"What happened?" Cedar asked, his voice croaking.

Ria shrugged, unable to explain. He tried to sit up and grimaced in pain, lying back before he'd risen an inch. Ria frowned, and then shivered. The sun had disappeared behind the trees and the evening chill was creeping up. More time had passed than she had thought.

"We have to get off the road, and make a fire," she said, injecting her voice with a cheerful authority she didn't feel.

"I'm game," Cedar smiled weakly. "Help me up."

With Ria's help he sat up, but she could not bear his weight when he tried to stand and they both sank down to sit on the road. Cedar passed his hand over his eyes.

"Where's…" he started to ask when he saw the splinters.

He didn't bother to finish the question and simply closed his eyes. The first strains of panic began to take hold of Ria, and then Cedar mumbled something.

"What?" she asked and leaned closer. He didn't answer.

"Cedar, you have to make yourself well," she said, trying not to whine and sound as frightened as she felt. He was her sole guiding light in this place; if he died, her future faded to black just as his did. "What if it comes back?"

Even in his injured state he managed a smile, shifting his leg slightly. "Ria, it's not that simple."

"You always say that," she said with a frown.

"Because it's true," he said, rising to his knees, and then falling back again.

No warning twinge of untruth tied her insides together, and that hurt more than knowing he was lying.

"You can have my blood," she blurted out.

He looked at her, surprised. "That is very kind of

you…" he began.

She stood up, put her hands on her hips and glared down at him. "You can't just leave me here!" she yelled. "You promised!"

He closed his eyes, breathing unevenly. "I never meant for this to happen," he said.

"I want to help," she said, grabbing his shoulder, forcing him to look at her. "It's OK. I don't mind."

"Like I said, it's not that simple," he said. "Your blood is no use anymore. I told you I used it all up, remember? It was the only way I could get back," he said, his eyes pleading with her to understand.

She didn't understand. "I have blood!" she said angrily. "You showed me!" She held up her finger to remind him.

He took her wrist and gently put her arm down to her side. The slight effort cost him visibly. "I know, but that blood has been changed. I can't use it anymore!"

"You have to meet them," Ria said, desperation leaking into her voice.

"Who?"

"The other Guardians. They told me so!"

"Ria." Cedar's voice broke, but she refused to look away, silently begging him not to give up.

He glanced away, his eyes falling on the jacket that lay where Ria had dropped it. He struggled to reach it, and his face became whiter. Ria retrieved it, and gave it to him. He reached into his pocket to pull out the little vial of blood. She took it from his open palm, and held it flat in her hand. It was still warm. It seemed so long ago that he had cut her arm.

"Ria, I saved this so I could send you back. It was part of the plan. I had no idea what sort of mess I was going to return to in Demona, so just in case I saved as much as I could. I couldn't save more. I had to make sure I had enough to get to Demona. I don't know what happened here, but it's different, the magyc is different, it's fading…"

His gold eyes willed her to understand. She nodded, even though she didn't understand at all. She held up the vial and examined the red liquid inside. It was thick and clung with stubborn sluggishness to the glass.

"Ria, I really was going to do it." He was speaking too fast. "I had it all planned out before we got here." He chuckled, a feeble sound. "But sometimes plans crumble and all you can do is watch. I really was going to do it," he repeated. His earnestness sapped his strength and his eyelids fluttered. "I still will. I promise. I will find a way to send you home, but I can't do it if I'm dead."

"I know," she said. She knelt next to him and pressed the vial into his hand, closing his cold fingers around it. "It's okay. Take it. We'll find another way."

"I promise I will. I will get you home." His gold eyes burned into hers. "But you have to do this. I can't."

She nodded, understanding. If she wanted it, she was the one who was going to have to make it so. It had nothing to do with whether Cedar was able to or not; he was refusing for reasons known only to him.

She closed her eyes and tried, but nothing came. She huffed in frustration. When she opened her eyes, he had fainted. She caught his limp body before it fell to the ground and let his head fall against her shoulder. She knew giving in to the panic would not help, but cold fingers prodded her belly and doubt whispered with its mean little voice in her ear. Gritting her teeth she tried again, ignoring the weight of him. Her tongue felt thick and clumsy.

Listen. The echo of the she-elf's voice whispered to her.

Ria clutched the whisper and rode it into a cool, calm

place until she heard the silent voice again clear as a bell. When she spoke the words were liquid gold on her tongue and the blood in the vial slowly transmuted into a similar light. No longer constrained, it blanketed the wound and seeped into Cedar's flesh. A blinding flash of light left Ria blinking and seeing black explosions. When she could see again, Cedar had pulled up the leg of his blood-stained pants to the knee and was examining his leg, flexing the muscles. His cheeks were flushed with color and his eyes were bright.

"Is it fixed?" she asked, hopeful.

"Feels almost as good as new," he said.

Ria could see that was a stretch, but the wound had stopped bleeding and even seemed a little less gaping. She had to help him to stand, but he bore his own weight and was able to walk on his own.

"Now, how about that fire?" he asked.

The flames shot sparks high into the sky. Ria's belly was full of cold pigeon and apples. She was warm and comfortable, and she lay on her back in a shallow, grassy indentation at the side of the road, using his jacket as a pillow. She gazed at the first star of the evening, a tiny point of light peeking through the dark blue sky. "What are we going to do now?"

He looked down at her. "Don't worry. You will go back. I promise. It's just going to take a little longer."

"You know, you can stop saying that," Ria said, shifting her head to a better position. "I believe you. I *can* tell when you're lying, remember?"

She looked up at him and smiled. His gold eyes turned iridescent green, hazel and grey in the light of the flames. The trees whispered to each other and the road wound away, an orange ribbon that twisted into nothingness in the dark trees. The sky above them was clear as blue gave way to black. More stars joined the first, sparkling like faint diamonds as a flock of birds winged their way towards the horizon.

"Could you always do that?"

Ria shook her head. "I don't think so."

Cedar nodded and though his expression was pensive, he offered no further comment.

"Will we go find the others?" Ria asked.

"Perhaps," Cedar said slowly. "Tell me Ria, how did they seem to you?"

"A little surprised at first, but they were nice. More than nice, actually," Ria said. "Except the one with black hair. He's darker than the others. I don't think I'll like him much."

Cedar chucked, but his humor was short-lived. "Did they say anything to you?"

"They said to listen," Ria said. She shifted to her side so she could look at him without straining her neck. "The Demon said something too. He said he would remember me, and then he said a word I don't know."

"What did it sound like?" Cedar asked, sitting straight and still, his face a mask of stone.

"Air whispering," Ria said immediately. The hair on her arm lifted just thinking back to it. "If the air could whisper, it would say that word."

"*Aethsiths*," Cedar said to himself, and he went to a place only his eyes could see, leaving Ria to speak to a body with a vacant expression.

"Yes! Ay…Ace-this…*Ayth-siths*." Her tongue didn't want to say the word, but when it finally came out right, it rang with powerful significance. Ria fell silent for a moment, reveling in the sound of it. "What does it mean?"

Cedar started and wrapped his arms around himself

as though he were warding off the cold. "I'm not sure. Right now, it is not very important. Maybe as we travel, there will be time to…Anyway, first we need to find the other Guardians."

He was lying; Ria knew it by the little flutter, a butterfly's tickle, in her chest and like a string being plucked a trickle of doubt entered her mind. It was as if the untruth made something inside her knock against something else, and like a row of dominoes falling to hit a little bell, she knew he was lying. She also knew now was not the time to press him for the truth.

"Where will we go?" she asked instead.

"I have to make a new guitar," Cedar said. "I will have to get wood and strings. For that, we will go to D'Ohera. Perhaps they will meet us there. If not, then we will see. Now go to sleep. I will keep watch."

Ria closed her eyes and drifted to sleep. She let the Path shape her dreams, both the comforting ones and the one that brought her awake with a gasp in time to see red eyes blink and disappear. It happened so quickly she thought it must have been a remnant from her dream playing tricks on her eyes.

GOLDEN GUITAR

Cedar Jal was tired of the endless road, little more than a well-worn track across the plain, that disappeared at the flat and unexciting horizon. His back felt cold and bare without the weight of his guitar and although he didn't want to admit it, his leg was killing him, itching like a Demon. That did mean it was healing, but right then he wanted to tear the skin off just to assuage the burn, damn the healing. *This wasn't exactly the homecoming I had been hoping for, but I suppose it could be worse.*

He looked down at the bobbing head of his solemn and taciturn traveling companion. Ria's auburn hair was greasy and covered in the dust that their feet kicked up with every step. She appeared to feel his gaze and looked up at him with a gaunt and sunburned face. Her grey eyes still sparkled with determination and she offered him a little smile with her chapped lips.

"Does your leg hurt?" she asked.

That girl is too perceptive by far for it to be quite natural. "Not much," he told her.

"You know," Ria said, giving him a long look before turning her gaze to the dusty road, "You're not a very good liar."

"So I've noticed," Cedar grumbled. "But there's nothing I can do about it right now."

"Your leg or your terrible lying?" Ria asked, her face perfectly straight, and Cedar wondered if she was making a joke or not.

"Both."

She slipped her hand into his and gave it a squeeze. He found the gesture comforting; even if he had not forgiven himself for the deception and violation, the girl seemed to have come to terms with it and did not bear a grudge, for which Cedar was grateful. He had no desire to scar the girl for life.

"How much further is it to D'Ohera?" Ria asked, squinting into the distance as if she would be able to see the city which had been their unchanging destination these long days.

"Damn if I know," Cedar said, his weariness pressing harder on his shoulders with every step. "I thought we would reach it days ago."

His stomach growled in agreement. As if in answer Ria's stomach gave a low gurgle and she giggled. He couldn't help it; he smiled back. Due to the untimely demise of his guitar, food had been limited to the few squirrels he managed to charm with increasing difficulty out of the trees and under-ripe berries. Fire had been equally scarce, the flames he had conjured more akin to a splutter than a blaze, though they hadn't yet been forced to suffer raw meat.

Numerous small streams twisted under the trees in the

forest, providing more than enough fresh water, but no fish. Cedar had looked. Then the forest had ended and given way to flat, arid plains which offered even less in the way of sustenance, and no water. Two days before, Cedar had given Ria the last meager handful of crushed berries. Neither of them had food or water since.

Ria trudged on stalwartly beside him though it was obvious the lack of food and water was taking its toll on her smaller-than-average twelve-year-old body. Cedar suspected the fact that she had technically almost died several days ago was exacerbating the situation, and guilt twisted uncomfortably in his gut. He tried not to let it show on his face; he didn't want to get into a discussion about it, especially now that he was unable to lie in a convincing manner.

I must find a way to send her back, and as soon as possible. It was stupid and foolhardy to bring her here like that.

Dealing with Death had taken its toll on Cedar as well. He had done it many times before, but never had his encounters occurred so close to each other or been so severe. Surprise still lingered when he thought about how he had managed to get out of them so cleanly, mitigated by the feeling the girl had more to do with both instances than it appeared.

Coming within an arm's breadth of Death wasn't so bad in the end, Cedar thought to himself, *just left you with a cold finger in your still-beating heart and a hazy spot in your mind.*

Two close shaves was more than enough, though only one was properly his, and Cedar determined to have no more for a good long time, until long after the girl was safely back to where she had come from. Wherever *that* was.

I would give my left arm to know how she managed to call the door and *pull us through so cleanly.*

Her lack of familiarity with magyc and walking between worlds told him that she hadn't done it before, which made her proficiency all the more astounding. Cedar entertained the idea of attempting to reproduce the circumstances that brought the two of them together and see if the girl could find her way back, but dismissed it. There were too many unknowns regarding the magycal mishap that had trapped him in the Void-like place between worlds to risk it.

Though he knew that he had done the only thing he could have, Cedar wished that some other, *any* other, way had presented itself. Sinking to the level that he had left a bad taste in his mouth and a blight on his dignity. Sending Ria back would hopefully expunge those.

That still left the problem of *how* to send her back. Only one kind existed who possessed the ability to walk between the worlds with any certainty, and only a few of those were able to make doors to other worlds. The Witches of Lii maintained a low profile, a polite way of saying they were impossible to find when you needed them, nor could they be bought with any amount of coin if they did not wish to be bought. There was also the inconvenient predicament that the Guardians weren't exactly on good terms with the Witches.

"There's someone coming," Ria said suddenly, pulling Cedar out of his dark reverie. "Maybe they can help us."

The black dot coming fast behind the pair grew into a horse and rider. Cedar and Ria stopped and stepped to the side of the narrow road and Cedar raised his hand to flag down the rider, a young, freckled boy with straw-blond hair sticking to his sweaty forehead.

Catching sight of the pair on foot waving him down,

the boy tried to veer away, urging the animal to greater speed. Cedar saw the boy had no intention of stopping to help them. *Not today, young sir.*

Kneeling, Cedar pressed his palm to the warm, dry earth, and searched for the subtle, driving rhythm that bound the world together. A few stubborn blades of spindly grass tickled his hands and a drop of sweat trickled down the side of his face. He almost couldn't feel the Path, a feeling as strange as not being able to feel his own heartbeat.

It shook him to the core, until Ria knelt down to put her warm hand over his. Brilliant gold light almost blinded Cedar and he whispered to the horse with forgotten words. Despite frantic yanks on the reins and several kicks, the horse slowed and trotted willingly to Cedar's outstretched hand.

The youth glared down at him, his dull eyes sullen. He wore old clothes in need of a good darning and no shoes. The horse on the other hand, was in remarkably good condition; strong and well fed, with thick muscles that bunched under a glossy, albeit sweaty, coat.

Cedar rubbed its soft nose and looked up at the rider. "Good day," he said cheerfully to the boy.

The youth grunted.

"I am Cedar Jal."

The youth said nothing.

"Do you perchance have a name?"

Muttering something, the boy would not look directly at him.

"You'll have to speak up," Cedar said, his manner still pleasant.

"Seca," the boy grumbled. "I have nothing for you to steal, thief."

"I would watch who you call thief," Cedar said, a cold

knife entering his voice. "You don't look much more than that yourself."

Seca drew back in fear, his pronounced Adam's apple bobbing as he swallowed.

"Now," Cedar continued, his manner returning to its former congeniality, "Let's talk about this horse, shall we?"

"I didn't steal it!" the youth burst out.

"He's a worse liar than you are," Ria commented, reaching up to pet the animal and giggling when it nibbled her hand with its big lips.

Seca glared at her, but at a look from Cedar the ugly scowl was replaced with a meek pout.

"It looks strong enough to carry two children and a man," Cedar said. "We are heading for D'Ohera and I am assuming you are doing the same?"

Seca did not look happy but he nodded.

"Perfect!" Cedar smiled widely.

Ria tugged on his arm and motioned for him to bend down. He did and she put her mouth close to his ear.

"What about food?" she whispered.

"Right," he said, standing and returning his gaze to Seca. "We are rather famished. You wouldn't have procured some food with that horse?"

Seca shook his head. Ria did not say anything so Cedar assumed the boy was telling the truth. Cedar shrugged. "Not to worry. We won't starve just yet."

Setting Ria behind the youth, he climbed up behind her, wanting to keep the youth where he could see him. The horse danced at the extra weight on his back and Cedar reached forward to pet the animal soothingly on the neck.

"You couldn't have stolen the saddle as well?" Cedar asked. The youth glowered silently over his shoulder.

"No matter," Cedar said. "This will do fine."

Gently nudging the horse forward, the chance companions set out again for D'Ohera. Cedar desperately hoped they would find it before too long and too late.

They rode without stopping until the moon rose round and silver in the dark sky. The two children had drifted to sleep hours before. First Ria, who leaned back against Cedar's chest. The boy fought sleep for longer but eventually his eyes drooped and his head began to bounce on his chest in time to the steady gait of the horse.

Finding a patch of relatively lush grass under three stunted trees, Cedar gently pulled Ria from the saddle. He lay her down under the middle tree and covered her with his jacket, which had somehow managed to remain a pristine white. The boy he had to shake awake and help off the horse. Seca ignored the arm Cedar extended and stumbled a few paces before dropping to the ground, snoring softly before his head came to rest.

Cedar led the horse to what he hoped was the sturdiest of the trees and tied it there, speaking calming words. The horse's dark eyes drank up moonlight as it nickered softly at him. Lying next to Ria, the last thing Cedar remembered was a streak of light as a star fell to the ground.

Ria's scream made him bolt awake and stand up even before his eyes were open. In the pale predawn light, it took him a moment to assimilate the scene that confronted his tired eyes. Seca was trying to put Ria on the horse while she kicked and clawed at his arms.

A glint of steel caught Cedar's eye, and his heart rate sped up as Ria screeched again. A moment later Seca gave a yell when Ria's teeth sank into his arm. The pair went down and Ria squirmed away from him as the boy scrabbled in the dewy grass to retrieve his knife.

Untied from the tree, the horse would have bolted at the commotion but Cedar managed to grab the reins with one hand and reach for Ria with the other. She was up before he could grab her, her lips smeared with blood, her teeth bared in a savage snarl and her hands balled into fists at her side.

Seca stood, one hand clutching his injured arm and the other bringing the knife up as he moved towards Ria. Quicker than a snake striking, Cedar grabbed the boy's wrist and twisted a little harder than was absolutely necessary. Seca screeched and dropped the knife. The boy cradled his wrist against his chest as he took a step back.

"You broke it!" he half-sobbed.

"It's no more than sprained," Cedar said mildly as he soothed the agitated horse with gentle strokes.

Seca froze for a fraction of a moment and then dropped his arm. Grabbing the knife, he took off running in the opposite direction without a backwards glance. Cedar watched his retreating form to make sure the boy wasn't coming back, and then turned to Ria.

She gave him a small smile, her face pale. Unclenching her fists, she tenderly touched her side before she slumped to the ground.

Pulling her shirt away from her side revealed a nasty cut running in a jagged tear from Ria's ribs to her hip. Cursing himself for allowing such a thing to happen, Cedar touched the wound and whispered. His connection to the Path weak and patchy and Ria was in no state to assist him, but it was enough. His words stopped the bleeding and woke Ria, who blinked at him with bemused eyes. The faint light of the sun hiding just below the horizon made her look like something risen from the grave.

"Sleep," he said softly with what he hoped was a

reassuring smile and touched her eyelids.

She did and Cedar took a deep breath as he tried to clear the sudden dizziness from his head. In that moment he realized he could no longer write off the strange laboriousness he experienced in calling the Path to having been trapped in the Void. Something was wrong, and Cedar had a strong inkling that it had to do with the perturbing incidents at the Crescent Temple and Akorgia.

The uncertainty made him an autumn leaf in the wind with nothing to ground him and he fumbled mentally for something to orient himself. His stomach clenched and hands shook with the need to reach D'Ohera without delay to find out what had transpired since he'd left. The girl's injury only added oil to that fire. Cedar grabbed onto the seriousness of her condition and used it to stop the world's wild spin. He was on his feet in a flash.

Riding is not going to be good for that wound, but I cannot help her any more than I have and she'll die if we stay here. Cedar lifted the unconscious girl onto the horse, climbed up behind her and held her fast with one arm.

Clucking softly, he pushed the horse as fast as he dared in the direction of the rising sun and D'Ohera. Sometime around midday her wound opened and he felt hot wetness through his sleeve. Nothing he tried would close it again, so he bit his tongue and continued. The flatness of the plains began to diminish and the land began to roll like the waves of the sea in a storm. Cedar's pulse quickened.

"Just a little further to go," he said, more to himself than to Ria, though at his words the girl muttered and stirred in her magyc sleep.

The hills seemed to go on forever, rising and falling steadily with the same monotony as the plains behind them as Cedar and Ria flew over the rolling terrain. As it sank toward the horizon, the sun's dying rays glinted off a smudge of something black.

Hardly daring to hope, Cedar slowed the horse. He shaded his eyes against the glare, and saw the shining black glass of the Necrolatry in D'Ohera. A relieved smile spread across his face. Urging the horse to a gallop, Cedar watched the Necrolatry grow from the tiny tip of an arrow to a giant black finger pointing at the sky as they rode. Cedar crested a hill and D'Ohera stretched out before him like a festering wound.

In the center of the City, the Pyramid of Light and the Gardens shone like a pale pearl. To the west lay the labyrinth of the Market, and to the north the Justice and the Prisons. The Pleasure District was a bright patchwork of gold, purple, blue and red rooftops and jutting spires, located conveniently next to the Justice and in the shadow of the Necrolatry, which was also known as Death's Temple.. All through the City, hovels, mud houses, tenements and mansions grew up next to each other like uneven stubble. It was one of the ugliest things in all of Demona and Cedar had never been so happy to see anything in all his life.

He nudged the horse onward and the smell hit as he neared the gates, making him remember with clarity the stench that could accompany this many people in this small an area. The better areas of D'Ohera had subterranean drainage systems, but unfortunately the majority of the city did not.

Gagging, Cedar made himself continue to breathe through his nose as he passed under the gates. In a few short moments his sense of smell was thankfully deadened. Emerging from the gates brought Cedar into the First Square.

Even in twilight the unpaved streets were full of

people: merchants, urchins, Ladies, soldiers or sell-swords, Scholars, priests, beggars and the rich going by in their elaborate palanquins or on bejeweled horses. Cedar even saw a few wild-men and one Thaumaturgist in the dark blue robes of the Cobalt Order. Cedar ignored them all as he pressed through the throngs, making for the Pleasure District. As Cedar made his way deeper into the city, more and more people filled the streets, and the less savory sorts started to appear. Forced to an agonizingly slow walk, Ria muttered and twitched as they were bumped and jostled from all sides.

Her fever burned hot enough to warm Cedar through his clothes and his worry deepened, a thousand little pins digging into his thoughts. Finally, he reined up in front of a tavern, an unimposing off-white building with a small porch in front and windows only on the upper level. A sign in the shape of a rearing horse read "Tales Mane".

"Victoria!" Cedar called, using the last of his strength to make his hoarse voice more compelling than an ordinary hail.

A form appeared instantly, a shape against the light spilling from the door. "Who calls?" a voice issued from the figure.

"Cedar Jal."

With a barely perceptible motion, the figure gave a discreet wave and disappeared. Cedar sighed in relief. He had feared in this weird world she wouldn't know or remember him, or worse, be gone.

He nudged the horse around to the back courtyard where a sadly dilapidated stable which stank of horse manure and rotten hay sagged against the two buildings on either side. He stopped at a small door in the white wall of the inn near the stable. The door was the same color as the wall, and it was practically invisible in the twilight. The horse nickered and the silver-white nose of a donkey appeared at the window to give a deafening bray in answer.

Cedar gave a tired smile as he dismounted, keeping one hand on Ria so she did not fall. "Good evening Silver. I trust you are as well as ever."

"So the ass gets a proper greeting, and what does the old friend get?" a gravelly voice grumbled behind him. "Orders in that voice you use on animals to make them obey!"

Victoria Meech was a woman whose age was impossible to guess but Cedar put her in her mid-sixties. She had a plain look that suggested she had never been a great beauty. Her hands trembled slightly and her dress was simple, undyed cotton, but there was iron in her spine and fire in her bright blue eyes. Her left eye sagged and wandered to the left a little, but she fixed the other on Cedar who embraced her fondly.

"You smell worse than my stable," she told him, wrinkling her nose as she looked him up and down, taking in his filthy clothes, long stubble and gaunt face.

He smiled ruefully. "Yes, I can imagine."

"Can you?" she asked, raising her eyebrow. "And I hope all this blood isn't yours?"

"Most of it is, thankfully," Cedar said, and Victoria frowned.

Her gaze moved to the horse and then the girl. "What have we got here?"

"She needs help. Now," Cedar said as he pulled the girl from the horse and cradled her in his arms.

Victoria shook her head, a resigned expression on her kind face. "Cedar Jal…" she did not finish her rebuke, but crooked a thin finger at him and shuffled into the tavern. Cedar followed with the unconscious Ria.

Victoria led him through the kitchen, which was hot with three cooking-fires burning. The smell of smoke and meat made Cedar lightheaded but he pushed aside his hunger and followed Victoria up the squeaky stairs. Opening a door at the close end of a long corridor, she stood back to let him enter. Two beds sat under the single, wide window and a plain screen hid one corner. Cedar lay Ria down on the first bed and gently arranged the blankets around her.

"I'll get someone to look at her," Victoria said from the door. She cupped a hand to her mouth and yelled in voice that carried surprisingly well for her slight frame. "Hey! Robbie, fetch Old Jacob!"

Cedar looked up. "Old Jacob is still around?"

"See for yourself," Victoria said and she stepped aside to let someone through.

Old Jacob was a stooped dwarf with dark eyes and grey streaks in his beard. His hands were large, calloused and gentle. A small dwarf boy with bright eyes accompanied him. The burlap sack the boy carried over his shoulder contained the needles and thread, herbs and medicine that Jacob needed and it rarely left his side. With quiet efficiency, he stitched up the cut in Ria's side and saw to her other cuts and bruises.

"She is not sleeping naturally," he remarked as he dabbed a cloth soaked in some infusion or other over a cut. Ria hardly stirred under his ministrations. "I trust that is your work and not something malevolent?"

Cedar nodded.

"She won't heal that way," Jacob said, his voice gravelly. "She must be allowed to rest properly, and she should eat something."

"They should both eat something," Victoria butted in, giving Cedar a mothering look.

"Nothing too rich," Old Jacob cautioned as he put his tools and medicines away. "Some broth, some fruit, maybe a little dry bread."

Cedar nodded and stood. "I'll get it."

Victoria shooed him away. "Nonsense. You stay here and watch the girl. Maybe take a bath. I'll be back shortly."

Cedar gave a tired nod and settled down on the edge of the bed. Jacob gracefully took his leave, picking up his sack and guiding the dwarf boy out. Ria was still caught fast in his commanded sleep. He touched her arm to release her, and her eyes flickered open. Ria fixed her gaze on him, then she shifted in the bed and looked around.

"Where are we?" she asked.

"In D'Ohera, at the Tales Mane," Cedar said, and gave her a reassuring smile.

Ria nodded and slid her hand down to touch her side, her fingers gently exploring the new stitches. "Is there food?"

At that moment Victoria came into the room bearing a tray which was almost the size of the bed. For Ria there was only broth, small apricots, sweet cherries and unbuttered bread as Old Jacob had ordered. For Cedar, there was roast meat of some sort, potatoes, turnips, dark bread with butter and beer. Placing the tray on the little bedside table, Victoria turned and left them to eat in peace.

Cedar helped Ria sit up and situated her food on her lap before turning to his own fare. His mouth was watering at the sight of the food but he knew he would end up with a stomachache if he wolfed it so he paced himself and chewed each bite many times before swallowing.

Ria brightened immediately at the food and ate hungrily. When she had finished every morsel, she lay back and closed her eyes, a contented smile on her face. Within moments she fell into a natural, healthy sleep and Cedar was pleased to see a pink glow on her cheeks.

Victoria returned just as he was putting the last bite of meat into his mouth. She brought a bowl of Two-Week pudding and cream. "This is the last piece," she said. "I saved it for you."

Cedar smiled at her as he took the bowl. "Are you sure it's not Eight- or Nine-Week pudding then?" he asked.

She did not smile at the joke. "More like four-year pudding," she said.

The smile fell from Cedar's face. "By the Path!" he muttered under his breath. *How can it have been so long?*

"What happened?" Victoria asked. "Timo came by at midnight one night, said he was signing on with his brother and then vanished. Luca has made neither peep nor appearance, but Timo mentioned he was going south. There was one message from Jæyd that said to lie low and keep safe, and nothing since. No one said anything about you, Cedar Jal. Wherever did you go off to?"

Cedar grimaced. "Nowhere that I wished to. It was a Void of sorts, but unlike any Demon Void."

Victoria shook her head. "You know all of that means naught to me, Cedar Jal. Demons are the stuff of Guardians, not plain folk such as I."

He sighed and put his head in his hand. "I know Victoria, yet I think I understand it even less than you do. I've thought about it from every conceivable angle and I have yet to make sense of it. I feel my head will soon explode."

"Sleep, Cedar," Victoria said, laying a hand on his shoulder and gently relieving him of the untouched pudding. "Perhaps in the morning it will be clearer to you."

Cedar nodded gratefully. He pulled the covers over Ria, who stirred but did not wake. Walking to the second bed in the room and sitting heavily, he slowly pulled off one shoe and then the other. He began to unbuckle his belt, but his fingers were thick and clumsy. In the end he simply gave up, threw back the covers and collapsed.

His eyes opened. Surrounded by a world of golden light, Cedar knew he was dreaming, but no ordinary dream. A familiar shape stepped out of the light and smiled at him. "It is good to see you again," Jæyd said, her blue-green eyes bright.

Cedar felt the weariness that had plagued him begin to dispel in the warmth of her smile.

"The others?" he asked.

Timo and Luca fell in place behind Jæyd. Timo's face was shining with his customary grin and even Luca did not appear as ill-natured as usual. Cedar wanted to embrace them, to reassure himself they were real and alive, but he knew that would have to wait until they were together in the material realms. The sight of their faces would have to suffice for the present.

"We have not much time," Jæyd said, flipping her plait over her shoulder.

"We seem to hear that a lot lately," Luca said, his mouth twisting in an angry grimace. "What happened? *Where did you go? Who is that girl? What are we supposed to* do?"

"He will have time to tell all later," Timo said with a long look Cedar pretended not to see. "When we are together."

The emphasis was not lost on Cedar.

"Indeed," he agreed quickly. "I am at the Tales Mane. I must forge another guitar for myself." He could see them all thinking the same thing, remembering the first golden encounter in the forest and the Demon. I was too out to notice anything, *he remembered ruefully.*

"That Demon. The one that you fought," Jæyd said, her expression and tone too careful. "Was that…?"

"One of the Nine?" Cedar finished the question, and he felt his insides go cold as he recalled the encounter. "It is possible. I am not

sure, but it is possible."

Cedar knew better. In old stories and old tongues the Demon would have been called The God of Blood. Now it was simply one of the Nine. The Nine Demons that had given Demona its name and brought about the birth of the Guardians of the Path. The Nine Demons that the First Guardian had banished with the Amber Torch. And now one has returned.

"And the girl?" Jæyd asked. "She truly banished it. Alone?"

"We will discuss that later," Cedar said curtly, not wishing to think about that now, or any of its many significances and ramifications. Above all, he didn't want to think about what the Demon had named the girl.

"What if she is the one?" Luca said, rubbing his pointed chin, his black eyes narrowed. His lips quirked up in a smile as though he had read Cedar's mind. "The Demon certainly seemed to think so."

"She is too young," Cedar said, a dangerous note in his voice.

The other three Guardians stared at him and he stared back defiantly. One by one, they dropped their gazes. Cedar knew the victory was a hollow one; he had not quashed their questions.

"Very well, Cedar," Jæyd said at last. "We will discuss it later." The golden light began to fade. "We will meet at the Tales Mane. Stay put, forge your guitar, and each of us shall fly there as fast as we are able. The Guardians will be together once again…"

Cedar woke abruptly awake and grimaced in the dim light of dawn. He felt unrested; his weariness had returned tenfold and his bones were tired. Getting up silently and taking pains not to wake Ria, he pulled on his shoes and went downstairs. Victoria was coaxing the fire back to life in the compressed bricks of sawdust and manure, the only cheap fuel available in the city. He stood in the doorway, waiting for her to finish. When the fire caught, she turned slowly and dusted her hands off.

"Well, Cedar Jal?" she asked. "Is the world clearer to you this morning?"

He gave a wry smile. "Somewhat."

"Very good. What is it that you now know?"

"I have to make a new guitar."

Victoria raised an eyebrow. "And this you did not already know? Your case was curiously absent and I am sure I am not the only one that noticed."

"Yes, but I told the others that I was here and that I was going to forge a guitar, so now I must do it. They are coming here," Cedar told her.

"And you will wait for them?"

"If you will have me," Cedar said.

"I could not turn you away if I wanted," Victoria said with an amused sniff. "Not with that girl you are dragging along. Besides, there are floors to be scrubbed, food to be moved to the cellar and the roof is leaking in six places."

Cedar smiled. "I'll get right on it."

"First the guitar," Victoria said, pointing a finger at him, a small smile on her lips. "Then the floors."

Cedar smiled. "The materials I need will not be cheap. I will need money and that means a trip to…"

"That means a bath and a new set of clothes," Victoria said, ever the practical voice, and gave the dirt and blood staining his clothes a pointed glance. "Now."

After a hot breakfast, a hotter bath, a shave and a change of clothes, Cedar felt ten years younger and ready to take on any one of the Nine. In a crisp white shirt and black slacks which brightened his obsidian hair, he made his way purposefully towards the Business District to obtain one very important thing that was needed to get anything done in any city, anywhere - money.

In sight of the pale grey walls of the imposing Justice, the street widened and Cedar was in the Business District of D'Ohera. Stone buildings took the place of wood and clay and the sun glinted off real glass windows, made by skilled Thaumaturgists in Isos or Samnara. Sitting between the Library and the Good Sons Hospital was the Coinage.

From his rough grasp of D'Oheran history, Cedar knew the Coinage was the second-oldest building in the city, second only to the Lion's Den, the indoor market with seven separate mazes of mud-brick suites. There were rumors of extensive underground tunnels for clandestine transactions, built by the Five Peddlers and the Stranger long before in the Time of Princes. No one knew why there were seven zones yet only six builders, though local legends abounded.

The Coinage had far simpler origins and no legends. It boasted over four thousand iron lockboxes and two hundred stone vaults in an underground labyrinth built in four levels that went a hundred feet down. Above ground, the Coinage appeared as a modest two-story building of veined, cream marble built in the style of the Esters and their Land-Beyond-The-Sea, with engraved columns supporting an overhanging roof and no windows. Gilded doors standing nine feet tall with handles of ivory and jade dominated the front of the Coinage.

Cedar paused as he read the sign over the door. He was certain it used to say, "The Path of Life is paved with Silver and Gold" in Old Hahlvetian. Now it proclaimed, "All roads are paved with Silver and Gold" in the Common tongue. It added to his growing disquiet about this strange new Demona that was not wholly familiar to him.

Cedar took the steps two at a time and pulled open the heavy doors. A gently murmuring fountain graced the center of the cool, dim foyer with impossibly high ceilings. As the door closed with a bang, the silence swallowing the echoes as a lion might swallow a mouse, Cedar gazed at the empty Coinage with a bemused expression.

The only person in sight was a fat, balding man waddling toward Cedar, perspiration adorning his brow, his hairless face twisted into an expression of simpering concern. "I'm sorry sir, can I help you?"

Cedar took an immediate dislike to him. Out of habit he answered the man pleasantly. "Perhaps. Where is everyone?" Cedar asked, gesturing around.

"I wouldn't know sir. Do you have an appointment?"

"No. I wasn't aware I needed an appointment where my money was concerned."

The man's eyes widened. "New policy, sir, I'm afraid…"

"New policy? Since when?"

"A year, more," the man said, twisting his hands. "I'm afraid you'll have to return with an appointment."

"I'd like to see the Magister," Cedar said, trying a different tactic.

"The Magister is currently occupied."

"I'd like to see him now," Cedar said. "I'm sure that Magister Lastar will be happy to see me."

A frown crossed the lumpy face of the clerk. "Jules Lastar has not been Magister for three years. It is Magister Holdun now."

Cedar pursed his lips and crossed his arms. Jules Lastar had been D'Ohera's Magister of Coin for over a dozen years. Under Lastar's sagacious care, D'Ohera had prospered with more merchants, craftsmen and artists flooding the Squares each day. Above that, he was a friend. *This keeps getting worse. And I* know *the name Holdun.*

"Why is that name familiar?"

The clerk nodded sagely. "He used to be the Magister of Arms. Perhaps that is why you know it."

"No, that's not it." Cedar remembered with an icy splash where he had heard that name.

During the cease-fire at the end of the Moonlight War between Demona and Ghor, the principality that lay just north of D'Ohera, Lan Holdun, the handsome Demonan general had led an attack on Erridon, the capital city of Ghor

Peace talks had just concluded in Erridon. Holdun destroyed the city, burning it to the ground. Four of the five Ghoris princes died, as well as seven Magisters of Demona and the two appointed Arbiters.

In retaliation, Ghor withdrew from the truce and attacked Torin, the capital of Demona, prolonging the war for another seven years. In the end, Demona crushed Ghor, which was subsequently annexed and the single remaining prince named Magister in accordance with the laws of Demona. Lan Holdun was tried for his actions, but an exceptionally brilliant and twisted lawyer named… the name escaped Cedar at the moment, but said lawyer saved Holdun from the death sentence and five years after Lan Holdun was imprisoned he was released and exiled. It was not a good omen that the name appeared here and now.

"How did Lan Holdun become the Magister of Arms and then of Coin?" Cedar asked, his hand shifting restlessly at his side.

The clerk sniffed disdainfully. "Where have you been, hiding under a rock? Lan Holdun rescued Demona when the Nitefolk attacked."

"The Nitefolk *attacked* Demona?" Cedar asked incredulously. *The world has turned upside down, left is right and right is left and the next thing they're going to tell me is the rivers flow up the mountains.*

"General Holdun crushed them in one fell swoop," the clerk explained condescendingly. "Then turned himself in to the Justice for crossing the border while exiled."

"*General* Holdun?" Cedar said. "Why not just ordain

him as a prince and be done with it?"

The clerk looked as though Cedar had just ordered him to remove all his clothes and dance naked through the Business District. After spluttering in incoherent bursts for several moments, the clerk straightened his jacket and fixed a cool glare on Cedar.

"Sir, I believe you may want to watch what you say. Lan Holdun is a hero and Demona is indebted to him. He has only ever tried to do what's best for her. He did a great service for the people of this land."

"And so he received a full pardon? Regaining all rights and privileges of a citizen of Demona, including eligibility to become a Magister?" Cedar said, his lips twisting. "How convenient for him."

"What would you have done?" the clerk said, his eyebrows rising. "He saved Demona!"

"I probably would have put an arrow in his heart," Cedar said. "Or if I couldn't find his heart, which is not out of the question, his eye would have worked just as well."

"It is treason to say so!" the clerk said, his hands at his chest.

"Then let's not say so," Cedar said, feeling any remaining warmth drain from his eyes as he glared at the clerk. "If *Magister* Holdun is not available, then perhaps *you* could help me? I simply wish to withdraw some of my money, if that's not *too* much to ask."

Cedar's sarcasm went over the head of the clerk, who twisted his face into an expression of extreme pain as he searched the empty foyer for someone to save him or a plausible way to escape. None immediately presented itself and the clerk sighed and beckoned Cedar with one pudgy finger as he waddled behind the gleaming marble counter.

"Name?"

"Cedar Jal."

"Box?"

"It's a vault actually," Cedar said smoothly. "B2."

Pulling a leather-bound ledger, one of many, from the shelves the clerk opened it with a practiced flourish and reverently turned the pages until he found one with B2 marked in the corner.

"That would be just the first page," Cedar said, a pleasant smile on his lips. "I believe you'll find seventeen more."

The clerk stared at him and then flipped the pages, all seventeen of them, until he came to a dark blue line drawn across the paper, the neat total drawn in the bottom corner in red ink. It said "Zero". A blue 'X' crossed the entire page, with the seal of a Demonan Magister stamped over it in blue ink.

"It appears you do not have any coin with us," the clerk said.

"I don't understand," Cedar said, blinking.

"I'm afraid your account was closed," the clerk said with a smirk and a look of relish.

"How can that be?" Cedar said, his knuckles going white as he gripped the marble bench.

"New policy," the clerk said, closing the ledger with a snap. "If an account shows no activity for six months it is closed."

"And my money?" Cedar asked through clenched teeth.

"There didn't appear to be any in the account at the time it was closed."

Because the Magister now had access to the funds of a defunct *account.* Cedar felt hot and cold flushes and he snatched the ledger out of the clerk's hands, ignoring his protestations, and reopened the book to the pages of his account. The last four transactions were all large withdrawals with a clumsy approximation of his Mark next to each, leaving zero in the balance. *It made no sense that the Magister would try to forge my mark. He could have just taken it. But now it matters not. There's nothing I can do.*

Cedar nodded and pasted a polite expression on his face. Handing the ledger back, he admirably controlled the urge to punch the clerk's haughty expression off his fat face, and walked away. He stood outside with his back to the Coinage and took deep breaths as he looked up at the cloudless blue sky. The curious stares of the well-to-do passing by did not help as Cedar tried to figure out what his next course of action should be.

He started to walk, his feet finding their way with no direction from him.

Cedar wandered out of the Business District, the clean, paved street becoming the wide dirt path that served as the main road of the Pleasure district, weeds growing in what passed for gutters. Tall, spindly buildings pressed over him and people in ragged, patched clothing crowded the road. It made the road seem narrower than he remembered, and nothing served to give him any hold in this strange city. *The D'Ohera I remember is no more. The* Demona *I remember is no more.*

Reenactions of his encounter at the Coinage went through his head as he walked and looked at it from every conceivable angle. *Too many things do not make sense, but I was gone for a very long time.* Perhaps there was something to the Nitefolk story, though what Cedar knew of the strange and xenophobic people who lived in the Mountains did not lead him to believe they would suddenly decide to attack Demona.

Coming upon an empty courtyard that stood at the corner of two crooked alleys, Cedar sat on the crumbling walls and rubbed his chin. Though familiar, the courtyard appeared to have been abandoned some years past. Idly, Cedar wondered what had happened there.

The whole world felt wrong, like a coat which had shrunk in the wash, but Cedar couldn't put his finger on exactly what it was that disturbed him so. His eyes roamed over the people walking by as if the answer to all his questions would somehow be written in the seams of their clothes, or the goods and parcels they carried on their person.

Something caught Cedar's eye. He looked closer. A small boy with skin browned from the sun peeped out from between two tenements catty-corner to the courtyard. The boy looked like he knew the place well. Cedar waved him over and the boy crept out with a shy smile.

Skinny legs stuck out from worn breeches which were too short and under his arm the boy carried a woven platter heaped with shiny candied nuts. Not one fell as the boy danced around the pedestrians in the street to stand in front of Cedar.

"A handful for a ten coppers, two handfuls for a half dozen Varyen," the boy told him, his voice pleasant and high. "Please sir, I have three sisters I have to feed."

"I'm sorry, but I don't have any money," Cedar told him.

The boy looked crestfallen, but Cedar caught him looking up at him from under thick lashes.

"You don't really have three sisters do you?" Cedar asked.

The boy pursed his lips, and then sighed. "No. But I have three younger brothers."

"Really," Cedar said, unimpressed.

The boy glared at him. "I'm not a liar!"

"Strange. You just told me you had three sisters who are now brothers," Cedar said. "Sounds like a liar to me."

"People just feel sorrier for girls," the urchin said with a frown.

"It is still a lie," Cedar admonished gently. "Why don't you just feed them those nuts?"

"I can't. I have to return the nuts or their worth in coin to the merchant or he'll whip me or turn me over to the Justice."

"I see," Cedar nodded. "What is your name?"

"Nadi," the urchin said. "And they aren't really my brothers. I just look after them."

"There is more than shared blood to a brother," Cedar said. "I have two brothers and share neither mother nor father with either. I am Cedar."

The urchin stuck his hand out and the two shook. Cedar smiled.

"What are you doing out here?" Nadi asked him.

"Wandering," Cedar said, his eyes following the lines of the courtyard to the little door in a shadowed recess and the stones where one could step through to a garden which was no longer there. Somewhere between the potted plants and the columns along the walk he realized how he knew this place.

"Perhaps you could help me," Cedar said. "There used to be a shop in that building there," he pointed at the other side of the courtyard. "An old dwarf used to sell his wares - poultices and tinctures and medicinal teas. Do you know where his shop moved to?"

"Why should I help you? You already said you don't have any money," Nadi said, a crafty look coming into his eyes. "What can you do for me?"

"I can give you some good advice," Cedar said mildly. "Help a stranger in need and one day, when *you* are the

81

stranger in need, someone may help you."

Nadi shook his head. "Man, you're crazy."

"This city no longer works like that does it?" Cedar asked, feeling something in his chest wither and turn grey.

Nadi shook his head emphatically. "No way. You never get something for nothing here. Unless you're a friend of a Magister."

"Alright, what if I tell you where you can sell all the nuts in ten minutes?" Cedar said.

Nadi considered him, his dusty brown hair blowing in the breeze. He brushed it off his forehead and nodded. "Okay. You tell me, I go sell them and then I come right back and take you where you want to go."

I doubt I'm going to get a better offer from this one. "Fine. You'll be wanting to go to the Tales Mane."

After giving Nadi his instructions, Cedar watched the kid run off and decided to lie down along the wall to take a nap. Something tugged at his arm and he started awake, sitting up so suddenly he fell off the wall. Cedar blinked in the sun and shaded his eyes. Nadi looked down at him suspiciously, the empty platter swinging from his fingertips. "How'd you know I was going to come back?"

Cedar smiled. "I didn't," he said. "But this was as good a place as any to take a nap."

"You really are crazy. Somebody could've robbed you."

"I have no money remember?" Cedar said.

"Your shoes are nice, and I know at least a dozen people who'd take that jacket in a heartbeat."

"You're hanging out with the wrong crowd, kid," Cedar said as he stood and dusted himself off. "Now, where are we going?"

Nadi smiled, his teeth white and straight against brown skin. "This way."

Cedar was led through the maze-like streets of the Pleasure District at a fast trot. Nadi ducked through crowds, into alleys and through weed-choked gardens, never once looking back to see if Cedar was following. He kept up a steady stream of chatter as they walked. Cedar only began to hear what he was being told when they drew abreast at a wide street.

"…helps me out sometimes, so I don't usually take people to him. You don't really know who you can trust, you know? Some Warden working for a Magister, or worse, the Justice, could come around to bother him. He's good at hiding, but sometimes they get lucky. Like last time. But I like you. In fact, you kind of remind me of him. So I'm gonna take you to him. But still, you can't be too careful, so," he stopped outside a brothel with white lace curtains scented with expensive smelling perfume hanging out the window, "you wait here, and I'll bring him. Then he can decide what to do with you."

Cedar did not have long to wait before Nadi reappeared with Old Jacob in tow. When the dwarf saw Cedar, he nodded.

"I thought you might be seeking me out some time soon," he said with a contented tug of his long beard. "How is the girl?"

"Better. She ate and was sleeping the last time I saw her," Cedar answered. "She'll be alright."

"Of course she will," Jacob said gruffly. "She's got some spirit, that one. Now, what is it that you need?"

"I need materials," Cedar said. "I have to make a new guitar. I need wood, lacquer, metal and ivory, the kind you have."

Old Jacob sighed and tugged on his long graying beard again. "I cannot help you. I wish I could, but Nadi here tells me you saw my store, my gardens. Destroyed, all of it."

"By who?" Cedar said. "Everyone came to Old Jacob…"

"Yes," Jacob agreed with a smile. "And then the Justice came to Old Jacob, and no one came after that."

Cedar threw his hands up in the air. "By the Path, what happened while I was gone? Did *everyone* completely lose their minds?"

"Not their minds," Jacob corrected gently. "Just their faith, perhaps."

"I thought it was just a rumor," Cedar muttered. "I cannot believe…" he stopped.

"Believe people would give up on magyc?" Jacob smiled.

"No. That anyone would believe that the Guardians of all people were unleashing the *Demons*," Cedar almost spat the word. "And turn against them overnight."

"Things were getting very bad," Jacob mused. "As I said, people simply lost faith."

"The Torch was broken!" Cedar said with an indignant look. "We sort of had our hands full with that."

"I know that and you know that, but people only know ruined crops, burned towns, starving families and dead children," Jacob said sadly. "I would not take it too much to heart, Cedar Jal. People are good, faith is difficult to kill and truth will come through in the end."

"I know," Cedar said. "I just hope the end is not too late!" He rubbed his smooth chin as he considered his problem. "I need to forge a new guitar."

"That will be difficult, Cedar," Jacob warned. "The Justice will not like to hear that you are doing that."

Cedar barked a mirthless laugh. "Perhaps not, but I will do it anyway. You say the Justice came and destroyed your shop?"

"He came with Wardens. They confiscated everything, and then burned it," Jacob said, a sad frown clouding his face.

"Then perhaps what I need is at the Justice!" Cedar said.

"I do not advise you to go looking for a fight with the Justice," Jacob said, shaking his head.

"Thank you Jacob," Cedar said, his gaze far away. "You've been very helpful."

Jacob grabbed his arm. "Cedar! Listen! The Justice, his name is Trem Descal. You recognize it?"

Cedar did recognize it, only because he had been trying to remember it ever since his conversation with the clerk at the Coinage. The name belonged to the lawyer who had defended Lan Holdun. Old Jacob looked at him with his deep-set eyes. "Demona is not the way you left it, Cedar. Be careful."

Cedar nodded and began walking back to the Business district and the Justice.

At the fringe of the Business District, sitting atop a hill surrounded by a low wall, the Justice was a squat grey building that glared out with small dark windows placed high up and far apart in the walls. A row of hedges along the base of the wall tried, and failed, to make the Justice less intimidating.

Cedar had no plan in mind other than to confront Justice Trem Descal about what had happened to Old Jacob. The Justice and his Magisters were servants of the people; they would have no choice but to listen to reason.

One hundred steps led up to a mean little mouth of a door. The steps supposedly represented the many steps to obtain and preserve true justice, but by the time Cedar reached the top he was convinced it was simply to prevent anyone from seeking the Justice. His suspicion was confirmed when he found the door was locked.

After several minutes of persistent banging a dark-haired man, wearing a grey uniform and a bland expression, opened the door. Before Cedar could say a word, the man beckoned him forward and Cedar was escorted inside. The cavernous audience hall was austere and imposing, all angles and dark shadows. Two doors sat in dark recesses on either side of the back wall, watching the room like veiled eyes.

"Cedar Jal," a voice echoed from the left doorway. "I have heard much about you. I didn't actually imagine I would ever have the honor of meeting you face to face, more so after the rumors of your death."

Cedar remained silent as the man made his way forward. Though Cedar had never seen him before, there was no doubt this man was the Justice. Trem Descal was a thin man in his mid-sixties, with light hair graying at the temples. His face was sharp and hard, his eyes pale and shrewd.

"Why did you destroy Old Jacob's store?" Cedar asked, not interested in any sort of pleasantries.

"Who?" Descal raised an eyebrow.

"The dwarf," Cedar explained. "He had a store in the Pleasure District. He helped a lot of people there."

"Ah. One of the Old Folk," Descal said, a slight flicker of understanding in his pale eyes. He sighed. "When witchcraft was outlawed, the purveyors thereof were shut down. It was nothing personal. Cedar…may I call you Cedar?"

"No." *This man knew little if he thought Old Jacob was a Witch.*

Descal looked surprised at the flat tone, but then he nodded and rubbed his brow with one long finger. "I understand why you don't like me, Mr. Jal, but I believe that is only because you don't know me very well yet. The world is mired in the past, lost in superstition. These things must die for the world to move on to a greater future."

"By burning Old Jacob's shop?"

"Him and others like him are chaining people to a way of life which no longer has a place in this world, and therefore must be eradicated."

"People like him?" Cedar repeated, seeing for the first time that the threads of inconsistency in Demona led to a much greater tangle than he had first imagined. "You mean people who use magyc - like me?"

"The Guardians are among those who must eventually recant, yes," Descal said without apology. "Though by no means do we have to remain on unfriendly terms, if you understand my meaning."

"I do understand your meaning," Cedar said. "And I'm afraid I don't like it."

"That is a pity," Descal said, seeming truly disappointed. "People like you Mr. Jal. They look to you for direction and they will follow you. But, if you will not cooperate I'm afraid I cannot just let a public threat walk out of here. Perhaps a stay in the Prison will help you to understand the wisdom in my offer."

Cedar sensed the pair of Wardens behind him a second before they pinned his arms at his side. He did not resist as they pulled him from the hall. Anything he could have done would have been an ineffectual demonstration at best. Four more of the stony, grey-clad Streetwardens joined the procession as Cedar was escorted to the Prisons.

Mirroring the Justice in form and color, the Prison was connected to the former by an arched bridge of milky glass. Crossing beneath the forbidding portcullis, Cedar emerged into the center keep of the Prison and looked up at the tall and impossibly smooth walls. He had a moment for a slight twinge of regret at his passive acceptance of his unwarranted arrest before he was led forward again.

Cedar and a contingent of five guards stepped onto a wooden platform disturbingly similar in form to a gallows, which left the remaining guard to lower them down, inch by inch. The first level consisted of cells which were clean and spacious, with fresh air and sunlight that came from above. All the cells were empty.

Below that the cells were smaller, and still empty. By the time they reached the third level, the sky was a small blue patch above them and the only light came from smoky torches. Many and more of these cells were filled with men and other creatures, all in rags, crowding close against the bars, yelling and jeering as Cedar went down. The fourth level did not have bars, but solid iron doors with small windows through which Cedar could see dirty faces. The breath from their cries misted on the filthy glass of the doors. The fifth level doors did not have windows at all, though some trembled slightly at blows from behind them.

As they continued down, Cedar felt a small sinking sensation in his stomach when he realized there were more levels than anyone knew about. It would be a simple thing to be lost in the depths of the Prisons for an eternity. When they finally stopped at the single door of the sixth level, Cedar grimaced. Having no fondness for closed spaces, he could imagine the next few hours or days were not going to be pleasant. When the Warden opened the door, a dark stair greeted them instead of a cell. Taking a torch from the sconce beside the door, the Warden thrust it inside, the light only penetrating far enough to illuminate the first three steps.

Cedar was shoved inside and the door closed with an echoing bang, leaving him in complete darkness. He sat on the top step and felt the cold of the stone leach through his trousers into his flesh. Cedar kept waiting for his eyes to adjust, but the blackness did not diminish, even after many minutes. It was deathly quiet and a smell of rot and excreta came from below.

Eventually, Cedar began to creep down, feeling his way with his toes. Steep and knee high, the steps seemed endless, and though Cedar tried to keep track he lost count at thirty-two.

When he came to a point where he could not find another step down despite stretching his leg as far out as he could with the sharp edge of the stair digging into his rump, he crawled on his hands and knees until his head brushed a wall. He felt his way along the cold, slime-covered stone. Suddenly, he bumped into something that gave under his foot. Cedar swallowed, his mind immediately conjuring every horror tale he had been told. In spite of his frantically beating heart, he knelt down closer to it.

Very faintly, he heard breathing.

"Hello?" Cedar said, the hair rising on his arm from something other than cold.

Whatever it was grunted softly and tried to move away. Afraid of losing it in the dark Cedar groped around for something to hold it here and his fingers closed around what felt like an arm. Skeletal fingers tried to pry Cedar's hand away, but Cedar was far stronger than the poor creature rotting down there.

"Who are you? What is your name?" Cedar asked.

A faint croak that sounded almost human was swallowed by the darkness.

"What was that?" Cedar bent closer, the smell of human filth and dying threatening to choke him.

"Lasssstarrrr," the man whispered.

"The Path take me!" Cedar said, and a surge of righteous indignation for the plight of the former Magister of Coin made the Guardian's throat tight. "Jules! What happened? How long have you been here?"

Lastar made a rumbling sound in his throat that dissolved into a painful cough. "Trem Descal happened. How long? Time has no meaning down here. A day, a week, a year, I do not know." His voice became stronger with every word.

"How are you still alive?" Cedar whispered, cold fingers crawling down his spine.

"They throw buckets of slop at us," Lastar said. "If they remember."

"Us?" Cedar asked, his skin crawling. "There's more of you?"

"Seventy or so, by my count," the harsh voice of a goblin came from behind Cedar. "And at least I can see."

It was common knowledge that goblins could see the infrared spectrum, and darkness was no barrier to their eyes.

"Who are you? Why are you here?"

"I am Cium," the goblin's voice said. "And I'm here for the same reason as everybody else. The Prince doesn't like us."

Cedar's blood froze. "You can't mean Descal…or…not *Holdun*?"

"Who else?"

"But Demona is not a principality, hasn't been for hundreds of years. We left those days behind!"

"Holdun doesn't call himself a prince, yet he is in everything but name. So what did you do to warrant being thrown down here with us?"

"I can think of a few things," Cedar said,

remembering the day at Erridon, pulling children from among the ruins smoking in the sunset, feeling his blood heat.

A beam of light pierced through the center of the room from above, bright white against black, making Cedar wince and blink as it assaulted his eyes. The sight of the lumps lying around the cell against the wall, stirring sluggishly toward the light, made bile rise in the back of his throat. He rose and stepped over them as he made his way to the stairs.

"Cedar Jal!" A voice he did not recognize echoed down the stair. "Cedar Jal!"

Cedar stood with one foot on the first step and his hands on his hips. "What do you want?" he yelled back.

"Come up the steps, you silly boy!" a different voice called, one Cedar knew instantly. "Quickly!"

Taking the steps without a backward glance, Cedar found Victoria in the doorway next to a young redheaded guard with a small scar over his eyebrow. Victoria grabbed Cedar and pulled him up the last step.

"Come. I've gotten you freed, but we must not linger. It is not safe."

"Yeah, I did get that impression, but," Cedar glanced back down the stairs. "There are people down there! *Lastar* is down there!"

"And you cannot help them if you are down there also," Victoria scolded. "Did you leave your wits in the Void of yours?"

"No," Cedar shook his head, unable to argue with the cold logic.

Taking her hand, he stepped out of the door and the guard closed it. The metallic bang tore through Cedar and he closed his eyes, glad for Victoria's warm hand on his elbow. He allowed her to guide him onto the platform and they were hoisted into the air with a jolt and the clanking of chains. Working the winches above them, the second guard was as young as the first, his blond hair cut close to his scalp.

"How did you acquire these two?" Cedar wondered aloud as he looked at the two young men, their fresh expressions so at odds with Cedar's conception of the grey uniforms.

"How any sensible person acquires anybody." Victoria smiled serenely. "I bought them."

"For how long?"

"Just to get you out, and then I was never here."

"You can't trust them," Cedar said, glaring coldly at the uniforms.

"I know this, Cedar Jal, but it cannot be helped." She nodded at the redheaded guard, her wandering eye crinkling as she smiled. "That one was born under Old Jacob's care. The blond one's little brother is one of the boys Nadi has taken under his wing. These are hard times, and hard times make hard men, but it does not mean that we should lose our faith in the good in men."

"You're right, Victoria. Your counsel is sound as always," Cedar said ruefully. "But something has to change. It cannot go on like this!"

"Of course," she agreed. "So what are you going to do to right things?"

"First I must forge another guitar for myself," Cedar said. "I'm afraid I feel all but useless without it."

"So we must arrange for you to make another, which has been done."

"You bought someone else?" Cedar asked, bemused. "You have been busy."

"Not quite. Actually, it was Nadi who suggested it," Victoria confessed.

"Nadi? The street urchin I sent to you with the candied nuts?" Cedar asked, an eyebrow raised. "You took to him faster than usual."

Victoria gave him a look. "I had him follow you. That boy has more eyes and ears than a nine-headed cat. It was he who came to fetch me to tell me where you were, so you should thank him next time you see him."

Cedar heard the unspoken reproach but something else in her voice made him look twice. She looked straight ahead and would not give him the chance to meet her eyes.

"Victoria, you knew where I was planning to get the supplies," Cedar said slowly. "Why did you not just tell me that Old Jacob had been put out?"

"You needed to see D'Ohera anew for yourself," Victoria said, her gaze still fixed ahead.

"To what purpose?"

Victoria finally looked at him. "I simply wanted to make certain you saw what was in front of you and not what you wished to remember." She frowned. "I did not think you were foolhardy enough to go running to the Justice." She gave his hand an affectionate squeeze. "But all is right now. Let us not brood on it."

Cedar smiled as they were let out of an unobtrusive door in the rear of the Justice. When the guards closed the door behind them, it was nearly invisible in the grey stone. The sight of the sky and the warm sunlight was like food to a starving man for Cedar. He gave Victoria his arm as they made their way around to the main road of the Business District.

Nadi was sitting on the corner of the wall surrounding the Justice, swinging his legs, his head turning in a way that reminded Cedar of a clock pendulum as the boy tried to watch all sides at once. Catching sight of them before they had taken two steps towards him, Nadi offered them a wave and a white smile. Cedar helped the boy down and returned his smile.

"I hear I have you to thank for getting me out."

Nadi nodded proudly. "Did you hear my other idea?" Cedar shook his head and the boy looked disappointed. "About the guitar?" he said and again Cedar shook his head.

"Victoria was about to tell me." Cedar turned his gaze to the woman.

"Not so loud." She leaned closer. "You have heard of the Yelndels?" Cedar gave her a blank look and she continued. "They are somewhat of a myth."

"They are not!" Nadi interjected hotly. "I've seen them!"

"And who are these people exactly?" Cedar said.

"A way to procure things that are frowned on by certain people," Victoria said. "A faction of them showed up in D'Ohera almost a year ago now."

Cedar looked at Nadi with a raised eyebrow and Nadi shrugged defensively. "I thought it was worth a try!"

Cedar nodded agreeably. "My recent experience leads me to believe you're correct, though it sounds expensive. Victoria, I know that you have done much and more for me but I need just one more thing from you. I have no money to buy what I need. I will pay back everything you have expended on my account."

"There is no need to do that, Cedar Jal," Victoria smiled at him, her good eye twinkling. "You owe nothing."

"But the guards?"

Victoria held up her hand, and then took a ribbon from around her neck. Three small iron keys clinked together softly as she placed it in his hand. "The guards were bought with your very own coin." Cedar's jaw dropped, and Victoria continued. "When Holdun became

Magister of Coin, any halfwit troll could see he would find some means of appropriating any coin he could and bankrupting the Coinage. You were not here, so in your absence I withdrew all your money and for a small fee, I have been keeping it safe until such a time when you should come to collect it."

"Where?"

"Where else?" Victoria lifted her skirts above her ankles so the hem did not get dirty and started down the street. "Those holes in the roof still need fixing."

Cedar found only three holes in the roof, not the six Victoria complained of. He patched them with slats of wood and tar before he carried the chests down and brought them to his room.

Young Robbie the dwarf boy sat in a chair with a large book in his lap, reading aloud to Ria and Jacob. He stopped when Cedar entered. Ria was sitting cross-legged on the bed, being examined by Old Jacob. The layers of dirt and grime had been scrubbed away, no doubt by Victoria's firm hand and Ria was pink and glowing. Victoria had also found the girl some proper clothes and she now wore a green tunic and suede trousers, though she still wore the odd, multi-hued shoes she had come to Demona with.

Ria flashed Cedar a bright smile when he walked in. "Hi!"

"Hello," he grunted amicably as he put the last of the three chests at the foot of the bed. "I see you're better."

"Jacob said I'll be as good as new in a couple of days," Ria said, and looked down at her side where a red line was crisscrossed with neat stitches.

The flesh did not tear as Old Jacob pulled the stitches out. It seemed the old dwarf had not lost his touch or his sense of the Path. Cedar felt a twinge of jealousy for the natural gift of the members of the Old Races - their connection with the Path was a birthright, not a talent or hard-won skill.

"That's good," Cedar said.

Taking the keys from around his neck, he opened the chests. In each were neat stacks of silver and gold, hexagonal Varyen, triangular Rabs, square Anar, and oval Fenns. A slim leather ledger rested upon the coins in the third, the pages filled with Victoria's account of the money.

"It is not as much as you were expecting, I know. I could not save all of it, and there were several expenditures," Victoria said.

Cedar leaped up and gave her a bone-crushing hug. "It is more than enough. Now, where can I find these Yelndels?"

Old Jacob did not look up from his work. "I made a list of everything you need on the pillow. Nadi will take you where you need to go. I suggest you take a lot of money, what you seek is not inexpensive. There is one other thing." He slowly pulled another stitch out. "I request that you retrieve something for me as well. The ones you seek will be able to help you with that."

"Certainly," Cedar said immediately. "What is it that you need?"

"There was an old dwarven chest carved of dragonbone, about as big as a shoe-box. It had been in my family for generations before it was 'appropriated', and I wish it to be returned to me."

"I will see that it is done," Cedar promised solemnly. "Nadi, let's go."

"Wait," Victoria interrupted. "They only come out after dark. There is time to eat, at least."

Cedar wanted to argue, but as he knew little about what they had planned, he chose to follow her advice.

Victoria served a supper of ham and pea soup, black bread, and butter and apples stewed with cinnamon. They all ate together in the warm, smoky kitchen but Cedar was preoccupied by the sun's agonizingly slow journey to the horizon. When the shadows stretched long, he stood, grabbed his jacket and the sack of gold coin, and walked to the door.

"I cannot wait anymore," he announced.

Nadi stuffed one more bite of bread into his mouth and scurried after him. Victoria saw them to the door, fussing like a mother hen. Cedar kissed her on the cheek.

"Promise me you won't do anything stupid," Victoria said, gripping his arm firmly.

"I promise," Cedar said in the most sincere voice he could muster.

Nadi grinned and allowed Victoria to scrub the food off his face before he ran after Cedar. Making their way to the edge of D'Ohera, Nadi led him to the great storehouses which sat like giant brooding chickens. Nadi crept around to the back with Cedar no more than a tall shadow on his tail. Mounds of junk and refuse were piled behind the storehouses, black hills in the twilight. As Nadi crept closer, a voice called out of the darkness.

"No farther boy. What do you want out here?"

"I want to find the Yelndels," Nadi said, his high voice shaking a little. "Old Jacob sent us, and we come with gold."

Grumbling erupted from the nearest pile, and seven shadows detached themselves from the darkness, becoming bat-eared goblins as they came closer. Their wiry torsos were bare and all of them had a variety of knives strapped to their chests and arms. The one in front had straight white hair down to his chin and a stylized rune tattooed on his neck. He smiled, sharp teeth glinting.

"We don't like Old Jacob, but we do like gold," he said as he looked them up and down. "Who might you be?"

Nadi puffed his chest out. "I'm Nadi," he said. "This is Cedar. Who are you?"

The goblin grinned wider. "I am Yelndel." He pointed at the second goblin. "And he is Yelndel, and he is Yelndel and…"

"We get it," Cedar said quickly, and the smile vanished off Yelndel's face.

"In a hurry are we?" the goblin sneered. "Don't worry, no one is coming out here."

"I've no doubt of that," Cedar said. "But my time is not unlimited."

Stepping forward, he reached a hand into his jacket to withdraw the drawstring sack. Fourteen knives flashed out and pointed in his direction. Cedar froze, held out the other hand and very slowly pulled out the bag of coin. The goblin motioned for Cedar to throw it. Cedar did and crossed his arms. "That should cover it."

The goblin leader hefted it and handed it to the goblin on his left. The goblin disappeared and Cedar realized he might have wanted to get his goods *before* handing over all of his money. He held his breath, but the first Yelndel jerked his chin at Cedar.

"What do you want?"

Cedar held up both hands then slowly stepped forward to hand the goblin the note Old Jacob had written in small, square letters. The goblin squinted at it, his dark lips moving as he deciphered it.

"The dwarf asks much of those who bear him no great respect."

"I do not know about your quarrel with Old Jacob, but I have no part in it," Cedar stated firmly.

"I have no quarrel with the dwarf," Yelndel said. "But

I have no love for the Magisters and them for me, so I cannot be faulted for my caution."

"But if we were the Magisters' men, you would be taken or dead," Nadi frowned.

The Yelndels threw their heads back and howled with laughter. "Boy, you know nothing," the white-haired goblin said, tears leaking from the corner of his eye. "We are shadows and myths. We do not exist. The Magisters could no more catch us than they could capture thunder in a glass. We will get these items for you, but the coin will not be enough."

"I have more." Cedar began.

"No, you do not have enough coin," Yelndel said. "I desire something else."

"What is that?" Cedar asked.

"The Prince."

Cedar started. "What prince?"

"I want Holdun," the goblin glowered. "You have been away a long time Guardian, but your eyes are still there, no?" Yelndel smiled at the surprise on Cedar's face. "Yes, Guardian, your name is still whispered in dark places, sometimes with love and often with hate, but you have not been forgotten." He bared his pointed teeth in an angry snarl as he continued. "How many goblins have you seen in the streets of D'Ohera? How many elves? How many dwarfs? Why do you think that is?"

The goblin's words came like blows, battering reality into Cedar's core, forcing this new Demona upon him. Tears glittered in his eyes as he looked down at Yelndel. "I wish I could grant your request but I have a claim on his life as well."

The goblin stared at him, his gaunt face hard. Cedar stayed very still as the goblin weighed him up lest he inadvertently tip the scales against his favor. Yelndel turned away and the other goblins followed him without a word. Cedar's heart sank. Before Yelndel completely disappeared into the shadows, he paused and spoke over his shoulder. "Wait here Guardian. We will return."

Stars twinkled and the moon rose as Cedar and Nadi waited. It was almost sunup by the time the Yelndels returned. Between them, they carried every item from Old Jacob's list. When the goods were piled next to Cedar, Yelndel stepped in front of him with his arms crossed, putting his large hooked nose in Cedar's face and glowering at him with flashing eyes.

"You still owe me, Guardian, and I promise you one day I will collect on your debt." He paused. "And if I see Holdun in the street, I do not intend to stay my hand, no matter the worth of your claim on his life."

Cedar opened his mouth to reply, but the Yelndels were already gone.

Cedar and Nadi trudged through back alleys and shortcuts known only to the streetwise urchin and his kind, laden with their treasures. When the sun finally rose over the tops of the roofs of D'Ohera's Pleasure District, all the materials the goblins had retrieved were piled around the chests in Cedar's room.

Cedar ordered everything, lining the items up neatly. Ria sat on the bed and watched with wide eyes as Cedar went through the supplies. Nadi sat beside her, sharing a raisin-studded muffin with Robbie, and Victoria sat with two other smaller boys on her lap. A third very blonde one crouched at her feet.

"You have everything you require?" Old Jacob asked, standing in the doorway.

"Yes," Cedar said. "Your friends were very helpful."

Jacob smiled. "The Yelndels are not friends to any but

their own."

"They did not seem to be overly fond of you."

"They are not," Jacob shrugged. "But we are useful to each other, so we tolerate each other."

Cedar tried to pay Jacob the value of the wares but the old dwarf waved away the gold with a smile. "You have paid already, with this."

Old and yellowed, the dragonbone chest had a rich glow which only came with great age. Runes were inlaid along the top and the front, the shapes familiar to Cedar though he was by no means fluent in Dwarven. While he was curious as to what it contained, a dwarf's dragonbone chest was more personal than flesh, so Cedar held his tongue and simply nodded. He began to pack what he needed into a burlap sack.

"You should sleep," Victoria said, a worried frown adding more lines to her face.

Cedar shook his head. "There is not enough time to sleep. The others will be here soon and we have much work to do. I must be ready. I do not know how long this will take, so don't worry if I am not back in a timely fashion."

Slinging the bag over his shoulder, Cedar walked out the back door of the Tales Mane. Doing his best to avoid people, he took the long way to Gardens.

The diamond gates were almost blinding in the midday sun. Slipping past the bored and inattentive Streetwardens took no more imagination or effort than a jaunty whistle and presently Cedar found himself surrounded by cool greenness. The Gardens were just as he remembered and he was glad they had not been violated by Descal or Holdun.

The trails spread out in a fan pattern, only to be swallowed by lush greens, purples, pinks and oranges.

Cedar started down the left-most path, walking easily, his steps long and smooth. At a large copse of willows which bent over the path, he ducked beneath the boughs and continued into the center of the trees where the fronds of a giant willow covered the ground in a sliver carpet. Nested amongst the roots like a mouse against a mountain was what appeared to be a groundskeeper's hut. Though the door had no handle or lock, it opened without a sound when Cedar waved his hand in front of it.

With the door closed, the hut was black as pitch, the shadows swallowing everything. In the dark, it felt like a small coffin. When Cedar had a fire going, the light flickered to the corners and filled the hut with warmth, revealing a space that was unnaturally larger than it appeared from outside.

Cedar set his bag on the long table in the center of the room. A bellows and forge sat at the far end in one corner and a large iron cook-stove and wide fireplace occupied the other. Pulling the materials from the pack, he carefully placed everything in a straight line. A cupboard concealed behind an engraved panel contained all the tools any artisan could want.

Cedar began to forge his guitar.

First, he shaved and sanded the two sheets of golden mahogany until the seam was all but invisible when he put them together. Only then did he glue them. When the glue dried, Cedar traced the shape he wanted, free form, the charcoal pencil curving the lines of water and air. A knife of dragonclaw cut through the wood as though it was whipped cream. From the center Cedar carved out a perfect circle.

The rosette was formed with the care of walking a rope stretched over a gorge, each tile placed exactly, laminated and cut to match the design in Cedar's head.

Cedar didn't think or plan, instead letting his feeling guide his hands. The pattern emerged under his fingers like rays of sunlight and tangled brambles. A ring was hollowed out in the soundboard and the design inlaid and shaved smooth.

The backboard followed in the same manner. Carving the braces took Cedar longer as each piece was meticulously brought forth by shaving minute flecks to scallop the edges and smooth the sides. He glued the x-brace to the soundboard and the backboard took a fan bracing that appeared as an eagle's wing outstretched.

Taking more sheets of wood, Cedar cut them to a width that felt right and then laminated them to the perfect thickness. He soaked them in water and then spent hours which flew by in a blink, slowly bending and shaping them to match the boards. While that dried, he carefully carved out the kerfing, cutting shallow notches so it became supple.

Wiping the sheen of sweat that graced his brow, Cedar continued, gluing the neck and tail blocks to the sides, and then leveling, trimming and gluing the kerfing in place. Placing boards along the top to prevent the clamps from crushing the sides, he set the opposing side in place to level the boards.

Planing the sides down to the correct height, Cedar took a moment to admire his work. The shell of the guitar was light yet sturdy, the curves pleasing to look at, the shapes matching like two lovers' lips.

Laminating the boards of the neck, he set the ebony strip for support, then began to carve the fretboard, hollowing out grooves for the fret wires and setting them with gilded ivory.

He pressed gold, obsidian, and purple dragonscale into a starburst and the rune for *power* at the first fret, a roaring island cat and the rune for *strength* at the third, a tongue of flame and the rune for *magyc* at the fifth. The runes of his name graced the seventh fret.

On the twelfth fret he made a series of overlapping rings and around the inside of the rings he cut a series of runes set out in ivory and obsidian. As he finished with the last rune, the chill which Cedar had ceased to notice lifted out of the air. He smiled a glad smile as he glued the fretboard to the neck.

The headstock took Cedar more time than he expected but the wooden block did not like the shape he was trying to force on it. Finally, he gave up and let the wood come as it wanted. When he had finished, Cedar held it up to the light and decided it was a good thing he had not tried to make it something it didn't want to be.

Drawn out of the wood in curving lines and tapering points was the aspect of a flame. He had planned on the pegs being smooth and unadorned, but the words of a childhood rhyme appeared in his head and he carved the appropriate runes as a little prayer of peace and hope.

After gluing the headstock to the neck and the neck to the body, he pulled a small clay bottle from the where it sat innocently at the other end of the table. Inside was a mixture of moonlight, powdered unicorn horn, witch's tears and a maiden's kiss, or so it was rumored.

Whatever it was made of, the end product was a powerful and long lasting sealant that would protect from more than simple blows, fire and time. Sealing and resealing with thin coats of the magycal varnish, Cedar finally laid the guitar on the table and watched as the final layer hardened, giving the guitar a sheen which was lightning and shadow.

He strung it with gut from a unicorn and tuned it. A crystal clear note hung in air as if suspended by magyc when he plucked a string. By this time, the lack of sleep was hammering him. Even the starkest of corners looked comfortable and beckoned with the promise of sleep. He could barely keep his eyes open, but one final thing remained to be done.

Cedar rolled up his sleeves and placed his hands on the instrument, concentrating as he called the Path to him and his creation, and -

- nothing happened.

Nor on the second or the tenth attempts until at last, exhausted and bewildered beyond tolerance, Cedar gave up and staggered home. The Path, as the foundation of this world, was still there – he could feel it faintly, but like something out of reach, he could not grasp it or use it. It was like a ship sinking slowly but surely behind the horizon, and when it disappeared, his connection to it would be severed completely. The expression on Victoria's face confirmed all that Cedar had discovered.

"How could this happen?" he whispered. He leaned against the doorframe as though it would support both his weight and his shattered belief. "*Why didn't you warn me?*"

"Would you have believed me Cedar Jal?" Victoria said, her one good eye glittering with unshed tears.

"I should have *known*," Cedar lamented bitterly, his voice low and rough. "How long? How long has it been…?" he could not finish the question.

"I know not," Victoria said. "Again, you ask me a question that is the in the realm of the Guardians, and they have disappeared."

Cedar nodded dumbly as he dropped the useless guitar and the empty burlap sack on the floor. Climbing up the attic stairs and through the broken window slats to the flat roof of the Tales Mane, he watched the stars come out.

He was no longer tired, just simply numb. Sleep no longer appealed to him.

Soft sounds behind him made him turn, but when he saw Ria he went back to gazing at the stars. She sat down next to him without a word, letting her legs dangle off the scalloped edge of the roof. Finally, she looked at him.

"What happened?" she asked softly.

"I can't make another guitar," Cedar said, the words falling heavily from his lips. "At least not here."

"Why not?"

It was the last thing in the world that he wanted to talk about, but Ria's earnest face would not allow him a sharp retort. "The Path is fading in Demona," he told her softly. "In D'Ohera it is almost gone. I felt it in the forest, but I didn't really know it, didn't *allow* myself to know it, until now."

"What will you do?"

"I don't know," he said. "I don't know."

It was only when Cedar heard the awkward notes that he noticed she had brought the guitar to the roof with her, and he winced. "Don't."

"You played for me once remember? You said you would teach me how to play," she said as her fingers moved hesitantly over the frets.

Listening as she played the simple riff over and over again, Cedar's eyes began to droop and his head fell on to her shoulder as exhaustion finally took hold. After a minute or an hour, Cedar didn't know which, gold light flared behind his eyelids and his eyes flew open.

Emanating from the guitar, the light surrounded him in sporadic bursts and beams. Cedar wondered for a moment if he was entering another golden dream, but the roof was still solid under him, the sky was black and the light was focused from a single point.

This is no dream, Cedar realized, *it is* her. He hesitated, unwilling to disturb her or interrupt whatever was happening, but he needed to understand. He gently touched her shoulder.

"What?" she asked when she saw his face, her fingers stopping.

She has no idea what she is doing. "Keep playing," Cedar said softly, putting his hands below the bridge and on the headstock. This time, when he called the Path, golden light flared like molten lava spewing from the terrible and awesome volcanoes found in the Wild Islands. Ria squealed, in delight or shock Cedar could not tell. The glow grew to surround the guitar, binding it in gold chains, binding everything around them in gold light until it was all Cedar could see, and then abruptly it faded.

Warm in his hand, the golden guitar was no longer just wood and lacquer. Now it shone with an unmistakable inner light which made Cedar's heart beat faster and a smile grow on his face. Ria smiled too and handed it to him with a reverent look on her face. Taking it, Cedar ran his hand over the fret-wires and then turned to look steadily at Ria. Her face was open but a trace of trepidation began to cloud her expression the longer he gazed at her.

"What?" she finally asked.

Cedar put his hand on her shoulder and turned her so they faced each other straight on. Putting his finger under her chin, he looked deep into her wide grey eyes. There was no doubt this girl was more than she appeared, but could she be the one the Demon said she was? Was it possible the Prophecy was coming to pass? Would she be the one to shape the future of this world? *But she is too young,* Cedar thought. *And would not be here but for an unfortunate mishap.*

"Why are you here?" he murmured.

"Because you brought me here," Ria stated without

hesitation.

"Yes, I did," he said pensively. "Let's go down."

With the guitar in one hand and Ria's warm hand in the other, Cedar made his way back down into the Common of the Tales Mane.

Trem Descal greeted him at the door.

Cedar gripped the neck of the guitar and felt the instrument throb in tandem with his own heart. "What are you doing here?"

"I could ask you the same thing," Descal said, his pale eyes shifting between Cedar, the guitar and Ria.

"I live here," Cedar said coldly. He felt Ria slide closer to him when the Justice's eyes fell on her and the guitar began to vibrate faster. "And I'm asking you to leave."

"You live in an inn?" Descal seemed bemused and ignored the second part. "How strange."

"Where I live is none of your concern," Cedar said. "Leave."

"Don't you want to know why I've come?"

"No."

"One of the Streetwardens reported seeing you come in and I came to see if it was true," Descal said. "I must admit I was surprised to hear you had any friends left."

"As you can see, it is true," Cedar replied coldly. "And apparently I do. Something you would be wise to take heed of."

"I take it you have not changed your mind."

"That is correct."

"Very well, I admit…"

"Please stop this farce," Cedar interrupted. "There is nothing further we have to say to each other and both of us know it."

"Mr. Jal, you do not know what is happening here,"

Descal said, his voice lowering dangerously. "You may be able walk away with your life. I am not disputing that, but think of the others that are not as…*capable*…as you are…"

A dull crack echoed around the room and Descal's eyes rolled back in his head. He slumped down, his hand going to his head with a groan.

"I wonder who he could be referring to," Victoria said, examining the slight dent in her cast-iron frying pan. "He ruined my pan."

Descal struggled to his knees, his pale eyes shooting flames. "Mr. Jal…"

Cedar's fist caught him square in the temple and Trem Descal was out.

Nadi appeared next to Victoria "We showed him," he said proudly with a crooked grin. "But there's more of them outside. I looked through the kitchen door."

"How many?" Cedar asked.

"A lot more," Nadi said, his little brown face solemn as he danced on two brown bare feet.

"We have to leave," Cedar said. "I cannot stay here and protect you."

"Cedar Jal, this is my home," Victoria said, her wrinkled face solemn. "I am not going to run away because some person with an overstated idea of his own importance tries to restrict what I can and cannot do. And as much as I love you, I do not need your help. I was here long before you came, and I'd be willing to bet I'll be here long after you've left."

Cedar looked at Nadi, and the little boy stepped close to the old woman, slipping his brown hand into her worn one. Old Jacob appeared with the young dwarf Robbie in tow and stood behind them, laying his large hand on Nadi's shoulder.

"We will take care of each other, Cedar Jal," Victoria

smiled. "You have no cause to worry."

On impulse, Cedar kissed her on the cheek. "Of course not," he said. "But what are we going to do with him?"

"Make sausage out of him," Victoria said with an impatient shrug. "And don't give me that look, Cedar Jal. As I said, we will take care of ourselves."

"It is not that simple," Cedar said. "Descal has many friends."

"And many enemies," Victoria said serenely.

"He has more friends, friends which are closer at hand," Cedar said sharply, nodding toward what lay beyond the walls of the inn.

"Well, you're not leaving just yet, are you?" Victoria said. "I can show them that I have friends too."

Cedar sighed, but a slight smile was tugging at the corner of his mouth. Arguing with Victoria was as effective as arguing with a pot of soup. He looked down at Ria and she smiled at him, a happy, innocent smile that made her look like the twelve-year-old girl she was.

"We should wait, Cedar," she said, giving his hand a squeeze. "The others are coming, remember?"

All Cedar could do was nod. He was out-numbered by their reason. *They have a point. All the Guardians will be together again, just like it was before, and we will figure out a way out of this mess.*

Lasting less than an instant, the moment of gladness fled and Cedar's insides became ice in a turn which left him breathless. The image of the very last time the Guardians were all together was burned into his mind with fire and weapons, and so much blood.

"The Path save us," Cedar whispered, his face twisted in anguish as all his suspicions of ill-intentioned meddling against the Guardians came back to him. "Not again."

THE FIDDLER

The liquor was terrible in this sorry, nameless tavern. Luca Lorisson knew this because it was taking him at least four times as long as usual to get drunk. Looking at his half-empty glass with a sour expression, Luca deliberated how badly he wanted to be drunk. In the end, it was not bad enough to drink whatever was in the glass and he pushed the watered down horse's piss away.

It was dark outside the windows of the Common of the tavern. In the tiny town far enough south anyone looking for it would have a good chance of missing it if they blinked, the one upside of the place was that for some reason a little pocket of the Path resided here. So, Luca stayed.

In a warped reflection off his glass, he caught sight of the inn-keep coming towards him, a giant hairless man dressed in a navy shirt, cordoned pants like the Esters wore and an apron which may have been white at one point early in its life. As Luca was in no mood to deal with the man, who happened to be his employer for the time being, Luca tried to disappear into the stool. Unfortunately, it didn't work. Luca was still sitting there when the inn-keep stopped at the table. Luca scowled darkly, his left hand automatically groping for the glass, which was no longer within reach.

"You see this?" the inn-keep began without preamble. "I do not pay you for this!"

Leaning to the side to see around the other man's bulk, Luca surveyed the room. He counted four customers, and none of them were drunk or even close to it. Two did not even have drinks in hand. Luca could see the inn-keep's point, but Luca was in a particularly foul mood that night and didn't feel like making the effort to be cooperative.

He shrugged. "You don't pay me at all."

Purple-red infused the inn-keep's very round face and Luca smirked. Infuriating the man was not much of a challenge.

"Play, or leave!" With that ultimatum hanging in the air, the inn-keep returned to his place behind the bar and continued to polish the glasses.

Luca thought about taking the second option, but he did need a bed for the night. He sighed and picked up his fiddle. Luca gave the instrument a loving glance. Sweet maplewood stained a purple so dark it was nearly black formed the body. It was adorned with silver strings and pegs, and runes set out in emerald dragonscale that read, "May the Path Keep All." The fingerboard had a worn, silver-gold sheen and the bow was unicorn and maple.

With practiced boredom Luca placed the fiddle under his chin and drew his bow across the strings, slowly at first and then faster. Rewarded with the faces of all five people in the room turning toward him, Luca smiled widely. His thin, pointed face brightened and lost some of the harshness.

A smattering of applause ended the improvised jig. Not too bad, considering the audience numbered only five, and Luca did not miss the drink. His mood improved considerably and he played a second song without being asked. When his stomach grumbled as the last notes died away, he got up and went to the bar.

"What's for dinner?" he said.

"For you?" the big inn-keep asked. His tone suggested he was considering whatever slop was rotting in the pig-trough.

However, a languid glance revealed all four customers now had a drink in hand, so the inn-keep returned from the kitchen with a heel of hard bread and stew. Twice Luca almost broke his teeth on something hard that he did not care to identify further, but the fare was passable and Luca finished it all, going so far as to lick the bowl.

"Play," the inn-keep demanded, taking the bowl and pointing at Luca's stool.

"Not with grease on my fingers," Luca said and was immediately handed the damp towel which ordinarily hung from the dirty apron's single pocket.

After a brief examination to make sure there was nothing unsavory hiding in the folds of the towel, Luca cleaned his hands and wiped his mouth.

"Go, go!" the bartender said, pulling the towel out of Luca's hands. "Play more!"

"I'm going," Luca replied. As he settled onto the stool, Luca wondered for a fleeting moment if he could get away with playing the same song. At times, the uncomfortable thought that someday he would run out of songs whispered subversively to him. It suggested there was a predetermined limit of magyc and he would find himself to be no more than a fraud and his good fortune no more than a dream. But tonight Luca felt like playing something new, something exiting and he ignored the voice. The first note had the beginnings of something great, and Luca latched onto it.

Closing his eyes, letting the feel of the strings under his fingers pull him into that place where he felt most himself - powerful, untouchable and benevolent - Luca gave himself to the song. Gold light began to filter through his eyelids, very slowly, until he was being blinded with his eyes closed. Even though somehow he could still see, he did not believe what his eyes were telling him.

Cedar Jal lay in the middle of a dirt road winding through an unfamiliar forest, looking not a day older or a hair different than the last time Luca had seen him. A small girl in strange garb stood at Cedar's side.

A Demon, almost as tall as two men, stood over them. Cold shivers chased each other down Luca's limbs, an instinctual reaction to the proximity of ancient evil. The other Guardians appeared out of gold light and the sight of them banished the chills.

He tried not to show it, but Luca was glad to see them. Most of his attention, though, was fixed on Cedar, who looked two steps from Death. There was some discussion which Luca didn't remember much of, too preoccupied with Cedar's predicament. Cedar was very quickly banished from Luca's mind when the girl started to sing.

Luca would not have thought to look twice at the girl. She was small, thin, and too pale, though her grey eyes were fierce. The Demon's hiss of *Aethsiths* echoed in the air long after the Demon disappeared. A ball of apprehension gathered in Luca's stomach. He had tried and succeeded in running away, remaining hidden for the last four years, but his little holiday was coming to an end it seemed.

Even if the Demon was mistaken, things are going to get very interesting, Luca thought as the glow faded to black…

Too much light in his face made Luca grimace. He began to plan the slow and painful demise of whoever was shining it in his eyes. Waving his hand in front of him, fingers groping for the person's throat, Luca came to the conclusion that there was no one there. He turned on his side to escape the torture and smashed his forehead into something hard. With a groan, he opened his eyes and was confronted with a dented table leg.

Blinking rapidly as he assimilated this piece of information, Luca decided he had better sit up and see what was going on. This was easier said than done and it took him the better part of a minute to drag himself up, inch by agonizing inch, until he was sitting, slumped over, and able to view his surroundings.

Luca's head brushed the underside of the table. His bow lay just beyond his left foot and the head of his violin was visible hanging over the edge of the table above him. The tavern was empty and it was a crack in the window shades that had allowed the sun to assault him in such a brutal fashion.

It was dim under the table and Luca was thankful for that. Not entirely certain he would be able to think in brighter light, Luca pulled his legs under him and scratched the stubble on his jaw with one finger as he considered what had happened.

Of course, I dreamed it, he told himself, though he didn't do a very good job convincing himself. *It is not possible that Cedar has returned. He is dead. I* saw *him die four years ago.*

Luca's fingers fell still and a slight frown drifted across his face as he recalled that day. It was a blur of night and day and night again as Luca had run as he had never run before. Scrabbling up the steep sides of the plateau, he'd gritted his teeth against the metallic screeching that had made his bones vibrate jarringly, not wishing to know what was at the top even as he moved towards it.

The ground had shaken, trying to throw him like a wild colt, but Luca had persevered, pulling himself over the lip of the plateau only to be blown back by a blast of biting wind. He had gotten one brief glimpse of the Crescent Temple, white against the blackness of a massive Rift into the Void, before he was tumbling head over heels back down the slope he had just ascended.

That one glimpse had included Cedar spinning into the Void, guitar in hand, golden sparks flickering around him like fireflies among green lightning. It seemed a lifetime ago, and Luca had done his best to forget it every day since. The melting pot of emotions included grief and regret, and he did his best to drown them in music and drink. Now it looked like he would have to face up. The thought was chilling and sobering, yet welcome in a strange way.

Luca looked around the tavern that he was now the sole inhabitant of. Most of the tables were splintered in some fashion or another and none of the chairs matched. Grease, liquor and vomit had stained every surface, the windows were smudged with dirt and the door and ceiling sagged. It made the whole place look like a block of ice on the brink of melting.

"What am I doing here?" Luca asked the table leg as though it would be able to answer.

He waited for a response for a long time, but all remained silent. Two pictures of Cedar, one in which he was lying on the ground with a Demon standing over him, the other where he was being sucked into oblivion vied for Luca's attention. Of course, there was also the mysterious girl who had shown up with the missing Guardian. S*he had called the Guardians of the Path from all corners of Demona to help protect one of their own. That had to mean something.*

The Guardians would be alright without me, Luca knew. *Jæyd and Timo will find Cedar, fill him in regarding what had happened in his absence and figure out what to do with that girl he'd brought with him.*

Luca's sense of duty was not as stalwart as the others', a fact he neither denied nor hid. Even sitting alone, Luca refused to let other people dictate what he did. He would do as he pleased and there was very little people could do about it, but something about this situation struck a sense of obligation deeper than he cared to fully admit. After what happened, Luca felt that abandoning Cedar now was something he could be put in Death's torture chamber for.

There's nothing for it. I'll have to go and see what this is all about.

With a groan, Luca scooted out from under the table and stood, stretching cramped muscles. Gathering his bow and fiddle took only a moment and a quick glance ascertained the instrument had survived the happenings of last night with nary a scratch or dent.

His jacket hung on a hook behind the door. A quick shake dislodged the accumulated dust of several weeks, making the purple and green threads shine through again. The jacket was Luca's most prized possession after his violin. It was a spectacular jacket of supple silk-lined leather which went down to the knees, with wide flaring cuffs and collar. It didn't do anything mysterious or magycal on its own, but it made people think it did.

Luca made a quick trip back to the little strongbox the bartender hid under a pile of dirty rags. It didn't take more than a whisper to charm the lock open and Luca smiled. *I've still got it.*

The smile fell from his face as he beheld the pittance inside. In total couldn't have been more than half of what Luca had been promised, yet Luca felt an absurd guilt work its way through his gut at the notion of taking the money. Before he could talk himself into another course of action, he took half the coins and clicked the lock shut. On the way out Luca stretched up and passed his fingers over the lintel, leaving an invisible mark, as the runes for *good fortune* and *protection* shone in a gold only seen in the Path.

He left without a look back.

The nameless town which had been Luca's home slowly diminished behind him. His black boots became duller with every layer of dust he kicked up from the small goat track that wound in a vaguely westward direction across the southern plain of Demona.

As Luca walked, his thoughts turned to one of the only two people in all of Demona which Luca Lorisson had any sort of affection for, at least in the way that people understood the word: Victoria Meech, the old woman who ran an inn in D'Ohera, and who also happened to be the only person Cedar would listen to.

Knowing Cedar, Luca would bet he'd make for the Tales Mane with all haste after returning from the dead. *If he gets up, that is. That Demon looked pretty annoyed while it picked Cedar's guitar out of its teeth.*

Luca smiled as he walked. Cedar had a habit of vexing those who attempted to thwart him, and it was one of the things which Luca admired most about the tall, slim man with gold eyes. Other than that, they didn't see eye to eye very often. Their relationship was built more on tolerance than great love.

Even so, Luca felt a weight lift off his conscience with the knowledge that Cedar had returned and in one piece.

Though Luca didn't let his hopes get too high. No sense in opening himself up to unpleasant feelings later.

Without really thinking about it, he found his feet leaving the track and taking him north to Torin, rather than west to D'Ohera. In the four years since the incident at the Crescent Temple, Luca had avoided the North with every ounce of willpower he possessed. Now it was intent on dragging him back. *Four years in the South. Nice weather, almost no people to bother me and plenty of places to hide and forget. Not to mention Demon-free. For the most part,* he amended. It was hard to get excited about returning to a place of such hostile memories, but something drove Luca towards the Mountains, and he decided to see where this feeling was taking him.

The fertile grasslands of the deep south began to give way to pine forests. At first only small stands sprung up here and there, but the farther Luca walked, the thicker they grew, their scent crisp and invigorating and not totally unwelcome.

Soon Luca was lost deep in the shadows of ancient pines as thick as oaks and as tall as mountains. The forest seemed to be in the grip of some timeless spell. Everything was quiet and looked to be made of colored glass. Shaking off the feeling that he was being bespelled simply by being there, Luca tread lightly, the carpet of needles deadening the sound of his footsteps.

Sometimes earth, trees and sky could hold a memory fast, as a portrait above a mantel, and though Luca tried not to, part of his mind slipped back to before. *When the Guardians walked this world in the light, with heads held high.* Luca shivered. *In a forest similar to this, the nightmare had begun. Ever since we have had to creep through shadows with faces hidden.*

Luca picked up his pace to leave those thoughts behind. Silent shadows crept after him, but he was confident they were no threat to him and his violin. He guessed they were bandits come down from the dead and dangerous North to see what mischief they could manage in the milder South.

Yet here he was doing the exact opposite. His fretting finger, a name Luca gave the sixth sense which he swore resided in the fingers of his left hand, throbbed numbly. It told him clearly that he was completely insane. It also told him Jæyd would remain where the need was the greatest and die before leaving her duty undone. Namely, the North and the Crescent Temple.

She would not need persuading to go to Cedar though, Luca mused, keeping half an eye on the trailing shadows and a hand on his fiddle, just in case. *And it would be safer to travel together.*

With his consent this time, his feet began to take him North with purposeful strides. As the pines thinned, the shadows gradually let him be, retreating to the imagined safety of their trees. He held no animosity for the less savory characters of this world. Indeed, there was a nostalgic comfort in their presence and wiles. He caught a glimpse of red hair and a feminine form melting into the trees and silently Luca wished her good health and fortune.

Ending more or less where the hills began, the Great Southern Pine Forest rapidly diminished until it was a green blur behind Luca, visible only when he reached the top of a particularly large hill.

The hills seemed to go on forever. As he crested one Luca could see a dozen others that he would have to pass. As the sun sank, he stopped in a small valley. Offering much in the way of kindling and little actual fuel, the hills were still far enough south that the nights were mild and could be endured without a fire. Luca wrapped himself in his jacket, his violin beside his head, and was asleep in a minute.

Sunrise woke him earlier than he wished, but he was not going to get to the Mountains by lying about. The day passed without event and the night was the same as the last, if perhaps a little cooler. Luca's stomach woke him the next morning and he chewed a sprig of wild mint he found growing among the other grasses, lamenting his lack of foresight to bring food from the tavern.

He kept an eye out for game as he went. Coming upon a small dirt path that wound through the hills, he set along it in hopes of finding someone with something resembling breakfast. It was midday before he heard anyone and an hour more before the sound of whip, harness and horses nickering materialized into a wagon.

Luca stood in the middle of the road determined to ask for something to eat, but when the wagon pulled to a stop in front of him he found two overlarge crossbows pointed at his chest, armed with what looked curiously like harpoons.

Luca tried to reassure himself that he was quick enough to stop the bolts from striking, but he was not feeling foolish. Instead, he slowly extended his hands, making sure to bare his violin prominently.

"Good day!" he called out, changing his voice to one more suited to a Southerner. "I am a poor wandering minstrel in dire need of a meal and to rest my weary feet in a fine wagon such as yours!"

The two men in the wagon looked at each other, their fingers twitching on the triggers, and Luca tightened his grip on his bow.

"We got no room," the driver muttered, a tall, thin man with skin darkened by sun and layers of dust, while he flipped the reins impatiently. A felt hat was pulled low over his ears. His cadence hinted strongly of the Southport of Isos.

"Maybe we do," said his companion, an equally tall and dirty man with bushy ginger eyebrows but only a few wisps atop his shiny and uncovered pate. His face was more genial than the driver's and Luca pegged him as the easier to sucker, though the first was obviously in charge. His accent was even more prominent.

"I have no money," Luca said, the white lie sliding off his tongue with an appropriately pitiful expression. "But I can play a fine tune and I don't take up much room."

They lowered the crossbows slowly and Luca allowed himself to breathe. After a moment of grumbling from the driver and an elbow nudge from the other it was decided Luca could come. Luca smiled, pleased with himself as he climbed behind the wagon. *And Jæyd says I only charm as well as ice down the front of a tunic,* he thought, taking pleasure in proving her wrong though she was not here to witness it.

Bouncing down the road was uncomfortable, but the sight of the road and the hills swiftly diminishing behind Luca made it worth it. He tucked his legs under him and felt the burn in his feet ease as he gave a contented sigh. Something hit him in the head and he turned to see an apple lying behind him. As he watched a second came flying toward him, which he caught easily. A shout came from up front. "I don't hear any music!"

Luca obliged, occasionally playing one-handed as he devoured the fruit, but still putting heart and soul into the song. He played without stopping until the wagon wobbled to a full halt. The sun had disappeared behind the hills, and the sky was the deep purple of a bruise, faint stars twinkling. The two men came around the rear of the wagon and stared at him.

"What're you playin'?" the bald one asked him.

"A violin," Luca said. "Or a fiddle, if you like."

"I know that," the man said with an easy smile. "I mean what song?"

"I couldn't really say," Luca told him. "I just made it up."

"Well, I swear there's somethin' in that music, 'cause we made double time today, and them horses aren't even tired," the driver said with awe in his voice. Luca mentally raised a fist in victory for winning over the grouch. "My names Bij and this is my brother Cov."

"Luca," he introduced himself with a bow. "Pleasure to be of service."

"Where you headin'?"

"North."

"So are we!"

I sort of figured that one out Luca almost said but managed to hold his tongue. "How far will you go?"

"Torin," Cov said. "My wife and the children went up there a month back and now my brother here is helpin' to bring furniture and seed for plantin'. The wagon's his."

Maybe they haven't heard the rumors. Then again, Torin isn't in the north proper. Perhaps things are not as bad there. "Where do you hail from?"

"Akorgia by birth, but Isos at present," Cov said, naming the port at the mouth of the river O'Rente.

An introspective look came onto Luca's face as he recalled the dark alleys in the heart of the sailor city and the wharves along the river-bank. Days spent in streets filled with sailors and pirates, whores and pickpockets, merchants and peddlers, men with skin as dark as night, small men the size of children, men with striped cats from the Wild Islands or White-bears from the heart of the Mountains. Nights had been filled with the smells of the sea, exotic spices and human filth, running along the rooftops and sharing his ragged bed with rats as big as cats and cats as mean as rabid wolves. Luca shuddered. He still didn't like cats. He realized Cov was still talking.

"...but there are strange things happenin' there. Storms come in with no warnin', more...what do you call 'em? Refeuggs...Refusees..."

"Refugees," Luca said helpfully.

"Yeah, those types! More of them comin' in from up the coast with stories of pirates fighting fierce, rapin', burnin', stealin', murderin', people seein' things in the water and sailors returnin' with stories of ghost ships floatin' in a fog with no crew!"

I'm gone for two blinks of an eye and the entire world starts falling apart Luca thought. "So you're heading inland to Torin?"

"Yeah. My brother's got a farm there, and I'm going start one of my own. Sorry the food is cold, but we don't have room for firewood in the wagon, see," Cov said as he handed Luca a heel of bread and some sort of salt fish so strong Luca was afraid his breath was going to smell for the next three weeks. However, it was solid food, so he gnawed at it without complaint.

"Well, I'd be much obliged if you could carry me as far as Torin," Luca said.

"O'course, sure," Cov agreed. "Always happy to 'elp, me and Bij are."

Looking slightly less than agreeable, Bij nodded slowly with a suspicious look which made Luca's skin crawl and the three travelers finished their dinner in silence.

"How are you 'bout takin' a watch?" Bij asked gruffly.

"I'm nocturnal by nature," Luca said cheerfully and received two confused stares. "I'd be happy to take the first watch," he amended.

"Right," Cov said. "And don't mind anything sounds

like a drownin' whale, is just Bij snorin'!"

He went off chuckling. Bij looked at Luca. "He's lyin'. I don't snore."

"Of course not," Luca said, his own face mirroring the man's seriousness. "Good night."

When the hour came to wake Cov for the next watch Luca did not budge from his perch atop the wagon. Gazing at the stars and letting slow, melancholic notes slip from under his bow, the Guardian kept watch through the night, enjoying the moonlight and solitude.

The next morning Luca found himself on the box between Cov and Bij as they continued towards Torin. Cramped and awkward, Luca found it difficult to play. He winced each time the wagon jumped over a rock that made the violin squeal with jarring harshness, but the brothers appeared not to notice.

Around midday, Bij lifted one bony arm and pointed. Luca squinted and his eyes widened as he saw what Bij had noticed. No more than a faint shape and sparkle on the horizon, Torin, the City of Stone, was before them.

Clouds scurried past in the blue sky and the midday sun made the pale stone glow. At one time Torin had been the wonder of Demona, a city of white light and golden wonder, green gardens and gilded squares. Now it was no more than an overgrown ruin, sitting on a slight rise in the middle of vast and empty plain.

Years ago, before Ghor had attacked the city in retaliation for the sack of Erridon, the Guardians had been in Torin, but Luca didn't remember very much. In those days the city had been loud and vibrant. Luca was finding it difficult to reconcile his broken memories to the desolate place he now traveled through. Making their way along the wide, paved street, the wagon swaying from side to side, the horses' shoes clattering sharply on the stones, Luca shivered in the cool silence that pressed in on all sides.

"The farm is just outside the city," Cov was saying. "When we get there, the wife'll have a good, hot meal. Eel and mussel stew, flatbread, baked apples."

"That sounds most welcome." The advertised fare was Isosian through and through. Though Luca had not been sorry to leave the fruits of the sea behind when he left Isos, the mention of a proper meal made his mouth water.

He looked up as a shadow fell over them. The Guardians of the Gate, two rampant unicorns of gilded ivory, raised forelegs crossing to form the arch of the gates, watched over the northern gate of Torin. Both were sadly pockmarked where looters and thieves had gouged away the layer of gold, and one unicorn was missing its horn and one proud foreleg. Holes which had once been gleaming ruby eyes stared out, black and empty. The other was intact but for the missing sapphires. Roughly the size of one of the unicorns' mighty hooves, the wagon rumbled past the Guardians of the Gate and onto the plains.

The plains which spread around Torin were quite flat but they had a disconcerting ability to hide from the eye what should have been plain to see for miles, and so it was they came upon the little homestead with a suddenness that startled Luca.

Built entirely of the umber clay bricks which were really the only thing to build with on the plains, it was a squat, square thing with a dark, square door. The white fence that Luca originally took for whitewashed wood turned out to be rib bones of what could have been a whale. A tendril of smoke curled out from the roof and when the wagon rumbled to a halt and Cov gave a hoarse shout, three small children barreled out of the doorway with shrieks of excitement, followed by a rather stout though pretty woman with fair hair and rosy cheeks.

Though he did not seem big enough to do so, Cov scooped all three children up in his arms and kissed the woman. "We're all starvin'. We have a guest for lunch, Karmel. Think we can fit an extra spot at the table?"

Karmel bobbed her head and took the smallest child from Cov. When she spoke, her accent was smoother than her husband's; it was the same as Luca's. "Of course. I'm glad you're hungry. There's eel stew and bread, and peaches and cream!"

"She makes the best eel stew," Cov told Luca as they made their way up the path that was little more than a worn line in the ground. "I don't know what we're gonna do when the jars of pickled eel runs out, as we're not anywhere near the water no more."

"There are caravans that go between the cities," Luca said. "Some of them go as far as the coast."

"I know. I sent her and the children on one. Perhaps that would work," Cov said as the child, who had the same red hair as Cov would have if he'd had any, played with Cov's bushy eyebrows. "It'd make Karmel happy, I know. She wants to start a place and make things like eel stew and fishcakes and mussels'n'dumplins and such for the folk here. She says they don't eat very well. All corn and potatoes and pork. I told her she could, but only after we get everything all fixed up proper here."

Luca could see what he meant the moment they stepped inside. It was cool, dark and almost completely bare. A crude fireplace had been dug, but there were no hearthstones. The kitchen appeared to consist of a kettle, a pot and a small chest. Onions and herbs hung from the ceiling rafters and small barrels and large jars were stacked next to the fireplace. Sitting in the middle of the room, the table was simply a slab of wood on two barrels and a stump served as the one chair. Hidden by a faded curtain, the bedroom was no more than a pile of straw and blankets. A painted jug filled with water for washing sat on a stool. Karmel noticed his glances and her cheeks reddened.

"It's not much now, I know, but now that Cov has brought all the things, I'll be able to make it a proper home." A child grabbed her skirt and peeked around her with a mischievous expression.

Luca smiled at the round-faced child. "Ma'am, it looks to me like you've already done a pretty nice job of that."

This time her blush was accompanied by a sweet and somewhat flustered smile. "Please call me Karmel," she said. "Come, the food's ready."

Lunch was a loud and confused affair. The brothers quickly unloaded chairs from the wagon but there still were not enough to go around. Cov took the old stump and Bij took the stool, which left Luca and Karmel with proper chairs. The children played change-chairs throughout the meal, though it was more properly change-laps. One of them always managed to be on Luca's knee. He had forgotten how nice it was to have family around. At some point during the small talk, Luca dropped the southern drawl and lapsed back into his Isosian lilt. Though the three hosts shared glances at the change, none made mention of it.

Afterward, with a dozing child on one knee and a belly full to bursting, Luca let out a satisfied sigh. "Karmel, I have never been overly fond of seafood but I believe your cooking may just have changed my mind."

"Thank you," she said. "It's funny to think of an Isosian not having a taste for seafood."

Luca smiled. "I suppose I had my fill when I was younger."

"When did you leave the Water City?" Karmel asked,

her blue eyes bright.

"I was eleven," Luca said.

"I miss it already," Karmel said softly with a homesick smile. "After all the Torinish in the last few weeks, it's so nice to hear someone speak the way they do on the docks."

Luca smiled and didn't say he never wanted to see the Water City again. "I will be happy to keep up a stream of chatter as long as I am here enjoying your hospitality."

"How long will you be stayin'?" Cov asked, gently bouncing the youngest child on his lap.

"I'm afraid not long at all," Luca said. "In fact, I must leave immediately."

"But the sun is going down," Karmel gasped, the color draining from her rosy cheeks.

"I'll 'ave to be goin' too," Bij said. "You can take your time unloadin' the wagon and bring it 'round when you got the chance. I won't be needin' it for a few weeks at least."

"But your farm is almost half a day's travel away!" Karmel clenched her fists in an attempt to maintain composure.

"Karmel, what's the matter?" Luca asked gently.

"Nothing," Karmel said in a voice barely above a whisper. "Just the darkness."

Luca shivered when she said it, the word *Demon* unspoken yet underlying her fear.

Cov frowned and rubbed his head. "It won't take but a minute to get some more blankets. There's no lack of space in front o'th'fire.."

Shaking his head, Bij stood silently. "Brother, I've been on the road away from 'ome for two long weeks." For the first time since meeting him, Luca saw him smile. "I know these plains like the back of my hand. I'll be alright, and I'll look after the young fellow 'ere until daybreak."

Not so young, but thank you kindly anyway, Luca thought

as he nodded at Bij. "And I'll take care of him," he promised Cov and Karmel.

In the end the couple acquiesced, but they wouldn't let Luca leave empty-handed.

"Where was it you said you were going?" Karmel asked as she bustled around the sparse kitchen.

"The Mountains," Luca said, gently sliding the child from his lap to Cov's outstretched hands. He picked up his instrument from the back of the chair.

Karmel nodded, counted something out on her fingers, and then began pulling out food. Bread, salt fish, dried fruit and warm fishcakes wrapped in paper, enough to last twelve men twice the distance to the Mountains by Luca's figures, was all bundled into a cheesecloth sack and tied with twine.

Cov and Karmel saw them off with hugs and well wishes. The sleepy-eyed children waved with one hand while hiding yawns with the other. Just as suddenly as the little home had appeared, it disappeared into the dark as the night took Luca and Bij.

No more talkative or companionable on foot than when traveling by wagon, Bij stalked along on his long, lean legs without a word. Luca was content to let the silence remain unmolested, even by song, though he kept a sharp eye out in case either violin or dirks were called for.

Covered by a blanket of clouds, the stars were not visible to guide them but somehow Bij kept going. Luca did not question his lead, careful not to fall behind lest he lose the faint outline of the man in the darkness. He kept even closer when the hint of acid reached his nose.

Bij suddenly stopped and sniffed. "It smells like something was burnin'," he said.

Not burning. Freezing. The Guardian had noticed the

same thing long before, but saying something would only have alarmed the other man. Now that Bij had noticed, there seemed to be no harm in hurrying him along to his destination.

"How far is your home?" Luca asked, sliding his forefinger up and down the neck of his violin.

Bij scratched his head. "Not really sure 'bout that. I thought we would've made it by now. See, the sun's comin' up."

There was indeed a faint pink glow on the horizon, so subtle Luca wondered how the man had been able to spot that and yet not smell the stink of Demons. Bij continued to look around, eyes narrowed, and then he smiled.

"Ah! We must've turned north somehow in the dark. This is where we part ways," Bij said. "You go on further north, my home is that way," he pointed toward the light on the horizon.

Remembering Karmel's words, Luca tried to ignore the uneasy feeling settling in his stomach. His gaze vacillated between the impending sunrise and the much darker north. "I should see you to your door," he said softly.

Bij scowled. "I can take care of myself, *minstrel*."

"I'm sure you can," Luca said, straining to keep the condescending strain out of his voice. Jæyd's face flashed before his eyes, her eyes laughing as she mouthed 'ice down the front of a tunic'. Luca strove harder to fill his voice with encouragement and patience. "But I believe it would be best if we continued together."

Bij did not stop scowling, but he shrugged. "Suit yourself, minstrel. I cannot stop you."

Luca rolled his eyes at the man's retreating back, then hurried after him, silently taking his violin in hand and debating whether it would be more prudent to simply unveil his weapons.

When the Demon's arm detached itself from the shadows and came sweeping towards Bij's head, the two dirks were already half formed in Luca's hands. It took but half a second more to send the first blade slicing through the air to bury itself in the Demon's flesh. Dissolving in a shower of gold sparks as the Demon screeched, the dirk reappeared in Luca's still outstretched hand.

"You may want to get behind me," Luca said to Bij as the Demon stalked forward.

Shock frozen on his face, Bij gaped as the Demon materialized beside him, its red eyes glowing in the dim light. Thin, angular and roughly the size of a man, to Luca's eyes it looked like an overgrown thorn bush. He fully intended to prune this one back. Now wary of Luca's blades, the Demon circled the two men. Luca kept between it and Bij, who was slowly recovering his wits.

"Not one of them things again," he muttered.

"I take it you're familiar with your average Demon," Luca said.

"Yeah," Bij said. "They come around sometimes."

"Really? And how exactly do you deal with them when they show up?" Luca asked, his eyes never leaving the Demon as it wove back and forth in front of him.

"I've got a special knife. A couple of other men have somethin' like it," Bij said. "But I don't have my knife with me. I didn't think I was gonna need it down South."

"Maybe for the time being, you should keep the knife on you wherever you go," Luca suggested conversationally, parrying the Demon's sudden swipe at him, the harsh crash of metal on bony plate making both men cringe.

"Yeah, I'll do that," Bij said. "Maybe I'll get one like

yours."

"I wouldn't count on it," Luca said. "These are very difficult to procure."

"Are they blooded?"

"Pardon?"

"Do they have blood on them?" Bij asked intently. "'Cause if they don't they won't work."

"I think they'll work fine," Luca said. "Just give me a minute, alright?"

Without waiting for a response, Luca bounded forward and engaged the Demon head on. The Demon could not have any attention on the other, completely defenseless, man because Luca's blade moved so quickly and fluidly.

The Demon was driven backwards, screeching and squealing. Luca pressed it back further. Hissing at Luca, the Demon raised its fore-claws in a familiar gesture and ripped a fissure in the air, the biting cold from the other side stinging Luca's eyes.

No, I really don't think you're getting off that easy.

Before the Demon could crawl back into the safety of its little Void, Luca darted forward and cut off one front limb with a clean swipe. Black blood spurted and the Demon howled, flailing the severed limb and hopping from one leg to the other.

After that, it was almost too easy to kill it. Luca felt as though it lay down to wait for his blade. He made two quick jabs which were simultaneously merciful and merciless and the Demon rattled its final breath. Dead, it looked more like a pile of oddly placed twigs than anything dangerous or menacing.

Luca leaned back on one leg, his bloody blades crossed on the other, breathing heavily. Bij came up softly behind him and looked at the carcass of the Demon. The details grew steadily clearer in the waxing light. The weird, almost misty, light from the Void spilled over the Demon and the two men, distorting the shapes.

Realizing belatedly that the Demon had not just laid down for him to kill, but had in fact been attempting to return to the Void, Luca saw he was now standing in the doorway to that Void. Cold shivers trickled down his skin and he hurriedly moved away until he could see the tear shining black against the sky.

"We can't just leave that open," he said to himself. He was surprised when Bij grunted an affirmative at him.

"They only close from the inside," Bij said.

"You've closed them before?" Luca was even more surprised. "I thought only a Demon could do that."

"A door is a door. If you can find the handle, you can close it. I would've expected a Guardian to know something like that," Bij said, unimpressed.

That was not entirely accurate, but Luca wasn't going to argue with the man, and certainly not after the man had just revealed he knew what Luca was.

"Right," Luca said, a warm flush passing through him at the voicing of the title. *It seems we have not been totally forgotten. Now, is that a blessing or a curse, I wonder?* "How long have you known?"

"I guessed the first day, but a minstrel with gold weapons that can fight a Demon without blood?" Bij looked at Luca with a knowing glance. "Not likely, by me. I figured you to be a Guardian come back from wherever you'd got to."

"I'm glad someone remembers those admirable people," Luca said. "So, how exactly do you close them from the inside?"

"Someone goes in, pullin' the Demon after, and closes it," Bij told him as if it were the simplest thing in the world.

So, somehow the dead Demon passing the threshold must close the rift, Luca reasoned to himself. *I must remember that.* He realized with an uncomfortable sensation in his stomach that left the question of…

"Who goes in?" Luca asked slowly as the reality of what the man was telling him sank in. "And how does he get out?"

"One time we took a murdering rapist, and threw him in," Bij said. "The other time, there wasn't one of those kinds 'round, Josas volunteered, and he didn't come back out."

Luca nodded, disgust and understanding melding into a hard lump in his stomach. It was callous. Callous, but practical.

"You're a Guardian, you've got a job to do, so I guess I'll be goin' in," Bij continued with the same inflection as if he were talking about eating dinner. "I have one thing to ask of you."

"Hold on one moment," Luca interrupted. "What makes you think I'm going to let you go in there?"

"The way I see it, you don't have a choice," Bij said. "If it weren't for you, I'd be dead by the Demon, so either which way it isn't really any different, except now I can close it so no more get out."

Luca could find no hole in the man's logic and this aggravated him more than a quip he could think of no clever retort to.

"Have you tried any other way?" he demanded, gripping his dirks tightly.

Bij scratched his head. "Well, I can't say I remember, but I wouldn't guess there was too much thinkin' goin' on at the time."

As Bij was distracted with trying to remember the exact sequence of events, Luca took but a fraction of a moment to steel himself and then stepped into the Void.

Cold seeped into his flesh, so deep and alien even Luca's hardy leather garb couldn't keep it out. He was drawn to the warm light of his own world and had to fight the urge to dive back out. His eyes filmed over, making everything unclear and immersing him in a dark grey cloud with no solid shapes, just undulating lines.

A Demon appeared in front of Luca as he was squinting around. Luca gripped both blades tightly, the golden glow making the Void a little more bearable. The Demon stared at him with a blank expression which did not change much when the blades pointed at its throat.

"Close it," Luca growled.

The Demon cocked its head, blinked its deep red eyes rapidly and then pointed at the yellow light that leaked weakly into the Void. Luca started to leave but then thought of something else. "You should bring the other one inside."

The Demon did not want to go near the Rift, but at the insistence of Luca's blades, it stepped closer and peered out. Muttering a mournful howl at the sight of its dead brethren, the Demon tried to slink away. Luca's blade helped it find its way out of the Rift. Once it was within Demona it seemed to increase in size. It growled at Bij but shrank back when the air was pierced with a golden gleam.

With repeated gestures and a few well-placed jabs with the pointed end of his dagger, Luca made the Demon pull the carcass inside the Void. It did not need to be told again to close the Rift. Watching the tear disappear, Luca felt the rising sun dispel the unnatural cold, though the stink still remained, and reflected on his incredible luck at the appearance of the second Demon after his reckless plunge into the Void. *Things could have turned out a bit more sour if it hadn't had the decency to show up.*

He wiped the blood from his blade on his pants. The dark blood was invisible against the black fabric except where it covered the glittering green and silver threads. A thought occurred to Luca as he gave a cursory examination to his clean blades. He looked at Bij.

Bij crossed his arms as the blades melted back into the violin that Luca swung over his shoulder.

"You're the first person I ever saw come back out," Bij volunteered after a moment.

"I'm just glad to be here," Luca said, rubbing his arms in an attempt to return some of their warmth, wondering how to phrase his question.

"I would be too," Bij said. "That was pure crazy, what you did."

"I've done worse." Luca almost smiled, though the cold of the Void still clung to his clothes and skin like wet slime. "You said something before, about blood? What did you mean?"

"If you put the right blood on the blade, the Demons don't like it," Bij shrugged. "One time Lyff accidentally cut one of his kids when they ran in front of him and the Demon just didn't like that blade at all. It just left. Lyff didn't have to do anything more than wave it at the thing."

"Is the child alright?" Luca frowned, not sure that he liked the idea of child-sacrifice, even if it was the only way the people of Demona were going to be able to handle the Demons. *At least until they stopped persecuting the Guardians.*

Bij shook his head. "No, no, he didn't die. But we put his blood on all the knives, hoes, shovels, anythin' sharp, and the Demons started to leave us alone."

Luca nodded. *Interesting. They're using First Magyc and they don't even know it. Granted, that kind of magyc hasn't been used in Demona since time immemorial, but it looks like it's back again. That could either be a good sign or a bad one.* "So you can take care of yourself?"

"Like I told you before," Bij said, a shade of his scowl returning.

Luca held out a pacifying hand. "Good. Then we should get you home, and I'll be on my way."

As they began to walk away, something caught Luca's attention. The arm Luca's blade had sliced from the Demon's body lay just to one side, hidden by a tuft of sienna grass. Luca blinked. He thought he saw something clutched in the severed hand of the Demon, but it swam in and out of his vision.

With a quick glance at Bij, who hadn't noticed anything and kept walking, Luca took two quick steps over and pried the sharp fingers from the object. It looked like a rock, so black it sucked the light out of the air around it, but it was much heavier than it looked like it should be. It gave Luca a distinctly uncomfortable feeling under his ribs and he had to fight the urge to drop it like a potato fresh from the fire. *I should probably leave this here, but what if someone else comes along and finds this, whatever it is?*

Luca paused, undecided, then realized it was more fool-hardy to leave a thing that felt the way this black stone felt out in the open than it was to take it with him, so he put it in the pocket of his jacket and hurried after the Torinish farmer.

Bij's home was a larger, more established version of his brother's. A garden with budding greens lay in the front and colored curtains hung in the windows. The two men stopped outside the gate.

"My wife will want me to offer you breakfast," Bij said, and the meaning of the precisely worded statement was not lost on Luca.

Luca shook his head. "Thank you, but no. I have food

from Karmel that I'll eat on the road. I have no time to waste."

"Good luck," Bij said with a long, penetrating look that made Luca edgy. "I hope you do what you came back to do."

So do I. "May the Path keep you," Luca said, relishing the old farewell which had disappeared with the Guardians, raising his hand in a brief farewell before turning north for the next leg of his journey.

Five days of flat plains and a cold that grew ever deeper passed before Luca found himself under the wing of the Mountains.

Grasped tight in the embrace of an eternal winter, the Mountains were made of stone and ice, tearing at the sky like claws on a beast. Seeming to touch the very sun, the tallest were wrapped in cloaks of glittering blues and silvers and their shadows stretched for leagues.

The Mountains were considered the northern border of Demona, at least by the cartographers of the past. In any event, people did not venture into them and those that did brave the frozen depths seldom returned, whole or sane at any rate. The Nitefolk - small, cat-like people who lived among the smaller of the rock giants - said that even at the summit of the baby peaks the air was too thin for a man to breathe, and one would die sooner of suffocation than cold. Luca would never admit to believing this but he had no great desire to test it either.

Though it was well into spring, the nights didn't know it and Luca knew freezing was a very real concern if he stopped moving. He walked through the night, warming his hands under his armpits and making up nonsense verse to entertain himself. When the sun came up and the first rays touched his frozen face, he was too numb to feel them but as the sun drifted higher, slowly warmth and sensation seeped back into his limbs.

Finally sure he was not going to die of cold or exposure, Luca stopped at the next place that looked to be a likely place to rest, a small copse of Everwood trees, the cotton-like covering on their thick, arching roots making the hollows perfect for napping. Exhausted, he chose the one that allowed the most sun through its outstretched limbs and collapsed into the soft oblivion of sleep.

Luca awoke to the sound of his teeth chattering and the sight of his breath misting in front of him. Standing with stiff limbs, Luca cursed himself in multiple tongues for sleeping so long and losing valuable traveling time.

A quick glance at the sky showed that the sun had passed its zenith and was beginning its descent, and Luca's rested eyes now noticed what his exhausted, sleep-deprived eyes had not: against the sharp angles of the Mountains, the beginning of a flat-topped mound was now visible.

Hope sprang up as Luca saw the end to his journey. He pulled a piece of bread and a strip of salt fish out to gnaw on as he walked, longing for the hot and savory eel stew that he had eaten what seemed a lifetime ago.

If anything, this night was worse than the previous, with more rocks and rises appearing in his path, but around dawn Luca felt a change that warmed him first from the outside in and then from the inside out as he remembered what it was.

In the ground around the plateau that the Crescent Temple sat upon was a network of hot-springs which brought heat from the center of the earth to the surface. The result was an undying spring in the midst of an endless winter.

The ground under his feet began to slope upwards and warm at the same time. Despite being tired and half-frozen, Luca felt an infusion of energy give his limbs speed and grace they had lacked previously.

At first Luca thought it was just his mind playing tricks on him, but as the light grew brighter and brighter and took on a golden hue, Luca realized what it was. He took a step forward and stumbled, grasping at a tuft of rough grass above him but failing to steady himself. Luca fell and hit the ground, but didn't feel it.

He opened his eyes to a familiar sight.

By the Path, I can't wait until we're all actually together again and this sudden wrenching into a world of golden light can be dispensed with. His stomach clenched as he realized if this had occurred the previous day, his body would have died while he was off parleying with his companions, the very same companions that were now before him. Including a very alive Cedar Jal.

The golden-eyed Guardian was tight-lipped about the girl; none of the others could get anything out of him about her or where she had come from. Luca could see they were dying of curiosity about the Demon's pronouncement, but all Cedar would say was that he was in D'Ohera.

Just like him, Luca thought irritably. *Letting everything rattle around in his head until he's absolutely certain he's figured it out while the world crashes down around him. Not like that's ever gotten us into any trouble.*

He returned from his thought to the sound of Jæyd's voice echoing faintly. "…meet at the Tales Mane. Stay put, forge your guitar and each of us shall fly there as fast as we are able."

Luca drowned in golden light and closed his eyes.

He opened them to find himself lying near the far edge of the plateau with no memory of moving there. The sun was going down, setting the mountains aflame. In the orange light, the Crescent Temple appeared whole and unmarred.

Luca picked himself up and tried to set his dream-muddled thoughts in order. He was compelled by Jæyd's words to set off for D'Ohera and the Tales Mane at once, but he had come all this way to find her. *I'll just have a look; see if she's still here.*

Approaching with silent and reverent steps, Luca recalled again the last time he had been there, the flashes of unnatural green lightning, the way the ground shook and trembled, blasts of hot and cold wind and the gaping holes in the air. The air shifted in waves over the Temple, and Luca saw with horror that the Rift, black and gaping, still floated over the west tower like a hovering dragon.

It made the whole place reek; acrid air filled his lungs with every breath And filthy shadows coated everything. Turning his head every so often to make sure the shadows were simply shadows and nothing more, Luca's heart sped up and his palms begin to sweat. *There is nothing here but evil memories,* he told himself, but still he clutched his violin tighter.

The Crescent Temple was an ancient building, built so long ago there was no record of who had built it, though the size and scope of the thing suggested that giants had designed it for their needs. Sitting atop a plateau, the Temple curved around like a marble tiara. The foremost towers were arranged in a triangle, the tallest in the center, the next lower and the next lower. The towers tapered into walls as tall as twelve men. The walls enclosed the Gardens.

Once more or less level, the ground had shifted and tilted, pulling half the temple with it. Huge blocks of stone stuck out of the ground like blunt teeth and trees which had stood for hundreds of years lay toppled, rich earth still clinging to their massive, spreading root system. Yet even with all the havoc that had been wreaked, somehow the Crescent Temple had avoided complete destruction.

An overgrowth of bushes and vines spilled over from the now wild Gardens. The spring which fed the fountains in the Gardens had been rerouted by the massive upheavals in the earth. A waterfall tricked through the western wall and down the rocks, the faint shadow of a rainbow arching across the wall to disappear behind the tallest of the towers.

Luca made his way slowly to the great oak doors that stood higher than three men. Still locked tight, they did not budge when Luca passed his hand lightly across the massive iron handles, nor did anything happen when Luca grasped them firmly and whispered for them to open and let him pass. The hair rose on the back of his neck. *This cannot be happening, not here.*

Swallowing the taste of fear, Luca stepped back and looked, reaching out for the source of magyc that had only ever been constant and comforting. Not a trace of the Path remained here, no faint spark or glow. Suddenly, Luca felt alone and powerless.

The violin hummed against his skin. The reassuring warmth traveled from his finger to his stomach and he began to breathe easier. *At least I still have that, no matter what else remains, or does* not *remain, I should say.*

The place was silent and somehow Luca knew that Jæyd was not here to spread her calm blanket of protection, traces of which still remained. His fretting finger told him she would return soon, from wherever she had gotten off to, but he couldn't tell when.

She would be the one to ignore common sense for the sake of duty, Luca mused, sitting down on a step. *Even as the whole world was consumed in insane blood lust, Jæyd would stay in the most obvious place to find a Guardian, just to save this same world from the Demons, as she was charged to.*

It was almost enough to make Luca feel slightly ashamed, but Luca was not Jæyd. Luca sat upon the great steps and watched the last sliver of sun disappear as he waited. He became increasingly anxious as night approached. Finally, he decided that today was not the day he would meet up with Jæyd.

I have to stay here for the night at least, Luca thought. *No way am I going out there in the cold.*

Luca stood and stretched for a brief moment before turning to face the giant Temple doors. He shook his head. Slinging the violin over his shoulder, he made his way toward the rear of the Temple. He clambered over the rocks, noting the state of each of the towers and turrets, where the walls were sound and where they had crumbled, for no other reason than it may prove useful at a later time. When he reached the haphazard waterfall, Luca found the rocks became too precarious for him to leap about on. Making his way back, he went upward, finding footholds and handholds aplenty in the cracked walls of the Gardens.

He pulled himself onto the top of the wall, which was as wide as a city street. After a few steps, he found the end of a huge oak's bough brushing the wall. Luca stared at it, rubbed his brow and leapt. Walking as a tightrope walker would, he danced into the leafy greenness, his feet as sure as a cat's. Swinging down from branch to branch, he landed in the dark recess of the Gardens.

By this time, night had thoroughly claimed the Gardens of the Temple, binding everything in shadow. No moon came out to light the way and Luca was almost blind. His breath came with effort and he waited a moment to allow his eyes to adjust to the gloom. He was relieved to find he was not totally without sight.

Remembering the tangle of pleasure-trails that wound through the Gardens and led back to the courtyard, Luca set out to find one. Making the best guess, he plunged through the plants, but everything was so overgrown he could no more have found a trail than he could find feathers growing on dog. He wandered aimlessly, branches slapping at his face and vines grabbing his ankles.

Luca didn't know this place anymore. All the plants were green yet completely dead, the leaves like fine spun cloth to his fingers, and the first small flowers of spring without smell. The obvious contradiction vexed Luca as he made his way through the Gardens, hopefully in the direction of the rear door of the Temple.

It was not until he tripped on the intricately carved leg of the sitting bench that he noticed he had entered the vast gazebo. The stout beams covered in thorny climbing vines were more like trees. Birds twittered sleepily at him from their roosts in the roof rafters now indistinguishable from the spreading canopy.

Overjoyed at the prospect of finally reaching the Temple and being free from the Gardens, Luca crossed to the other side of the gazebo and took the steps down two at a time until he emerged into the open.

The lack of a moon made the stars shine all the brighter, though the absence of their sparkle in the Rift overhead was not pleasant. Rising up a short distance ahead, the Temple sat like a slumbering behemoth, all detail lost in shadow.

All but untouched by decay and neglect though the Gardens' advance pressed on three sides, the courtyard was just as Luca remembered it, the smooth stones, high walls, the fountain in the center gleaming in the faint light, quiet and still now, its water long since gone.

Luca slowly circled the silent fountain and it was then that he saw a shape emerge from the open archway in the cloister which ringed the courtyard. The two froze at the same time.

Luca felt the other sizing him up even as he tried to determine if it meant mischief or would simply turn tail and leave him in peace. The proximity of the Rift would give strength to a Demon, and something told Luca this was no ordinary foe to begin with. The two stared at each other from across the wide, yet somehow too short a distance, that separated them.

Making no sound Luca remained still, but the other began to move stealthily across the stones toward him. Crouching, Luca slipped the violin from his shoulder. A second later, the ring of blades being crossed reverberated through the courtyard. The silver shadow paused, but only for a second.

Luca took a slow, deep breath, feeling his lungs expand and the blades hum pleasantly in his hands. Luca didn't hold with any god and didn't believe in prayer, but something had to be said. *If I die here tonight, may whatever Path is left in this place keep me and may Death treat me well.*

Luca Lorisson moved forward to meet the advancing shadow.

THE PIPER

Jæyd Elvenborn crouched with one knee pressed into the ground, balancing with the opposite hand. Wisps of auburn hair stuck to her temple and her white trousers were splattered with mud and blood, some of it her own, but she did not mind, not now. A sense of urgency pressed her forward on her present course despite the weary feeling in her bones and the memory of Cedar outlined in golden light commanding her to make for D'Ohera at once.

It was well past twilight and the world was just settling into the stillness. Jæyd's gaze returned to the trail of her quarry. After running across the entire northwestern peninsula of Demona, her Demon had returned to where it started. The Demon was nowhere in sight.

The Crescent Temple loomed up before Jæyd, the cold stone still somehow warm to her, and the grand front doors still a sign of home after a long journey despite the acid tingle in the air. The air was thin here, and the ground still not fully recovered from whatever Cedar had done to it four years ago.

Dancing with light steps up the uneven stairs, the elf waved her hand over the long handle in the middle of the door. A quiet groan slipped from the hinges, but the door did not move. Dismayed, Jæyd tried again, this time with more force, her fingers brushing the cold metal.

She breathed a sigh of relief when a stream of gold light snaked across the door and it opened for her. Compounded with the events of the past few days, this small mishap troubled the elf. Here, even with the Rift that Cedar had left gaping over the Temple, she had always been able to find the Path, no matter how faint. Though she had sworn not to dwell on the incident, it sat in her consciousness, ready to taunt her with uncertainty at any moment.

Too many signs to ignore. Jæyd pushed the thought away and stepped inside the Great Entrance Hall.

As always, memories tumbled through her mind as she passed through the passages and halls of the ancient building. Luca and Timo dueling up and down the stairs, the metallic thunder punctuated with taunts and laughter; meals in the Great Hall, the candles on the table tiny pinpricks of light in the cavernous room; Cedar practicing in the long Eastwing passages, hitting the center every time; Luca dancing along the roof beams in the armory, agile as a cat while he threw insults at her; Timo singing old battle songs of the Dale during the thunderstorms, his baritone ringing in the rookery while lightning flashed above.

Not even a whisper sounded to lead Jæyd onward as she walked through the empty halls, but she was pulled out of her memories by a shadow slipping around a corner at the end of the passage.

Rounding the corner, Jæyd came upon the Gardens, black as the sky. The Gardens of the Crescent Temple had gone feral, overgrown and half in ruins and rubble, relinquishing majesty for a wild magnificence. Above, the Rift shifted and reformed like black lips over a blacker maw.

An open cloister surrounded the Gardens, latticework supported by slender columns. An archway in the center of the cloister led out to a stone courtyard. Once a gazebo sat between the courtyard and the trees, but now the trees had retaken much of it. The overgrown gazebo was as much a part of the Gardens as the trees themselves.

It is going to be a task to set it right, Jæyd thought as her eyes examined the cracked stone and uprooted trees, and she smiled to herself. *Most of the battle will be convincing the others but after Cedar and his Library project, I do not doubt I will be able make them come around.*

The elf walked along the cloister, stepping over thick vines that lay like trunks of small trees across the path. Starlight made the courtyard glow in rich silvers and deep blues. Jæyd stepped through the tiered archway into the open and a world of diamond-edged blackness.

Even as she stepped into the courtyard, a shadow blacker than the lightless night slipped from the gazebo on the other side and she paused. Seeing the shadow pause as well, she sensed fear and a sense of finality exuding from it. Instinct urged her to drift into her Old-Sight, but in the presence of the Rift and the influence of the Void, her eyes burned and blurred, so the elf resisted the temptation, instead relying only on her normal vision. Lost in the shadow, Jæyd could not make out detail, but the Rift repulsed most living things for a league, so this shadow could be just one thing – her quarry. She grasped her flute tightly and her palm tingled.

I cannot lose it this time, not in this place.

The shape crouched and Jæyd stepped forward as she slowed her breathing to an even rhythm. A distinctive ring of metal reverberated through the night, causing her to freeze in place. *I know the sound of those blades.* The realization she was not facing a Demon made her memory stutter for a moment, but then it came to her.

"Luca?" she called out, the question full of hope and joy.

A pause.

"*Jæyd?*" a voice with a strong Isosian Northport lilt came back incredulously.

"Luca!" Jæyd flew across the courtyard.

The shape materialized in front of her, becoming the thin, sharp-eyed man with purple, silver and green streaks in his hair and clothes. His two blades were crossed in front of him and he managed to pull them out of the way just in time to avoid impaling her as she rushed him. Jæyd squeezed him tightly.

"By the Path, it is good to see you!" she said. "It has been so long."

"Jæyd, you're suffocating me," he moaned, his voice muffled in her hair.

"I apologize," she said without contrition, and tightened her squeeze for a moment before she released him.

Rubbing his ribs with a pained expression on his face, Luca squinted at her. "What are you doing out here at this time? I thought I was going to die!"

"Pursuing a Demon," Jæyd replied easily, placing her hand on her hip. "What are *you* doing here? The last I heard you had gone South."

"I was getting a touch of wanderlust," Luca said. "Then Cedar showed up and figured I'd drop by to keep you company on the way to D'Ohera, and see what you thought about the whole thing."

"And how did you know I would be here for you to find?"

"You're like a ghost, Jæyd," Luca explained. "You don't let go of places easily."

"I see," she said, but could not argue with him. "Well, before we set out for D'Ohera, there is something I must finish. You did not happen to see a Demon walking around have you?"

"Not recently," Luca said. "Not here."

Jæyd scowled and turned her head first one way, then the other, trying to pinpoint the direction toward the Demon. The Gardens were brimming with Demon scat coming and going every which way. It was impossible to pick out one trail, even with her fuzzy and uncomfortable Old-Sight. She may as well have been in the Voide.

"I do not understand it," Jæyd complained, crossing her arms. "It does not make any sense!"

"What doesn't make any sense?" Luca asked, slinging his violin over his shoulder and trying to see what she was looking at.

"The Demon!"

"They generally don't," Luca said as he ran a hand through his spiked and colored hair. "Why should this one be any different?"

Jæyd gave him an impatient look. "She refuses to return to the Voide. I do not think she *can* go back. *And* she did not kill me when she had the chance."

"And you want to go back and demand satisfaction, is that it?" Luca asked, his eyes incredulous. "Are you insane?"

"That is what I like about you, Luca," Jæyd said as she walked in tight circles. "You never try to drown the truth in honey."

"You're welcome," Luca said. "But in all seriousness, you're not going chasing after this Demon to find out why it *didn't* kill you?"

"I am, and I mean to solve this mystery or die in the attempt."

Luca looked at her, his face deadpan and his jaw set in that stubborn way he had. "What about Cedar?"

Jæyd stopped pacing. "What do you mean?"

"The girl? The Prophecy? Are you just going to desert him?"

She started pacing again. "Do you know how long I have been here Luca?"

"About five minutes," Luca said, and rolled his eyes when she glanced at him with an irritated grimace. "Oh, alright. Since Cedar disappeared, so…four years."

"Yes. And in that time, *nothing* like this Demon has ever appeared. I have chased her across half of Demona and nothing she does is expected. She is obsessed with something. She does not kill. *She avoids people.* Demons never *avoid* people, and in all my years of chasing Demons, I have seen only a handful of females."

Luca stared at her in shock. "What?"

"It is a fe-mal-le," she enunciated, in no mood to be patient with him.

Luca blinked, processing that information. "What does that mean?"

"Well, Luca, females possess certain features that allow them to bear young and…"

"I know *that*," Luca grumbled. "What does that have to do with *the Demon?*"

"The one I am looking for is female," Jæyd said and knew at once that she had vexed him more than usual.

"So, you can tell the difference between a male and

female Demon?" Luca said with an expression akin to that of finding half a worm in his fruit.

"Yes. You cannot?" Jæyd knew she should not have been surprised yet it was so natural she assumed everyone could.

"It's not that I can't," Luca began defensively. "It's just that I never thought about it. Like you said, they never show up here."

"Typical," Jæyd gave a delicate snort. "How did you think they breed?"

"I didn't ever think about it," Luca said loftily. "Why would I want to think about that?"

"It might expand your understanding of Demons. Did it ever occur to you that not all Demons are the same?"

"Of course. Some are mainly evil, some are pure evil, and some are the ultimate evil," Luca said with a smirk. "And then of course, you have the Nine."

"And where do they fit on your little scale of evil?" Jæyd asked, finding Luca's groupings humorous if not truly useful.

"They are the essence of evil," Luca said, crossing his arms and looking at her triumphantly.

"That is very poetic, but irrelevant in this case," she told him.

A split second was all the warning given, a faint whistle through the air, a biting cold which did not come from the blackness of the night, and Luca disappeared before her eyes.

Cursing, Jæyd leapt into the darkness after Luca and the Demon. The shape moving in front of her crashed among the trees, zigzagging through the gaps and making gaps when they were not readily available. Vines and branches flew into Jæyd's face and roots grabbed her feet but Luca's panicked shouts spurred her on, her arms and legs pumping as she raced after the Demon.

With every step, Jæyd gained on it despite the tangled plants, until it was close enough to touch and she could see sweat steaming off it. Darting up a low spreading branch, the elf leapt onto the Demon's hard back. In a reflexive action, the Demon whirled and the two Guardians went flying into a tangle of bushes. The Demon paused for a moment, its eyes shining in the dark. Then it plunged into the trees without a look back. Soon only the sound of their breathing and the faint call of an owl somewhere in the Gardens could be heard.

"I think we found your Demon," Luca said, his voice thick as he picked himself up and retrieved his instrument, which had fallen a short distance away. "Nice of it to drop by."

"Are you hurt?"

"Only my pride, fortunately," Luca said, a fuzzy, bewildered expression fading from his eyes. He gave himself a pat as if to reassure himself that he was still all there. "It didn't stay long, must have jumped through the Rift."

Jæyd knew otherwise. "No, she did not. I have seen her run that way before. She is still searching. Come on."

"You're actually going after it?" Luca grimaced. "What am *I* supposed to do?"

"You may come if you wish," Jæyd said. She glanced at him briefly with the smile she reserved for when he was in one of his bad moods, a smile which had equal chance of placating him or goading him into a worse temper.

"That's not what I meant," he said.

"I am going with or without you," she said. "I will not be long. I suppose we shall meet again at the Tales Mane."

The elf turned and walked away through the trees

towards the courtyard and the Temple. After a moment, she heard slow, begrudging steps following her. Jæyd smiled again.

"You're going in the wrong direction," Luca informed her, coming up to her elbow. "It's this way."

He pointed to Jæyd's left. Through a gap in the trees, something that could be grey stone peeked from the blackness.

"I am glad you are here," she said, perfectly sincere.

He glared at her.

Walking through the ghostly halls of the Crescent Temple side by side, the man's boots clicking in time to the elf's strides, Jæyd watched Luca's eyes flit from the columns to the windows to the statues in the recesses and the doorways. She could almost see his memories flash by just as her own did.

"It is strange being back here," he whispered, the sound eerie in the empty halls. "Everything is the same and yet something is missing."

"Yes," Jæyd said. "But one day the Guardians will return. Just as it was before."

"Of course," Luca agreed absently and Jæyd saw that it would never be as it was, at least for herself and her three companion Guardians.

She shivered, the twilight of the First Age an incorporeal presence always near, dogging her steps. A slow, drawn feeling of fatality made Jæyd's bones feel old in a way they had not before. She walked faster to leave it behind.

Further along the hall Jæyd saw the slit of a shadow from which came the faint smell of pine. Usually she avoided this part of the Temple; it was too empty without the others, but now Luca was there. She nudged him and they went into the tiny passage that forced their shoulders together, barely wide enough for them to walk abreast.

Together the pair of Guardians stopped in the doorway of the Guardians' Hall. The Hall had not taken much damage. In the dark, it was like some ghostly realm, long and rectangular, the thick columns like ribs, moonlight shining off the checked tiles. Jæyd's sharp eyes were able to make out the tattered and singed remains of the Prophetic Tapestry hanging on the far wall. Through the rips, the faded colors of the mural from which the tapestry had been copied were visible.

From that point, spreading out in both direction along the walls in haphazard bursts of colors, were painting after painting of Guardians, young and old, their visages captured in timeless form. They were an eclectic bunch. Jæyd saw paintings of goblins from X'Kpögh, with long white hair holding gilded xuärtans, harp-like instruments they played with stone-filled metal tubes; Elves in traditional garb, tights and flowing tunics, and elves in classic Demonan clothes and shorn hair; High dwarves in helm and mail and Wild dwarves in loose breeches with fierce painted faces, their long bone-horns engraved with carved faces; bearded men from Samnara in patchwork pants who could have been pirates in another life, the bows of their fiddles made of whalebone; Torinish, Isosian, Akorgian, and D'Oheran men and women with drums, flutes, guitars, harps, and bells. Even Nyicans in bright knee-length robes were pictured here and there, tattooed arms bare.

Luca only had eyes for the nearest painting. Like some twisted testament to history, icy Demon fires had blackened the face of the fifth Guardian, obscuring his features. The other four stood shoulder to shoulder.

The long-gone Artist had done a remarkable job of capturing the finer nuances of the character of each, not surprising as he most likely called upon the Path for his artistic endeavor; the sardonic twist to Luca's mouth, the pride in the lift of Timo's chin, the hard gleam in Cedar's gold eyes. Jæyd avoided looking at the painted version of herself, not liking the fact that her ears appeared too large and the lace on her tunic made it look as though there was an unbecoming bulge around her midsection.

"How did Cedar look to you?" Luca asked.

An image of Cedar in the middle of the road flashed into Jæyd's mind, with the Demon and the girl. The Demon was familiar and Jæyd shivered. *One of the Nine has finally returned to Demona. As has the missing Guardian. A final page in the story of the First Age turns.*

There had undoubtedly been other signs and for a moment Jæyd regretted the decision to seclude herself in the Temple, but there had been no other choice of action. When Cedar Jal had disappeared, a permanent Rift had ebbed and flowed in and out of Demona at the Crescent Temple and Jæyd had taken it upon herself to take care of anything that came through.

"It is a fair reproduction," Jæyd said with half a glance at the portrait as she replaited her hair, swiftly catching the strands that had come free in the battle. "His nose should be a touch larger."

"Not the picture. Now."

"All I have seen I have seen through a golden haze. It was difficult to tell."

"And what about the girl?"

"What about her?" Jæyd deflected the question with her own.

"Where did she come from? What is he doing with her?"

"I do not know, but I will be sure to ask him when we next see each other," Jæyd answered and turned away from the image. She did not want to think about the girl or the Prophecy.

"It seems the girl is a touchy subject for everyone," Luca grumbled. "Turns everyone into dithering, defensive imbeciles."

"What do you make of her, then?" Jæyd said, the slight edge in her voice cutting Luca's harangue short.

She realized sheepishly she had just proven his point.

"I think everyone is overreacting," Luca said at last. "Fate is Fate. It cannot be changed, even by Cedar."

"Just do not tell him that," Jæyd said as they stepped out into the night. "It did not go well for the last who tried to tell him that."

Luca grimaced but had nothing to say. They left the Guardians' Hall and exited the Crescent Temple through the south postern.

Past the Mountains, the sky was as clear as the Thaumaturgists' best glass and the stars appeared as big as diamonds. Jæyd looked around and sniffed. The air was chilly and sharp with the smell of stone, ice and Demons. The spring-warmed ground steamed, giving off ghostly tendrils which floated around their feet. In the perfect stillness of the night, something occurred to her that she should have thought of before.

"Why did she come here and then leave?"

"Who? Oh." Luca coughed, a nervous sound which piqued the elf's curiosity. "Is that relevant? It's a Demon. Kill it. End of story."

"It is relevant," Jæyd insisted. "She has been relentlessly pursing something, yet she came here and then left. There is nothing here! What could have caused her to do that?"

"I don't know," Luca said, tugging his ear. "Why are you over-thinking this?"

"Because Demons do not act this way!"

A curious expression passed across his face and then blew away as if by the wind. Jæyd waited for him to say something but Luca did not speak.

"What is it?" she prompted.

"I might have possibly done something…"

Jæyd put a hand on her hip and glared at him intently. She'd had enough mysteries and Luca's agitated state was wearing on her thin nerves. Luca sighed.

"It's probably nothing," he said. His mouth worked as he thought of what to say. He threw up his hands. "I don't know. Nothing makes sense anymore. Up is down and left is right."

Jæyd continued to glare at him, but the dark Guardian only stared forlornly at the sky, his hands in his jacket pocket.

"So you do not know *any* reason why this Demon may be acting this strangely?"

Luca pursed his lips. "Right now I wouldn't be too sure of my own name if you asked me what it was with regard to Demons or magyc."

Jæyd put a hand on his shoulder, as much to give strength as to receive it. The elf hadn't acknowledged that she was so tired before the incident at Akorgia, but looking at it now, she supposed she had been tired for quite a while. She had done everything she was required to, but it lacked purpose, a series of pointless events which had no connection and she had no control over. Her life continued to spiral in that direction, ever more mysteries, never answers or satisfaction. Dwelling on it would no more change the past or future than a whistle would change a thunderstorm, but sometimes it was so hard to pull her thoughts from the mire. She did so now, and found Luca gazing at her with glittering eyes.

"Well, we will not make it right it by standing here," she said, and turned away.

Luca followed Jæyd as she walked away from the Crescent Temple on the fresh trail of the Demon. He grimaced as they left the warm plateau.

The Mountains loomed up over them, black giants eating the stars. The hillocks rolled under their feet, the chill air spiced with the musk of Everwoods. Jæyd's boots navigated the rocky terrain with ease, finding the worn trails through the tough grass. They walked in silence for a time before Luca spoke.

"So you don't know who or what the girl is?"

"I do not know," Jæyd repeated in a patient voice. "Why would I know more than what Cedar has told us?"

"Because you know everything," Luca said.

Jæyd laughed. It felt good to laugh, despite the cold and the stink of Demons. "I do not know everything, not even close. The girl is as much a mystery to me as she is to you."

"You know, I think you might be lying." Luca looked at her, his black eyes serious. "I have a feeling you *do* know."

"Perhaps you are right," Jæyd admitted. "But it matters not at this point in time. The whole thing is strange, disjointed, like a dream upon waking. I cannot tell you until I have seen the girl and spoken with Cedar."

"Cannot or will not?" Luca pressed.

"My friend, how many years have we known each other?" Jæyd said.

"I can't count that high," Luca answered with a laugh.

"True. And in that time, how many things have I hidden from you?"

"That I know about?" Luca thought for a moment.

"Three."

Jæyd frowned, certain he was playing with her.

Luca smiled, held up his hand and proceeded to enumerate on his fingers. "You won't tell me how old you truly are, you didn't tell me the gesture I made when we met the High-lords at Carallión after the end of the Moonlight War was possibly the most inappropriate thing I could have done, and you never told me that it was your brother's death that convinced you to become a Guardian and not a vision of a stag with gilded antlers or whatever it was you said."

The mention of her brother brought a wash of emotions that writhed in Jæyd's stomach even after all this time, but now it was like the echo of distant thunder rather than a mountain-slide coming down around her ears. "How do you know that?"

"Cedar told me."

"That was not for him to tell," Jæyd said with a frown.

"I suppose not," Luca allowed. "He didn't want to but he thought it would help me with something I was having trouble wrapping my mind around."

"I see," Jæyd said with a nod. "Did it?"

"Yes," Luca told her after a moment's consideration.

"Then it was wise of Cedar to do that. Well, aside from those, would you say that I have kept things from you?"

"No," Luca admitted.

"And I am not keeping anything from you now. If anything, I am keeping something from myself."

Luca nodded. "Alright. But when you figure it out, you'll tell me what it is?"

"If I am able, then I shall," Jæyd assured him.

"Damn elves, with their twisty words and empty promises," Luca said and Jæyd smiled.

"It is good to see you again," she said. "I am glad I no longer walk alone."

"Good to hear," Luca said. "Where are we going?"

"Wherever the Demon goes."

"And how long will this take? We do have a *little* bit of a pressing matter back in D'Ohera."

Jæyd stopped. Cedar's inert form flashed into her head again and she found herself chewing her lips with her sharp teeth, just as her mother told her not to.

"Trust me, I know the truth of your words. Yet, something about this Demon will not let me leave this alone."

Luca rolled his eyes. "You do realize we potentially have *Aethsiths* and one of the Nine in Demona? Do you know what that means?"

"I know better than most what that means," Jæyd said softly. "Remember, it is I who have walked the halls of the Crescent Temple all these long days. Something tells me this is a branch of the same tree and I will find out what it means. As I said before, you may come or not as you choose. I will not speak of it anymore."

Luca gave a slow nod, stuck his hands in the pockets of his long black jacket and matched her stride as she continued east, following the Demon.

The pair of Guardians walked, sometimes gaining, sometimes falling behind by Jæyd's estimation, but always following in the Demon's steps. When the sun began to rise, the Guardians stopped and Luca brought down a hare with a flick of his wrist that sent the gold dirk flashing through the air. The creature was stringy, lean and lacking flavor but it was nourishment. Luca attacked it as though he had not eaten in a year.

"So, what is so special about this Demon of yours

anyway?" Luca asked, pausing between bites. "Apart from it being a she-Demon? And wanting to kill you?"

Jæyd considered the question for a moment, staring at the roasted meat in her hands. When one dealt with Demons for as long as she had, one made classifications within one's own experience. In Jæyd's experience, Demons fit into three categories: the first not any more or less than mere beasts, their minds grasping only hunt, eat, sleep and reproduce.

The second had intelligence on the order of a dull person, enough to speak, follow orders and create mischief, but not so much as to plan complex schemes or coordinate many facts.

The third were vastly powerful and cunning, with an old magyc of their own that Jæyd neither understood nor wished to. To her knowledge, only nine of the third existed and for that she was extremely grateful. This one appeared to be the first type who had been given the powers of the second. A curious mix, mute yet more intelligent than an ordinary beast.

"I think I can talk to her," Jæyd said. "I have tried before and she has not answered, but I feel as though she understands my questions."

"What would you possibly need to talk to it about?"

"She is on a mission. It holds her here in Demona. I think she is searching for something, and she cannot go back until she finds it."

"What do you suppose she's searching for?" Luca asked, his food suddenly forgotten.

"I could not begin to imagine," Jæyd said. "But I think it is important."

"Something to do with the Nine?"

"Yes," Jæyd said. "I cannot say for certain, but I believe she is held here by their bidding. I do not know why. And now that Cedar has returned…" She didn't know how to finish the thought.

Luca nodded and tossed the remains of his meal into the small fire. "Well, I don't think I've done enough running to suit me at all. My muscles are just cramping with the insatiable desire to continue."

The sarcasm made Jæyd smile. As the sun rose, the Guardians gained on the Demon. She ran at an easy speed, meaning to pace herself and cover a large distance. They crested the last of the hills, plains spreading out below them.

Dark patches of isolated trees, forests too small to have a name, dotted the plains like bruises, darker when they fell in the shadow of the Mountains. On the horizon, the river O'Rente glittered like a ribbon of diamond.

Jæyd pointed to the small black dot speeding across the plain. "We will catch her when she reaches the river. Demons do not like running water."

Jæyd's former words proved true, though the latter did not. The Guardians ran, forking to flank the Demon and reaching it as it paced back and forth on an overhang, the bank dropping steeply to the river below. The Demon lifted its head, sniffing with rapid, almost frantic breaths, and then leaped into the rushing water of the O'Rente. Jæyd could only gape as the Demon swam clumsily to the other side.

"I thought you said they didn't like running water," Luca said, sheathing his dirks and putting his violin on his back.

"They do not," Jæyd whispered.

"Now I suppose we have to get across," Luca said, his tone jovial, his expression sardonic. "You do know the nearest ferry is a good two miles downstream?"

"Yes, I know this," Jæyd said. "We must hurry."

Jæyd and Luca went south along the bank until they reached the ferry. Fortunately, the ferryman was on their side of the river, though the old man had to be woken from his late-afternoon nap. He grumbled as he pulled on his boots and a coarse coat which smelled like salt and sweet pipe smoke.

"That'll be a Katon apiece," he said, pulling the ropes from the post on the bank.

Jæyd looked at Luca, hoping he had money. She'd had no use for it, cloistered at the Temple, and had fallen out of the habit of carrying it. Luca rolled his eyes and pulled out his wallet. He made their fare with Rabs and Varyen, counting each coin with painstaking slowness until even the ferryman just gestured for him to hand over whatever he had already counted out so they could be on their way.

The ferry bobbed against the current and Jæyd let it lull her into a state halfway between sleep and waking. Luca and the ferryman chatted to pass the time, but she didn't hear much of what they said. When the ferry jarred against the opposite bank, her eyes flew open. Luca had already jumped from the ferry and was mooring it to the poles. The ferryman leaned against the ropes.

"You two seem to be in a hurry to get somewhere," he said. "You should be careful. There's been some trouble around these parts. Demon trouble." The ferryman tapped his nose.

"We'll keep an eye out," Luca said.

The Guardians walked away.

"Where to now, fearless leader?" Luca asked.

Jæyd took her flute and sounded a gentle note. It floated in the air in front of her, glowing and spinning in lazy circles before it gave a few half-hearted sparks and died. No trail was illuminated. Only the flat grass answered with a small ripple in the breeze, then all was still. Luca saw the look on her face and patted her shoulder.

"That should have worked," she lamented, and couldn't stop a hint of bitterness from tainting the words. "Even at the Temple, near the Rift."

"Welcome to how the other half lives," Luca said, unsympathetic to her plight. "We never have the benefit of old blood. Come on. You said she was flying straight as an arrow, so she probably crossed and kept going."

They made their way back up the river. The sun was high in the sky and it had burnt away all the clouds, leaving nothing to block the intensity of its rays. Sweat ran down Jæyd's face and made her shirt stick to her skin in an itchy embrace. Though it was tempting to take a quick dip in the singing waters of the O'Rente, she resisted, pushing herself harder. In front of her, a winding trail of gold sparks appeared at the exact place the Demon had climbed from the river. She gave a cry of excitement.

"What is it?" Luca demanded, gold dirks coming to hand at once.

"I can see her trail!"

"So your Path-magyc works, sort of, despite the, whatever it is going on in Demona," Luca said, and sheathed his blades. "Interesting."

"Yes," Jæyd murmured. "Very interesting."

They followed the Demon to a small forest. Jæyd went into the trees without pause, the cool shade beneath the trees soothing her feverish brow. The trees were young, sprouting up in haphazard bursts of enthusiasm as though they had just happened to meet and did not plan to stay long.

Not far into the forest, Jæyd's sharp eyes picked out the Demon sitting, hunched against a fold in the trunk of an oak, its long arms wrapped around her angular body.

The slits of its red eyes glared out like thin moons in a starless sky, and when it saw them, its eyes widened. Like a flower unfolding, the Demon stood and took off. Jæyd followed, darting around a tree with long strides, her fist clenched tight around her flute. As Luca vaulted down from a bough and Jæyd cleared a tangle of roots with a flying leap, the Demon spun and hissed, her gaze vacillating between the Guardians.

Jæyd circled, crouched low to the ground, her flute held against her lips, fingers poised over the keys. Smells of fresh earth, cool air and spring buds invigorated her.

The She-Demon was wounded, and spots of black blood stained the trunk it leaned against like dappled shadows. It had its multi-jointed arms wrapped around one side, trying to stem the flow of blood from a deep cut in her abdomen. She was panting with exertion and bared her teeth at Jæyd and Luca in pain and anger.

Jæyd bared her own pointed teeth and was rewarded with a scream of defiance from the Demon. Once again, Jæyd attempted to discern a reason, some explanation for the odd behavior, as she took in every scrape, bruise and cut on the Demon's skeletal body.

Luca waited, his knives unsheathed. Before Jæyd could do more than unveil her blade, the Demon began to screech, a series of short, ear-piercing screams directed at Luca. It left Jæyd too discombobulated to react when the Demon leaped at them, clearing Jæyd's head. A taloned foot caught her in the chin and she crumpled to the ground and blacked out.

She became aware of Luca's voice in fits and starts. When her eyes fluttered open, his face swam in and out of focus. She sat up, her head throbbing. A stinging pain drove into her temple when she touched it, her fingers came away red.

167

Evidence of a recent battle stood out like a bonfire at night - a gashed tree limb here, bloody mud there, an entire bush uprooted and thrown across the clearing. The clearing was empty and the Demon nowhere in sight.

Luca crouched beside her, his arms around his knees.

"Did you…?" Jæyd began, fearing the worst.

"No." He paused. "Jæyd," he began. "When you first put this crazy desire of yours to me, I went along with it but this is getting ridiculous. Instead of going where we need to be going, we are heading in the opposite direction and I am trying *not* to kill a Demon. Is this really what we need to be doing right now?"

His gaze burned into her. Jæyd's frown deepened as she tried to puzzle it out, her gaze wandering to the path of destruction left by the Demon's hasty retreat. Standing slowly, aware of every ache and pain in her body, Jæyd limped several feet and reclaimed her flute, the silver cool and comforting in her hand. Two trees had been uprooted and tossed aside in the Demon's haste to get away, illuminating the path with a wide 'V', and taunting her to follow.

Yet how long can I justify chasing her with Cedar in D'Ohera and at the very least one of the Nine returned?

"You are right," she said at last.

"I am?" Luca's eyebrows flew up. "Really?"

"Yes, but I am so close," she said. "You must go onto D'Ohera. Tell Cedar I will be there shortly."

Luca shook his head. "No. You might need me to save your skin again. Let's just get this over with, okay?"

Jæyd nodded, too exhausted to argue. Ignoring her body's protests, she plunged into the forest, Luca on her heels. The Demon had left a trail of torn branches and uprooted saplings that a blind and witless troll could have followed, leaving Jæyd more than enough attention to mull over the Demon's increasingly inexplicable behavior.

She paused and scratched the tip of her pointed ear, a slight frown on her face as she attempted to reason why the Demon could be so determined. They were unnatural in this world; there was nothing here that they needed. Yet this one continued to stay and search, a treasure-hunter with an incomplete map who refused to give up. Jæyd sighed and shook her head in frustration as she walked around a tree.

She took a step to continue and an arrow buried itself at her feet.

Jæyd's first startled thought was that Cedar had somehow traversed the space between them in an instant, but the arrow remained fixed in the ground and did not melt into golden sparks

She looked up to find half a dozen men standing in the trees a short distance away. Most of them had a motley assortment of sharp objects, the majority of them farm tools. Only one actual blade was visible, though the nearest man had a bow, drawn tight with a second arrow.

"I don't want to shoot, but I will if you leave me no choice!" the bowman called to her, his voice strong and determined, giving no reason to doubt his words.

Jæyd put her hands up. "No need to waste the arrow, good sir," she said.

"Doesn't look like much of a sir," Luca said, his voice soft but his words carried farther than he'd intended and Jæyd cringed inside.

"You are correct. I'm a far cry from any sort of *sir*," the man agreed without releasing his grip on his bow. "Who are you?"

"I am called Jæyd Elvenborn," she said. "This is Luca Lorisson."

"What's your business this way?"

"A suicide mission," Luca said, and Jæyd thanked the stars that he lowered his voice enough so only she could hear this time.

"Tracking a Demon," Jæyd replied.

Dark looks were directed at her, and she frowned. She had come to accept the bigoted attitude most people had towards the Guardians but these men could not know they were Guardians. It had been at least seven passings of the moon since she had seen or spoken with another person, but this was different. She had done nothing to deserve mistrust, yet it hung tangible in the air. Hostility simmered in the men's bearings and the twist of their mouths as they muttered to one another.

"Where do you hail from?" the man with the bow asked. Of all the men, he was the calmest, though his arrow remained nocked and pointed at Jæyd.

Jæyd paused. Once it had been easy. When meeting a fellow traveler on the road, it was custom to simply share where you were from. In the present, the truth was as likely to make you enemies as it was to gain you friends. *Especially for a Guardian.*

"I have been in the North for four years now," she said, her voice soothing, sensing the men would snap at the slightest provocation. She had no desire to provide the trigger.

Luca had no such compunction. "I'm from Isos, unfortunately," he said with a nonchalant shrug. "Heard of it?"

Jæyd grimaced. Another man, short, dark with a black beard and a barrel chest stepped closer and muttered something to the bowman, who lowered his weapon. Then a net descended from above Jæyd, its weight bearing her to the ground. Something hard slammed into her head and everything went black.

Jæyd woke with wrists chaffed and raw, tied to a thick sapling. She was sitting on the ground, legs under her, arms stretched out above her head. Luca was tied in a similar fashion next to her, one tree over. Open air was visible through the far-spread trees at the edge of the forest. The sounds of fires, tin dishes, horses and tent flaps fluttering in the breeze behind her told her this was no more than a temporary campsite.

So, the men are far from home and not happy about something, Jæyd thought, but that was all she could discern.

She and Luca had been tied with their backs to the camp and a cloud of smoky haze from the fires hung over them, limiting Jæyd's vision. Her body was protesting at the ungainly angle they had placed her in and dried blood had crusted in the corner of her eye. Jæyd scowled. *Someone will pay for that.*

Looking around, she tried to get her bearings. They must have taken her to the edge of the forest where they had set up a camp. Faint stars were visible in the clear sky showing through the boughs above her and pink and orange clouds were scattered on the horizon, but the throbbing in her head muddled her sense of direction and time. *Sunup or sundown? Either way, I have been out for too long.*

She tried to call out, but her throat didn't work and all she managed was a low, inarticulate sound. Luca stirred next to her, straining at his bonds in a semiconscious haze. Someone had heard her groaning and came to see her. It was a younger man, his clothes loose on his lanky frame, a reddish beard beginning on his jaw.

"Who are you?" Jæyd asked, forcing her lips and tongue to work, her voice raspy. "Why am I being treated in such a fashion?"

The man did not answer, but a sun-browned arm offered her water from an earthenware jug. Jæyd accepted the offered water, drinking thirstily and spilling a fair amount of it down her shirt. She cleared her throat. "Thank you," she said as the empty jug was withdrawn, but the bearer did not so much as nod.

Jæyd shrugged. She waited until he had disappeared before getting to her knees, then went to work on the rope with her sharp teeth. It was soon no more than tatters of fiber. She rubbed the numbness out of her wrists as she turned and observed where she had been taken.

Around and within a small glade in the forest, a handful of low tents, all dust brown in color, had been set up around a central fire. Vague shapes gathered around the fire, the soft murmur of their voice a soothing lullaby in the weak light.

"Jæyd," Luca mumbled. "Where in the three inner Hells are we?"

She turned back to him. He leaned against the tree, with only the ropes around his wrists above him keeping him from falling to the ground as he squinted at her with one eye. The other was glued shut with dried blood. Gently, she rubbed some of it away with her thumb so he could look at her with a lopsided gaze.

"Shh. Stay here," she told him.

"Don't leave me!" Luca said, coming more awake.

He staggered to his feet, his movements made ungainly by his bonds. He gave his hands an ineffectual shake.

"Untie me now," he demanded, glaring at her.

Jæyd sighed. He would make a fuss and that would bring the men running. She took the small knife out of her suede boot and cut through Luca's bonds. Luca braced himself against the tree for a moment then pushed himself upright, standing shakily but unassisted. He looked down.

"Seidon pull me under!" he swore, the sailor's curse from his dockside days in Isos slipping out in his wrath. "Look what they did to my jacket!"

The jacket was covered in dirt. Luca showed Jæyd a rip up the side.

"It looks dashing," Jæyd tried to sooth him.

"Don't, just don't. And where is my violin?" Luca said, throwing his hands up in disgust. "If there is a single scratch on it, just *one*…"

Jæyd's hands went to the pocket in her breeches but her flute wasn't there. *Demonfire.*

"We need to find our instruments," she said. "Follow me."

They walked towards the tents, treading carefully. A pair of wolf-like dogs with thick, dark grey fur were lounging in the carpet of needles and leaves outside the closest of the tents, pink tongues lolling. Eying her with interest as she walked on silent feet towards them, one of them stood, ears forward and Jæyd froze.

Putting out her hand, Jæyd eased into the greyness of the Old-Sight. For a heartbeat, she was afraid it would elude her. Then she saw their Auras as a golden glow that surrounded the heart of each dog.

Easily manipulating the now visible Aura, she smiled when the dogs gave small whines and lay down with their heads on their paws. The dogs did no more than watch with big yellow eyes as she crept among the tents, feeling for the warm spark which would show where the instruments were.

Within the largest of the tents, Jæyd found what she was searching for. Ducking under the back flap, she found herself in a sparse sleeping place, empty of everything but a bedroll tucked against one side, and their instruments.

Luca's violin case sat in the corner and on the pillow was Jæyd's flute. She snatched it up with a lighting quick motion and smiled in satisfaction. That flute had been with her for almost half a century, and while it was not the end of things if she had to make another, she had become attached to this one. Grabbing the violin on the way out of the tent, Jæyd emerged beside Luca, a determined look hardening her features.

Now, it is time to find out what is going on here.

Tossing the violin to Luca, Jæyd moved with liquid grace, stalking into the circle of light around the fire. The ten or twelve men sitting at the fire stopped eating and looked up. Shocked gazes greeted her and the silence was total. Not even an insect had anything to add.

"Someone is going to explain to me what you are doing," Jæyd said smoothly. "And why my friend and I warrant being treated in such an abominable fashion."

One of the men spoke, and she recognized the bowman from earlier. "How did you get out?"

She bared her teeth. "These are not for decoration. Now, who is going to tell me what I wish to know?"

The next person to speak was the burly dark-haired man and Jæyd frowned, noting with distaste the shadowy discoloration of his Aura, which told her all she needed to know and more. Dressed in leather, mail gleaming below his breastbone, he was the only one adequately equipped to fight anything more than a weedy garden.

"We've heard stories from the cities, Guardian. We aren't afraid of you," he said, getting to his feet and looking at the other men, who were nodding their agreement.

"Well, that would be your biggest mistake," Jæyd purred, her fingers beginning to tingle pleasantly against the flute.

Not given to rash action, stupid people were the one thing that could instantly heat her blood to the boiling point. Luca grabbed her arm from behind, saying her name in a low voice. The bowman rose, one hand making placating gestures, the other still holding his plate of dinner.

"Now, miss…er…Guardian…"

"Jæyd will do fine, thank you sir," she said.

The man opened his mouth, perhaps to remind her that he was not a sir, but he changed his mind and closed his mouth, instead looking among his companions for direction. None was forthcoming and a spongy silence stretched out. Several men tried to go on eating their dinner, but after a few half-hearted bites the plates were set aside and they sat avoiding each other's eyes.

"We will start with something simple," Jæyd announced, deciding they needed a little guiding. "What are you all doing out here, far from your home?"

"A-hunting Demons," one of the younger men said, sounding like he was quoting one of the great hero-legends of Past-times, firelight flickering off his simple face.

The golden light which undulated in his chest was large but not very bright. Weariness began creeping into Jæyd's bones.

"I see," Jæyd said. "And do I look like a Demon to any of you?"

"Some might say the Old Races are simply Demons in fair form," the one in chainmail spoke up, his mouth twisting unpleasantly. "And perhaps the Guardians as well."

"Okay, now you can kill him," Luca said in her ear.

Despite herself, Jæyd's mouth twitched. Her wariness was replaced by another familiar sensation in her gut - twisting exasperation. She fell out of the Old-sight and the world regained its usual hues, clothed in the smoky colors of dusk.

Disbelief that anyone could be so stupid fought with the desire to pound the truth into the man's little skull. Instead, Jæyd took a deep breath and counted to ten in three different languages and twice in elvish, then directed her next words to the bowman.

"I do not know who you have been listening to, but I would not believe all words that are spoken nowadays," she said, making an attempt to be cordial.

"Perhaps we should not believe the words of a…" the dark one began.

The rapier seemed to grow from the elf's fingers and ended suddenly against the tender flesh under the man's jaw.

"One more word," Jæyd stated without emotion. "Just one."

The man blinked rapidly, his tongue flicking out to moisten his trembling lips, but fortunately for him no sound issued forth. Jæyd withdrew the blade.

"I am looking for a Demon as well," she said. "A female, heading west. Perhaps you have encountered her?"

"If we have, I'm afraid she isn't heading anywhere anymore," the bowman said with traces of apology and defiance in his voice. "We've come upon only one Demon, just a day ago, and Utto here," he gestured to the unpleasant man, "killed it."

"Where?"

The bowman hesitated, then answered. "North of Akorgia, in the shadow of the Dalemounts. We are looking for a missing child," he added in the same careful tone. "We think the Demon took it north."

Jæyd frowned. The many long years of her life had taught her that true coincidence was rare and unlikely, and two Demons acting strangely in the same time and place was too much coincidence. "That would be very strange behavior for a Demon."

The man sighed. "We know, but no blood or body was found and there is no other explanation we can think of."

"The one that I am hunting has no children with it," Jæyd said. "But perhaps I can help you find your missing child."

The words of the dark man the bowman named Utto were tinged with poorly concealed hate. "We don't need any help from…"

The hilt of Jæyd's blade caught him square in the temple and Utto uttered a small moan before sinking down to his knees, a trickle of blood slowly rolling into his hair. His hand felt the now tender spot on his head as he glared up at her, the bigoted condemnation in his eyes only held in check by his newfound appreciation for the consequences of pushing her.

"I warned you, one more word," Jæyd said, lowering her blade just a little now that her point had been made.

"That was very impressive, and I'm sure it was equally satisfying, but maybe not the most intelligent thing to…," Luca said, stepping closer to Jæyd.

He fell silent when the men jumped up and grabbed for their motley assortment of what passed for weapons. Jæyd realized she may have acted a little too rashly, but the weapons were not pointed at her and Luca.

Then the cold crept up on her.

The Demon came upon the group at the edge of the forest, emerging out of the growing darkness without a sound. Jæyd knew immediately it was her Demon, with its familiar red eyes and gangly limbs with more scars than when it had first appeared in Demona. The men were afraid but they held their ground as the Demon came towards the fire, the light making its eyes flash gold and red.

The Demon was limping, and Jæyd remembered the slashing blow which had given the she-Demon the wound in her thigh. The Demon's left leg could barely support her weight as she stood and searched their faces for something. Red eyes fixed on Jæyd and the Demon hissed. *She recognizes me too, for whatever that is worth.*

Utto had risen to his feet and was now yelling orders to the men. In that moment, Jæyd saw why the men looked to him for direction; he kept his head despite the sudden appearance of their foe and offered a stable point in the confusion. The bowman released an arrow before Jæyd could say anything, but the shaft sped past the Demon's ear and she did not even have to duck.

"Wait!" Jæyd commanded, laying a hand on the arm of the bowman. "This one is mine."

The men looked confused, some lowered their weapons and others glanced to the men on either side of them. Finally they turned to the bowman and Utto. Utto glared but the bowman nodded. "As you will Guardian, but if it comes to it we will kill it."

Jæyd nodded. She walked towards the Demon, rapier out, the silver flashing in the firelight. The Demon took a step backwards, and then another as the elf came forward, herding the Demon away from the men.

Jæyd was in a bind. She did not want to kill it, but with the temperament of these men, if she tried to talk to it as she had before and it hurt one of them, she did not know how they would react. It would undoubtedly be unfavorable if the bigoted Utto had any say in it.

"Come on, leave!" Jæyd muttered under her breath.

"What are you up to?"

The Demon tried to edge to the side and return to the fire, but Jæyd blocked her, trying to make it look like a fight. This dance continued for a time, but the Demon would not be deterred. *I do not understand. All this time simply running away and now she will not go.*

Distracted by her confusion, Jæyd was not prepared when the Demon barreled straight at her and knocked her over, making straight for the campsite. Jæyd was up in a flash, but it was too late. The men were already defending themselves, the bowman firing with wild abandon. An arrow struck the Demon in the forearm and another grazed her knee, but she did not slow.

Jæyd ran after the Demon, her feet swiftly covering the distance, but as fleet as the elf was she was not fast enough. Two of the men advanced, one baring a pitchfork, the other a knife bound to a stick. Both held thick shields that were little more than pieces of wood and rope bound clumsily on their arms.

They slashed in tandem, the attack unsuitable for battling Demons, aiming for the chest and the abdomen. Jæyd smiled grimly. That would buy her just a few seconds. No ordinary sword was going to pierce the thick armor which protected a Demon's midsection.

Utto swaggered into her peripheral vision and her heart sank. He carried his sword and even though Jæyd was a hundred feet away, the gleam on the edge and the waves which rang out from the metal as he unsheathed it said that his was not an ordinary blade. Jæyd put on a burst of speed, running as she had never run before.

Although Utto fought like a man chopping wood, his form blunt and unrefined, he was fortunate. His thrust carried the blade forward to slip between the plates of the Demon's armor at the shoulder and neck and she howled.

The man went in for a second blow, but a silver rapier blocked his strike. His eyes widened and then he smiled savagely.

"So the stories are true then," he said hatefully.

Jæyd flicked her sword and threw his blade away easily. "The stories are *not* true," she said. "But as I said, this one is mine."

"Then kill it." The burly man stepped back with his unsettling smile. "Kill it and prove the stories are just lies."

The Demon swayed behind her, one clawed paw touching the newest wound on her shoulder, the firelight gleaming off fresh blood. Jæyd ground her teeth together. *I will not allow this man to twist my words or my mind.*

The other men were confused and could not understand why the elf did not just kill the Demon. The mistrust grew and thickened like porridge, hanging heavy and unpleasant in the air. Utto's smile grew and he lifted his sword once again, swinging it low and circling in front of the elf. "So it is the brave men of Demona against a Guardian and its pet Demon."

Jæyd growled low in her throat. "Do not tempt me."

"Guardian, why do you not just slay it?" the bowman asked, true concern sitting on the curve of his brow as he took a step closer to her, unwittingly putting himself between the Demon and Utto.

"It is complicated," Jæyd sighed, keeping half an eye on the Demon and both eyes on the dark man in front of her, frustrated by her inability to explain.

"Don't listen to her, Corman," Utto spat. "Her tongue is coated with poison."

"And your mind is coated with manure if you truly believe what you are saying," Jæyd shot back before better judgment could temper her words.

As the words left her tongue, the Demon shot

forward like a dark arrow. The bowman could not get his bow drawn in time and the Demon raised one arm, its claws poised to take off the man's head. Jæyd screamed and leaped forward. She swung her rapier, no more gracefully than Utto and cut off the foreclaw. It flew some distance and landed with a thud. The Demon echoed Jæyd's scream, flailing the stump and her remaining arm as she spun in a half circle and fell back.

Seeing his opening, Utto darted forward and came at the Demon from behind it. Jæyd gently tapped his blade with her own, turning it slightly so that it slipped harmlessly along the plates of the Demon's back.

The Demon spun to face the man and grabbed his blade with her good hand, yanking it out of the man's grip. She threw the sword aside with a cry of pain, though her eyes never left the man. His face contorted with fear, a silent scream escaping his frozen mouth as the Demon stalked forward and tore open his throat. In the blink of an eye, the Demon disappeared into the darkness, dragging the still-twitching body with her.

The silence of the night was slowly filled with chirping tree crickets and the sound of the wind blowing through the leaves and dry grass. Jæyd could feel the eyes of the men on her as she stood with her back to them, breathing heavily. She slowly turned to face them.

"Where did it go?" one of them asked, looking nervously into the night.

"Don't worry, it won't be coming back, will it Guardian?" the bowman called Corman said slowly as he took a step towards her.

Jæyd shook her head tiredly; the rapier was already a sliver flute in her hand and Luca followed her lead. "No, I think not. She was just hungry."

Two of the men promptly began to heave, spilling

their semi-digested dinner onto their shoes, and Jæyd felt a twinge of sympathy. Something like that was not easy for men to acknowledge, though fundamentally it was no more repulsive than a wolf hunting sheep. The rest of the men began to glare at her. Jæyd got the distinct impression she was going to be tied with something more secure than rope this time.

Corman stepped forward and picked up Utto's bloodstained sword, hefting it in one hand as he looked between it and the Guardian. "You saved me Guardian and I thank you for that, but what about Utto?"

"I am afraid I will not mourn his death," Jæyd said with a frown. "The world could do with less troublemakers and stirrers of his kind."

Corman was hesitant in his defense of the other man. "I know you did not see the best of him, but he has aided and protected us for many days."

"Many people have at least one worthwhile quality," Jæyd said with a smile that flashed pointed teeth. "This does not necessarily make them worthwhile people."

"But you cannot just let them die."

Jæyd sighed, a burning urge tangling her wits, an urge to explain to him the entirety of her life, how many people had lived and died because of her, how many summers and winters had passed without seeing her own home because she was protecting the homes of others who did not even know it, how many nights she had sat up looking at the moon and praying for a sign that it was her time to hand over the mantle, but the men in front of her could never comprehend this life without living it and so Jæyd was left only with the simple, shallow reason of here and now.

"I told him the Demon was mine," she said firmly. "And I do not speak lightly on matters such as those."

Corman nodded quickly. She sensed he did not wish

to anger her. Jæyd felt sad and a little wistful for the days when the Guardians had been respected and admired, not feared or reviled. She placed her hand over her heart, her fingers crossing in the Elven gesture of oath and truth.

"Corman, I never intended that any of you die," she told him. "If Utto had heeded me, I would have done my best to protect him, even if it meant destroying the Demon."

"I believe you," he said, and he meant it. But, there was something else, something he was not saying. She did not say anything and waited for him to speak in his own time.

"Guardian, there is one other thing."

"What is that?" Jæyd asked.

"The child. We have been searching for seven days now. We tracked it this far and I am sure she is close but so far we have had no luck finding her. We have found no body and there is always a body." Corman paused and swallowed. "Did you offer your help in earnest?"

"Please, Guardian," another man stepped forward. He had a plain face lined with more than age. His rough clothes were loose on his frame. His voice broke. "It is my daughter. She is only four and a half years old."

Jæyd paused, now torn between three different quests, all legitimate for a Guardian, duty telling her she was honor-bound to fulfill all three. Luca gave the elf a stern look and then rolled his eyes. Corman's pleading expression quickly made up her mind.

"We will try, but we must be quick for we do not have much time."

Corman chose five men to accompany them; the rest would remain at the camp. Luca brought up the rear. The men followed Jæyd as she led them away from the camp and the scene of the recent battle. They carried torches to light their way.

Her eyes could see with perfect clarity in the dark and the flickering light dancing off the trunks was more distracting than helpful, but Jæyd pursed her lips and continued through the trees.

Emerging into the open, Jæyd strode forward until the black sky was completely clear above her, the stars clear and bright. Putting her flute to her lips, she offered a prayer to those stars and blew one, low haunting note which hung in the air like a frozen raindrop waiting to fall.

The note held true. Listening to the complex echoes and following the sounds, her finger stretched out, pointing into darkness. All the men looked in that direction, half hopeful the child would be there, and half fearful it was a Demon. There was nothing but the night and the flat plain.

"It is not far, but neither is it close," Jæyd said. "We must not tarry."

She set out at a fast jog, pressing the men as fast as they could go. Corman jogged beside her, his bow on his back and held against his side with his elbow, eyes narrowed against the darkness. He did not carry a torch and though his breathing was strained, he did not break into a sweat.

Observing him from the corner of her eye, Jæyd noted he was younger than the lines on his face told. His hair was long and dark, framing his angular face. A neat beard grew on his square jaw, while clothes of a simple weave sat on his frame. The touch of a woman was evident in the tidy stitches of the darning in his trousers and the pattern sewn down his rolled sleeves.

"Tell me what happened," Jæyd said.

"The Demon had been plaguing us for several weeks.

We heard about the Blood Magyc coming back but none of our village had it. We put watches through the night, but at dawn they retired. The Demon came through the town before the sun came up. Devan's girl must have heard the dog barking and gone out to quiet him. The dog we found, torn bloody and dead, but of the child no sign was left. We can only hope…" Corman's voice broke. "Utto came to us and offered his sword and his aid."

A sell-sword. That would explain a lot, his attitude and *his cool head in battle,* Jæyd thought with a frown.

The frown on Jæyd's face deepened as she considered Corman's tale and tried to fit it together with hers. It fit about as well as a troll foot in an elven glove and Jæyd sighed.

"It is not the same Demon I have been chasing, for she has been far north, but this is not usual Demon behavior."

The flare of hope in the man beside her was so swift and bright Jæyd felt faint for just a moment. She laid a hand on his elbow. "Still, do not fall too hard into hope, for the blow will be that much harder if we find ill."

A gentle echo of the note she had played rang through the still air. They had reached the place. Jæyd halted and the men stopped behind her, milling around, looking at her expectantly. In the darkness, they could not see what her sharp eyes discerned with ease.

A stone formation stood on a small rise. Something in Jæyd's stomach twisted when she looked at it, whispers of old magyc tingling on her skin. When she pointed it out, the men took several steps back.

"It is a Standing," Corman said, his voice low and his eyes wide. "Some say it is a Door between worlds."

Jæyd had some experience with Doors and understood the men's trepidation. Unless one was a Witch, trained until they were given black robes in place of white, magyc Doors did not function at will. Unlike regular doors, they were unpredictable. Sometimes they would open, but only once, or lead to a different place the second time. Luca did not look happy, but he came to join her.

"I will go and look," Jæyd said.

"I'm coming with you," Luca spoke up.

The men were content to let them go alone. The Guardians left the group of men standing close together and ventured up the rise. Once the stones might have formed a monument beautiful in simplicity, but something, whether time, man or Demon, had ravaged the stones leaving them little more than a pile of rubble.

Jumping over long stones which hummed faintly when she put her hands upon them, Jæyd noticed the stones grew colder as she journeyed toward the center of the Standing. When she emerged into the empty space that the stones surrounded, Jæyd gasped as the frigid air hit her in the face. A small area, no more than five paces across, was bathed in dark light that radiated from a tear in the very air.

"Well, this is just lovely," Luca said.

"This is no Door," Jæyd whispered to herself, awe filling her.

The Standing was ancient magyc that Jæyd knew by a different name, an *Aegiswær.* The sole purpose was to encyst an unclosable Rift to the Demon Voide within a ring of stones and seal it with the Path to prevent anything from falling in or coming out.

The Standings, or *Aegiswæri,* were created by the first Guardian, Cedar Rün. This one was failing as shown by the fresh, clear track leading to and away from the rift. A Demon had escaped recently, and then returned.

"The end truly is coming," she said to herself. *Unless*

the Demon Cedar had fought was not one of the Nine. That was the only hope.

A whimpering sigh caused Jæyd to glance around. Almost invisible in the black light, a child sat just outside the Rift, white and wide-eyed, something clutched in her hand. When Jæyd pried it from the stiff grip, it took a moment for her to determine what it was.

The doll was warm and sticky, and the metallic smell of blood mixed with the cold of the rift began to filter down Jæyd's throat, choking her. Jæyd tossed the toy away and knelt in front of the child to brush her fingers across the soft, porcelain cheek. Stirring at Jæyd's touch, the child looked up and blinked slowly.

"It's so cold," the little girl whispered, her eyes blank.

"It is alright, sweetheart," Jæyd said. "Let us go somewhere warmer."

The little girl could barely move so Jæyd picked her up and set her on a hip. Luca helped them over the fallen stones, taking the girl from Jæyd while the elf clambered over. The men let out a collective breath when they saw the Guardians reemerge from the Standing and a few hoarse cheers went up when they saw the little girl.

The child's father threw down his weapon, broke from the crowd and ran to the Guardians, taking the girl from them, the worried lines melting from his face. He touched her hair, her face and her arms. The little girl stood there numbly, eyes vacant and unfocused.

"Guardian, what's wrong with her?" the man asked, his voice frantic.

The back of Jæyd's neck began to prickle, the warning of impending danger making her muscles tense.

"Jæyd," Luca said, his voice low.

The little girl gazed blankly ahead as Jæyd fingered the holes in her flute. With one hand Jæyd reached out to touch the girl's cheek again and the child finally moved, her hand coming up as quick as lightning to grasp Jæyd's wrist in a bruising grip.

"Guardian," the child said in a voice that was not her own.

"Demon. What do you want?" Jæyd demanded and clenched her teeth against the crushing pain in her wrist. She gripped her flute tighter with her other hand.

"Things are a-changing," the child said sing-song. "The sands are a-shifting beneath your feet."

Jæyd shivered. Something, the ghost of a memory sang to her from long ago. *A-shifting a-shifting, a-shifting beneath your feet.* She shook off the cold fingers of dread that clutched at her heart and composed her features into a neutral mask.

"And the ground beneath yours is steady?" Jæyd replied with practiced skepticism.

A little frown of confusion crossed the pale face before her. "The sands are a-shifting," the child repeated.

"What have you done with the girl?" Jæyd asked, trying to pull her arm from the grip to no avail.

"The child is lost," the voice issuing from the little mouth told her.

The child's father stumbled back and uttered a pitiful moan.

"Truly?" Jæyd said, her heart sinking.

The child nodded and did not flinch when the shining rapier appeared in the elf's hand. "Your weapon will not avail you, Guardian," the child-that-was-no-longer-a-child said, a strain of foreign sadness in the voice. "The child is lost."

Sharp fangs elongated from the mouth of the child, forcing the jaws open and a foul smelling breath exuded from deep inside. Without hesitation, the rapier bit into flesh that gave like cold butter. The child gave a small, high shriek and collapsed. Some color returned to her face, but only for a moment before it leaked into the ground along with her lifeblood.

A high keening from behind Jæyd made her turn to face the man leaping at her, his face twisted with grief and rage. His movements were hindered by tears and clumsy enough for Jæyd to avoid, twisting aside for him to collapse beside the small, still body of the child, his body wracked with sobs.

In the face of the man's crushing grief a helpless weight infused Jæyd. Grief such as this should not be allowed to exist in the world. The only thing the elf could think of to ease his pain was something she had not done since she was with her family in the forests of Carallión. Unsure the man would understand or accept the gesture, she still had to try.

Jæyd took a breath and knelt next to him, letting the grey film fall across her eyes. Touching the man gently on the shoulder, Jæyd warmed him with her own Aura, her sympathy and certainty that the Path was watching over his daughter expressed in a way words could not. The man's sobs quieted and he wiped the wetness from his face.

"Thank you, Guardian," the man said, his voice hoarse.

He gathered the child's body in his arms and carried it away, hunched over it. The other men gathered around him, the light from their torches sending shadows flickering over their faces. Turning as one, they walked into the night, towards the camp. Jæyd knew they would make for their homes at first light and no more talk of a-hunting Demons would pass their lips.

Corman appeared at her elbow and she turned to look

at him.

"What happened to the girl?" he asked her.

"It was not the girl any longer," Jæyd said. "It was a Thrall. A Demon in another form."

"Was she…was her passing easy?" Corman said. "Her family will ask," he added at Jæyd's look.

"I cannot say, but I do not believe it would be a terrible thing to tell them that she was not frightened and it was over quickly."

"I will do that," Corman said. His eyes fell on the blade in her hand. "I shall say also the Guardians have returned to Demona, and that the stories about them are not true."

"Thank you," Jæyd replied, surprised how much the words meant to her.

Corman nodded. "Where will you go now?" he asked.

Luca crossed his arms. His expression conveyed his concern accurately, a concern Jæyd shared. The Thrall was another very bad sign and one that the other Guardians should know about right away.

"I will follow the Demon I have been pursuing," she told Corman, the flute replacing the rapier with a delicate gold shimmer. "I must catch her before there is any more death."

Corman nodded and lifted a hand in farewell. "Guardian, may…may the Path keep you."

"May it keep us all," Jæyd replied as she turned and headed into the night after the Demon.

Through the night and the following sunrise Jæyd and Luca followed the Demon's trail, always moving steadily west. Luca's complaints were held at bay only because they were headed in the right direction, towards D'Ohera. The Demon was stronger, moving faster than before, no doubt thanks to the recent nourishment. The memory gave Jæyd mixed feelings of righteousness and queasiness in the pit of her stomach.

They crossed back over the O'Rente at the ferry south of the one they had used before. After they crossed the river, familiar rock-strewn, hilly terrain greeted them. Jæyd's eyes saw the flat plains and the rolling hills and the dark line of Mountains to the north.

On the second day, grey clouds rolled in, gathering in front of them and on the third day she ran through sheeting rain, welcoming the refreshing cleansing that rinsed the dirt and blood from her skin and returned her clothes to their original color.

Luca's pointed face was more drawn than usual. He tugged at the hem of his sleeve, an agitated motion she had not observed before. The chase was wearing on his nerves, nerves already worn thin from the encounter with the Thrall child. "Come, the Demon cannot run forever. Eventually it will find what it is after," Jæyd said, infusing her voice with as much encouragement as she could muster against her exhaustion.

The Demon's trail finally lead them to a section of the main road that lead south toward Torin, the dull white stones reflecting a dim version of the midmorning sun.

Neglected for a long time, many of the roads of Demona had been reclaimed by nature. Whole stretches had been lost, but fortunately for the pair of Guardians, the roads surrounding Torin were mostly intact.

"At least the City is empty," Jæyd said as she peered down the road, the Demon spore obvious and unpleasant to her eyes. "She cannot do much harm to forgotten stone."

"Not quite empty," Luca cheerlessly contradicted her, digging at loose stones at the edge of the road with the toe of his boot. "At least, I heard some people had moved back the last time I was there."

"Then we must move quickly," Jæyd said, pushing away the tiredness which welled up when she realized that nothing would ever be easy or simple. "We must head her off."

The city loomed over them before she saw it. It always irked the elf that something so large could be so invisible.

"It is as though the ground swallows it and spits it back up," she muttered and Luca snorted with laughter.

She stalked ahead of him and he followed at a more leisurely pace. They skirted the outer wall until they came upon one of the smaller gates. The City was quiet and still from the gates to the First Square. A lone bird glided on an invisible current of air in a cloudless sky. It was majestic and a little melancholy but Jæyd noticed none of it. Her attention was consumed by the fact that the Demon's trail had simply disappeared. It was as if a giant bird had swooped down and plucked it off the ground and carried it away. *Or it has gone back to the Voide.*

Jæyd snapped her teeth impatiently as she considered the possibilities. She was distracted by Luca tapping the ground with his violin bow, his eyes vacant. She wondered if he was trying to solve the puzzle of why the Demon's trail ended. She doubted it when she heard the complex, syncopated rhythm of his tapping.

Luca noticed her gaze and smiled. Putting the instrument firmly under his chin and using his now free hand to flick his fingers across the strings he sent three quick pizzicato notes off, the fourth lingering in the air with a touch of vibrato. In a blinding flash of gold Jæyd saw the Demon in a Square, the rubble of a fountain splayed about in the center. The grey-white walls of Torin were unmistakable.

"This way," she said and took off running.

The courtyard was a huge, square expanse that seemed horribly empty to Jæyd. Cracks spider-webbed across the walls and the huge stones in the ground, providing fertile ground for all manner of greenery and growth. A crumbling fountain sat in the center. Scattered at one end of the Square was the wreckage of a carriage and the carcasses of six creatures emaciated beyond recognition, a few black hairs clinging to grey skin.

Jæyd felt a shiver dance up and down her spine as she made her way past the scattered debris and behind the fountain in the middle of the Square. Splinters of dark wood littered the ground and she gravitated towards them like a moth to a flame. *Something is familiar about those splinters.*

"This has been here for a while," Luca commented, his voice carrying from across the courtyard. "Days, at least."

"Yes," Jæyd agreed absently, still hung up on the shards of wood. She could not grasp the insubstantial wisp flitting around the corners of her mind.

"So?" Luca prompted. "I don't think the Demon is here. Unless it's hiding in a crack."

"Very amusing," Jæyd muttered. "If you are not going to help, you could go find a hole and fall into it."

For a moment Luca looked like he was going to respond in kind, but then he paused, a smile playing on the corner of his mouth.

"Jæyd," he began almost conversationally. "When was the last time you had a real meal?"

Jæyd bit into the pasty surrounding the pie. Buttery flakes stuck to her lips and gravy ran down her chin. She thought she might have possibly died and gone to join the moon. Luca was attacking his pie with a vengeance, somehow managing not to spill most of it over himself. After he devoured it and licked his fingers clean, he shot Jæyd a grin.

"Good?"

"Very," Jæyd agreed. "What exactly was that?"

"Eel," Luca said. "An Isosian treat and Karmel's specialty." Jæyd raised her eyebrow and Luca smiled.

"I met her and her husband on my way north," he told her. "She said she wanted to make eel stew and mussels'n'dumplins for the people of Torin because in her opinion the food here was terrible."

"A typical charitable Isosian opinion," Jæyd grinned at him.

"Of course," Luca said. "You have gravy on your chin."

Jæyd wiped the gravy away with her finger and then froze. Four people had come into the street in a headlong rush, a woman and two men, the elder of the two carrying a child clutching a painted wooden doll. Upon catching sight of the Guardians, they stopped suddenly, something like terror in the gazes. The child pointed.

"Luca, we are being observed," she said out of the corner of her mouth.

"Naturally," Luca said with a smirk, spreading his arms wide. "Who wouldn't want to observe this?"

"I am being serious," Jæyd said, her eyes flicking between the group of people and the closest escape route should the situation turn hostile.

Luca glanced across the way. "Jæyd, it's a child. I don't think it merits panicking over."

The child pointed at them again. The woman tried to quiet the child, but she saw Jæyd watching and a flush entered her cheeks. She looked away. The man carrying the child started towards the Guardians. The rest hesitantly followed. Jæyd's fingers twitched by her side, and she considered pulling out her flute and unveiling her rapier.

"Are you Guardians?" the elder man asked hesitantly.

"Yes," Luca said before Jæyd could stop him. "Why do you ask?"

"You must come with me." The man turned to the others and bade them to stay.

He handed the child to the woman and began to run back the way he had come. Luca was already following the man and Jæyd had no choice but to follow as well. They were led along wide streets to a different, even less populated district of the City.

Here the empty street was haunted by the wind that whistled through loose stones and sent leaves racing down the gutters, but curtains, open doors, carts of wares and a tray of fresh baked tarts showed people had been there only moments before.

"It's that way," the man pointed, clearly unwilling to go further.

Luca patted the man on the shoulder. "Thank you. Go back to your family."

Jæyd was hyper-aware and leapt without thinking into the Old-Sight, but something was shielding the area so thoroughly not even a hint of the faint grey haze appeared to her eyes.

She was so preoccupied with the temperamental failing of her sense of the Path that it took Luca cursing and grabbing her arm to call her attention to the spectacle in the middle of the street.

A dead donkey lay in the street, congealed blood pooling in the cracks between the stones like black mortar. A little way off, a black chest lay still entangled in the harness around the donkey. It looked as though someone had tried to drag it away. The body of a Demon lay not too far beyond that, arms and legs akimbo, its chest caved inward. The whole thing almost looked like a stage set for a play, only all the actors had taken their bows and left.

The chest grabbed Jæyd's attention and tried to escape her gaze at the same time, wavering like the flame of a candle in a draft while the rest of the world seemed to be fixed even more solidly in place. A strange pressure began to build behind Jæyd's eyes and she swallowed, feeling her ears equalize.

I have seen this before.

Pushing past the heaviness in her mind, she saw through her mental fog to emerge in the past. A memory came to her, a memory from her long-gone youth…

A winding stair above her disappeared in the dark green shadow of the thick boughs. Slipping between the bars of the balustrade, Jæyd peeped into the crack of the great Farseer doors of the Council Chamber. Hushed voices spoke in urgent tones as a living shadow pulsed with a dark heartbeat among them.

In the center of the chamber, sitting in the middle of an empty space everyone within the chamber avoided, was the wooden chest, her father's handiwork evident in the design and pattern. Darker even than the shadow, the chest was totally devoid of life. Strange, for when her father worked with wood, it would always retain a portion of the life it had when it was still a living tree. Something was very wrong here.

When Jæyd closed her eyes she could see nothing, not even the grey of her Vision and this was more disquieting than the dead wood and the dark shadow. She opened her eyes and watched as the source of the pulsing shadow, something hidden within the grip of a High Elf, was placed inside and sealed against perception and detection. The heartbeat disappeared and only the life-sucking chest remained.

When the Elven leaders took up the chest and began to traipse towards the door of the Council chamber, Jæyd tried to back down the stairs quietly so they would not know that she had seen. Her foot caught on a knot in the wood and she gasped as she fought for balance. Her effort was in vain and she fell back, landing on her side, a little cry of pain escaping her lips.

A heavy thud and footsteps reached her ears as the chest was dropped and the elves came rushing forward. Thrown open from the other side, the Farseer doors parted to reveal seventeen proud, pale faces gazing at her. Jæyd saw with shock that one of them belonged to her father.

"Jæyd! What are you doing here?" he demanded as he pushed his way out of the crowd and pulled her to her feet. "The Council Chamber is no place for a child."

"I saw the man," she whispered. "I...I had to know." She glanced at the chest. "What is it?"

Her father sighed. "Jæyd, you must remind me to tell you the story of the curious raven and what became of him."

"Haliel," a strong voice said. "Who is that?"

"May I present my daughter Jæyd, My Lord," her father said with dignity, though the tips of his ears colored and he gripped Jæyd's shoulder hard.

A tall Elf with dark hair and grey eyes stepped forward. A spun circlet of gold and ebony sat on his brow and a sapphire broach pinned his long fur-trimmed cloak at his throat. Jæyd remembered her courtesy and dipped a quick bow to the High-Elf Lord.

"My Lord," she said.

His keen eyes bore into hers. "What brings you here, Jæyd Elvenborn, daughter of Haliel?"

Jæyd lifted her chin. Curious she may be, but no one would ever say she was a liar or coward. "I came to find the Demon-touched man."

"The man is gone," the High-Elf told her, a small smile on his red lips as he looked down at her. "Does that satisfy you?"

"No," Jæyd said, trying not to feel small under his gaze. "What is that chest?"

"*That is dark magyc. It is a Darkwood chest, sired by First Magyc and holding a space out of time and sight and even memory. It will be taken far away and no mortal will find it or open it.*"

Jæyd swallowed as she realized where the man had gone, and she felt a moment of pity. He had not been very bright and was more than a little crazy, but he should not have died.

"*He came here for help,*" *she said, wishing there had been something she could do for him.*

The High-Elf Lord's eyes narrowed. "Perhaps putting him out of his misery was all the help he deserved. However, it could not be avoided. He was more dead than alive as it was."

Before Jæyd could ask for clarification of the cryptic remark, her father put his hand on her shoulder. "Come, Jæyd, my work is done here. Let us go."

Jæyd waited until they had put half a hundred paces between themselves and the Council Tree before turning to her father. "How could you do that?"

Her father knelt in front of her, teal eyes very similar to her own looking at her a little sternly and a little sadly. "Jæyd, listen to me. One day, this world and its peoples may be perfect. Today is not that day. Perhaps it was not the kindest or the noblest or the rightest thing that could have been done, but believe me when I say that every person in that Chamber thought it was the best thing they could do in very bad circumstances."

"*What will happen to the chest?*" *Jæyd said, thinking back to the Council Chamber and found the memory fuzzy and hard to keep a hold of.*

"*It will be placed far into the Wastelands beyond Carallión, so the Path will not be touched and it will not invite Demons here.*"

"*Are you certain?*"

"*As certain as I can be in an imperfect world,*" *her father said as he stood. "Now, let us think on it no longer and see what your mother has prepared for dinner."*

Jæyd looked back, the memory of the Darkwood chest already fading, and then followed her father home…

Luca's strong arms caught Jæyd as she almost fainted. She had not thought of that incident afterwards, not even when Jhæveæn had been taken.

"What happened?" Luca asked as he steadied her on her feet, his black eyes searching her face.

"That chest is evil," Jæyd whispered, gripping his arm with white fingers. "We must destroy it!"

The elf ran towards the chest with awkward steps, her mind still struggling to recall the details of the incident in her childhood, searching for anything that would help her. Reaching the chest, Jæyd tried to lift it but all she managed to do was shift it half a centimeter to the left.

"Here, let me," Luca said but for all his masculine bravado, he too was unable to move it more than an inch.

A chittering sound, like insect mandibles or dry paper rustling came from inside the chest and made Jæyd feel as though her ears were bleeding. She stepped backwards.

"What in the eleven Hells is that?" Luca asked, grinding his teeth, teetering on his feet like he had just been spinning.

"You can hear it too?"

"Hear it? Of course I can hear it!" Luca said. "Make it stop!"

Through the haze of uncomfortable physical sensation, something caught Jæyd's attention, a tiny part of the memory which had brightened in her mind.

"Strange," she muttered. "We should not be able to hear anything at all."

The sound from the box increased in volume but before either Guardian could exclaim or question, what could only be an answering scream sounded from behind them.

NICOLE DRAGONBECK

Jæyd's Demon appeared suddenly, tearing around a corner like a terrier after a rat and at last Jæyd knew what the Demon had been chasing after. Seeing the pair of Guardians, the Demon hesitated, slowing abruptly, talons tearing into the stone. A whine issued from behind razor sharp teeth and her hand-less arm pawed beseechingly in the air.

Jæyd's rapier was in her hand even as Luca's knives appeared in his. In a dark blur, the Demon raced up the wall, scrambling from eave to eave, and then leaped down from the rooftop to land right behind the Guardians.

"Don't let her touch the chest!" Jæyd cried out.

"Way ahead of you," Luca said, already balancing, albeit somewhat drunkenly, on the chest, still grimacing at the racket coming from within it.

Jæyd dashed forward, stepping into the well-worn dance with the Demon and backing her up against the wall. Spilled fruit from an overturned cart made the elf's footing treacherous, but she persisted, pushing the Demon back along the street.

The Demon stepped into the shadow of an awning and Jæyd followed. With a hiss, the Demon reached up and pulled at the flapping cover, ripping it half off its frame and throwing it at Jæyd. When the elf tried to get out of it, the blue tarp tangled around her shoulders and pinned her in place. The Demon dashed away.

Jæyd struggled as she cut it away with quick slashes of her rapier, throwing it over her shoulder like a cloak before dashing after the Demon.

The Demon had run back to the chest. Luca was throwing his knives at it, keeping it at bay. He was still somehow standing on the chest, which rocked unsteadily on the uneven stones.

"Get off! Keep it back!" Jæyd ordered, and he obliged,

leaping off like a dancer and pressing the Demon back. Jæyd noticed he was not intending to kill, just to keep it distracted, and made a mental not to thank him for that, though he would of course deny it.

Jæyd reached a hand towards the chest and brought her rapier up, intending to destroy it on the spot by chopping it apart but the sharp end of a spear was suddenly digging into the tender flesh just below her ribs.

"I would not touch that if I were you," a voice warned.

Jæyd realized two things simultaneously, the first being that the person belonging to the deep voice had no idea what the chest meant or was capable of doing. The second was that if she did not do something drastic immediately, Torin and eventually the whole of Demona would once more be a city where the only company for the weeds in the streets would be the wind and sighing ghosts.

THE DRUMMER

Timo of the Dale stood placidly at the bow of the ship, the *Summer Snow,* wrapped in a cloak that was as wet as the sea itself, his bulging arms crossed, his face upturned in the rain, invigorated by the sheer power all around him.

The storm was magnificent in its rage, the lightning illuminating the sky in a ghostly pink and freezing the sheeting rain in glittering diamonds with each flash. The sea swelled like a giant shifting in its sleep and the foam swam like spirits of the dead under the bank of oars straining at the sea and attempting to guide the ship into calmer waters.

It was times such as these when Timo missed his fellow Guardians and the adventures of their calling the most, but he had abandoned that life when the Torch broke and the Guardians were disavowed.

Dark gazes from the crewmen were directed at him as they rowed and bailed, but he paid the dirty looks no more heed than he would a butterfly among spring flowers. The superstitious sailors blamed him for the unnatural weather, though it was not his doing. Timo smiled a little at the way people made mountains of things they did not understand.

A streak of lightning cut the sky in two like a sword from the heavens, burning a white strip in his vision. Timo balanced easily on the rolling deck, watching the lightning and the rain against the sea. It felt good to be back on the water again, the pattern of sailing up the coast a soothing balm to the burning hole that had been left when his previous life had come to a sudden end. The Daleman did not like to dwell on it, but thoughts of the others, the Torch and the confusing events had been thick on his mind of late.

He took a deep breath of moist, salty air…

…and then was suddenly standing on a grassy patch made of golden light. The golden light diminished and a road running through a forest took its place. A figure that Timo hadn't seen in four years or more lay in the middle of the road, blood seeping from his leg.

Beside him, a small girl was whispering words only known to a few and chills ran down Timo's back. The dream only lasted for a brief moment, enough time for Timo to realize that his whole world was about to change again. Then his companions faded away completely…

Timo's eyes opened to the sight of four lined and weather-beaten faces hovering over him in the captain's small, close cabin. In the windowless room the only light came from a spluttering candle lantern in the hands of a bald sailor in dripping clothes.

When Timo sat up with a sudden lunge, all four of them leaped back, all but one muttering prayers to their gods and making the Sign with their hands. Timo felt no fear from the fourth, the first mate.

The first mate was a short, wiry man with deep eyes, dark, shaggy hair and a scar that stretched from temple to jaw across his face. It left him with half a nose, one eye permanently closed and a mouth which curved up in grimace. He never spoke, but when he nodded sharply one of the other sailors ran off immediately. The sailor returned presently with the captain.

Captain Haldar was as tall as the mate was short, stocky as the mate was thin, and as comely as the mate was not. Deep blue eyes and white blonde hair tied back in a tail behind his head showed him to be a Daleman like Timo. A laughing mermaid on his arm undulated as he crossed his arms and looked down at Timo as he might look at a rotten fish on his deck.

"What is the meaning of this?" he asked in his booming voice.

Timo stood and at once noticed the absence of weight upon his back. He looked around and the first mate wordlessly handed Timo his drums, looking glad to be rid of them. After they were strapped to his back, Timo did not feel so naked. Captain Haldar was tapping his foot impatiently, annoyance clouding his face like thunder and Timo realized the storm in his eyes was about to fill the cabin.

"It was nothing," Timo tried to placate him.

"Nothing?" the Captain almost shouted. "You come back aboard after a fortnight on land and as many days of easy sailing for us, and the first night you are back, the mother of all storms descends upon us like a spurned lover! And if that is not bad enough, the storm disappears in the blink of an eye after you faint like a maiden who has sighted blood!"

Timo noticed for the first time the deck was steady

under his feet, and he smiled.

"Don't smile. You won't be smiling when we've been becalmed for weeks, moving like a turtle on land under oars only. You will be praying for a storm and the feel of the deck trying to heave you overboard," Captain Haldar warned.

Timo smiled wider. "At that point, I *would* conjure up a storm."

"Captain!" one of the tattooed sailors began, his face paling to a greenish tinge in the lamplight, but Haldar held up his hand.

"Leave us. I would speak with him alone."

Grumbling and casting poisoned glances behind them, the sailors left. The first mate ducked out last and closed the door with a whisper-soft click.

Captain Haldar sighed and let his hands fall to his sides. "It is already bad enough that my crew sees you as bringer of bad luck, this talk of conjuring a storm does not help."

Timo pulled a disgusted face. "I never understood why they are all so superstitious."

"And I don't understand how any brother of mine could have such flimsy sea legs and faint at the slightest wave under the keel," Haldar said, some of the clouds leaving his face.

"I didn't faint and *I* don't understand how a brother of mine could stand to stink of fish, salt water and grog all the time. When do you bathe?" Timo returned, flopping down on the tiny bunk and pulling his drums into his lap.

He began to tap and it took him a minute to recognize that he was playing again the rhythm he had played for the girl in the golden dream, the girl the Demon had called *Aethsiths*.

Haldar snorted. "You still have not answered my

question."

"What question, little brother?" Timo asked, only half-aware of the boat and Haldar in front of him as his fingers began to add to the rhythm, the heel of his hand reinforcing it.

"What is the meaning of this little episode?" Haldar said. "You scared the crew half to death."

"You'd think they wouldn't scare so easily," Timo mused. "They sail on this treacherous water and do not fear storms or drowning or mammoths-of-the-sea, yet one man faints and they pray for strength and courage from Seidn, the mighty Lord of Water and Waves or the Lady-of-the-Deep."

Haldar knelt beside him, eyes as dark as the sea at midnight burning into eyes as fresh as the sky at dawn. "They do not fear storms or mammoths-of-the-sea because they can see and touch these things. The *know* them, and can fight against them with their own wits and hands and knives. Against you, they can do nothing."

"I bleed the same as any other man," Timo said.

"If they can reach you with a blade," Haldar countered. "They have seen you fight the pirates, Timo. It is the only reason I can convince them to let you stay aboard."

Timo had to smile. "You have a point there, brother."

"Bah!" Haldar stood and threw his arms in the air. "You take nothing seriously!"

Timo sobered. "Some things I do."

Haldar grimaced. "I know. But sometimes I wish you wouldn't smile so much."

Timo replied with his biggest grin. "Well, soon you'll no longer be burdened with my beautiful face. I must go ashore."

"Again? For how long?" Haldar asked.

"Indefinitely," Timo said, his blood tingling with gladness. Cedar had returned and soon Timo would see the others again.

Few Dalefolk ventured beyond their jewel-like valley and fewer still took to an outsider's life as Timo had. Haldar was one of the few who did not judge his brother harshly for the decision to take up the mantle of Guardian. For that Timo had always been grateful.

Nor did his brother ask why Timo had to leave all of a sudden and Timo smiled again. Though Timo was older by five years, not even their mother would believe it, swearing the Joker had switched their bodies in the night. Haldar was ever the protector, the teacher, the strong tree in a gale, while Timo was the adventurous, insouciant one.

"Where are you going?" Haldar asked.

"D'Ohera," Timo said, watching with childish delight as distaste filled his brother's face.

"That place," Haldar snorted. "And you say I stink!"

"You do," Timo said.

"Why on earth do you want to go there?" Haldar asked, ignoring the jibe.

"There is a woman there who runs an inn. Or at least she calls it an inn," Timo said. "I believe that is where the other Guardians will meet, so there I will go as well."

"It is very far inland," Haldar mused, either not hearing mention of Timo's companions, or choosing not to comment. Politics of any kind were irrelevant out here on the water, and Haldar paid little attention to the ebb and flow of opinions on land, as long as it did not interfere with his ability to dock, load and unload his ship. The big Daleman walked to his desk and shifted some charts about. "We are nearer to Samnara than Isos."

Timo got up and stood behind Haldar to peer over his brother's shoulder. His heart sank when he saw the tiny finger of land over in the corner under Haldar's finger and the black dot far to the west labeled 'D'Ohera'.

"It is far from D'Ohera, but there is a caravan merchant in Samnara who owes me a favor. He is not the most savory sort, but it is the fastest way I know," Haldar continued. "Perhaps I can convince him to help you. But you should not come. If he sees your face he might run or worse, lose his wits and become a gibbering idiot similar to yourself."

"Thank you, brother," Timo said and grinned, throwing his arm around Haldar. "I knew there must have been a reason I did not drown you when you were born, loud, ugly thing that you were."

Three days later the *Summer Snow* drifted in the darkness towards Samnara. Known as the City of Iniquity, Samnara was the northern-most inhabited point of Demona unless you counted Gulmira, home of the dwarves. Perching atop a sheer stone cliff, the city watched over its large port as an eagle watches its eaglets.

Any ship or person was welcome regardless of standard or affiliation, the one stipulation being that to enter was to agree to rule by Samnaran law. The city was well-equipped to enforce the agreement, housing the largest garrison and militia in all of Demona.

This did not deter an unusually high percentage of villainous characters from calling Samnara home. More dead men had started anew in this City and a person could find any number of reformed pirates, thieves, murderers or smugglers willing to turn back for the right price.

Cloaked in predawn shadow and fog, the cliff loomed in front of them, the lighthouse beacon a broadsword of light above their heads. Thick mist deadened all sound, and the waves whispering under the hull sounded like sinister voices in a dark alley.

Haldar stood solid as an oak with his arms crossed, saying not a word as the boat was guided in by a wizened man baring toothless gums at the invisible shore while his gnarled hands grappled with the slippery tiller. Timo paced restlessly up and down the deck. His fingers itched to play, and the thought of solid land under his feet once again was so strong it caused a physical sensation in the pit of his stomach.

Like a black arm stretching into dark water, one of the docks appeared beside the boat. Faint shouts, ghostly and incorporeal, carried up to the deck as the *Summer Snow* was brought in. The first off the ship, Timo half skidded down the plank to the creaking planks of the dock where he waited with increasing impatience for Haldar to conclude his business with the mate and the dock master.

After placing a small pouch that clinked with the unmistakable music of coins into the outstretched hand of the first mate, Haldar pulled up the hood of his cloak and strode past Timo. Timo hurried after him, pulling his own hood over his head, concealing his face in shadow.

The streets wound back and forth up the cliff. The colors all bled grey in the dawn. Glowing halos surrounded the torches on the corners and lanterns in the windows. Disembodied voices called to and from hulking buildings which sat over the street like crones over a crystal.

Timo shivered and pulled his cloak tighter about his bulky frame. This was a City that never truly slept and the night harbored more than simply dark dreams and shadows.

The brothers made their way to a tavern housed in the hull of an old ship, the mermaid on the prow missing one eye and the cheek below it. The sign said "The Shipwreck Inn".

"An unlucky choice for the name of an Inn," Timo muttered, and Haldar gave him a curt nod of agreement.

It seemed as though the fog from outside had seeped through the cracks in the planks and filled the tavern. Tables which were little more than boards on barrels were surrounded by silent and sullen men of all kinds, Southrons, Cantons from J'Erd, the Little Men, and even several Nitefolk in the corner, ghostly pale and cat-eyed. A lone Elf stood silent in the corner, orange-gold hair braided tightly, filigree greaves over his forearms and leather armor marking him as a sell-sword.

Timo followed Haldar as the captain made his way to the bar. Although they were the only people waiting, the bartender did not move until Haldar slammed his fist down, making the glasses and bottles rattle like a crystal rain. Ice green eyes under heavy lids flicked to the two Dalemen, and a slow, wheezing sigh slipped from fat lips. "What do you want?"

"I am looking for a man who goes by many names," Haldar said. "Last I knew he was called The Panther."

After a long pause, the bartender gave a slow nod towards the back of the room, at the huge hulking form of a red and black pipe organ. In the shadow of the pipes, the figure of a man sat alone, moving only to lift a clouded glass to his lips. He gave only the slightest sign that he noticed when Timo and Haldar sat across from him, a pause in the motion, and then he settled the glass down over a rough glyph gouged into the tabletop. "Captain Haldar. A pleasure to see you again."

Prickles crept over Timo's flesh at the high voice which spoke with an inflection that was most often heard in D'Ohera. No shape or feature of The Panther could be discerned through the fog and dimness, and Timo wondered if there was in truth no man under the cloak, but a Shade or a ghoul instead.

Haldar nodded curtly. "I recall that you owe me a favor," he began without preamble.

The Panther did not move or speak for a long moment. "Do you now?"

Haldar did not back down. "Yes."

"Well, it is fortunate our memories are the same, Captain Haldar of the Dale, for if they differed, I fear I would lose any confrontation which resulted from our disagreement."

"I doubt that," Haldar said, an unhappy ring of truth in his words.

"Ordinarily I would agree with you, but not with a Guardian by your side."

Shock flickered over Haldar's face, then resignation when he saw no further point in hiding Timo's identity. "He must go to D'Ohera."

"That is a long way," The Panther observed.

"It is," Haldar agreed. "But it is not out of your way and it would satisfy your debt."

A warm flush of gratitude crept into Timo's belly as he comprehended what his brother was doing for him. Debt was as good as gold or a life in the shadowy parts of the world. That did not diminish the cold feeling in his heart which crept like ice over a lake when the shadow at the table spoke.

"Then it is done."

The Dalemen's farewell was short and brisk, the brothers embracing before standing back. Timo pulled on Haldar's ponytail with affection.

"Another day, brother."

"Another day," Haldar replied, his face long as he grasped Timo's shoulder. "Be careful."

"I am always careful," Timo said.

"No, I mean, be careful with The Panther," Haldar insisted, his grip tightening. "He was always a cunning man but now he is different, something more than he seems."

Timo laid a comforting hand on his brother's shoulder. "I know," Timo said. "I will be careful."

"And take this." Haldar gave him a purse heavy with coin, and stopped Timo's protests before they could be voiced. "The world is not what it was brother, and being a Guardian no longer carries privilege or assurance of aid."

"Thank you," Timo said, gripping the purse tight in his hand.

"Fair skies, fair tides," Haldar gave the old farewell, a little smile showing through the worry on his face.

Timo watched Haldar disappear into the mist, the grey light of dawn only serving to make the air more ethereal, as though they walked with ghosts in the Great Valley of the gods and not upon the earth. Timo did not need to turn to know the dark shape of The Panther now stood beside him, watching from under the hood.

"Are you ready, Guardian?"

"Of course," Timo said.

"Then let us be off."

The black wagon that was to carry them across land to D'Ohera was hitched to six black stallions, draft-horses bigger even than the ones the Southrons used to plow their fertile fields. Strapped to the back of the wagon was the sparse cargo - two luggage cases, a white burlap bag and an iron lockbox. In amongst these, half hidden under a fold of tarp, Timo spied three small chests, made of wood darker than midnight. He found his eyes sliding from them after looking at them for too long, and he realized the chests were full of some strange magyc that made him very uncomfortable, a strange sensation for the sure and steady

Daleman.

"Do I wish to know what you are transporting?" Timo asked, running a finger lightly over the polished wood, but pulling his fingers away when it burned like hot metal.

"No."

Timo accepted this simple and sinister answer with no more than a lift of an eyebrow and stepped into the black wagon as The Panther climbed to the box. Inside, the wagon was as full as the luggage rack was empty.

Twin girls, blonde and dressed in pale silk, had taken the seats against the window. They looked like ghosts and were just as silent. An olive skinned man who smelled like jasmine and blood, dressed in the fiery togas of the Wild Islands, sat cross-legged next to the first girl.

Beside the islander sat one of the Nitefolk, his barely pointed ears visible under a mop of thick hair. His sharp and dainty face clouded with suspicion as his slitted-green eyes watched Timo climb in. Across from these was a family in travel-soiled clothes, a tired-looking man, his thin and pale wife, and four scrawny children close in age and appearance.

Timo sat in the only remaining seat beside the Nitefolk, trying not to stare at the impossible sight of a solitary Nitefolk. They rarely ventured out of the mountains, and then only in pairs. He did not succeed and received a low growl from the creature, after which he quickly averted his eyes.

No change could be felt for some minutes, and the mismatched travelers waited with increasing restlessness, until finally Timo stood, half-crouched in the cramped coach and opened the door, meaning to ask The Panther what the delay was. This was unnecessary as the ground was flying in a blur under him, the wind almost strong enough to pull Timo from the coach.

He struggled to pull the door closed for almost a minute until the Nitefolk slipped under his arm and grabbed hold of the door, his sharp nails digging into the wood. Together they managed to close it, and the Nitefolk slipped silently back to his seat, retracting his nails.

When the door next opened, after what could have been an hour or a day, The Panther stood there. Behind him, a line of scraggly buildings which all looked the same in the dying light of the sun huddled together on the plain under a small copse of equally scraggly pine and birch.

"We'll stay here for the night, to allow the horses to rest, and continue as soon as the sun is up," The Panther told them and gestured for the passengers to get out.

Timo was the last to disembark. He stepped out and stood tall, feeling every muscle, tendon and even his skin protest. *Those horses don't look like they need to rest, but the passengers look like they could use about a year of sleep,* Timo thought.

The horses stood quietly without a trace of lather or sweat. The Panther pointed at one of the buildings set a little apart from the others and the passengers made their slow, heavy way to it. Timo waited until all the other passengers were inside before entering the sorry excuse for an inn.

Standing in the doorway, Timo glanced back and saw The Panther climbing into the coach. Timo watched until The Panther turned and looked at him and then Timo shut the door to the inn.

The innkeeper was a fat woman with greasy hair who half-sourly gave them one room for the night. If it hadn't been for the sweet twins and the four children, it would have been all sour. The room held one large bed and a stacked bunk. A pile of mismatched blankets were folded at the foot of the bed.

The twins collapsed on the bottom bunk and were asleep in moments. The islander took the top, the family took the large bed and the Nitefolk curled up in the corner, covering his face with one hand. Timo was left with a ragged blanket on the floor.

He slept fitfully, his dreams full of storms and Shades who called him 'Guardian' in high-pitched voices.

Timo woke to a loud banging. Standing at the door, his face still hidden by the dark hood, The Panther waved at them impatiently.

"The sun has risen, it is time to be off!" his voice rang out, grating on Timo's nerves. He struggled to sit up, rubbing his raw eyes, his yawn almost cracking his jaw.

The other passengers stirred and struggled out of bed, looking worse and twice as unrested as Timo felt. They staggered out while rubbing eyes sunken in shadow, the twins holding hands and the children hanging onto the threadbare coats of their mother and father.

"Are we to have any breakfast?" Timo asked The Panther.

"I do not provide meals. The fee covered passage and rooms only."

Timo decided not to mention the fact that he had not paid in coin but the canceling of a debt. His fellow travelers looked disheartened at the news, the islander grumbled something in his chirpy tongue and the Nitefolk drew his lips back in a silent hiss.

"Wait for me," Timo said, making certain The Panther nodded, however reluctantly, before he went to seek out the woman from the previous evening.

The fare was as bad as the room, but the sour inn-keep would not tell Timo where else to get food and he had no wish to test The Panther's patience or trustworthiness. After buying two small loaves of hard bread and a sack of assorted fruit, he remembered the Nitefolk and bought some sliced ham and a wedge of pale cheese. Timo stacked everything in one arm and hurried out to the coach.

Once again, Timo made sure everyone else was inside the coach before he climbed in and closed the door. This time he noticed a small pull and a jerk when the coach started.

The other passengers accepted the food eagerly and even the Nitefolk seemed to lose some of his disdain for the Guardian. Every crumb disappeared and the passengers settled into silence. A dull and heavy feeling infused the air of the carriage, pressing on Timo like a thick blanket on a summer night. There was much restless shifting and several times Timo caught someone's eyes drooping or head nodding, but sleep would not come even to the children, who looked miserable but did not cry.

Eventually, Timo pulled his drums to his lap and started to play. At first nothing happened, but then the Nitefolk shifted to look at Timo's fingers gently tapping the skin, cat-eyes bright in the dark and a rumble not unlike purring came from deep in his throat.

Gently swaying in time to the beat, the islander pulled one of the children into his lap where the little girl promptly fell asleep. Pink infused the twins' pale cheeks, and they sat a little straighter. Timo took all of this in with half-closed eyes and did not stop playing.

Only when the door was thrown open did Timo's fingers fall still. The setting sun was shining directly into his face and he lifted his hand to shade his eyes. The Panther stood there, steam rising from the folds of his cloak.

The Nitefolk slipped past Timo and stepped outside.

In the distance the dark Mountains rose up, casting a shadow for leagues, and an immense dark forest grew like a bushy beard at the foothills. The Nitefolk took nothing with him as he scampered into the trees.

Timo stood and looked out of the doorway of the coach to watch the Nitefolk disappear from view, his mind trying to comprehend how they could be this far from Samnara after only a day and a half of traveling. Unbidden, the image of the three chests came to the front of his mind and Timo's fingers tingled where they had met the strange wooden chests.

"How long until we stop?" he asked.

"We will travel through the night," The Panther muttered.

Timo caught a slight edge to his voice. When the faceless shadow turned to him as he closed the door, Timo shivered under the cold gaze and ducked back into his seat without a word.

One of the children murmured fitfully in his sleep and the mother looked pleadingly at Timo. "Please play for us."

Timo obliged. At some indefinable point later, he began to suspect the carriage was no longer moving. When he tried to open the door he found it locked from the outside and forcing it did no good at all. Timo held the drums, his fingers glowing with a pleasant heat as the drums were replaced with a bronze and gold halberd. Red oak, smooth from years of use, was worn soft under his hand and runes along the side of the head burned black.

"Stay back," he warned, and watched the other passengers cringe as far into the corner as they could, but the halberd did not have a chance to smash the door open before it opened from without. The Panther stood there, outlined in past-noon sun.

"Put away your weapon, Guardian," he rasped.

217

"There is no need. We are come to our journey's end."

Everyone spilled out onto the sun-warmed grass of an old courtyard. Great, flat stones could still be seen under the grass. Huge chunks were missing from the tall stone wall and moss grew over the towers and turrets. A little way off, a crumbling fountain stood like a forlorn lover. The luggage had been unloaded and piled next to the coach.

"I give you Torin, the wonder of Demona," The Panther said.

"And now nothing but a ruin," Timo said. "Why do we stop here?"

"This is as far as I can go," the Panther told him. "Most of the city is deserted but in the Gardens there are people, and more come every day."

This was glad news to Timo. Since the end of the Moonlight War, Torin had been a ghost city, where rats were kings and only the vines thrived, but the other passengers were not so glad.

"Doheerah!" the islander insisted, speaking in the Common tongue for the first time the entire journey, his thick accent making it difficult to understand what he was saying. "Eez wat wee paheed for."

"I am sorry," The Panther said, and he sounded truly distraught. "But there is nothing more I can do."

Timo watched The Panther climb back onto the carriage box and noticed the horses. No longer resembling the large draft-horses, they looked like half-starved cats, bones showing through desiccated flesh. Bloody foam frothed as they restlessly chewed at their bits and clumps of hair fell off, revealing skin covered with scabs and sores oozing pus. Only one thing could do that and it was not safe to have it running unchecked across Demona.

"Wait!" Timo yelled as The Panther took the reins.

The Panther did not heed the shout, snapping the

reins over the horses, which lunged forward. The other passengers stood like statues as Timo charged after the carriage. With a last burst of speed, Timo grabbed the baggage rack. His feet left the ground and he was pulled along.

Timo tried to undo the straps that held the chests in place, knowing that The Panther was not about to leave them behind, but the expert knots defied his attempts. He pulled the knife from his belt and slashed through the straps with one blow. The first chest bounced behind him.

Releasing the second two proved more complicated and the Daleman almost lost his grip several times before he thought to put the knife between his teeth to leave two hands free to maneuver. When the second chest tumbled free, an anguished cry came from the front and Timo was almost dislodged as the carriage swerved violently, the left two wheels leaving the ground.

The knife went spinning out into the air and Timo would have followed had he not caught a strap, which he had fortunately not had time to slice all the way through. The tear ripped further and further and as Timo watched, the entire thing came free. Suspended in mid-air for a heartbeat, dust filling his eyes and ears, Timo had time see his life flash before his eyes and curl himself into a ball.

Hitting the ground made everything inside of him jar against everything else and left him breathless, the taste of blood rising in his throat. The sound of the carriage careening away faded until the sound of Timo's ragged breathing was all that was left.

Then a child's scream split the air.

Huddled together, the passengers watched Timo warily as he staggered up as fast as he could. Two Darkwood chests lay in front of them like coffins, one tipped over on its side, the other upside down. Timo coughed, still trying to dislodge the dust in his throat.

"Who found these?" he asked, his voice rasping in his raw throat.

One of the children stepped forward and one of the twins. Tears ran down the child's face and any color the twin may have regained had drained from her face.

"What happened?" Timo demanded.

The child would not say anything, and the twin did not look at Timo as she spoke, her voice whispery and light. "The child found the first chest. He tried to carry it. We found him curled around it, screaming, unable to let go. I don't remember much, but it was easy to lift and impossible to let go."

"We had to pull her away from it," the mother of the child said. "The chests burn when you touch them."

She held the child's hands to show Timo the angry red wounds. She had similar marks on her own hands, as did the twins and the father. Timo glanced down at his fingers, but they were free of redness or wound. Then Timo noticed that the party was one short.

"What happened to the islander?" he asked.

"He ran off with the third one," the other twin said. "It didn't seem to harm him and we couldn't stop him."

"Let's have a look inside the other two then, shall we?" Timo said, his voice grim. "Find out what this is all about."

The father went paler and pulled his children closer. Timo could not fault him for his fear and the Daleman nodded kindly. "You should take your family where they will be safe. You and your sister should go as well," he included the twins.

He watched them gather their meager belongings and hurry away, making sure there was no trace of them before he turned back to the chests. Neither had a clasp or a lock and the waves of dark magyc coming off them made Timo nauseous.

"Why does this feel like a very bad idea?" Timo muttered to himself, poking the nearest chest with one end of his halberd.

After a moment of deliberation, Timo took his halberd in hand and gave the chest a firm tap squarely in the middle. At the impact, lightning shot up his arm and his numbed fingers let go of the weapon. Timo jumped into the air, shaking his tingling arm and mumbling curses in every language he could think of, making up a few of his own when he ran out of the usual.

Smoke rose from the chest, and a thick chunk of wood had been chopped off, though the halberd was still embedded in the wood. Gritting his teeth, Timo grabbed it and pulled it free. The next blow shattered the lid into large splinters, the sides of the chest bowing under the impact. It also paralyzed his arm with pins and needles of flame that danced up and down his flesh.

Using his good hand, Timo flipped the decimated lid open. Covered in a spiderweb of cracks, a round black stone the size of a man's head lay inside. Brushing his fingers over it, Timo felt the breath pulled from his lungs as he stared at whatever it was that lay in front of him.

Hefting his halberd with his other hand, Timo hesitated for only a second before he brought it crashing down on the second chest. Although he was prepared for the shock, he spent some minutes cursing and shaking his arm to restore circulation. Feeling like he now had two tree branches strapped to his shoulders, Timo clumsily opened the second chest and found a second stone, though this one was smooth and unblemished.

So engrossed was the Daleman in the contents of the

chests that he failed to notice the shadow that slipped up behind him, only realizing it when he felt something cold press against him, trying to choke him with ice and ash.

Timo fought back as much as he was able, his fingers thick and stupid as they struggled to bring the halberd up. It connected with a solid thud and a golden flash of light made his attacker howl and stagger away.

Timo spun on his knees to face the next attack, swinging the halberd up in a graceful arc that sent The Panther spinning backward, hissing and cursing. Timo was on his feet in an instant, halberd poised, eyes narrowed as he considered the form before him.

"Are you truly the man known as The Panther?"

"Once I was," the creature said. "No more."

"What are you?" Timo asked. "What are you doing with these chests?"

"It matters not," the creature called The Panther rasped. Its body was unbalanced, one limb hanging down, rendered useless from the halberd blow.

With a grating snarl, The Panther leapt for Timo who spun away easily. The Panther reached for Timo, missed, stumbled and fell. Timo placed a boot on The Panther's back and pressed him to the ground where he squirmed like a large black bug, kicking ineffectually.

Timo flipped The Panther and ripped the cloak away, baring the thing's face. Bloodshot eyes sunken in pale flesh blotchy with purple bruises stared back at him, squinting in the sunlight. A mouth so swollen and misshapen it was more akin to the snout of an animal, flecked with spittle and raw with cuts inflicted by its own teeth, snapped at him and then whimpered.

"Guardian, help me. Please."

Timo gazed down at the Thrall, a thing that used to be a man but was now something else, the flesh and blood warped by an additional entity housed in the body that was slowly decaying. It was held together only with powerful magyc, and under his revulsion, the Guardian couldn't help but feel sorry for it.

A wet crunching sound behind them made the Thrall shudder and cry out in pain. Timo spun around to see the stone which had been covered in cracks collapse into a pile of bloody yellow goo. Judging The Panther no longer a threat, Timo left him and went to tip the mess out of the chest onto the ground, gagging from the smell. The liquid seeped into the ground, leaving pieces of black stone and a black mass that quivered when Timo nudged it with his boot.

"Leave it," the Thrall behind him whispered. "It is already dead."

"And the other one?"

"Soon it too will be dead, but there were three. The third I can no longer see."

"One of your passengers ran off with the third one," Timo said. "The islander."

The Thrall sighed, still lying on the floor. "It does not matter. He cannot do anything with it."

"Maybe, but he could give it to someone who can," Timo said, grim words falling like hail. "How could you be so stupid, to bring dark magyc like that among people?"

"They were necessary. We had no choice."

"Why?" Timo asked, crouching beside the pitiful creature.

The Thrall coughed, phlegm rattling in its chest. "We needed to travel quickly. The passengers were brought along to keep the cargo we were charged with from coming to harm," The Panther struggled for words. "We didn't have enough power alone. You and your drums did not help as we'd hoped. You almost killed us."

"That was not my intention," Timo said mildly. "I was playing to keep the children comfortable."

"No matter. The Darkwood also has properties that served our needs, which is fortunate for us. But now they are all open, and they will die…instead of…instead of being…"

"Sold?" Timo supplied.

The Thrall shook his head, its throat working in a spindly neck. "No, they were never for sale. They were to be…," The Thrall mimed something breaking in two.

"Hatched," Timo breathed, bile rising in his throat.

"Hatched," the Thrall agreed. "In D'Ohera."

Timo remembered the golden-eyed Guardian's last words at the terrible battle outside Akorgia. *This did not happen by chance.* Timo had a sneaking suspicion that Cedar may have been more right than the other Guardians had first supposed. *But what did three Demon-spawn have to do with any of it?*

"Who in their right senses would have anything to do with Demons?" Timo asked. "And why? Nothing good could ever come of it!"

When the Thrall did not answer, Timo grabbed him by his frail shoulders and shook him.

"Who were they going to?" the Daleman asked again, his blue eyes hard.

"I know not, but they are coming," the Thrall said, his bloodshot eyes eerily Demon-like. "Even the Guardians cannot stop them."

"But there is one that could," Timo said, thinking of the grey-eyed girl the Demon called *Aethsiths.*

The Thrall sucked in a rattling breath but said nothing. Timo glanced back at the open chests, one empty and the other still holding the second egg. Fine lines were already appearing over the surface of the egg. Pounding its fist on the ground, the Thrall let out a keening cry that for all its pain did not sound human.

"What happened to you?" Timo said. "Why did you do this?"

"They told me I would be able to see them again," a shadow of the man-that-had-been coming into the thing's pained eyes, a lone tear running down a ravaged cheek. "I…"

Before he could say more, a fury rent his face and the body jerked. "I told you, you would not wish to know what it was I carried," the Thrall continued in its high-pitched rasp, slowly rising to its feet.

Timo turned towards the Thrall and faced the mutilated thing. The Guardian's face set as stone, strong hands gripping the halberd. There was only one thing to do. *For its sake. For the sake of the man that was.*

Killing it was easy, the halberd falling with molten grace. Only one blow was necessary. The creature crumpled in on itself much like a sail when the wind dies, its death rattle a sigh entwined with a scream which made Timo's skin crawl. It was not possible to bury it for there was solid stone under his feet, so Timo dragged the body to the wall and made do with piling rubble over the body.

The large Daleman stood for a long time, contemplating what to do with the remaining egg. In the end, he simply watched the egg collapse into rotten-smelling goo. There had been more form to the black thing inside, divisions where legs and arms would eventually be. Timo looked at it for a long time, before turning away and heading into the city. *I had never given it a thought,* he realized. *How it is that Demons came to be.*

The hair on the back of his neck stood on end as he remembered there was yet another of the repulsive things.

I must find the third one before it is too late.

Dusk had fallen by the time Timo chanced to run into another person. The small but allegedly growing population of Torin had worked industriously to patch up one section of the destroyed city between the First and Second Square.

Rubble had been cleared out of the streets and used to fortify the remaining buildings. No vines crawled the walls, and the fountain in the Second Square was bubbling merrily from five of seven spouts. Children splashed in the water, hung out of windows and dashed across the street, squealing and chasing each other as men and women bid others goodnight, closing up storefronts and packing away wares.

"Hey!" Timo called out to a particularly noisy group of children.

Two or three turned to stare at him and then bolted away. A braver boy paused and then took several steps towards him.

"Do you know where a stranger could get a room for the night and get a hot meal?" Timo asked him.

"The Traveler, just down the road and up Main," the boy told him, rubbing his dark blue eye with a dirt-smudged hand. "It's the only tavern in Torin. Food's good too." The boy smiled and revealed two missing teeth. "We get all sorts of people coming through. Where are you from?"

"A place called the Dale," Timo replied, thinking fondly of his home.

Shouts from within a crumbling church made the boy turn his head. His friends hung out from over the balcony waving at him.

"I have to go now," the boy said and ran off, leaping

over the low wall in front of the church like a hare and pelting across the statue-filled front garden.

"Thank you," Timo said to the empty air.

The boy's directions proved accurate and Timo found himself at the tavern on Main in moments. Light spilled out of a large square building with one remaining tower which perched to one side like a crooked hat. On the wall, someone had painted a likeness of a smiling young man with a dark beard and a walking stick. "The Traveler" was written over his head.

Inside the tavern was just like the Torin that Timo had known years before. The light came from ornate oil lamps, which gave a rich yellow glow that reflected in the glass and polished wood. Drapes and cushions of dark velvet absorbed the sounds, and the voices blended to a soft rumble as people ate off fine crockery and heavy glassware.

It did not take Timo much time to learn the islander had been here. Not many strangers came into town wearing a bright orange toga. Every person Timo spoke to nodded and said they had seen the islander sitting in front of the tavern, walking down the street, buying a sausage in the Square, speaking with another man in a grey robe, but no one could tell him where the man was now. The tavern keeper, a cheery man with a fringe of white hair and calloused hands who wore the dark, cropped jacket with large buttons and corded pants Timo had only seen true-born Isosians wear, said the Islander had not taken a room.

"Though I don't know where else he can go," the man said with a bemused frown. "No coaches left tonight and this is the only tavern in town, unless one sprung up this morning."

"Well, I'd like a room," Timo said. "And the islander has something which belongs to me, so I would appreciate any information you might have on his whereabouts."

"Of course," the tavern keeper said, his rosy cheeks bunching in a smile.

The room the tavern keeper showed him was as grand as the Common, albeit as small as a closet, with silk sheets, thick carpets and a mirror on the vanity framed in gilded iron. Timo had not really thought that he would sleep, but as soon as his head touched the pillow the Daleman knew no more, until a slight scratching sound invaded his sleep. Bathed in silver moonlight that only made the shadows darker, the unfamiliar room vexed Timo for a moment until he remembered where he was.

Once more, the scratching sound came and Timo's head whipped towards the tiny window. When he tried to open it, he found it locked and it was too dark for him to easily see the latch. By running his hands along the frame, he did eventually manage to unlatch the window, but even then it resisted being opened. A harsh squeal came as he pushed it and Timo saw the source of the scratching.

The window opened onto a dilapidated courtyard. A dead tree stood in one corner and a leafless twig had been tapping against the window in a cool night breeze. Leaving the window open, Timo returned to bed and once again closed his eyes, drifting into a sleep which was not truly sleep…

His dreams were golden. Cedar and the others appeared. Cedar looked terrible. He was in D'Ohera, as Timo had thought. Jæyd said that they would meet at the Tales Mane. Timo managed to nod at her before she disappeared and then he was floating alone…

Tales Mane was on Timo's lips as his eyes opened. The tavern room was bathed in early morning sun through the open window. He sat up and stretched his arms above his head. A pleasant warmth in his whole body from a good night's sleep made him feel capable of anything. A quick wash strengthened his vigor and he made his way downstairs on light feet.

Breakfast was a bowl of cooked grain with cream and honey. It was not as good as Victoria's but Timo was hungry and he had a long day ahead of him. The innkeeper said that there had been no word of the islander, but he directed Timo to the Western Gardens.

"If the man you are searching for is in Torin that is where you will find him or news of him."

Timo set off immediately through the revived streets of the City. Torin was a shadow of its former glorious self. Most of the buildings were still in the ruins left from the Moonlight War and the ones still standing were in a state of disrepair which was hard on the eyes, but the sight of people in the dead capitol of Demona gave Timo hope the city would bloom again.

Torin had been one of the few cities in Demona to boast multiple Gardens, six in total, but after the Ghor's retaliation at the end of the war, that number was reduced to zero. Now, it appeared at least one was being reclaimed and maintained.

In the Gardens, most of the ancient trees had been burned away and the trees now were hardly more than saplings. Like a lake in the middle, the huge fountain reflected the pristine sky. The paving stones of the paths had been swept clean and straightened, at least in the main part.

A market had been set up within the walls of the Gardens, rows of stalls overflowing with goods leading through to the Main Road on the other side. The Main led to the First Square, where the shops had been rebuilt to an extent and painted.

Wares were on display, artfully concealing the cracks and collapsed walls. Headless statues were used to hold up tables and roofless buildings that had half collapsed now served as pleasant outdoor eateries. Timo saw woodcrafts from Akorgia and Elba, a man displaying switches from the magyc trees of Balmar's Fire Gardens and a woman selling seafood from Isos, much to the delight of her customers.

Cool morning air stirred colored fabrics and clothes as Timo walked by a tailor and a weaver who had set up shop beside each other. A little way down, brass pots and jugs shone in the sunlight. Across the way, fragrant wax candles tied together by the wicks lay in piles.

In amongst all the color and life there was no sign of the bright orange toga of the islander. Fortunately for Timo, he found someone who had spoken to the islander. The blacksmith, who doubled as a farrier when the need came, wiped the sweat from his florid brow and shook his head, a giant pair of tongs dangling at his side.

"He came here yesterday evening, dragging a chest behind him and asking me to open it. At least that's what I think he wanted," the man admitted. "It was difficult to understand what he was saying."

"Did you open it?" Timo asked, fearing the worst.

The blacksmith shook his head. "No. I did not even want to try, but the money the islander offered was too much not to."

Turning, the man bent down and retrieved a twisted hulk of metal, scorched black. "This was my hammer," he said and tossed it to the ground, a look of disgust on his face. "Now I can't even melt it down to reform it!"

Timo tried not to let his relief show. "Do you know where he went?"

The blacksmith shook his head. "I'm sorry." He looked thoughtful. "Though I would check with Eselma the sculptress." He pointed down the way. "She has a stall just down the way. I saw her speaking with the islander after he left here."

"Thank you," Timo said, and hurried towards the small stall sheltered under the spring-clad boughs of one of the larger trees in the Gardens.

Statues small and large, most of fine marble, fewer of jade or obsidian lined the low wall that made one side of the little stall. Even larger ones sat on the ground. Some were crude, mere forms with no features, others Timo half expected to turn their heads and look at him.

Though none of them moved, Timo felt a presence amongst the statues, watching him. Men, elves, fauns, animals and the occasional tree or castle depicted in stone created a magycal stillness which sucked Timo in the farther he went back into the stall.

When a statue of a woman with long hair bent over something turned to face Timo, his breath left and his heart sped up, drumming against his ribs. It was a handsome woman in a long pale yellow dress, her silver-blonde hair almost indistinguishable from the marble. Her pale face seemed to be carved from the same. In one hand, she held a tiny pick and in the other was a fine brush.

"I'm sorry, did I startle you?" the woman said and smiled, her voice reminiscent of the ring of miners' hammers echoing deep in the earth. "Can I help you?"

"Are you Eselma?" Timo asked, his heart still pounding in his chest.

"I am indeed," the woman said and inclined her head in a graceful nod. "What can I do for you, Daleman?"

"I am looking for a man from the Wild Islands, wearing a bright orange toga," Timo began. "I was told he came here."

"He did," Eselma said, leaning back against the large

and unformed piece of marble behind her. "What of it?"

"He has something that does not belong to him," Timo said.

"The chest," the sculptress stated and Timo nodded.

"Do you know where he is?" Timo asked.

The woman gave a slow nod, her eyes glittering. "What is it worth to you?"

"I have money," Timo said, the blacksmith's words about the islander's money making his own words sound hollow to his ears. Haldar had been generous but his brother was by no means rolling in gold.

Eselma looked unimpressed but considered his offer for a moment before speaking.

"I would rather you bought something," she finally told him.

Timo gave the statues nearest him a quick glance. All of them were too large for him to carry comfortably.

The woman laughed and set her delicate tools on the stone. "How about one from the front?"

The little figures on the wall were cloaked in shadow from the cloth above, yet seemed to gleam with light all the same. Timo grabbed the nearest one, a cat crouching with its tail wound around it. "How much is this?"

"That is not for you," Eselma said with a disquieting gleam in her eye that matched the gleam of the stone.

Her pale grey eyes lazily looked over the statues, one red-tipped finger tapping each before moving to the next. Hovering over a statue in the center and obscuring it from Timo's view, the sculptress gave him a close-lipped smile and pressed it into his hand.

Timo looked down and found the likeness of… "What is it?"

"It can be whatever you need it to be," Eselma said. "It is, I think, much more suited to you than a cat."

Timo examined the rough stone that he held. It appeared to be two pieces of grey stone, one pale as dawn, the other dark as shadow, somehow joined without a seam. Twisted like flame, jagged like a mountain, with no symmetry that he could see, the statue meant nothing to Timo.

"How much is it?" he asked.

"How much is it worth to you?" she countered.

Her cryptic remarks were beginning to wear Timo's nerves thin and he rattled the purse hanging on his belt. "Three Katons."

She pursed her lips. "That is all?"

"Four Katons," Timo said, still bemused, but the expression on her face prompted him to raise his bid at once. "One Fenn."

Eselma sighed. "I can tell your mind is not on this. Very well. One gold Fenn and it is yours."

Timo dug the oval coin from his purse. As the sculptress extended her hand to take the money, the sleeve of her long dress pulled up and the Guardian noticed several pale marks down her thumb and up her arm. Eselma noticed his gaze and pulled the hem up to cover her wrist.

Timo dropped the coin into her palm and then grabbed her arm, exposing the scars and everything came together, the tale of the sculptress and her strange statues. The one he still clenched in his fist seemed to warm at his realization.

Eselma glared at him and jerked her arm away, pulling up the sleeve once again. "That was very rude."

"How long?" Timo asked, watching her face very carefully. *I should have known, should have been paying more attention.*

"Almost a year," Eselma said with a boastful

expression. "I was probably the first to discover it."

"That is doubtful," Timo said. "Blood magyc has been around for a long time."

"Rediscover it then," the sculptress said. "What is it to you anyway?"

Blood Magyc was almost Sorcery and that was almost dark magyc, but Timo didn't say that. To the sculptress, magyc was magyc. "Did you open the chest?"

"I had better luck than the blacksmith," the woman said. "But still the chest would not open."

Timo gently tossed the statuette in his hand, glancing at it with doubt in his sky-blue eyes. A Daleman to the core, he did not trust magyc outside of the Path completely, especially when it was forced on him by a strange woman who made statuettes with a magyc not far from Sorcery.

"It will not harm you, Daleman," Eselma said and then she sighed. "I sent the islander to my quarry, or what used to be the Festival Square of Torin. There you will find him and the chest."

With these words, she turned and disappeared into the gloom at the back of the stall, becoming invisible among her statues.

Finding the place Eselma had told him of took Timo most of the remainder of the day. He wandered through the demolished streets of Torin, backtracking when he ran into impasses of rubble and found himself going in circles. In the end, Timo scaled a wall and took the faster though more risky route across what was left of the rooftops of Torin. He skirted gaping holes, slid down sloping roofs and balanced across uncertain bridges of piled wreckage.

The Festival Square was no longer recognizable as anything that might have been made by men, much less a Square of the capital of Demona. Everything had crumbled and not one wall remained standing. Huge blocks of granite, marble, slate and quartz made a broken maze in the open space. Here and there smaller chunks and chips of other semi-precious stones littered the ground. Coming upon the center of the square, Timo understood why the sculptress would refer to it as a quarry.

A fantastic contraption of pulleys and weights had been set up to break the stone into more manageable pieces. Timo glanced at it, then a flash of orange dashed out of sight behind the elaborate device. Following, Timo caught the little islander easily.

The islander was winding the winch, which creaked like an old man's back, and he did not notice Timo until the side of a halberd caught him in the backside and sent him sprawling. Spitting out a mouthful of dust, the islander glared.

"Ahee do nutheen rrong," he said petulantly as he rubbed his bruised bottom. "Eet eez maheen. Ahee hadd eet ferst."

Timo took a long moment to work out the gist of what the man had said and when he did, he did not follow the logic, but he nodded anyway and refrained from pointing out that the Thrall had it first. Perhaps ownership was defined differently in the Wild Islands.

"Do you even know what's inside it?"

"No," the islander said, the stubborn look still on his face. Standing and smoothing his glaring toga, the islander stared loftily up at Timo, dust and sweat forming a thick paste on his olive face.

Timo sighed. "What is your name?"

The sound that issued from the islander's mouth was too full of clicks and gurgles for Timo to reproduce and the Islander smirked. "Dey culla mee Zhweendl."

Again, it took a moment for Timo to understand

through the thick accent and he couldn't help smiling. "Do they now? Well, Swindle, you are going to have to give up on the chest. Where is it?"

The olive-skinned man glared at Timo silently. The large Daleman grabbed the swath of orange fabric over the islander's left shoulder and hoisted him against a wall of marble.

"Where is it?" Timo repeated. "I do not have time to play games."

The islander pursed his lips and glared off over Timo's shoulder, until the Daleman prodded him in the stomach with the pointy end of a halberd.

"Dere, *dere,*" the islander squeaked with a nod towards the contraption.

Though it bore signs of abuse, scuffs and dents from numerous attempts to open it and long chipped scratches from the force of weights dropping on it, the chest remained sound and unopened.

Untying the convoluted knots the islander had employed to secure it to the contraption proved to be nigh impossible and after several moments spent struggling with them, the islander watching with his skinny arms crossed and refusing to help, Timo simply cut the knots, being careful not to touch the chest itself with his halberd.

Now that he had the third chest in his possession, Timo had to make a decision about what to do with it. Something told him that the appearance of this dark magyc in Demona had more to do with what was happing than he could figure out alone. Simply destroying the chest, though the obvious course of action, may not be the thing to do.

The Daleman was not as familiar with magyc as an elf would be. He had taken the mantle of Guardian and accepted the subtle powers of the Path only a dozen years before and he still approved of the bluntness of a fist over magyc, despite what most of his kinfolk thought of him. Timo decided it would be best to take the chest to D'Ohera where the other Guardians would be more capable of deciding what to do with it.

The moon had risen and set before Timo made it back to The Traveler. He hauled the heavy chest up the stairs and collapsed into bed, too tired to eat or bathe. In the morning, he was awoken by a slight chattering that came from inside the chest. When he picked it up Timo discovered it weighed more than twice what it had weighed the day before, and the kernel of worry grew into a pit in his stomach.

Putting the chest on his shoulder, he grunted with every step down the stairs. The innkeeper took his money with disturbed glances at the chest that lay at Timo's feet.

"Is there a stable in Torin?" Timo asked.

"Yes, but more in name than in practice," the innkeeper said. "It is just across the street."

The stable-master, an overly-thin man with thin hair and a thin mustache greeted him with a sad look. "Not enough people come through here to warrant keeping horses. Maybe as the city grows."

"What else do you have?" Timo asked.

"There is nothing," the man protested.

"What is that?" Timo nodded toward the last stall where a long grey nose poked out.

"That's a donkey," the stable-master said. "Good for nothing, eats too much and bites anyone who comes near him."

"I will take it," Timo said, smiling. "How much?"

"If you can manage to walk out with it, you can just take it."

Looking doubtful, the stable-master opened the stall

and leaped back. The donkey wandered out and turned its head from side to side. When it saw Timo it brayed in a very obnoxious manner.

Timo didn't say anything. His fingers lightly brushed the soft hair on the donkey's nose and the poor creature froze. Its eyelids drooped and it stood complacently while a rope and saddle was put on its back.

"I don't believe I've ever seen it do that," the stable-master said, still keeping back a safe distance and watching Timo work.

"I am good with animals," Timo said.

The purse Haldar had given him was almost empty but he wouldn't take the animal without paying for it. Though his purse was now uncomfortably light, Timo was smiling as he walked out. He was too large to ride the donkey, but the donkey bore the heavy chest easily, clip-clopping beside Timo as he made his way along the stone road of Torin, gathering strange looks like a dead rat gathers flies.

Then the donkey brayed, planted its feet and refused to budge, even with Timo's gentle persuasions. A faint stink and a dark blur was all the warning Timo had and then the donkey's bray of distress turned into a faint whine. When Timo looked down at it, he saw red blood gushing from its neck, spilling down its side. It looked at Timo with one soft eye before it crumpled. The dark chest rang as it hit the stone street, the ropes sliced.

The Demon appeared in a crouch in front of Timo.

Rearing in front of Timo, the Demon's red eyes rabbited between the blond Guardian and the black chest entangled in the ropes half-tied to the dead donkey. The Demon hissed, the short spikes on its neck raising, making it look like an agitated cat. Timo's immediate concern was not for himself but for the five dozen Torinish gaping at the Demon.

A small breeze blew through the street. The Demon's chest rose and fell rapidly. With a sudden leap, it cleared the distance between itself and Timo in a blink, pulling down a display of fruit in front of a small greengrocer in the process.

Small apples, round pears and dark spiky lichee fruit spilled every which way. The street erupted in panic when a second Demon appeared. Children stood frozen in awe as women screamed and men attempted to flee with their families.

The halberd appeared in Timo's hand like a rose appearing out of a jester's sleeve, too fast for the eye to follow. It blurred in his hands, golden sparks flying as he parried Demon blows. It took all his effort and attention to keep the Demons away from the chest, and Timo felt trapped. He would edge away a step and then one of the Demons would dash around behind him and attempt to snatch the chest.

It did not take a Scholar to put two and two together and understand that it would be very bad if the Demons got what they had come for. In trying to give equal attention to both Demons, Timo felt like a dog being teased and he growled in frustration, hurling his halberd at the nearest Demon. Luck carried the halberd straight through it and the Demon dropped where it stood, splayed out on the stones, a marionette with no master.

Without warning, the second Demon disappeared, running around the corner of the market. Screams reached Timo's ears a split second before he grabbed the chest and tried to follow the Demon.

The chest had grown too heavy and Timo only managed three paces before he dropped it, his muscles burning with effort. A chorus of screams made up his mind and Timo left the chest where it lay. He took off, grabbing his weapon on the run. He rounded the corner and found a small group of Torinish huddled against a crumbling wall, trapped in a dead-end, faces white with panic.

This day cannot get any worse, Timo grumbled to himself. *I should have left last night.*

The Demon skidded around the corner in front of him, leaping at him and he ducked. The Demon flew into the wall and it clung there, its talons latching into cracks as it scrabbled for a grip, sending a hail of dust and pebbles onto the people below before it leapt at Timo again. Timo spun away low, rounding the corner and coming up as the Demon flew at him.

Timo sent his halberd flying through the air a second time to pierce the Demon through the abdomen. Dark blood stained the weapon as the Demon's eyes dimmed. The family edged along the wall and ran, the father scooping up the child and carrying him away. The child called something back to Timo, but he didn't catch the words.

Timo leaned over, his hands on his knees. Just as he was starting to gain his breath, prying the halberd from the sticky grip of the corpse, movement in the corner of his eye made him start.

The halberd came free with a spray of dark Demon blood and Timo turned.

A dozen people had gathered at the mouth of the street, staring wide-eyed at Timo in complete silence. Their eyes moved from the Guardian to the corpse of the Demon and Timo's bloody halberd. Timo waited, the wind blowing in the corners of the dead-end like a forlorn fanfare to a pauper king.

The moment stretched out as the crowd slowly swelled to several dozen, gazing at the spectacle in front of them. Wonder dawned in their eyes as they saw what had happened.

"Guardian," a man began as he took his hat off. "Thank you for your protection."

Timo nodded once, unsure of what he should do. Since Akorgia, the Guardians had learned it was better to be safe than sorry where people were concerned, avoid all recognition as a Guardian if possible, and do their good deeds where they could, quietly with no recompense or reward.

Though it is a little late for that, you fool, Timo berated himself. *You can only hope they do not revert to the popular misguided mindset of Demona and stone you.*

"We have killed Demons here before, but not without loss of life," the man continued. "For this we are grateful."

An old man with silver hair and dark streaks in his silver beards stepped forward, leaning on a crooked walking stick. "The Guardians have returned!"

"So it seems," Timo said, hesitant but unwilling to contradict them for fear it would lead to a confrontation, a confrontation he did not need or want.

"Can he stay with us?" a young boy asked, eyes shining.

"Yes! The old tales say that at the beginning of the First Age of the Guardians, every city had Guardians to watch over its people," the old man said. "Will you be the Guardian of the people of New Torin?"

"I am afraid I cannot," Timo said. "I must go west…"

He trailed off. He did not have time to explain to these people that he wasn't able to protect them, that there was a greater need waiting for him in D'Ohera. People reluctantly stepped out of the way to let him pass.

"Please," a woman said, putting a hand on his arm. "You must at least accept a meal for what you have done."

"As it was before!" the old man chimed in, still enraptured with his dreams of the past and present meeting.

Unsure of what to make of the enthusiastic acceptance from the people of Torin and with no faith they would not turn on him with equal suddenness, Timo only wanted to leave and get to D'Ohera as quickly as possible.

"The people of Torin are not safe while I am here with the chest…oh, hells, the chest!"

Another Demonic scream made Timo's breath catch in his throat.

Timo sprinted back to the Main Road. He rounded the corner and saw a figure in a tattered blue cloak crouched over the chest, reaching out for it. In one bound, Timo was behind the person and he nudged them away with his halberd.

"I would not touch that if I were you," he said.

"You do not know what this is," a feminine voice said, the melodic tones giving Timo pause but he did not have time for further contemplation as he saw yet another Demon barreling towards him. It was smaller than others he noted, already wounded in multiple places and missing a forepaw.

The Demon was breathing heavily, foam at the corners of its mouth, a film making its eyes more pink than red. It hissed almost plaintively at him and howled when something hit it in the back. All Timo saw were golden sparks splutter and disappear and his heart leaped in his chest.

"Luca!" the figure in front of the chest yelled, still with the point of Timo's halberd firmly against her side. "You are supposed to be chasing it *away!*"

"Sorry!" a sardonically chipper voice with a familiar lilt called out, slightly breathlessly. "But I swear this thing is demented! I will *never* doubt your female intuition again! But I still think I should kill it before it kills me!"

The figure in blue pushed Timo's weapon away and stood, her own silver rapier held *en garde*. She pushed back the blue cloak, which Timo saw was actually the oilcloth cover of a stall, revealing cream suede and elven lace.

"Greetings, Daleman," Jæyd said, her eyes never leaving the Demon though she reached out and brushed her finger across his shoulder. Luca Lorisson skidded to a halt beside them, both dirks reappearing in his hands in golden flashes.

"Elf," Timo said a smile spread over his lips. "Little-One."

Luca grimaced at the nickname. "After four years, you couldn't have forgotten that one?" he said.

"By the Path it is good to see you!" Timo said, a glad warmth settling in his chest and dispelling a measure of the stress of the past days.

"Delightful," Luca muttered. "This reunion would be perfect except for this little problem we have here. And she won't let me kill it."

"Jæyd?" Timo inquired, looking between the Demon and the elf with a confused expression.

"I do not know why yet," the elf said, her blue-green eyes pensive and still fixed on the Demon. "But we must not kill it."

"Incredible," Luca sighed, rolling his black eyes. "So what are you going to do with it?"

"I want to talk to her," Jæyd said. "I have found out what she was searching for. Now I want to know what she wants with it and how it got into Demona. I chased her across the whole of Demona, half a dozen times almost forcing her to return to her Voide and half a dozen times, she did not. You will not kill her before I get my answers!"

The elf took her eyes from the Demon and turned her piercing gaze on the dark Guardian. Luca shrugged.

"I've been very accommodating, remember that," he said, waving a dirk under her nose. He shrugged to Timo. "Next she'll want to be getting recipes from it, or teaching it to darn socks."

Jæyd snarled and gnashed her pointed teeth. Luca smirked.

"She holds the answer to what is happening."

Timo's head was spinning and he blinked rapidly, assimilating Jæyd's use of *she* in what could only be a reference to the Demon. He was going to have to be filled in, but now was not the time.

"You want to talk to it?" Timo asked, trying to direct the argument back to something useful while keeping an eye on the Demon pacing back and forth just out of reach of his halberd. "How? Can it even understand you?"

"I do not know," Jæyd said. "But I know I cannot find out if Luca kills it."

In a sudden motion which caught them off guard, the Demon barreled past Jæyd, ignoring the slash from the rapier and Luca's dirks grazing off her armored torso, and set upon the chest.

Timo acted without thinking, batting away the Demon's paw from the chest and beating it back with a series of thrusts and slashes of his halberd. The Demon retreated, giving a plaintive hiss, its dull eyes watching the three Guardians warily. It made no move to attack them, instead sitting back on its haunches, wrapping its thin arms around itself, soft snarls punctuating heavy breathing.

The chest now bore the claw marks of the Demon in addition to the gouges the islander had inflicted trying to open it, but remained whole. Timo's arm trembled slightly as he remembered the force the chest had discharged when the halberd struck it, and he gripped the weapon tighter. *Dark magyc indeed.*

Jæyd stepped up beside Timo, her rapier out and shining silver. Her pale face, pinched into an expression of obsession, unsettled the Daleman more than the Thrall, the Demons and the chest combined.

"What could the Darkwood conceal that the Demon could want so badly?" the elf whispered to herself.

"Demonspawn," Timo told her, recalling the Thrall had called the chest Darkwood as well.

The elf turned a startled face to him. "That would explain much. How do you know this?"

"There were two others, in the care of a Thrall," Timo said. "I broke them open and destroyed the contents."

Relief swept over the beautiful features of the elf. Then she frowned. "How did you manage to destroy a Darkwood chest?"

"I hit it with my halberd," Timo said. "Hurt like all eleven hells."

"And that worked?" Jæyd was surprised.

Timo nodded. Jæyd accepted this and glanced at the chest.

"It is true, this chest is poorly made, hardly worthy of the name Darkwood, yet still…"

"Wait, what's all this about Darkwood?" Luca asked. "If that name is supposed to make me feel better, it's doing a horrible job."

"A Darkwood chest is a receptacle made by powerful Dark magyc. True Darkwood would be impermeable once sealed. My father crafted one, a long time ago in Carallión,"

Jæyd said. "It was ferried far into the Wastelands and left there, or so I believe."

"I take it this is not the same one," Luca said, tossing a knife in the air and catching it by the hilt, feinting at the Demon tauntingly, but it just snarled at him.

Jæyd shook her head. "No. This is crude, the work of a child or an idiot."

Luca snorted. "Or a man is what you mean to say."

A smile tugged at the corner of Jæyd's lips. "Perhaps. No elven craftsman would put his Mark on that. I suggest you destroy it as you did the others."

Timo nodded, raised his blade and sent it crashing down on the lid of the chest. A jagged flash of light threw him to the ground and the Demon howled, surging to her feet. Timo gasped for breath, an iron vice around his chest, his body numb to the core. The Demon screamed at them again. Luca held it back with his dirks as Jæyd helped Timo from the ground. Another notch graced the chest but it was sound.

"This one is more resilient than the others," Timo grunted, staggering as he tried to get his feet under him, his fingers tingling as feeling returned. "Perhaps it was made by a different person."

"Or it was the first to be made," Jæyd mused. "When the maker was at his most powerful."

"Whatever is inside has shut up, at least," Luca observed. "But your Demon is *not* happy."

A thought crept stealthily into Timo's mind, forming like a figure emerging out of mist but he put words to it hesitantly, unsure if the other Guardians, particularly the elf, would consider it wise. "What if we simply gave the Demon the chest and be done with it?"

The other Guardians looked at him, and as Timo had suspected Luca was the first to agree. "Sounds good to me."

Jæyd didn't look convinced. "I do not know."

"Jæyd, what do you expect will happen?" Luca asked impatiently. "It technically belongs to the Demon anyway, doesn't it? You've found your answers. This will solve all our problems. At least let's see what happens."

"Come," Timo said, taking her elbow and leading her away with deliberate steps, watching the Demon the whole time.

As soon as the Guardians began to move away, the Demon shot forward and set upon the chest without hesitation. Using its teeth and claws, it began to weaken the chest. The going was slow, black sawdust flying off. The Demon growled and flung it against a stone wall. The chest gave an audible groan and the sides bowed outward as it bounced.

The Demon jumped in surprise when a dirk shattered into gold light against the side of the chest. Luca yelped and jumped as though he had been hit by a lightning bolt.

"Wow!" the dark Guardian squeaked and then shook it off.

Luca clenched his jaw and sent another dirk after the first. The Demon tore into the wood, heedless of the dirks Luca continued to throw. Suddenly the chest split down the middle with a black and white flash that burned their eyes.

With a shriek of triumph, the Demon reached into the chest. Timo watched in horror as it picked up the black thing within and proceeded to tear it to pieces. Jæyd gaped beside him and even Luca averted his eyes.

Tossing the mutilated and unrecognizable thing away, the Demon turned and fixed red eyes which now shone brighter on the Guardians. The Demon reared up to full height and bared its teeth at them. The weight of the halberd increased in Timo's hand and gold light flickered along the lethal edge.

"Jæyd, what do we do now?" Luca asked, his hands white around the hilts of his blades. "Now that it's acting normal and everything?"

The Demon did not give the elf time to answer and attacked the Guardians. There was no battle, the Demon had barely moved before a golden halberd and two dirks embedded themselves in its body and it fell.

Jæyd said nothing, her blue-green eyes without emotion as she looked at the form of the dead Demon. Timo noted with displeasure that the crowd had followed him and continued to grow, spilling from the side streets as people pointed and came over. They pointed and exclaimed at the third dead Demon.

"The Guardians have returned!" someone from the crowd called out. "Hail!"

"Hail!" the rest of the crowd cried out.

Luca looked bemused. "What is this?" he said. "What am I supposed to do again?"

"I am not sure," Jæyd said, looking from one eager and awestruck face to another.

"Blast," Timo muttered. "They're probably going to try and convince us all to stay."

Luca looked horrified. "No."

"Well, they probably won't want you to stay." Timo's grin flashed through before his face settled into a frown again.

"Guardian! Who are your companions?" the old man Timo recognized from before called out.

The crowd parted and allowed the man through. Timo noticed the metal chain peeking through his beard. *A Magister,* he realized. Luca and Jæyd shrunk behind

Timo, leaving him to deal with the question. Timo took a deep breath and a leap of faith.

"Fellow Guardians, Magister."

"Then they are welcome." The Magister held out his hands. "I know you cannot stay, but know you *are* welcome. And there is something else."

The Magister turned and beckoned with a long, knobby finger. A young man, hardly more than a boy, walked forward leading a horse. He hesitated for a moment as his eyes went from one Guardian to the other, then he presented it to Jæyd, and bowed clumsily, his fresh face awestruck. "My lady, you must take this."

"I cannot pay," Jæyd said as she reached out and stroked the velvet nose.

"It is a gift," the boy said.

For a moment Jæyd looked disoriented, and Timo knew she felt as he did - thrown back in time to when the Guardians had been treated as honored guests and given anything they needed by those they aided and served. It had been so many years since that had been the way of things that the elf did not know what to make of it.

"Thank you," Jæyd said. "But all three of us cannot ride a single horse, and we cannot take more from you."

The boy looked crestfallen and looked to the other Torinish for guidance. They shifted and muttered to themselves, their faces clouding. Timo realized something had to be done, and quickly. He thrust his chest out and walked forward with long strides. Using the voice honed at gatherings in the Dale, Timo addressed the crowd.

"People of Torin! We do not wish to offend, but we cannot linger. We leave our blessing for New Torin and one day we shall return and partake of your generous hospitality."

In a sudden burst of joyous energy, the crowd

cheered. Timo kept the regal expression on his face even as bemused expressions stole over the other Guardians.

"Go," he told them out of the corner of his mouth. "Wave once and then do *not* look back."

Jæyd and Luca lifted their hands and the crowd cheered in a voice like thunder that shook the walls. Jæyd turned on her heel and strode away, pausing only to pluck one piece of the Darkwood chest and put it with her flute. Looking over the crowd, Luca shook his head a little and then followed Jæyd. Timo followed the pair of them. The crowd parted to let them pass, whispering amongst themselves words that Timo could not hear.

"That was very odd," Luca said, once they had passed into a still ruined and deserted district, the people of New Torin far behind.

"Yes," Jæyd agreed quietly.

"How do you explain all that?" Luca continued. "It is almost as though they believed the Guardians were," he struggled to find the right word, "*redeemed*. But we haven't done anything. I don't understand the way some people's minds work."

Timo shared the sentiment. While it was good not to be despised for the present, the mystery of Cedar's disappearance, the demon spawn and the Darkwood chests cast a long shadow over a small victory.

"We must make for D'Ohera at once," Timo said. "There is much we have to tell Cedar."

The Guardians made their way through Torin to the Western Gates. They departed from the white walls of Torin and made their way northwest, leaving the city to be swallowed by the plains. It was so natural to be together, even after four years, and just their presence brought a lightness to Timo's spirit. He felt no need to speak on it, to inquire how each of the others was or what they had been doing, and Luca and Jæyd shared his contentment to simply be together without words.

However, recent events were a different matter. Along the way, they traded stories about the Thralls each had encountered. Timo was disturbed to hear what the one had said to Jæyd, words resonating out of time and memory-*the sands are a-shifting* – to haunt them in the present. Jæyd's mood blackened when Timo told of the man who shared his body with an influence that was Demonic but not a Demon, a false Thrall.

"Seems pretty real to me," Luca muttered, but he too could not mask his disquiet.

None of it would sit easily in Timo's mind. A Thrall carrying Demonspawn to D'Ohera yet tracked by Demons who only wanted to destroy it, appearing at precisely the same time the Guardian returned with a girl the Demon called *Aethsiths* was too ominous to be inconsequential.

Perhaps it had not really been Demonspawn in the Darkwood chests. Maybe the Demon in the forest wasn't one of the Nine. But what if it was? When it was all taken together, what did it mean? The possibilities made Timo's head ache.

With the pace the elf set, it was not long before they entered the shade of the trees. The light turned green and thick, the leaves swallowing the sound and leaving them in a private world. The road appeared out of nowhere, starting from a small copse and snaking forward into the trees.

Timo remembered the forest and the road from the first golden dream. From Luca's clenched jaw and the shadow in the elf's eyes, he saw they had similar memories. They hurried through the forest, the rank evidence of Demons everywhere, the trees crowding close, making the air dark and difficult to breath.

Though the trees were clothed in the vibrant greens of spring, there was a stillness to the forest that made Timo shiver. He didn't see a single animal as they journeyed, only slight fluttering in the dark confines of the forest and an occasional birdsong, far off and timorous. It was stifling, like walking through Death's Realm, and Timo could not wait to be free from it.

As the sun began to go down, they rounded a bend in the road and Timo saw a familiar sight. Mundane when not bathed in a golden glow, and morbid yet somehow heartening nonetheless, was evidence that Cedar had indeed returned - dark smears of blood marking the place where Cedar and the Demon had fought.

The Guardians made camp just off the road, on a soft pine carpet. No game presented itself and the day passed without dinner. Unused to going without a solid meal for that long, Timo's stomach grumbled at him constantly, and he began to amuse himself with visions of the food Victoria would serve him when he arrived, beef stew, black bread, cider, apples and plums if she had them and two-week pudding with mounds of sweet cream on top.

By midmorning the following day, Timo and his companions had left the forest and started across the plains on the other side. The sporadic road through the rolling grassland was long and dusty. Jæyd did not tire, the fire still pushing her heels and the men struggled to keep up with her pace. Timo knew Luca would never admit to being tired, certainly not to Jæyd, but he did not think he had the same compunction himself.

However, when the Daleman saw the light in Jæyd's eyes, he thought perhaps he could continue a little more and then still more. The night brought the hills and no sleep. Their way was lit by stars which shone brightly above them and their tireless pace was rewarded in the morning when the sun rose over the sprawling disfigurement of D'Ohera, the Rainbow City.

The trio of Guardians stood looking down at it, each lost in their own thoughts. Timo could scarcely believe he had returned. Four years was a long time to be away and the prospect of seeing Cedar again warmed his heart as only a friend back from the dead could.

"Let's go then," Luca spoke first. "Cedar is…"

All motion seemed to cease as Luca spoke, his word rolling into a low blur. Everything moved in front of Timo's eyes at mind-numbingly slow speed. At first he thought perhaps the Path was calling them again and they were about to enter a world of golden light, but the light did not change and he remained firmly where he was, his feet solidly on the ground. Timo watched, his own head turning too slowly, as Luca took a step forward.

The ground rumbled underneath them, the shock building as a tear slowly began to form directly in front of Luca, who threw his hands up. Timo shouted a warning, too slow as the tear widened into a gaping wound revealing the cold misty world behind it.

Everything crashed down around him, returning to normal speed. Jæyd grabbed Luca and pulled him away as a Demon stepped through the Rift. The Void closed behind it with a crash, leaving Timo's ears ringing.

Over eight feet of muscle and sinew stood glowering over them, almost indistinguishable from the one Cedar had fought, though this one was covered in spines down its back and at the joints. Two long pointed horns jutted ungracefully from its brow.

One of the Nine. *In the old days it would have been known as the God of Blood,* Timo's mind noted numbly, even as his body responded without guidance from him, stepping away and bringing up his halberd.

The Guardians moved as one, Jæyd taking point with Luca and Timo at her flank. The Demon smiled. Shivers ran down Timo's spine when the Demon turned and moved its red eyes from the elf and glared at Luca. The dark Guardian looked startled and shifted his grip on the blades in his hands uncertainly.

The Demon paused, and Timo thought he saw a flicker of indecision in its ruby eyes. Then, as though it had not even seen them, the Demon turned and bounded for D'Ohera, leaving the Guardians gaping at its rapidly retreating back.

Jæyd threw up her hands. "All of them are doing it now!" she growled and this time Timo knew what she meant.

"We have to stop it before it reaches the city!" he cried.

"Too late for that," Luca said grimly, his mouth a thin, pinched line and his dark brows pulled low over his eyes as he watched the Demon stalk through D'Ohera's Gates.

"We still have to try."

Timo's words flew over his shoulder as he ran, wishing there was some way to warn the Guardian in the City, who was the only protection for the people from a horror long since banished from Demona.

The God of Blood disappeared behind the wall, and the first screams pierced the air.

WITCH, ASSASSIN, PRINCESS

Ria's eyes traveled over the newly forged guitar. The wood gleamed gold and beige, similar in color to Cedar's eyes. It was never far from his reach. At the moment, it was under his hand as he sat on the end of the divan in the Common of the Tales Mane.

Cedar's golden eyes never ceased to fascinate Ria. They could go warm and cold, narrowed when he concentrated and twinkled when he smiled or laughed. Now they were fixed on Ria, but she doubted he actually saw her. Cedar was far away, probably thinking about the other Guardians and what would happen when they got here. Or brooding on the things he brooded on and wouldn't tell her about.

Even though Ria had helped convince Cedar to stay here and sworn to herself she would be patient, being cooped up in the tavern was making Ria edgy. Her eyes flicked to the door every so often, longing to know what was happening outside.

It was obvious Cedar was of the same mind. He would have been pacing like a nervous cat, but with impressive self-control he held himself completely still, the only sign of his restlessness a rhythmic twitching of his left hand on his knee.

For the past three days he had been getting more and more agitated, and the more agitated he became the stiller and colder he became. He hardly spoke to anyone. At times he did not even thank Victoria for meals, which he ate robotically. His eyes glanced towards the cellar door with increasing frequency.

The prisoner's presence was tangible, a tight pressure which sucked warmth and sound from the air. Ria did not like the Justice Trem Descal, the way his pale eyes never blinked and the way he spoke to Cedar. She shuddered. She did not even like thinking about him, but she did, too often.

They had put a blindfold over his eyes and a gag between his teeth when Cedar had hauled Descal by his heels into the cellar while the Justice was still unconscious. The door was firmly bolted from the outside, but a strange sort of terror still wormed its way through Ria and she half expected to find the man standing in front of her whenever she turned a corner. Cedar told her there was nothing to worry about, but Cedar had been strange himself and his words did not comfort her.

Once Cedar had decided to stay at the Tales Mane and wait for the other Guardians, he immediately went into a frenzy, moving furniture to different places for reasons only he understood and nailing boards over the windows on the second story of the inn. The three chests of money had disappeared, food and supplies were stacked in the corner of the Common and Ria and Nadi were given strict warning not to stray out of sight.

Cedar had pursed his lips in exasperation when Ria had very practically brought up the issue of the bathroom. Nadi started giggling, though his ears were red and even Old Jacob smiled. Victoria had come to the rescue again.

"You will use the washroom past the kitchen, just not the one in your room. And yes, you may go alone," she told the children. "Now, let's leave Cedar in peace. He has work to do."

Ria knew better than to ask "what work?", but the next time she caught a glimpse of Cedar was hours later just as she was drifting to sleep. He had walked in and dropped wearily onto a chair he'd moved into the corner, leaned his head back and stared at the ceiling. Ria had wanted to go to him and ask what was going on, but she was afraid of the answer and Cedar's blank look.

Today, the Common was quiet, as it had been since they had retreated there after imprisoning Trem Descal in the cellar. The curtains were drawn and Victoria stood behind the bar, washing glasses and setting them in neat, straight lines with only the faintest of tinkles.

Old Jacob was sitting in a chair that was twice his height and five times his width puffing on a long, dark pipe. The smoke smelled good, thick and spicy, and Ria breathed in deeply, putting it in the place in her memory where she kept all things of Demona.

Because one day Cedar is going to send me home. Even if I don't want to go. Not that he bothered to ask me.

Ria knew she was going to have to deal with that at some point, but for now she pushed the thought away and looked instead at the others in the Common. Robbie, the curly-haired dwarf boy with bright eyes who had fetched Old Jacob to see to Ria's wound, which was now no more than the faintest pink line down her side, sat beside the old dwarf's chair, building towers and bridges with wooden blocks, lost in a world of his own creation.

Little Nadi was playing some game with bright tiles and little carved creatures by himself in front of the fire, his forehead creased with a long line as he contemplated his next move. His hand moved first to a bright blue square, then a red one and then what looked like a tiger, his fingers twitching slightly as he figured out which to choose.

"Don't move the Cat," Cedar said, his eyes still distant. "It will be taken by the White."

Nadi looked at the white piece sitting in the corner and grimaced. His hand moved away from the Cat.

Victoria frowned at Cedar from behind the bar. "Let the boy play. How will he learn if he never makes a mistake?"

Cedar stirred from his reverie to smile at Victoria. "I am still convinced there is a way to learn without making a single mistake."

Old Jacob looked up from the book he was reading. "And what way is that, young Cedar?"

"I am not totally sure yet," Cedar admitted. "But I am certain it must exist."

"The eternal hope of youth," Old Jacob said with a grimace which was more of a smile and puffed out a cloud of smoke.

"I am not that young," Cedar said and smiled back.

Then his fingers tightened on the neck of his guitar, his head snapped up and his eyes went cold. The lightness of the moment dissipated as the smile fell from his face. "Something is happening outside."

Ria felt a tingle run through her body and she sat up straighter. *Finally.*

"What is it?" Victoria asked. "Have the others

arrived?"

Cedar did not answer and took up his guitar. "Wait here."

Ria's heart sank. If it were the other Guardians, Cedar would have just said so. It must be something else. Ria thought about the Justice in the cellar and all the men outside, but they had been there for three days. *It must be something else, something bigger.* A shiver ran through Ria. She leaped out of the chair and ran to him, catching his arm before he could leave the Common.

"Is it another Demon?" she demanded.

He looked down at her, his hand turning white as the blood was slowly forced from it by his too-tight grip on the neck of the guitar.

"I don't know," he said softly. "Stay here."

She chewed on her lower lip and watched as he slipped away down the passage.

"Where's he going?" Nadi asked Victoria, his game forgotten.

"Where he goes," she answered, serenely continuing to polish the glasses, though her eyes lingered on the doorway long after Cedar disappeared.

Ria remembered the last time Cedar had told her to *stay here.* If she remembered correctly, a Demon had been involved. A cold feeling spread through her, starting somewhere in her stomach and running down to her fingers and toes.

The feeling told her she needed to be near him so she could protect him. Tangled up with that was the fear that she was going to lose him, and that he was going to die if she wasn't there to help him. It was an old feeling, as if it had been with Ria for a hundred years, but she was only twelve and had just met Cedar a fortnight ago.

She tried to shake it off, telling herself that Cedar had

been doing this for a really long time and knew what he was doing, but the feeling clung to her stubbornly, like hair covered in honey that she couldn't let go of.

I can't stay here. I have to do something.

Ria took a quick glance around the room. Victoria was absorbed in the glasses and Old Jacob looked like he had fallen asleep. Crouching down, Ria scooted silently through the Common and went along the passage to the kitchen. Cold ashes sat in the fireplaces and the door and windows were barred with slats of pale wood and nails. Ria crept over and peeked through a crack in the wood.

Shadowy figures milled about the courtyard in front of the stable. The grey nose of Silver the donkey poked out of the stable door for a moment before it disappeared inside again. Ria's heart was pattering so loudly in her ears she was sure the others must be able to hear, but they did not come running or call out.

Someone grabbed her elbow and a small squeak escaped her lips. She turned to find Nadi behind her, his brown eyes wide.

"Where are you going?" he whispered.

"Nowhere," she said sharply. "Go back to the Common."

"I'm coming with you," he said stubbornly.

"No." She tried to glare at him with parental sternness. She was older after all, and would be responsible for him, but when he stuck his tongue out at her, she couldn't help the smile that escaped. "No," she said again. "Victoria will be mad."

"I *am* coming," he told her. "You don't know the way around the city. I do."

Ria tapped her foot and tried to think of something she could say to make the boy go back, but there was nothing. He was right. She rolled her eyes at him, then turned back to the window and peered through.

Nadi fidgeted behind her. "What do you see?" he whispered.

"Not much," Ria told him, frowning. "There are people there. I don't know how we can get away without being seen."

Nadi looked at her with bright eyes and a wide smile spread across his face.

"I know a way," he whispered. "Come with me!"

Nadi took Ria to the second floor. The children ran up the stairs as fast and as quietly as they could. They weren't supposed to go up there; everything but the Common and the bathroom had been deemed off limits since the horrible man and his Streetwardens had shown up.

"Hey!" Nadi said and gave her a poke. "It's this one."

The room at the end was never used and the door had no handle or lock. It opened without a sound on well-oiled hinges. Pushed up against the wall, the bed had no mattress. If something didn't have a place of its own Victoria put it in here, which explained the odd range of things from the porcelain foot-bath to the harp with only four strings to the pile of mismatched floral curtains in the corner.

Nadi pointed to a trapdoor in the ceiling in the corner of the room. He got down on his hands and knees for Ria to stand on his back and she reached up to pull the ladder to the attic. It came down with a creak and Ria cringed, but no one came running. The children scrambled up the ladder to the attic.

Cedar had boarded the windows in the attic too, but a board came free when they tugged on it together. Too heavy for the both of them to hold, it slid down out of their hands, landing on the floor with a dusty thud and giving Ria a splinter in the heel of her hand. She pulled away with a yelp.

"Just pull it out with your teeth," Nadi encouraged.

"My teeth?" Ria asked, looking uncertainly at the dark sliver in her pale hand.

"Yeah, like peeling a grape with your teeth, except you're getting a splinter out," Nadi said. "It's easy."

Ria slowly bit her hand but all she accomplished was putting a red bite mark over the dark stripe. It looked like an eye and she rubbed her hand on her pants to make it go away.

Then they clambered out the window and onto the flat roof. Ria was glad for the clothes Victoria had given her. They were comfortable, smelled good and were easier to climb around in than jeans.

The sun was almost directly above them. Ria was very happy to see it after what felt like a year being cooped up inside. Nadi turned his face upwards, bathing in its warmth for a moment before he turned away and beckoned.

Creeping to the edge of the roof, the pair peered over and saw the tops of the Streetwardens' heads. Some wore grey caps. One was bald. Ria counted seven in total. All of them carried weapons and Ria felt a little thrill of fear. She reminded herself to be brave for Cedar's sake.

"So, where do we go?" Nadi asked her.

"I thought you were the one who knew how to get around here," Ria retorted. "Wasn't that the reason you came?"

"No, I said I knew my way around the town and I do," Nadi corrected. "I just don't know where to go. That's your job."

"Why do you think I know where to go any more than you do?" Ria asked, a bit crossly. "Cedar didn't tell me anything either."

Nadi was silent and when she looked at him, he turned his face away. Ria caught the uncomfortable look on his face, the little crease between his eyes.

"What?" she demanded.

"I heard them talking the other night," Nadi confessed.

"Who?" Ria asked, though she already knew.

"Cedar and Victoria and Old Jacob."

"What did they say?"

"A lot of stuff I didn't understand," Nadi answered vaguely.

Ria grabbed his shoulder and gave it a shake. "Tell me!" she insisted.

Nadi looked unhappy, but he did as she asked. "Cedar told them what happened when he found you. They said that Cedar would have to leave D'Ohera to send you back, because of the Path and all, and something about Witches," he said as he shook off her hand. "Victoria asked about a prophecy and Cedar got mad."

"What did he say?" Ria asked, her voice small. She hated when Cedar got mad, and it was worse when he was mad because of her.

"He said that everyone should stop seeing what they want to see. He said there is no doubt that you are special, but you're too young and you're going back and that was final." Nadi sounded a lot like a grown up when he repeated their words, but he looked at her sympathetically. "I'm sorry. I know you want to stay."

Ria shrugged and put on the same neutral expression she'd used back home whenever someone tried to question her about her feelings, and she didn't want to give them anything to make more of than was actually there. "I don't care. He always said he was going to send me back."

"Old Jacob also said something else," Nadi said. "Something about Demons and the Old Races seeing thing differently, and that you might be able to do the same thing, which could explain your talent." He looked at her curiously. "Can you?"

"I don't know. What are the Old Races?"

"Elves, goblins and the others."

"Don't be silly," Ria said with a frown. "I see things exactly the same as you."

"Maybe you just need someone to show you how," a voice said from behind them and the two spun around.

Ria's elbow slipped off the edge and she gave a little shriek as she began to slide.

Robbie the dwarf-boy grabbed Ria and pulled her firmly back onto the roof, looking at her apologetically, his curly brown hair falling over his protruding forehead into his eyes. "I didn't mean to scare you."

"That's okay," Ria began, but a yell came from below them. The three of them peered over the side to see one of the Streetwardens pointing up at them.

"I think we should go," Robbie said. "Now."

"Which way?" Nadi asked as he leaped up.

Ria didn't have time to think; the answer came to her and she just knew.

"That way." Ria pointed to the building next to the Tales Mane with the purple roof.

"Come on!" Nadi cried, not questioning Ria.

Nadi led them over the flat roof, the shouts of the Streetwardens fading behind them as they ran between a row of chimneys and leaped over a tiny alley to a dark green roof that sloped down. A wide road full of people and horses separated it from the next roof. Nadi slid down without hesitation and fell off the edge.

"Come down!" his voice floated up to them.

Robbie and Ria looked at each other. The little dwarf shrugged and slid down after Nadi. Ria swallowed and slowly followed, using her hands to hold herself back. When her legs dangled over the side, she risked a glance down and found Robbie and Nadi looking up at her from amidst a pile of what looked like dirty clouds. With a gasp she slipped over the edge and fell to join them, her landing soft albeit a little smelly.

"What are these?" she asked, wrinkling her nose.

"Fleece!" Nadi grinned. "Wasn't that fun?"

"How did you know it would be here?" Ria asked, swimming in thick fluff as she tried to get to the edge of the cart.

"The sheep farmer comes every fifth day with a load for the spinsters." Nadi pointed to a window in the building beside them. Inside, two old ladies in lace bonnets and a young woman were talking to a man in overalls and rubber boots.

Ria shook her head, extracted herself from the whitish mass and climbed out of the wagon. "Where are we?"

"At the edge of the Pleasure District. The Business District is that way, the First Square is that way and the Second Square is just there," Nadi said. "Which way from here?"

Robbie looked expectantly at Ria, his expression hopeful and encouraging.

Ria looked around, her eyes traveling along the road. People walked here and there, going in and out of shops. A Streetwarden passed by, driving in a large horse-drawn cart marked with the likeness of a grey wolf and filled with something smelly, and though his eyes glanced over Ria and the boys, he did not stop or call out. Ria followed the creaking path of the Warden's cart and its entourage of flies, until it stopped at the end of the road beside a strange wooden box where the two roads met. A tall, dark building with a spiral sun on the door sat on the corner. Something just beyond it called Ria forward, but a rising wall of terror pushed her back. The feeling grew stronger the longer Ria looked down the street, the hair raising on her arms.

"Something is coming," Ria said, shivering. "We'd better…"

As she spoke, a commotion spilled around the sunburst building and into the street. Screaming people were running, pushing and crying as they went. Some of the slower ones in front were trampled by those behind them, and no one stopped to help them up. The people overran the Streetwarden and his cart and did not seem to notice the flashing hooves of the horses rearing in fright. Behind Ria, another human flood rushed out from one street down. In a moment, Ria and the two boys were caught up in the flow, swept along by pounding feet, and carried away. The two masses crushed into each other and the world shook.

It was overwhelming, like a waterfall of icy water over Ria's head. She went blank, losing sight of Nadi and Robbie at once, fighting to keep her feet and not be crushed. Dust got into her throat and she started to cough and choke. Through breaks in the crowd, a dark crack between a low wall and a wooden building flashed between arms and legs. Shelter.

I have to get there, was all Ria's numbed mind could focus on.

She began to struggle against the crowd, people brushing by her, stepping on her feet, elbows and frantic hands in her face. More dust got into her nose. Something hit her in the ribs, and she couldn't breathe.

Then she ran up against the rough, sweet-smelling

wood. Inching along, her fingers found the crack and she pulled herself towards it, heaving breaths and racking her throat, making tears come to her eyes.

Ria slipped into the safety of the crack, shaking and clawing at her watering eyes. The frantic beating of her heart in her ears overshadowed the noise of the panicked mass. When her eyes cleared and she could breathe properly again, Ria poked her head out into the street and surveyed the mayhem, searching for a way through it.

The street was a tumult of confusion, but past the sea of swirling colors and sounds, one thing stood out and made her heart leap. Cedar, his white jacket somehow still spotless and shining, was balanced with one foot atop a lantern-pole and the other on the blue eaves of a pale yellow, cottage-like shop. Ria briefly wondered how he had managed to get into that position, then she saw that he no longer held a guitar in his hands but his golden bow and her stomach clenched. *Demon.*

Ria's eyes followed the direction of the streaks of light which were Cedar's arrows and a slow numbness settled around her, smothering her in a blanket of muted grey sounds.

A pair of Demons trampled through the crowd, head and shoulders above the fleeing people. Ria knew suddenly and inexplicably that the black creatures were looking for her. One of them would smell her as it stalked by, reach into the crack with a razor clawed hand…

Claustrophobia washed over Ria. It wasn't safe in this crack. She had to get out, she had to get out *now*. Her eyes lifted to the wall. Her fingers could just brush the top. She jumped, grabbed hold and scrabbled up. The wall was wide, a green garden on the other side. Ria stood with a hand on the side of the building for balance and peeked around it. The Demons were still advancing, people rushing from under their feet.

Ria looked up. Maybe she could climb to the roof and go back the way Nadi had taken her, but the eaves were out of her reach. She gave a cry of dismay which was drowned out in the screams from below.

Somehow, Cedar heard or sensed her and his golden eyes lighted on her, widening in frantic shock. He waved his arm and shouted something to her but she could not hear over the noise. She watched as he drew his bow, sending a gleaming gold streak of light at her. She ducked, covering her face with her arms and tilting on the edge of the wall, but the arrow did not hit her.

A strangled scream came from behind her sending cold splinters into her chest. Slowly, Ria rose and turned to see the arrow disappear into golden dust in the shoulder of a Demon standing in the garden, almost close enough for her to reach out and touch. Green plants wilted under its feet, but neither Ria nor the Demon noticed as they stared eye to eye, deep red shining into cool grey.

"Greetings *Aethsiths,*" the Demon growled as it reached for her with black razor-tipped claws. "We have been waiting to meet you."

Ria stood frozen as the Demon came for her, unable to breathe, unable to think, and she closed her eyes, praying the end didn't hurt too much. A breath of air fanned her hair back as the Demon's claws passed over her head and it howled. Ria's eyes flew open. A dagger was sticking out of the creature's forearm and as she watched, the dagger transmuted into golden light.

Another Guardian, she thought, without connecting the thought to anything real until she saw the small man appear beside her, surefooted as a cat on the wall, the green and purple thread in his black clothes shimmering in the sunlight.

The dark Guardian, the one who wasn't so nice with a funny accent.

"Hello, darling," the man said. His voice was lilting and sardonic and his black eyes glittered. "Perhaps we should be getting out of here, what do you say?"

His arm came up in a blur to block a long black forearm from descending on Ria's head and he flipped the other dagger into the Demon's torso. The crack of metal and bone echoed in Ria's ears and the Demon staggered back a few paces, tripped on a vine-laden arch and fell over, a comical sight if the situation had not been so dire.

"We have to go to Cedar," Ria heard herself say, taking a step away from the other Guardian, her voice detached. "I have to help him."

"I'm sure Cedar can take care of himself," the man replied. "And I don't think you can die just yet, not until we figure out why these thornbushes want you so badly and call you names. Let's go."

Ria was not impressed. The strange protective feeling from earlier had increased ten-fold, and it made her chest tight and her hands shake. Ria only knew she had to be there if Cedar needed her. *Needed her to sing.*

She opened her mouth to argue, but a woman's voice butted in from above them. "Guardian, your place is here."

Turning to see who the newcomer was, Ria and the Guardian saw a woman with a long braid down her back crouched, balancing on the corner of the roof Ria had been unable to reach. It was not the woman that Ria had met in the golden dream.

This woman was shorter with dark hair and black breaches which laced up the sides with leather strips. Her blouse and jerkin were black as well. A small broach glittered with rubies and emeralds, the only color on her person. Her calm eyes were like black topaz, dark with flecks of deep purple and blue.

"And who might you be?" the dark Guardian asked, surprise flitting across his sharp face.

"I am called Liæna Nati," the woman said, jumping down to join the pair on the wall. "But that is not important. Let me take the girl. I will take her away from here and keep her safe from the Demon while you take care of it."

"An excellent plan," the man said with a grin.

"No," Ria said firmly, searching for Cedar, but he had disappeared. "I want to stay here."

"You are a piece of work," the man grumbled. "Everyone else would rather be anywhere else and you want to stay here. Unbelievable."

"I have to help Cedar," Ria stated.

The man opened his mouth to say something, but the Demon's backhand caught him full in the shoulder and sent him spinning away. His arms flailed and he fell into the thinning crowd below.

Liæna jumped in front of Ria, reaching over her shoulder and pulling out a long, wicked sword that curved at the end. She parried the Demon's attempts to grab Ria while the girl scrambled down to the Guardian before she thought about it, surprised to feel the same protective urge that Cedar evoked welling up in her and urging her to come to the second Guardian's aid, though she still didn't like him all that much.

The Guardian was lying on his side, his blades under him. For an moment Ria was afraid he had stabbed himself, but when she touched his back he spun around and grabbed her, a wild, disoriented look on his face. She stared at him with wide eyes until he let her go. The Guardian stood with a groan and scooped up his weapons in a clumsy snatch. He glared at Ria and his tone brooked no argument.

"You need to go with that woman. I have work to do."

He pushed her aside, shielding her body with his and Ria saw a straggler sprinting down the road, drenched in sweat and terror.

"Where's that lovely Demon?" the Guardian called up to the woman on the wall. He took a running leap and flipped himself into a sitting position next to her. Then he reached a hand down and hauled Ria up beside him. "Have you dispatched it while I was resting?"

"Another Guardian came and rescued me," Liæna said with a graceful bow of her head. "She led the Demon off. I believe you should go and rescue her and I will take the girl."

"Good idea," he agreed and he jumped up, pulling his legs under him so he crouched on the wall. "Where will you take the girl? I will have to find her afterwards."

"Not far," Liæna told him, putting her sword on her back and taking Ria by the hand. "We have taken a room at the Tavern of Roses. Meet me there."

Ria frowned. She really should be with Cedar, but if that wasn't going to happen, she needed to be with a Guardian, as much as she didn't particularly like the Guardian in question. It was not an articulate need but primal and basic, the same as knowing she needed to hold her breath when she was underwater. As she was trying to think of a way to explain this to them, someone took her elbow. Ria turned and saw the woman Liæna. Ria pulled away and grabbed the Guardian's arm.

"I'm coming with you. I can help!" She spoke firmly though inside she wondered if it was the truth. She knew she had to help, she didn't know if she was able to. *But with the Guardians here, maybe I can.*

"No," the dark Guardian said bluntly. "Not…"

Liæna touched the Guardian on the shoulder with a pacifying look before bending close to Ria and speaking earnestly. "Listen to me. I know that you wish to stay and help the Guardians. Believe me, I want to do the same myself, but we will just be distractions for them. Come with me, and leave them to do their work. It will be alright."

Ria looked into her eyes, sensing nothing but truth in the dark orbs, and Ria nodded slowly. "Okay."

"Good." Liæna took Ria's hand.

The Guardian looked at Ria, his black eyes narrowed. "Keep her safe," he said. "Cedar will undoubtedly be furious if she's hurt in any way and it will be my head, which I like where it is, thank you very much."

"I will," Liæna promised. "Until we meet again."

"Until we meet again." the Guardian saluted with his blade and vaulted into the street, turning in the direction Liæna had said the third Guardian had lured the Demon, and running off.

"Until we meet again," Ria called softly after him.

Gripping Liæna Nati's hand tight and looking out from her vantage place on the wall, Ria saw six Demons. Terrified people were seething around them, scrambling over each other in their efforts to get away. None of the Demons looked as big as the one who had spoken to Ria, and Ria got the impression these were no more than animals, starving wolves let loose upon sheep.

"How are we going to get away?" Ria asked.

"Let's go this way," Liæna said.

She helped Ria up onto the roof and they ran over the rooftops until they reached a gap too big to jump. A ladder led down to an alley. Liæna went first and Ria followed. When her feet were on the ground, Ria took Liæna's hand and they ran down the alley. It opened into a small roundabout. Hedges ringed the roundabout, broken in even intervals where more streets entered the circle. A fountain sat in the center. Liæna and Ria took one step and then froze.

Stepping from behind the thick hedge across the roundabout, the Demon grimaced in a gruesome abuse of a smile. Ria wasn't sure if it was the same one as the one in the forest or the one in the Square or an entirely different Demon altogether. They all looked the same, sharp black angles, red eyes, too many joints, and they all moved like snakes, sliding forward on over-longs legs, ready to strike.

"*Aethsiths,*" the Demon said with a mocking bow. "We have come for you. Your presence has been requested."

Liæna took a step backward and pulled Ria behind her as she brought out her blade. The weapon gave the Demon pause, but only for a second. It hissed and moved closer.

Two more women appeared, running out from behind a yellow building on the corner of the street halfway between Ria and the Demons. Ria was worried for them for a moment, but their fierce expressions as they took in the scene before them showed they had intended to come upon the Demon.

The women took half a glance at it, then sprinted for Liæna as three more Demons appeared in the alley behind Ria. Liæna stepped closer to Ria as the women flanked them, the blonde one facing the Demons advancing up the alley, the other the Demon in the roundabout.

"We heard screaming in the streets," the dark-haired one announced. "We could not just sit and do nothing."

She was tall and beautiful in a distant, regal way. She wore burgundy satin trousers and a sleeveless blouse and slippers of the same color. A dark red cloak tied at her throat with a chain of rubies came down to her heels. Her hair fell in ringlets to her waist and warm brown eyes were framed in long lashes.

"You are just in time. Berria, take the girl," Liæna said with a nod at the dark-haired woman, her voice calm and crisp. "S'Aris. Those Demons, if you please."

S'Aris was shorter than Liæna by a nose. She wore a long, white dress with embroidered sleeves that flared just above her elbows and an intricately braided and beaded cord tied at the waist. Her face was fresh and innocent, with grey-blue eyes and soft dark-blond hair which fell in waves to her chin. A series of interlocking half-circles were tattooed on the back of her left hand.

Berria, the dark-haired woman, took Ria's hand and pulled her from Liæna. The others advanced in opposite directions to meet the Demons without a backwards glance, Liæna with her sword held at an angle, the woman called S'Aris pulling the braided rope around her waist tight, wrapping it around her hand, fingering one of the beads.

Berria tried to pull Ria away, but Ria planted her feet. She was done with strange people pushing her around. Knowledge and wordless conviction floated up from a dreamy place deep in Ria's mind that wasn't really there, the same place that knew when people were lying and had helped her pull the door out of the wall for Cedar.

"No," she whispered. "We have to help them."

Ria watched Liæna, wanting to call out and give warning, but the words stuck in her throat. The woman would not be able to defeat *that* Demon, any more than she would be able to put out the sun.

Ria flinched as the first blow struck. Gold sparks flared wherever Liæna's sword touched, but the wounds only angered the Demon. It feinted left and low and Liæna leaped back. Her foot caught on a cobblestone and she twisted. Ria tried to take a step towards her, but Berria held her back.

Liæna caught herself, flipping her legs over her head and turning the blunder into a tight back spring. Her foot caught the demon in the shoulder and she landed wrong, on her back with a thud. She did not get up. The Demon stood over her and reached down.

Three streaks of gold light came from behind it, hitting the Demon in quick succession, causing it to stagger and turn with a howl. Cedar vaulted over a low wall into the roundabout, the auburn-haired elf on his heels. Whipping its head back and forth, the Demon tried to swipe at the Guardians circling around it, Liæna forgotten.

Behind Ria, the dark Guardian skidded around the corner into the alley, followed by the tall blond one who no longer carried the drums, but a weird ax with a spear on it. The three Demons in the alley were dispatched almost as a passing whim. The Guardians each cut one down without breaking stride.

The third was confronted by S'Aris. They stared at each other for a moment. Then the Demon began to shake in agony. Though the woman in white did not touch it, its chest split open and parts of it began to melt into steaming puddles as it howled.

The two Guardians did not stop to help or admire her handiwork. They rushed past Ria and Berria and joined Cedar and the elf. As one, the four Guardians attacked the last and biggest Demon, the looks of intense resolution on the faces making them breathtaking and deadly. Ria peeked around Berria and watched with an open mouth as they danced and slashed, spun and parried in a deadly four-way waltz of death.

Working together, it took several prolonged moments for the Guardians to kill the Demon. Each time it tried to retreat to the Void, they cut it off and kept it occupied defending itself from blows which landed time and time again. The elf's rapier slashed at the Demon's abdomen, and arrows and knives bit into its shoulders. Howling, it sank to its first set of knees, still fighting, then the second set. With the last of its strength, it made two weak swipes at the arrows riding on golden streaks. The arrows struck home, and the Demon whined, a lost and plaintive sound, looking around for aid or reinforcements, or something else. Two more arrows found their mark, and the Demon shuddered. The fire in its red eyes dimmed, and it fell, dying where it lay. The four Guardians stood around the black mound, weapons pointed at the ground, heads bowed.

The world stood as if stunned in the wake of the passing of this creature, observing with wordless respect a momentous occurrence which had not happened in all time since the Beginning. Something inside Ria sensed the subtle shift in the world, the tiny tipping of an innate balance. The faces of the Guardians expressed the same awareness and reverence, and the single instant stood stark and solitary in the minds of every person there, pure and crystalline, stretching into forever. The feeling faded, and one by one, they shook off the spell, blinking as they reoriented themselves to the here and now.

Ria pulled her hand from the grasp of the woman and dashed across the courtyard to Cedar. When she touched his elbow, he turned, looked down and knelt. Cedar's face was flushed and sweat beaded his temple. Ria threw her arms around his neck and he gave her a tired smile as he returned her hug. "One down, eight to go."

"One of the Nine," Berria exclaimed from where she

stood. Her face went pale and she glanced at her fallen companion. "Liæna!"

Cedar stood in a flash, spun smartly on his heel, his bow drawn before he had finished moving, a gold arrow pointed at the woman's heart. Ria grabbed his arm. "Stop!"

Cedar stood tense as Liæna stirred and got to her feet, grabbing her sword. She waved to her companion and Berria sighed in relief. S'Aris appeared out of the alley and the two hurried to Liæna. The three woman gathered together, straining under Cedar's glare and gaining strength from each other's presence.

"We meet again," the dark Guardian said, glancing at Liæna. "Thank you for keeping the girl in one piece, though I can't say I was expecting that."

Ria turned to glare at him. "Then why did you let her take me?"

The Guardian looked at her in surprise. "I didn't have much of a choice at the time. I'm sure no harm would have come to you. I remember you being very capable of dealing with Demons."

"It is his way of giving a compliment," the elf stepped forward. "I would not take it personally if I were you. I am Jæyd Elvenborn." The Elf made a fist on her left shoulder and made a strange clawing motion.

Ria smiled and made a clumsy attempt at the elf's gesture, sure there was some deep significance in the motion. "I am Ria Westerfield."

"Well met, Ria Westerfield. Cedar, why are you threatening those poor women?"

Cedar did not stand down. "Who are you?" he called out, his voice as frightening as the hard expression on his face. "What do you want?"

Liæna made a move to step forward and a golden arrow split the cobblestone at her feet in two. Ria gasped.

The woman froze and slowly put her hands out in front of her. "I am Liæna Nati, of Torin. I mean no harm."

"And what of that insignia you bear so brazenly?" Cedar called back, his voice biting. "You do know what it means?"

All eyes fell to the pin on Liæna's breast. A brittle silence infused the air as all but the elf tightened their grip on their weapons.

"What does your pin mean?" Ria asked, looking from Cedar to Liæna.

"And more importantly, how did you come by it?" Cedar asked.

Liæna looked down at her chest, and then slowly took off the brooch and held it out to Ria. Cedar almost caught Ria by the shoulder, but Ria dashed out from under him and went to take the pin. It was a scorpion, set out in rubies with two glittering green eyes and a green stinger. A tiny "3" was etched in the red stone just under the creatures tail and filled with black. With a pensive expression on her face, Liæna watched Ria examine it.

"It belonged to my father," the woman finally said.

"And did he tell you what it means?" Cedar's question bit like ice.

"It is the mark of an assassins' guild called Spyne that formed in Torin a long time ago. They killed to keep order and maintain the balance for all people."

"And they used Demon magic."

"Not always," Liæna countered, the small flash of anger on her face quickly buried beneath a smooth and impassive expression. "And not all of them."

"I don't understand. What's the matter?" Ria asked, looking between Cedar and Liæna.

"For many years the assassins' guild honored the virtuous ways of its founder, but then it was infiltrated.

Only then did *some* assassins begin using dark magyc, Demon magyc, as you call it." Liæna clenched her fists at her side, but maintained a level voice. "When the Guardians discovered that, they hunted the assassins down, ran them out and murdered them. The remains of the guild retreated to the twin cities of Catmar and Balmar and waited, hiding, until the time they could exact their revenge."

Ria took a step away and Liæna smiled.

"It is not what you think," the woman continued, unclenching her hands. "My father *was* an assassin but he kept the Theory of Three and disavowed Spyne's Demon related practices. He gave me this before he was killed. The remainder of Spyne cast me out because of who my father was and because I too disavowed the Demon magyc."

"So you say," Cedar said. "How did you know where to find us?"

Liæna paused. "We heard there was a Guardian returned to D'Ohera."

"From whom?"

"Does it matter?" Berria asked.

Liæna put a hand on her arm and Berria relaxed. It took visible effort for the dark-haired woman to submit to Cedar's leery scrutiny, and Berria held herself proudly as she answered. "Streetwardens that we paid off and a goblin named Yelndel."

"We traced you to the Tales Mane," Liæna explained. "All the Wardens watching the tavern made contact impossible. We were almost desperate enough to try something stupid, when we saw you slip out."

Cedar did not look convinced.

"I know what you think," Liæna said, her voice as calm as ever. "Still, if I meant you harm, I would not have aided you in the Square."

The street was silent as Cedar evaluated her words.

"She has a point," the dark Guardian spoke up. "They did help us kill the Demons."

"She almost got Ria killed," Cedar grumbled, but he lowered his bow with a little help from Jæyd.

"Ria is tougher than she appears. Are you not? You did not come close to dying." Jæyd smiled at Ria and Ria nodded. "Then we are in their debt." Jæyd turned to the women. "Come and present yourselves."

The women slowly approached and arrayed themselves before the Guardians. Liæna pointed to each of her companions and named them with proud formality.

"May I present Her Highness Berria In'Orain of the former principality of Ghor and S'Aris of Lii."

S'Aris dipped a curtsy without lowering her eyes and Berria touched her lips with her fingers.

"The girl is Ria, and *Aethsiths*," Liæna told her companions. "As named by one of the Nine."

S'Aris and Berria raised their eyebrows and shared a glance before turning to Ria.

"May the Path keep you," they chorused.

Ria smiled, unsure of how to respond. Berria nodded once, a slow, proper gesture. Ria felt she should curtsy or something, but she was wearing dirty trousers in some Demonan style and not a skirt, so she just copied the beautiful woman.

"Your Highness," she mumbled.

The three woman laughed, not unkindly.

"Please call me Berria," the tall woman said. "I have not been a princess for so many years, I have forgotten *how* to be one."

"She lies," S'Aris said, a faint twinkle in her blue eyes. "She is still every bit the princess as the day I met her."

"A princess of Ghor who still names herself such," the tall, blond Guardian said with a curious frown. "Why?"

"I did not name myself as such," Berria countered, lifting her chin defiantly. "I believe it was Liæna who said that."

"There is a story there," Jæyd said. "One I would like to hear."

"Of course, but it is a story for another day," Berria said, her manner thawing when she addressed the elf. "We have more urgent business."

Cedar had not released his grip on his bow though the arrow was aimed at the floor. He started when Liæna held out her blade, but all the woman did was kneel and present it to Cedar. He looked at it with an uncomfortable expression until Timo nudged him with a broad shoulder and Jæyd spoke in soft tones, yet loud enough for all to hear.

"Cedar, you will offend her if you leave her on her knees all afternoon."

"Of course," Cedar said abruptly.

He took the blade, gave it a cursory look and then handed it back. Jæyd snorted and stepped forward, intercepting the blade. She turned it this way and that, testing the balance, and the sharpness of the curved blade against her thumb, the thoroughness of her examination conveying a deep respect for the weapon and the bearer who offered it. When she was done, the elf flashed a smile sharper than her teeth at Liæna, a dark curiosity gleaming in her eyes.

"An elven blade in the hands of a human assassin. That has not been for an age now. Tell me, how did you come by this sword?"

Liæna's ears colored and for the first time she looked flustered. "A friend gave it to me before he died."

"I see," Jæyd said and handed the blade back.

"Now we have told our names," Liæna said with a pointed look at Cedar. "And you have accepted my blade."

Cedar gave an irritated sigh and dipped in a quick bow. "I am Cedar Jal, Guardian of the Path. These are my fellow Guardians. Jæyd Elvenborn." Jæyd gracefully dipped her chin. "Timo of the Dale." The tall blond man raised his ax-like weapon in salute. "And Luca Lorisson of Isos." Luca touched his brow with the back of his hand. "You've met Ria."

"Well met," Berria said, her serene acceptance of his uncivil manner somehow more condemning of Cedar's discourtesy than open disapproval.

"Well met," Cedar said shortly. "Now, what is the business you spoke of?"

"We've been searching for the Guardians," Liæna told them.

"Well, you've found them," Luca quipped. "I'd say that was a job well done."

A tiny smile tugged at Cedar's mouth, but Jæyd glared at him and Luca.

"How may we be of service?" she asked Berria.

"More correctly, it is we who can be of service to you," Liæna stepped in.

"How do you mean?" Cedar's frown deepened when the three women shared a conspiratorial glance.

"We come with tidings of the Amber Torch."

Everything was still and silent as the Guardians stared at the three woman in shock. The women smiled at each other and the Guardians, pleased with the effect of their words.

"How...?" Timo began but he stopped, unable to complete the question.

"How is that possible?" Luca said with a frown. "Only Guardians know of the Amber Torch."

"No, others are aware of the existence of the artifact," Berria said. "Such as the Royal family of Ghor."

"And the Witches of Lii," S'Aris added.

"And Spyne, the assassins' guild of Torin," Liæna said with a bow.

"Oh," Luca said. "And who exactly *doesn't* know about it?"

The three women gave him blank looks, the same look Ria would give her father when he tried to make a cool joke but just didn't manage it.

"Never mind. I can tell when my humor is not appreciated," Luca said, and pursed his lips in a silent whistle, his eyes distant. "Still, the Torch was supposed to be somewhat of a secret."

"This is not the time or place," Cedar said, his eyes chips of smoldering ice. "You obviously know of what you speak. It is true. Ghoris royalty, the Witches of Lii and Spyne all know of some facet or another of the Torch, and there are more you have not named such as the elvish High Lords and the Nitefolk."

"How do you know that?" Luca said, honest surprise in his voice.

"I read," Cedar replied tersely.

Luca nodded. "Of course. That damn library project of yours."

Cedar shot him a glare then turned his stern expression on the women. A series of distinct expressions followed his thoughts, mistrust, curiosity and finally a resigned acceptance. "Streetwardens will be here soon. We cannot linger. Come with me."

Cedar led the group along the twisting backstreets, keeping to the shadows of doorways and covered walkways. Few people were out, and none noticed the Guardians creeping along. Ria didn't know where they were going, but it was not back to the Tales Mane. More people were in the streets, and whispers of *Demon* and *Guardians* had already made it this far, but Cedar led them true and they remained unnoticed. He took them to an abandoned courtyard surrounded by a low wall and decorated with broken pottery and cracked latticework. Crowding close in the shadow of the crumbling doorway, Cedar gave the other Guardians a chance to glance around and recognize where they were.

"Old Jacob's place," the elf said with a sad look. "Is he…?"

"He's fine," Cedar assured her, then turned his attention to the matter the woman had brought them. "Now, what of the Torch?"

"The walls of D'Ohera have ears and eyes," Berria said. "We should return to the inn where we have a room and discuss it there."

"This place is safe enough to talk," Cedar said. "Despite appearances."

"Why not the Tales Mane?" Timo said. "I would very much like to see Victoria."

"I second that," Luca agreed. "If anyone needs a second opinion."

"We do not," Jæyd said, baring her pointed teeth at him with affection. "I would like to see Victoria as well. It has been too long."

"No," Cedar said.

The three Guardians stared at him.

"Why?" Jæyd asked. "What happened?"

Cedar gave a cold smile. "Well, it's a bit of a long story, but the short version is that I got on the wrong side of the Justice and now he's tied up in the cellar. Meanwhile, the

Tales Mane is watched by Streetwardens who are too scared to do anything because inside there is a Guardian and one hell of a feisty old woman who can do some damage with a frying pan."

Luca gave a snort of laughter. "I can see I've been missing out on all the fun!"

"Indeed," Timo said. "But we can sneak inside. There are half a dozen ways to get in and out of the Tales Mane undetected."

"No," Cedar repeated.

"Cedar," Jæyd said, an exasperated twist to her lips. "You must tell us more than that."

"We cannot go to the Tales Mane, because of Akorgia."

The Guardians were dismayed by his words, but wholly unenlightened. Cedar looked agitated. He began to pace, a haunted look on his face and a tense, agitation in his movements. He stopped with his back to them, his head down. His words were directed to the three women. "I am going to take a chance and trust you because I see no other choice right now. Just know that if you betray us, I will hunt you down and make you regret the day you heard my name. Do not doubt my word." His voice shifted, now directed to his fellow Guardians. "Do you remember when we were last together? *All* of us?"

Luca's dark eyes narrowed and Jæyd unconsciously rubbed her pointed ear. A flush entered Timo's cheeks and his eyes glistened for a moment before he blinked away the wetness.

"Do you?" Cedar asked, spinning on his heel to face them squarely.

"Of course we do," Jæyd said softly. "How could we forget?"

"No, I don't mean that," Cedar said, striding forward

and grabbing her shoulder, looking directly into her eyes. "When we were together, what do you remember? What's the *last* thing you remember?"

The three Guardians looked uncomfortable and shaken. Jæyd's skin was paler than usual and she gnawed on her lower lip. Every muscle in Timo's body was taught, his face clouded. Luca's eyes were filmed and dull and he sat slumped like a rag doll. Ria waited, nervous energy balled in her stomach. Something important was about to be revealed and she held her breath, hanging on every word and every silence.

"Well?" Cedar prompted.

"I don't know," Timo said hollowly.

"I do not like to think about it," Jæyd's voice was soft.

"I know," Cedar said. "I know. I don't like it either, but you need to remember. I arrived after everyone else. I almost have it figured out, but I am missing pieces and I need you to remember!"

"Running," Luca spoke up, for once his voice entirely deadpan. "Running while the world burned, and…" His head drooped. "And men burned with it."

"Before that." Cedar was relentless. "Before the fire."

Ria looked back and forth between the Guardians, her confusion slowly seeping into their expressions as they stared uncomprehendingly at Cedar. He was gesturing with his hands, trying to draw the answer out of them. No answer was forthcoming, and he pursed his lips, crossing his arms. "Okay. Where were we? A little over four years ago, where were we?"

"The O'Rente, near Akorgia," Timo said immediately. "I could see the bridges."

"Yes!" Cedar said, gesturing for more information. "What else?"

"I came from Torin," Jæyd told him, a small frown on

her face. "I could see Luca coming from the east."

"Yes, as soon as Chesko called, I headed inland from the coast," Luca concurred. "He said it was important and he sounded desperate."

"Chesko said he was hurt, something about a child, and that he needed help," Jæyd remembered, her eyes clouded with the past. "I arrived first."

"What did you see?" Cedar asked.

"A child, of sorts," Jæyd said. "It was strange, some sort of Thrall, as Chesko said, but it was confused, not sure if it was human or something else. It said something."

"The sands are a-shifting," Timo added suddenly, looking at Jæyd with wide eyes. "It told us the sands are a-shifting beneath our feet."

Jæyd went pale. "The same thing the child-Thrall told me! A Thrall of the usual kind," she added for Cedar's benefit. "This one was a Demon for certain. Not like the first…"

"And I encountered a Thrall somewhat like the child," Timo put in, his low voice grave. "He knew what he was, but it was as though there was a battle inside him."

Cedar looked troubled. "That's not good," he muttered. He gave himself a shake. "What happened after that?"

"We all met in the clearing," Jæyd said. "Except for Cedar, who was late."

"We were attacked," Luca said simply.

"There was no warning," Timo continued. "It would have been our undoing if not for Cedar and Chesko."

Luca's mouth twisted bitterly. "It was a gamble, a stupid gamble. And Chesko lost his life for it."

"Chesko knew what he was doing," Timo said. "Still, all those lives."

"All those men," Cedar said. "They were *men*, not

287

Demons or Thralls."

"That was the first we had heard of the lies," Jæyd recalled, a faint frown on her brow and pain in her eyes. "People said the Guardians were responsible for the Demons, that we had become rotten, not to be trusted. That was why they attacked. They had strange magyc, and only Chesko's sacrifice allowed us to escape."

"It was a drastic effort on Chesko's part," Cedar agreed. "I'm certain that if not for his actions, we would have all died there, as was the plan."

Silence met his words, until Luca spoke, skepticism all over his face. "*Whose* plan exactly?"

Cedar looked unhappy. "I'm not certain, but I believe it was the plan of Lan Holdun."

Luca laughed, but his smile died quickly when Cedar did not join him. Jæyd and Timo said nothing for some time, processing the information.

"How do you know this?" Timo finally asked, a troubled look in his eye.

"Holdun has become the prince of D'Ohera in all but name, and installed his pet as Justice."

"You are referring to the same Justice who is in the cellar of the Tales Mane?" Jæyd asked, her eyebrows arched.

Cedar nodded.

"Then let us go and ask him outright," Jæyd said, but Cedar shook his head fiercely.

"Then what is the point of this?" Timo said.

"The point is, I believe there is a similar trap in place for us at the Tales Mane."

"Impossible!" Jæyd said. "How could that be? No one could have known we would be here!"

"I don't know," Cedar snapped at her. "I just have a feeling."

"Well, that's enough for me," Luca said, tossing a golden dirk up and catching it in a carefree gesture. "What? I mean it. If Cedar thinks something will be waiting for us at the Tales Mane, I would not go to the Tales Mane. He may be aggravating, but he's not stupid."

"Then what can we do?" Jæyd asked.

"Leave D'Ohera," Cedar said. "Quickly, quietly and immediately."

"We cannot just leave Victoria," Timo said firmly. "If the Justice is in the cellar and the inn is surrounded with Streetwardens, then she is in more danger than she knows."

"I know, I know, I tried to tell her the same thing myself," Cedar muttered to himself. "But how can we meet with her and avoid the trap?"

"Perhaps we can help?" Liæna spoke up.

"How?" Luca asked. "Assassinate them all? That will just draw more of them. Maybe we can princess them to death?"

"We have a better idea," Liæna said softly, drawing the attention of all the Guardians.

"This is not the desperate plan you were talking about earlier?" Cedar said, raising an eyebrow.

The women were silent. Cedar gave a slow nod.

"Gods help us," Luca said.

"We can create a diversion," S'Aris said, tucking a strand of dark blonde hair behind her ear and ignoring the dark Guardian. "Lead the Streetwardens away and set them on a false trail. You can sneak in and warn your Victoria."

"And do something with this Trem Descal," Liæna said.

"We can meet up outside the city," Berria added, flipping her cloak behind her with a sharp swish. "And

289

continue from there."

The Guardians looked at each other.

"We have the element of surprise," Luca said. "And if they don't see us, how will they know when to spring their trap?"

One by one the Guardians gave a nod. Cedar was the last to acquiesce.

"We're still going to split up," he said with a look which brooked no argument. "Jæyd and I will go first, and Timo and Luca will follow after. If anything appears amiss, forget it and get out of D'Ohera."

"What if we meet more Demons on the way?" Luca said. "They seem to be as common as cats today. What if another of the *Nine* comes after us again?"

"We cannot fight on seven fronts at once, so we'll have to pray they don't," Cedar said.

"Usually when someone says that, thing don't go well," Timo said, his face serious.

Luca nodded. "And I don't believe in prayer. Timo's right. In this instance, I think we ignore Demons if we see them and run if they see us. There are more important things at stake here."

"But we are Guardians," Jæyd said, her voice soft. "If we disregard our most basic purpose, what have we left?"

"We are Guardians of the Path," Timo said, laying a hand on her shoulder. "If our actions are right by that, we have not lost anything."

"Right," Luca said, giving Jæyd a hard look with his black eyes. "And we can't guard much of anything if we're *dead*."

"So it is decided," Cedar said. "We do *not* take on any Demon. We see Victoria, warn her, and get out of the city."

"Any Demon," Luca reiterated with a pointed look at Jæyd.

The elf nodded, though her eyes were distant and sorrowful.

Ria looked at Cedar, wondering what was going to happen to her now. The conversation hadn't been as enlightening as she'd hoped, and now things were happening, though she didn't follow the plan exactly. She did know she wasn't supposed to be out here. Suddenly she remembered Nadi and Robbie, and she whipped her head around, knowing she wouldn't see them but looking anyway.

Twisting her hands in her lap, she tried to think of what to do. *They can probably take care of themselves, but they might be lost, they might be in trouble. I should at least say something.*

Ria tugged on Cedar's sleeve and he looked down at her, and read the concern in her face. "You'll go with Timo and Luca. It's safer."

"No, I can't!" Ria said. "There's a problem."

"What problem?" Cedar asked, with an unhappy frown.

Ria shuffled her foot, and couldn't meet his eyes. "I lost Nadi. And Robbie."

"What do you mean *you lost Nadi and Robbie*?" Cedar demanded.

"They came out with me, but we got separated when we saw the Demons and now I don't know where they are."

Cedar stared at her and rubbed his jaw. Ria waited, hoping he wasn't too angry. Though it was far too late for it, she was having second thoughts about following him. It was easy to do that when there were no Demons around to invoke her protective instincts.

"Alright, this is what we're going to do," Cedar said at last. "Ria, Luca and I are going to get Nadi and Robbie and return them to the Tales Mane and Victoria's care. You three, wait for half an hour and then make your diversion to lead the Streetwardens away. Jæyd and Timo will go to Victoria and explain what is going on. We will meet up outside D'Ohera in the eastern hills."

Cedar did not give anyone a chance to say anything before he grabbed Ria's hand and pulled her away. She had to run to keep up with him. Luca strode along easily, his strides smooth next to her, his black eyes gleaming and an easy half-smile on his lips.

They walked back the way they came, jogging where Cedar deemed it safe, less worried about drawing attention now that there weren't so many in their party. As they drew closer to the scene of the Demonic incident, they saw fewer and fewer people and more and more Wardens. The Guardians and the girl took to slinking between one hiding spot and another, and finally they arrived at the street where they had met the three women. The Demon carcass had been removed and the street was deserted, but Cedar still kept tight in a niche in the wall, eyes roaming the streets and rooftops.

"Now, where did you lose Nadi?" Cedar asked.

Ria had to think for a moment. "Before the Second Square."

"They could be anywhere," Luca said. "How are we going to find them?"

"Ria's going to tell us where to find them," Cedar said simply.

Ria's throat seized up. "What do you mean?" she squeaked. "I don't know where they are!"

"Neither do I," Cedar said. "And you lost them."

Cedar gazed at her, his expression closed and final. He was waiting. Ria's heart sank as she realized both Guardians were watching her expectantly and she had no idea what they meant for her to do.

Ria swallowed. She felt something squirming in her stomach, a nervous memory of what had happened in the forest with the first Demon, the magyc which had taken hold of her. She took a deep breath and closed her eyes, because she seemed to remember doing that. After several long moments of nothing but blackness Ria opened her eyes and looked up at Cedar with a woebegone expression.

"I can't *see* anything," she said.

"Well, I imagine not, what with your eyes closed," Luca said.

Ria glared at him. "I don't know what to do," she said. "And making fun of me isn't going to help."

"I wasn't making fun of you," Luca said. "I was merely trying to point out why you possibly couldn't see anything."

"Why did he have to come anyway?" Ria grumbled as she started to sidle along the wall, a little bit to look like she knew what she was doing and mostly to get away from Luca.

Cedar followed, a frown on his face. Luca came behind, soundlessly whistling and kicking his feet high. Ria didn't look at either of them, instead concentrating on not stepping on any cracks. When she realized where Nadi and Robbie were, she stopped and looked up at them, a big smile on her face.

"Nadi said he knows his way around the town. They'll just go back to the Tales Mane!"

Cedar looked at her. "Are you sure?"

"Yes," Ria said, but a slow nagging feeling in her chest made her look away from the intense golden gaze. They wouldn't go back to the inn. Not Nadi, not with all the excitement, and not after they lost Ria.

Luca smiled. "She's not sure at all."

Ria punched him in the arm as hard as she could. He looked surprised.

"Girl throws a better punch than most dockhands," he said as he rubbed his arm where she'd hit him. "Still, if you're going to say you're certain, at least try to look like it. Sometimes, that's enough."

Ria ignored him. "I think Nadi would go back," she said. "If he was able. But he wouldn't leave me out here by myself, and if he couldn't find me…"

Ria took off running back down the alley, the same direction that Liæna had led her away from the Demon. Ria's legs burned and she couldn't breathe properly, but she didn't stop. She was about to run out into the street, but Cedar caught her and pulled her close to the wall.

"Something is not right," he said, holding his hand up to stop Luca. "It's too quiet."

They peered out of the alley into the streets. Ria remembered the place in the road well enough. It was deserted now, except for the patrols of Streetwardens walking two by two. Their boots made no sound on the stone, and the silence was unnatural.

"How did they get here so fast?" Luca said. "I mean, they're supposed to be able to do that, but they're public servants – they aren't that good at their jobs!"

"They were waiting," Cedar said, his tone making the words ominous.

Smoke drifted above the roofs like flags in a dull wind. Ria was closer to the building with the sunburst on the door than she remembered being before. Nadi and Robbie were nowhere in sight. Despite it being broad daylight, there was a twilight feel in the air and Ria shivered.

"We got separated there," she pointed down the street. "I lost them in the middle of everyone running and screaming."

"Excuse me, what are you doing here?"

The trio straightened and turned to find a pair of Streetwardens standing in the middle of the street behind them. The Wardens had a gold insignia, an inverted 'v' over a wolf's head, on the shoulder of their uniforms. One had his hand resting on the hilt of a sword.

"Just doing some shopping," Luca said at once. "This jacket is just so out of style, I can hardly show my face in public. It's a disgrace."

Ria stifled a giggle. The Streetwardens did not look amused.

"Sorry, sir, but we're clearing this district out."

"What happened?"

"I'm not at liberty to discuss it sir, but the Second Square will be closed until further notice."

Luca nodded and pulled Ria away. Cedar followed.

"Wait a moment. Any of you happen to see a man with a gold long bow?" the Streetwarden with the sword asked, looked at them with narrowed eyes. "Or an elf with a silver sword?"

Ria held her breath, sure a fight was about to break out. The two Guardians did not move, but somehow they seemed to shrink and pale, fading into something which would blend into a grey cloud. The instruments on their backs were suddenly difficult to see clearly and could have been haversacks or a canvas bag. A similar film dropped over Ria, and she imagined herself becoming invisible to unfriendly eyes.

"No," Luca said, his face perfectly straight. "No, I don't think so. What did they do?"

"They're wanted by the Magisters. Be careful if you see them, they're very dangerous. Don't speak to them. Just report it immediately."

"We will most certainly do that," Luca said, and

bowed. "Good day."

They walked away at a leisurely pace, Ria between Cedar and Luca. When they had rounded the first bend in the road, the Guardians broke into a trot, each with a hand on Ria's shoulder to propel her along.

"I would bet my left arm Nadi and Robbie found a way into the Second Square," Cedar said as they went. "The Wardens must have seen Jæyd and I when we went through chasing the Demon and closed it off."

"That's why I try to stay away from you," Luca commented with an airy wave. "Trouble always finds you. Hopefully the boys had enough sense to find someplace to hide."

"But how are we going to get in?" Ria asked. "The Streetwardens will catch us."

"Only if they see us." Luca winked. "Follow me."

The dark Guardian led them through several tiny streets and winding alleys, through doors which led to dim passages and dingy rooms with more hidden doors. At the end of the journey they found themselves in a small, dark store that smelled like oil and fur. As Ria's eyes adjusted to the dimness she saw racks of coats, all different kinds, made of fur, wool and leather. Luca brushed these aside and strode to the front.

The storekeeper was a little man with spectacles and a bright yellow bow tie.

"You can't be in here!" he spluttered.

Luca held up a finger to his lips and the man's protests died. The three took no notice of him as they crouched beside the door. Cedar peered through the window next to the door and gave Luca a sharp nod. Balancing on the balls of his feet, Luca eased the door open a crack. Taking a quick look outside, Luca took Ria's hand in a firm grip and pulled her out the door into the Second Square.

They concealed themselves behind a statue of a giant stag and a fox just beside the door. Groups of Streetwardens milled around, several of them piling rubble at the far end of the Square. Others dragged casualties to the opposite end where the bodies, some more bloody than others, lay in uneven rows right in front of the Guardians. Ria stared at the bodies in revulsion.

"It's better if you don't look at them," Cedar whispered.

"I can't help it," Ria said, her eyes wide.

She knew Cedar meant well, but his words held the tiny chime of untruth. Ria dimly recalled her mother had told her if you avoided looking at something, when you finally did see it, it would still be horrible, but if you just looked at it straight on, it lost its power over you. Besides, these were not the first dead bodies she had seen.

Ria got the distinct impression death was very common around here and suddenly she wondered if going home wasn't such a bad idea after all. She buried the thought at once and looked closer at the bodies, trying to see if she could remember what each was as Cedar had told her that day in the forest. They all looked like men to her, despite the disarray obscuring some of their features. Ria squinted at their noses and then their ears but those were all perfectly rounded, not a point in sight.

"Are there any elves?" she asked.

"What's that?" Cedar asked.

Ria pointed at the bodies. "Are any of those elves?"

Cedar glanced at them for half a second. "No."

"Dwarfs?"

"No."

"Trolls?"

Cedar smiled. "Trolls don't often frequent the cities."

Ria looked at the bodies sadly. "So there aren't any

dwarfs or elves?"

"Do you have something against the Old Races?" Luca said. "Why do you want a dead elf in front of you so badly?"

"I don't," Ria said and glared at him. "I was trying to see if I could remember what Cedar told me."

"About what?"

"He showed me what elves and dwarfs and trolls and goblins look like. But none of those look like any of them."

Luca looked at the bodies and a frown began to tighten his face. "She's right. It is a bit strange that none of the Old Races were out today."

Cedar didn't take his eyes off the Streetwardens as he answered. "Descal made a point of providing lodging for them in his Prison. They don't come out anymore, at least in the daytime."

"I see," Luca said. "Won't Jæyd be a bit out of place then?"

"She's supposed to be sneaking," Ria said.

"Right." Luca turned his attention back to the Second Square. "So, those boys are somewhere in that mess?"

"I think so," Ria said.

She frowned as she looked from the shops whose closed doors and darkened windows looked as dead as the bodies lined up at the sides of the Square to the Streetwardens in grey and black slowly putting the Second Square back into some semblance of order.

A man came out of a shop across the Square, looked around and walked up to a group of three wardens and began gesturing and waving his hands. All the wardens did was shake their heads and walk away. The man kicked a chunk of rock and winced before disappearing back inside.

"He's not happy," Luca grinned. "But I think he's missed the fact that at least he's not dead."

Cedar glared at him. "It's not funny, Luca."

"Everything's funny if you look at it the right way," Luca retorted. "You should lighten up."

"Later." Cedar's voice was terse. "Ria?"

"I can't see them," Ria said.

"Well then, maybe we should just go home and…" Luca began but stopped of his own accord and gave a sigh, rolling his eyes.

Ria rubbed her chin. She thought of Robbie, how he thought that she might be able to see how he saw, the same way the Old Folk saw things. Unfortunately, she still had no idea exactly what that meant.

"How do the dwarfs see things?" she asked Cedar.

"I don't know," he said, giving her a puzzled look. "I'm not a dwarf. Why do you ask?"

Ria grimaced. "It's nothing, just something Robbie said about seeing things differently."

Luca smiled at her grimace, but for some reason, he chose to take pity on her. "Jæyd says there is something her people have called the Old-Sight. She described it to me once. Basically she can see people as they appear in Path-light or something like that."

Ria clung to every word, but that was all Luca said and she understood none of it. She sighed and looked around, hoping to catch a glimpse of the boys somewhere obvious. The Second Square had the same cold, waiting feeling as the road in the forest. Something had tainted the air. The more Ria thought about it, the more it seeped into her bones like water into sand and she shivered.

Ria put her hand on the statue, against the cold head of the fox curled around one of the stag's forelegs. Cedar was warm beside her as was Luca on her other side. The warmth from her hand made the fox's head warm in turn, and a solid thought trickled through the blankness in her mind. *Warm…it's something about the* warmth *of things, I think.*

Ria looked around, looking for something she could only describe as "warm". With this thought in mind, things did begin to look different. At first she thought it was her imagination, or her eyes playing tricks on her, but as she continued, she became convinced it was something more. If she tilted her head and concentrated, a few of the Streetwardens looked "warmer" than others. Birds fluttered by, and to Ria's eyes, they had a spluttering "warmth" as well. When she squinted and almost crossed her eyes they appeared to have a gold halo about them, but it died quickly. She heard a snort beside her and her eyes flew open to see Luca almost crying with mirth.

"I'm sorry," he said, biting his knuckles in an attempt to contain his laughter. "I just thought…ha! Descal might mistake *you* for a small troll if he saw you like that and throw you in the Prisons."

"Whose idea was it to bring him along?" Ria huffed and Cedar gave a sigh.

"Try to be helpful," the golden-eyed Guardian told the dark one.

Luca sighed. "This is probably the stupidest thing I have ever done. We're trying to remain unnoticed, remember?"

He slid his violin out, and while on his knees, he began to play, very softly.

"Anytime you want to join in," Luca told Cedar, an annoyed expression on his face, scooting further behind the statue as if that would shield the music from the Wardens' ears.

Cedar obliged, the guitar appearing in his hands in the blink of an eye, the soft strum gentle as a breeze

"That's more like it," Luca said, quick notes dancing out from under his bow.

Ria tuned them both out and went back to squinting at the Square, drifting along on the music behind her, letting it carry her and listening for words to come. All she heard was the music vibrating within her chest. She tried different things, holding her breath, clenching her fists then her teeth, biting her lip and the gold seemed to get brighter or dimmer depending on what she was doing, but it was sporadic, and she didn't know what *she* was doing to cause the change.

A small robin perched nearby. She stared at it until she saw the gold light glimmering over its feathers. She watched as it flitted around erratically over the tops of the buildings, a glittering spark shining pale, almost invisible, like a star in the sunlight. Then she saw the lost boys.

They were lying on the grey roof of a dark blue shop, peering over the eaves with sparkling eyes. For the briefest instant, Ria saw a bright gold flare around their heads, but then she blinked and the light disappeared.

"Cedar!" Ria grabbed his elbow and pointed.

The corner of Cedar's lips lifted when he saw what she had. The Guardians slung their instruments over their shoulders in a synchronized motion and the three crept back through the coat shop to a small alley between the shops in the Square, then behind the shops until they reached dark blue walls.

Cedar gave Luca a leg up and the dark Guardian leaped up the wall with a fierce grace, clutching the eave and pulling himself onto the roof. He disappeared over the peak. Ria heard two startled squeals, then silence.

Luca reappeared with the boys in tow. They slid down after him without a word, falling into Cedar's arms and he set them down. Luca landed on his own feet, crouched like a cat and stood smoothly.

"We lost you in all the people," Nadi told Ria when

they were all on the ground. "We tried to follow you, but we got swept away!"

"You should've stuck with us," Robbie admonished.

"We saw everything!" Nadi continued, his eyes bright. "There was a Demon!"

He faltered at the frown on Cedar's face, and looked down at his feet.

"I'm sure Victoria will want to hear all about it," Cedar said.

"Oh, let him be," Luca said, putting a hand on the little boy's shoulder. "Boys will be boys. Weren't you a boy once? Or were you always a stick in the mud?

Cedar gave him a cool look. "We have to return to the Tales Mane. We're running out of time."

The Tales Mane was a modest building, two stories painted a pale blue with a covered porch. Three steps led to the door. The roof was flat with white eaves, and all the windows on the second story save one were closed and dark, boarded up from the inside.

It was nothing that anyone would look twice at, but Cedar's eyes were fixed on it. Twelve Streetwardens in the grey of D'Ohera wandered back and forth in front of the inn. Pedestrians gave them a wide berth as they hurried past as though if they didn't notice anything, it couldn't hurt them.

"How did you three get out?" Cedar asked the children.

"We climbed out the window." Ria pointed to the single open window.

Four Streetwardens were stationed on the roof, sometimes peering into the window, sometimes peering over the edge.

"Why don't they go inside?" Nadi wondered. "Don't

they want to rescue the Justice?"

"They're waiting for something," Luca replied. "You're right, Cedar. I don't like it."

Cedar nodded. "I thought those three were going to cause a diversion."

As he spoke, something exploded a short distance away. Some of the Streetwardens took an automatic step towards the noise, while the rest took several steps backwards. Silver and blue sparks shot into the air and shimmered out of existence.

"What are those?" Nadi wondered.

"Fireworks!" Ria exclaimed, then clapped a hand over her mouth, horrified she had spoken too loud.

The Streetwardens didn't notice. A shower of red and purple shimmers drifted towards the earth, disappearing behind the buildings.

"Even with that, there are too many Wardens," Cedar muttered.

"Let's go to the courtyard around the back," Luca suggested.

Silver the Donkey let out a deafening bray, making the three Streetwardens in the courtyard look up. The two Guardians and the children froze, crouching behind the short wall beside the stable. Cedar and Luca clutched their instruments, ready to call forth the weapons.

Another firework went off, and another. Angry shouts came from outside in the street, and then a far off cheering. The cheering was cut off by more shouts, then a second celebratory cry was taken up from the opposite direction. Cedar risked a look, and his eyes widened. He nudged Luca in the ribs, and jerked his head over the wall. Luca turned to look, and Ria followed his gaze.

Giant gold letters floating over D'Ohera spelled the words "Long Live the Guardians". Silver stars popped behind the message and feathers of purple and blue raced up beside it. The Streetwardens pointed and then ran out to join their fellows in the front.

Luca grinned wickedly, his eyes eating the words with a hungry gleam. "I think I just might get to like those women."

Ria waited for Cedar to move but he stayed in the shadows of the stable, peering right and left, a pensive expression on his face. The courtyard was still deserted. Ria fidgeted for a moment, wondering what he was waiting for and then she poked Cedar.

"There's no one here. Quick!" she whispered and dashed towards the door that would let them into the kitchens.

It was locked. Ria looked about, biting her lip. She was about to run back to Cedar when she heard voices and immediately sank down behind the water barrel just beside the door.

A pair of Streetwardens trotted back into the courtyard. They came and stood by the kitchen door and spoke in soft tones. Ria inched back as far against the wall as she could and tried to blend into the cold stone. The sound of metal on metal scraping softly and some indistinguishable muttering reached Ria's ears. She strained to hear what was being said, to no avail.

When silence fell, she took a deep breath and peeked out. The Streetwardens were gone. Ria leaned a bit further out, and a little bit more. Someone grabbed her arm but before she could scream, a hand clamped over her mouth.

"Shhh!" Cedar said. "It's only me."

Ria relaxed and Cedar let go of her. Ria jumped up and opened the now unlocked door, staring into the dark kitchen.

"Demonfire!" Cedar swore softly and ran inside,

Luca, Ria and the two boys behind him.

Cedar slipped through the hall and stopped outside the Common. Ria tried to dash around him into the room but he put his arm out to bar her. A steak knife buried itself in the wall behind them.

"Victoria?" Cedar called. "It's just us!"

"Cedar!" Victoria came out. "I am so sorry! Come in!"

Cedar, Ria, Luca, Nadi and Robbie spilled into the Common. Everything was dark. The shades were drawn. Old Jacob was standing beside his chair with four more knives. Victoria brandished a frying pan, this one dent-free. She beamed at Cedar and embraced Nadi and Robbie before gazing at them sternly.

"Where did you two boys run off to?"

"It was my fault," Ria spoke up. "They came after me when I went to go find Cedar. I'm sorry," she gave the elderly woman a beseeching look. "I know I wasn't supposed to leave, but I had to help Cedar."

"Well, everyone is back, safe and sound, and that's what matters," Victoria said.

"There may be trouble yet. Where did the Streetwardens go?" Cedar demanded, tightening his grip on his guitar.

"They ran off when things started exploding," Victoria said, looking surprised at his harsh tone.

"No, the two that came in here," Cedar stated.

"I didn't see anyone come in," Victoria said.

"Demonfire," Ria whispered as Cedar dashed out of the Common towards the cellar.

A crash and Cedar's shout sounded from the hall. Ria forgot everything else and ran towards the commotion to find one Streetwarden bleeding over the green rug in the hallway and the other brandishing a sword in Cedar's direction. Cedar stood with his back to the cellar door as something, or rather, someone on the other side thudded against the door.

A moment later, Luca stood at Ria's shoulder. A golden knife appeared in the chest of the Streetwarden with the sword and he sank down to join his companion on the floor. Two more Streetwardens appeared in the doorway leading to the kitchen. Cedar turned to face the new foes as Luca slipped past Ria, two golden dirks in his hands.

"Where are Jæyd and Timo when you need them?" Luca muttered as he stalked forward.

"Hopefully they had the sense to remember what I said and get far away from here," Cedar replied, his face grim as he used his bow to beat the Streetwardens back, parrying with efficient grace.

"Indeed," Luca said, his first dirk barely missing the Streetwarden, who ducked, and burying itself in the wall behind him instead.

Cedar dealt a hard blow to one of the men in grey who went cross-eyed and slumped to the floor. Then fifteen more Wardens came streaming into the hall like thick grey smoke. Ria's eyes widened and she ducked back into the Common.

Nadi and Robbie beckoned to her from under the low table in the center of the room, their faces pale and frightened. She started towards them, but shadows in the hall warned of the coming Streetwardens. Ria dropped beside the sofa, scooting around as grey legs thundered past, praying they didn't look over the furniture and find her hiding there.

Ria remained crouched beside the sofa as things crashed around her. It sounded like they were tearing the wood from the windows and smashing anything they could reach. She covered her ears as she peered over the sofa to find Cedar in the confusion, but he had disappeared down the hall.

At that moment, more people appeared in the doorway and Ria's breath froze in her throat. She struggled to remember how to breathe, her lungs unwilling to accept the air as these new people ran past and she sank into herself to make herself as small as possible. These people weren't dressed in the grey uniform of the Streetwardens. They wore white with an insignia on the right side of the chest, a red rose half in full bloom, half black and wilted.

As Ria stared at the rose, unable to move her eyes away, something uncoiled inside her and bleached her vision to a cloudy grey. She winced from the brightness of a flaring golden warmth just visible down the hall which some instinct told her was Cedar. Beside Cedar was Luca, his gold more akin to a dark bronze amid a sea of dull umber and washed-out yellow throbbing like a heartbeat.

Now gathered around the cellar door, the Men in White were vague grey shapes blurring into the walls and furniture through the film over Ria's eyes. The air was becoming colder, which didn't help with breathing and fear held her rigid. She watched as the men forced open the cellar door and pulled out the man called Trem Descal.

Even though she didn't want to, Ria couldn't help but see that Trem Descal didn't appear to be there at all, just a faint black outline and empty space. *I don't know very much about magyc in Demona, but that can't be a good sign at all. He shouldn't leave. I should do something.*

Standing as though she were balancing on stilts, Ria tried to take a step towards the Men. The nothingness that was Trem Descal pointed at her and said something which to Ria's ears was only a low rumble.

One of the Men in White stepped towards her, raising

a crossbow. Something hit her from the side, carrying her over the sofa to crash into the floor, strong arms breaking impact of the fall. Squirming away, the grey faded from her eyes, and she found Timo crouched over her as three crossbow bolts winged over his head.

"Stay here," he said and then leaped over the sofa.

Ria lay there for a moment to catch her breath, the world sounding as though it were crashing down around her. *Can't let him get away.* She looked at her hand. It was trembling. She clenched it into a fist against her side, and then stood up, using the sofa as cover.

All four Guardians were now engaged with Streetwardens in the Common, Jæyd in the corner, her rapier shining red and silver as it darted about like a rabid dog, Timo in front of the fireplace, his halberd a blurring fan blade in his hand, Cedar balancing on the arms of Old Jacob's chair as he shot arrow after arrow of gold light into the crowded room, Luca grinning manically as he danced and parried in the doorway.

As she watched, searching for an opening, Ria became aware of an underlying current in the air which made the hair on her arms stand up. The ground under her feet began to shake, so slightly at first she thought she was imagining it. The Guardians, with all their attention on the Streetwardens, did not appear to notice it. Ria grabbed the sofa for support as the trembling grew.

Trem Descal is doing this, Ria thought, the knowledge fuzzy as she concentrated on moving forward without running into a body or getting an arm or head chopped off by a stray blade.

She stumbled towards the doorway, ducking past Luca and miraculously managed to avoid getting sliced up by his blades. He didn't see her as she slipped into the hallway. It was deserted and Ria quickened her pace, frantically looking for any sign of the Justice or the Men in White.

The kitchen was as empty as the hall, but a flicker of movement beckoned Ria outside. She stumbled into the bright light of day, momentarily blinded.

Silver the Donkey let out a deafening bray of annoyance from the stable, which brought Ria out of the strange half-dream and firmly into the courtyard, which was full of horses and Men in White.

Trem Descal stood beside a coal black stallion. A shout from one of his men made him turn and look at Ria, a cold surprise in his pale eyes. A cold stab of dread pierced Ria's chest as Trem Descal walked towards her, holding out his hand. Ria backed away until she felt the wall at her back which was heaving like an unbalanced washing machine.

"I would step away from the wall, child," Trem Descal said, his voice flat to her ears. "It's about to collapse."

As bright as the flash after a nuclear explosion, a picture of the Tales Mane in ruins, dust obscuring most of the rubble popped into Ria's head.

"*Cedar!*" she screamed as loudly as she could.

The same thing that made her eyes go funny gave extra power to her voice and it reverberated long after she stopped screaming. A crack appeared in the wall next to her. Ria glared at it.

No. It mustn't fall until they're all out, she thought with fierce determination.

Before her eyes, the crack disappeared. Ria blinked. Some part of her knew that she had made it happen and the knowledge both terrified and thrilled her. Concentrating on the whole inn, brick by brick, she made the shaking dull down to a slight tremor and the inn began to settle back into place.

Although Ria's focus was on the Tales Mane she was hyper-aware of the man standing close enough for her to touch. A fine crease appeared between Trem Descal's eyes and a vein pulsed in his temple. He was frozen, held in place like the magnet men on the fridge at home.

With a shriek and a groan the Tales Mane became still and Trem Descal fell to his knees. Two of the Men in White pulled Trem Descal up and put him on his horse. Only Trem Descal looked back as they galloped away, and Ria felt a curious sensation in her stomach at the knowing look in his pale eyes. The Guardians rushed out of the doorway to crowd around Ria, Victoria and Old Jacob following half a step behind and they watched the horses gallop away in a cloud of dust.

"No doubt that's our friend Descal," Luca commented.

"He's not our friend," Ria whispered, her voice strained. "He tried to kill you."

"I know he's not our friend," Luca said, an uncharacteristic soberness in his demeanor.

"What happened out here?" Timo asked.

Ria looked around and noted with surprise the state of her surroundings. The courtyard was in ruins, and barn had half collapsed, its door hanging askew like a drunk at a bar. Giant cracks ran through the stones. As she watched, the keystone of the arch to the courtyard teetered and toppled to the ground with a crash. After a moment, three familiar figures clambered over the chunks of rock and surveyed the wreckage.

"What are you doing here?" Cedar demanded as the three women walked over to the Guardians, a little snap in his voice. "You're supposed to be leading the Wardens away!"

"We tried," S'Aris said. The look she gave Cedar was a little hurt. "We thought it had worked because they started chasing us. We led them off, but they fell off after half a dozen blocks. We waited but then we saw the dust over the Tales Mane and came to make sure you were alright."

Cedar sighed. "I'm sorry. You're right. Everything turned out as well as could be expected." He looked at the courtyard, his eyes haunted. "At least, no one died here today."

Ria tugged at S'Aris's sleeve and then at Cedar's white sleeve, both somehow still unsullied, though the front of Cedar's jacket was splattered with red.

"They're going to come back."

She hoped he didn't ask how she knew because she would never be able to explain it. Trem Descal's pale eyes, full of dark knowing, flashed in front of her. Cedar did not ask, just gave a sharp nod.

"I suggest we get out of here," Luca said. "We can go to the place these three have been staying at and wait out the aftermath until things have settled enough for us to leave unnoticed."

Liæna shook her head. "No. We have to leave D'Ohera. Now."

Jæyd gestured at the courtyard around them. "But what about Victoria and Jacob and the Tales Mane? If the Streetwardens return, how will they defend themselves?"

"Go," Victoria said, a steely glint in her good eye. "I already had this argument with Cedar once before. I'll take care of this."

No one would argue with the old lady. The farewells were brief and hurried.

"I'm sorry we could not stay longer," Luca told Victoria.

"Ah, it is a good thing, or nothing of my inn would be left standing," Victoria said as she gave the Guardian a squeeze. "And you'll be back."

"Come." Cedar grabbed Ria's hand and pulled her along. "We'll go through the South Square. They won't be watching that one. I hope."

Ria was in a state of giddy disbelief as she trotted along behind Cedar. *I stopped an earthquake.* She couldn't wrap her mind completely around the thought, it just kept sliding out of her mental grasp, and decided that she wouldn't tell Cedar. He would just freak out. *She* was freaking out and she wasn't worried about this *Aethsiths* business like he was. At least the color in her vision was the normal color she was used to. Ria decided to keep her mouth shut until she had some quiet time to think about it.

Too bad I don't have my iPod, she lamented. *That would help me think.*

Staying close to the walls, the group went quickly along small twisting side streets with Cedar and Ria in the lead. When they reached the end of the black-stone paved street, Cedar peered around the corner and jerked back.

"Wardens," he said. "Demonfire and thrice curse them."

"How many?" Luca asked, taking a step forward to look around the corner but Cedar grabbed his arm and held him back.

"Fifty, if not more," Cedar told him with a grim frown. "We can't take all of them."

"Well, we can always go around," Luca said, turning on his heal. "And...wait, where did the assassin and the Witch go?"

"I apologize for this," Berria said. "There was no time to explain. When the coast is clear, leave. We will catch up." She paused. "If we don't make it, go to the City of Fire. Find a man by the name of Dirsh of Ghor. He will help you as much as he can."

With those instructions she hurried off, disappearing around the nearest corner with a swish of burgundy satin.

"Look!" Luca said with a jerk of his pointed chin.

Ria peeked around Cedar and saw half the Streetwardens move off en mass. After another minute the force of Wardens halved again. Timo and Luca made a move to cross the Square, but Cedar shook his head.

"Wait," he said. "There's one more. And, there we go."

The third time only two Wardens left, but this still left a dozen in the South Square. Cedar watched with a frown. The freedom visible through the South Gate enticed them onwards.

"What are we waiting for?" Luca grumbled.

"He is looking for a way that does not involve the death of these men," Jæyd said, weary compassion in her voice.

"Well, it doesn't look like you have much of a choice," Luca said. "But if you like I will do it."

"No, I can do it faster and cleaner."

Before Luca could open his mouth to contradict him, Cedar had already sent his arrows streaking to their mark and set his bow to the ground. He lifted an eyebrow and smirked briefly for Luca's benefit. The amusement did not quite make it to his golden eyes and his expression was drawn. Luca rolled his eyes in return.

"Let's go," he said.

Outside the South Gate, the hills that Ria knew but didn't remember seeing rolled away to the horizon. They ran for the largest hill, dropping behind the crest, out of sight but with the City still in view. Grey figures manned the walls and the gates, but no alarm was raised.

Watching the others as they waited, Ria pulled blades of grass out and made a pile in front of her, glancing at each of the Guardians in turn. Cedar had sunk back into his stillness, crouched close to the ground, his arms around his knees as he stared at nothing in particular. Luca walked around idly, whistling fragments of different songs, none of which Ria recognized. Timo stood as still and strong as a mountain, his eyes fixed on D'Ohera and anything that came to or from the city. Jæyd paced with long, slow strides around the others.

"How much longer will we wait?" Luca eventually asked.

Ria looked up. *He wasn't actually thinking of leaving them behind?*

"For a bit longer," Cedar said, looking up.

"We may have to go back in there if they don't turn up soon," Timo said.

"Of course we will," Jæyd agreed in her calm voice. "But it is folly to recklessly dash back in when they may be on their way as we speak."

Ria listened carefully, understanding the news about the Amber Torch had banished from Cedar's mind the thoughts of sending Ria home, at least for a little while. This made a happy glow settle in her stomach and she tried not to let it show on her face.

"I still can't believe they *all* know about the Torch," Luca grumbled.

"You are like the boy who finds out all his friends knew about the hidden glade that was his and his alone," Timo said without moving his eyes from the City.

"Is that a Dalemen metaphor?" Luca snapped. "Because it's about the stupidest thing I've ever heard."

Timo smiled. "Relax, Little-One. It doesn't make you any less important."

"I am glad we are together again," Jæyd said, glancing fondly between the two bickering men. "I love to see you two play together so nicely."

"If they truly do know where the pieces of the Torch are," Cedar said, his voice only slightly less distant than his gaze. "everything can be put right at once."

"That," Luca replied, raising an eyebrow, "sounds too good to be true."

Jæyd ended her pacing next to Cedar and sat down. "Do not expect too much, Cedar," she told him. "If they have but one piece, it brings us one step closer and that is a good thing."

"I know," Cedar said. "But I can hope."

"Someone is coming," Timo said, moving for the first time in an hour, bringing his arm up to point.

First Berria came into view, dashing over a low rise. A moment later Liæna came up, her left leg bloody from a gash in her thigh and her face pale, filmed with a sheen of sweat. Even limping, the young assassin overtook the princess and reached the Guardians several paces ahead of her companion.

"We must hurry," Liæna began without preamble. "We set a false trail, but there is a good chance it will not hold them for long."

"How long?" Jæyd asked.

"A day, no longer," Liæna said and the Guardians' faces fell.

"We tried," Berria said. "But they had some magyc with them. Someone that we could not hope to fool."

"S'Aris stayed behind to confuse them even more," Liæna said.

"You left that girl by herself?" Luca asked, his black

315

eyes narrowed. "Will she be alright?"

"Of course," Jæyd and Liæna said as one.

Ria smiled to herself. Though Luca tried to hide it, a sliver of concern showed in his black eyes and Ria began to see a pattern to the dark Guardian's moods through his strange manner of dealing with the world. He was almost growing on her. With that thought came the faint conviction that everything was going to turn out alright, no matter how terrible it seemed now.

"Then let's go," Cedar said as he stood in a fluid movement, slinging his guitar over his shoulder. Ria stood with him, her pile of grass clippings scattering.

"They will not expect us to go south, at the very least, and it will buy us some time," Liæna said.

"Which we are going to need," Berria added.

All looked to where the princess pointed. A white-robed woman crested the nearest hill. She waved, and then pointed urgently behind her. From D'Ohera, a small grey and white smudge appeared and began to drift away to the North. They all knew that sooner or later it would find the true trail.

S'Aris came up, flushed and gasping, but no worse for wear. "I'm sorry," she said breathlessly. "For the moment, they think we went north, but there was nothing further I could do." The Witch took a deep breath, and gazed at them with wide eyes. "I think they have a sorcerer with them!"

EPILOGUE

That night, Ria Westerfield lay in the grass of the magycal world that she had found herself in, her head pillowed on the crook of her arm, every bone and muscle in her body aching in protest of the demands she was placing on it.

A strange kind of déjà vu infused her thoughts about what had happened to her over the last few days, as if someone had told her in great detail of these events but she had forgotten their words, or she'd read it in a book long ago, and it was with a detached equilibrium that she went through the incredible yet unsurprising twists and turns. It made her feel like a thief, taking a part of someone else's life and at the same time she felt like it already belonged to her and that she was not really stealing it, but taking back what had been stolen from her.

The mention of sorcerer had sent the Guardians on swift feet away from D'Ohera. From their grim looks and terse comments, Ria gleaned that because sorcery did not come from the Path, if the Guardians came up against this sorcerer and had to fight, they would be at a severe disadvantage, like a boxer with one hand tied behind his back. The situation was more complicated than this, but the details were woven so far out of the reach of her understanding that she did not even try to make sense of it, much like the atoms and electrons she learned the names of and not much else about. She was not sure the Guardians could even make sense of it, though the tangle of it was never out of their minds, and they pulled and worried the threads endlessly.

Especially Cedar.

Ria knew he was awake even though Luca and Timo had the watch on the brief respite which was called so the weary band of fugitives could recover a little of their strength. Moonlight gleamed in his eyes, and she wondered what he was thinking, which tangled threads he was trying to pull apart and straighten. She suspected most of them had her name on them. As they should. Her throat still burned with the tingle of metal and magyc whenever she thought about what he'd done to bring them both here, but her fingers still found nothing but unmarred skin, an empty reassurance and yet comforting at the same time.

Part of Ria - the normal part that knew cars and TV and school and dingy apartments and nothing of sorcery or the Path or worlds like Demona – berated her choices and lack of common sense in wanting to remain in the company of a man with no apparent compunction against killing her. Arguments that she was safer with him than alone in a strange world filled with other dangers far more likely to cause her death fell on deaf ears of what normal people would call her rational mind as it attempted to convince her Cedar was dangerous and unpredictable.

The trepidation and very real warnings were blurred and softened by another part of her – the part that knew when people were lying, that part which could hear voices on golden light and music, that part which saw Doors appear in walls and didn't question her sanity – which felt the acute need to make sure Cedar and the Guardians were alright. It was this part which felt at home in this world, and it held more sway regarding Cedar.

The longer she stayed here, the stronger it became, but even so it didn't feel entirely right. Something powerful had awakened within her, but like a wild lion pacing in a cage, she wasn't sure she wanted to let it out. If she opened the bars, she knew that she wouldn't be able to put it back in again. This feeling followed her to an uneasy sleep, uncertain of what Cedar, the world, and Fate held in store for her tomorrow.

*****

Cedar Jal sat apart from the others, his back to the sleeping bodies huddled together for warmth as they caught a few moments of much needed sleep. The Men in White were still far away on the wrong trail, but Cedar remained vigilant. All around him, the gently rolling hills between D'Ohera and the Sister Cities were bathed in moonlight, frozen in midnight's bewitching grip. Nothing moved, not even the air.

He was drowning in fatigue but his eyes would not close, electrified by what the three women had told him. They brought welcome news and had proven themselves in D'Ohera, but their timely appearance was tainted by much older suspicions. They seemed to be a god-sent aid whose story fit too perfectly to be real: that after fleeing Ghor, the princess spent the next four years seeking out others of like mind and unique knowledge so together they could gather the lost pieces of the Torch in hopes of the

Guardians' return. Despite its improbability, the story must nevertheless have been true. Ria would have said something if the words had been false.

The thought of the girl made Cedar feel even more exhausted. Every moment she remained was a constant reminder of what he had done and another moment in which her life could very well end. He had a Witch now, but she did not wear the black, and only a Blackrobe could trespass into the Void between worlds with any certainty of getting out again. Cedar decided he would ask S'Aris about contacting one of the Blackrobes when he found a private moment. Still, the problem of Ria would have to take a back seat now that the Guardians had a trail, a trail Cedar had stared on four years before, when the world had started to unravel. Someone, or some*thing*, had tried to steal the Amber Torch, and though the attempt had failed , right before Cedar's eyes the Torch had fallen from its pedestal, shattering into twelve pieces. While he watched, the pieces were gathered in a swath of golden light and when the light withdrew, the pieces were gone.

A chill raced across Cedar's skin as he recalled it. He had seen the Path often, of course, but never like that. That had not been the Path as called by mortals, but the Path as the elemental, omnipresent force that it was. Only something very powerful would cause the Path to manifest like that.

While Cedar had yet to wrap his mind around what had happened, he knew without doubt that what must be done before all else was to restore the Torch. The magycal artifact had been created by Cedar Rün, the first Guardian, to shield Demona from Demon eyes and keep the Path safe. Without it, Demona and the Path were vulnerable, and as the Prophecy foretold, only *Aethsiths* would be able to avert some terrible fate. *The Prophecy says she will inevitably fall.*

He spoke the words under his breath, with only the silent stars above to hear him. "The Path everlasting, shall ne'er perish, yet waxes and wanes as day's light gives way to night's dark… One day will vanish, forsaken by people…faded, then put out the final spark… without the power of Life all shall turn to Death… the Guardians as named, though strong and true…cannot rekindle a dead fire… In a place devoid of the Path, their most dire need will bring forth one …known as… *Aethsiths*…"

Cedar stopped. Perhaps that dire hour had not yet come. Demona was not completely *devoid* of the Path.

If they retrieved the pieces of the Amber Torch and remade it at the Crescent Temple, perhaps that dire hour the Prophecy spoke of would not come to pass.

Cedar hoped.

*****

A man sat against a small tree on the rolling grassland between D'Ohera and the Sister Cities of Catmar and Balmar. He was close to eighty years old but no one would guess that by looking at him. He was thin and muscular, with dark curly hair, green eyes and unlined skin. He wore clothes he had acquired on his extensive travels through different lands, his white shirt threaded with blue and dark pants held up with black cord making him look like a mutt. His half-shin boots were pointed, with snakes carved up the sides. His name was Llaem Bli.

He sat outside for no other reason than to enjoy the day, drawing idly in his treasured journal and generally being contented with life. On some days his thoughts were smaller and more tangible, on other days like this one his head was filled with impossibilities such as did the world itself have a Mark? Could a Maker's mind be widened enough to see the Mark of the whole world, and if so, what would it look like? He thought it might be the shadow of the Marks of those who had built the world, Fyr and Eyrth and the others. He thought those Marks, if they existed, would likely burn the eyes out of his head.

The big thoughts made him feel strangely small and insignificant. He looked over the vast rolling plains of Demona, and the wanderlust bubbled up from where it lay dormant, reminding him of the times he set out with nothing but his pack and trusty walking stick and left everything behind without a backwards glance. Those were the times he felt bigger and more meaningful than anything else in the world. Just as soon as it came, the pull of the road untraveled disappeared, and Llaem looked at the world with eyes that only saw the appeal of a settled life.

A whispery sigh drew his eyes to the figure beside him, what appeared to be a young woman, little more than a girl, slight as a wisp and, dressed in overlarge clothes. Her hair was brown with splashes of red, green, blue, and purple, and cropped short, sticking out like a dandelion. Her large eyes were the same iridescent brown color, sparkling with reds and blues which shifted with her mood. She plaited strands of wild grass, nimble fingers coaxing the blades to grow as she wove them, green stalks flowering and sprouting at her will. Llaem marveled at the effect, and at the same time, lamented the small creature's fall.

The nymph was capable of so much more, at least according to the small mentions regarding nymphs in the vast collection of books in his library which Llaem had poured through when he found Kwik. The sparse paragraphs didn't tell him very much, only that nymphs were reclusive and powerful. He could see something he assumed was her Mark, but it was too strange for his mind to comprehend and interpret, the way it did with men's Marks. That probably goes the same for the world's Mark, he thought, and the insight brought a smile to his face.

"What makes you happy so?" the nymph asked without looking up, her voice as soft as leaves rustling in a breeze.

"Oh, just the secrets of the universe," Llaem replied.

She turned to him, her hands falling still, a puzzled frown fixed on her face as she tried to understand his words.

Llaem smiled and patted her arm. "Never mind."

She looked down at where he had touched her, still trying to figure out what he had meant. Llaem knew she didn't understand most, if not all, of his jokes. Her literal thinking, grounded in roots and water, soil and air, did not lend itself to a sense of humor.

Finally, Kwik gave a small shrug, a gesture she had picked up from him, and went back to her weaving. Llaem watched her, wondering at the point of the endless rope of grass, but the nymph was content and relaxed for a change and he didn't want to vex her by asking.

The nymph stiffened suddenly, and the ends of the grass turned yellow, wilted and died. She didn't notice, her attention fixed on something in the distance. Llaem followed her gaze, but saw nothing.

"Something Ungrowing comes," the nymph stated, the emotions of hate and fear bringing the red and green hues in her eyes into focus.

"What sort of Ungrowing?" Llaem asked.

"All Ungrowing is Ungrowing," the nymph whispered as if this clarified something. "But this Ungrowing is familiar to me."

Her words evoked a sense of personal violation, and Llaem's skin crawled. Several times, he'd tried to get the story out of her, to get a feel for her life before he'd taken her in, but a nymph's concept of time was warped by the life span of the trees and forests that they protected and were intimately connected to, and she sometimes spoke of the incident as though it had happened a few days ago and other times as if it were a hundred years past. But no matter when it happened, the look in her eyes was always the same.

"The ones who took you after your tree fell?" Llaem asked, his eyes riveted on the exquisite face of the creature.

Kwik nodded fiercely, her eyes alternating between red and orange, to yellow-green, in a terrible mix of emotions found in a wounded and cornered animal. He laid a hand on her arm, and to his wonder she did not jump or shudder or pull away. Instead she leaned into him, drawing comfort from his presence.

"What will we do?" she asked, her voice calmer now.

Llaem opened his mouth to answer, when the nymph jerked forward again, the glowing purple and gold drowning out the reds and greens as she peered into the distance with almost predatory interest and curiosity.

"Something else comes," she said. "Something Growing."

Llaem searched the flatness of the plains, but saw nothing but grass and a few stunted trees all the way to the hazy, undulating horizon. He glanced at Kwik, and the nymph's gaze had not moved from the point to the north. D'Ohera, Llaem realized, and his mouth twisted unpleasantly. The rumors from the Rainbow City continued to filter down with those seeking to escape the ruthless measures of the Justice by heading for what they hoped was more tolerance in the Sister Cities.

It was folly, but Llaem couldn't do anything about it, just as he couldn't do anything about people getting wet in the rain. They would run to the Sisters, and be met with more of the same, but they wouldn't believe it until it had happened to them.

"The trouble with problems is that they usually just cling to your ankles when you run from them," Llaem said aloud.

Kwik looked up at him, head tilted in confusion. She still had yet to become used to his habit of uttering the tail end of a series of thoughts. He looked for something more subtle, and for a moment he wasn't sure what he was looking at. They were too far away for him to distinguish one Mark from the other, it was all a blur of determined thoughts. Behind it was the grey, sucking emptiness that made Llaem go cold inside, the thing the nymph called Ungrowing.

He gave her a quick reassuring smile. "Kwik, go back to the house. We're about to have company."

She gave him a doubtful look. "They are coming," she insisted. "The Growing and the Ungrowing. You cannot stand against the second, it will swallow you in a storm strong enough to tear an oak from the earth."

He offered her a lopsided smile. "Don't worry about me, Kwik. I've withstood a storm or two in my time. Nothing is going to tear this oak from the ground, I promise."

She didn't look convinced, but she stood and put her twig-like arms around his neck, pressing her cheek against his, and the gesture banished the cold sitting in his stomach. He watched the nymph float through the grass, which he swore bowed to her as she passed. Then he turned his eyes back to the two groups converging, both probably unknowing of the full consequences of their meeting, and was struck with the foreboding that the Mark of the world was changing as he stood there.

"The sands are a-shifting, yes they are a-shifting," he sang under his breath, and made himself comfortable, propping his journal on his knees and preparing to wait for the beast from the dark to come up for air.

*****

ABOUT THE AUTHOR

Nicole DragonBeck was born in California one snowy summer long ago, the illegitimate offspring of an elf and a troll. At a young age her powers exploded and she was banished to the wilderness of South Africa because her spells kept going inexplicably awry. There she was raised by a tribe of pygmy Dragons and had tremendous adventures, including defeating a terrible Fire-Demon that had been tormenting a sect of Dwarf priests. In gratitude they taught her the arcane magic of writing and the rest is horribly misinterpreted history. She reads as much as she writes, is obsessed with dragons and Italians, enjoys cooking, listening to music and can often be heard fiddling on a keyboard or guitar. She currently lives in Clearwater, Florida, is a member of The Ink Slingers' Guild and is working on several novels, all of which have at least one mention of a dragon. She lists friends, music and life among her greatest influences.

Connect with Nicole online:
www.NicoleDragonBeck.com
facebook.com/nicolebeckauthor
twitter.com: @DragonBeck
Instagram: authordragonbeck

Made in the USA
Middletown, DE
21 April 2019